THE NEGOTIATOR

Books by Frederick Forsyth

FREDERICK FORSYTH

THE NEGOTIATOR

BANTAM BOOKS
NEW YORK · TORONTO · LONDON · SYDNEY · AUCKLAND

THE NEGOTIATOR

A Bantam Book / May 1989

Library of Congress Cataloging-in-Publication Data

Forsyth, Frederick, 1938–
  The negotiator.

  I. Title.
PR6056.0699N44   1989   823'.914   88–43346
ISBN 0-553-05361-2

Bantam Books are published by Bantam Books, a division of Bantam
Doubleday Dell Publishing Group, Inc. Its trademark, consisting of the
words "Bantam Books" and the portrayal of a rooster, is Registered in
U.S. Patent and Trademark Office and in other countries. Marca Regis-
trada. Bantam Books, 666 Fifth Avenue, New York, New York 10103.

PRINTED IN THE UNITED STATES OF AMERICA

THE NEGOTIATOR

CAST OF CHARACTERS

THE AMERICANS

JOHN J. CORMACK	President of the United States
MICHAEL ODELL	Vice President of the United States
JAMES DONALDSON	Secretary of State
MORTON STANNARD	Secretary of Defense
WILLIAM WALTERS	Attorney General
HUBERT REED	Secretary of the Treasury
BRAD JOHNSON	National Security Adviser
DONALD EDMONDS	Director, FBI
PHILIP KELLY	Assistant Director, Criminal Investigations Division, FBI
KEVIN BROWN	Deputy Assistant Director, CID, FBI
LEE ALEXANDER	Director, CIA
DAVID WEINTRAUB	Deputy Director (Operations), FBI
QUINN	The negotiator
DUNCAN MCCREA	Junior field agent, CIA
IRVING MOSS	Discharged CIA agent
SAM SOMERVILLE	Field agent, FBI
CYRUS V. MILLER	Oil tycoon
MELVILLE SCANLON	Shipping tycoon
PETER COBB	Armaments industrialist
BEN SALKIND	Armaments industrialist
LIONEL MOIR	Armaments industrialist
CREIGHTON BURBANK	Director, Secret Service
ROBERT EASTERHOUSE	Free-lance security consultant and Saudi expert
ANDREW LAING	Bank official, Saudi Arabian Investment Bank
SIMON	American student at Balliol College, Oxford
PATRICK SEYMOUR	Legal counselor and FBI agent, American embassy, London
LOU COLLINS	Liaison officer, CIA, London

THE BRITISH

MARGARET THATCHER	Prime Minister
SIR HARRY MARRIOTT	Home Secretary
SIR PETER IMBERT	Commissioner, Metropolitan Police
NIGEL CRAMER	Deputy Assistant Commissioner, Specialist Operations Department, Metropolitan Police
JULIAN HAYMAN	Free-lance security company chairman
COMMANDER PETER WILLIAMS	Investigation officer, Specialist Operations Department, Metropolitan Police

THE RUSSIANS

MIKHAIL GORBACHEV	General Secretary, Communist Party of the Soviet Union
GENERAL VLADIMIR KRYUCHKOV	Chairman, KGB
MAJOR PAVEL KERKORIAN	KGB *rezident* in Belgrade
GENERAL VADIM KIRPICHENKO	Deputy Head, First Chief Directorate, KGB
IVAN KOSLOV	Marshal of the U.S.S.R.
MAJOR GENERAL ZEMSKOV	Chief planner, Soviet General Staff
ANDREI	Field agent, KGB

THE EUROPEANS

KUYPER	Belgian thug
BERTIE VAN EYCK	Director, Walibi Theme Park, Belgium
DIETER LUTZ	Hamburg journalist
HANS MORITZ	Dortmund brewer
HORST LENZLINGER	Oldenburg arms dealer
WERNER BERNHARDT	Former Congo mercenary
PAPA DE GROOT	Dutch provincial police chief
CHIEF INSPECTOR DYKSTRA	Dutch provincial detective

PROLOGUE

The dream came again, just before the rain. He did not hear the rain. In his sleep the dream possessed him.

There was the clearing again, in the forest in Sicily, high above Taormina. He emerged from the forest and walked slowly toward the center of the space, as agreed. The attaché case was in his right hand. In the middle of the clearing he stopped, placed the case on the ground, went back six paces, and dropped to his knees. As agreed. The case contained a billion lire.

It had taken six weeks to negotiate the child's release, quick by most precedents. Sometimes these cases went on for months. For six weeks he had sat beside the expert from the *carabinieri*'s Rome office—another Sicilian but on the side of the angels—and had advised on tactics. The *carabinieri* officer did all the talking. Finally the release of the daughter of the Milan jeweler, snatched from the family's summer home near Cefalù beach, had been arranged. A ransom of close to a million U.S. dollars, after a start-off demand for five times that sum, but finally the Mafia had agreed.

From the other side of the clearing a man emerged, unshaven, rough-looking, masked, with a Lupara shotgun slung over his shoulder. He held the ten-year-old girl by one hand. She was barefoot, frightened, pale, but she looked unharmed. Physically, at least. The pair walked toward him; he could see the bandit's eyes staring at him through the mask, then flickering across the forest behind him.

The Mafioso stopped at the case, growled at the girl to stand still. She obeyed. But she stared across at her rescuer with huge dark eyes. Not long now, kid. Hang in there, baby.

The bandit flicked through the rolls of bills in the case until satisfied he had not been cheated. The tall man and the girl looked at each other. He winked; she gave a small flicker of a smile. The bandit closed the case and began to retreat, facing forward, to his side of the clearing. He had reached the trees when it happened.

It was not the *carabinieri* man from Rome; it was the local fool. There was a clatter of rifle fire; the bandit with the case stumbled and fell. Of course his friends were strung out through the pine trees behind him, in cover. They fired back. In a second the clearing was torn by chains of flying bullets. He screamed, *"Down!"* in Italian but she did not hear, or panicked and tried to run toward him. He came off his knees and hurled himself across the twenty feet between them.

He almost made it. He could see her there, just beyond his fingertips, inches beyond the hard right hand that would drag her down to safety in the long grass. He could see the fright in her huge eyes, the little white teeth in her screaming mouth . . . and then the bright crimson rose that bloomed on the front of her thin cotton dress. She went down then as if punched in the back and he recalled lying over her, covering her with his body until the firing stopped and the Mafiosi escaped through the forest. He remembered sitting there holding her, cradling the tiny limp body in his arms, weeping and shouting at the uncomprehending and too-late-apologetic local police: "No, no, sweet Jesus, not again . . ."

CHAPTER ONE

November 1989   Winter had come early that year. Already by the end of the month the first forward scouts, borne on a bitter wind out of the northeastern steppes, were racing across the rooftops to probe Moscow's defenses.

The Soviet General Staff headquarters building stands at 19, Frunze Street, a gray stone edifice from the 1930s facing its much more modern eight-story high-rise annex across the street. At his window on the top floor of the old block the Soviet Chief of Staff stood, staring out at the icy flurries, and his mood was as bleak as the coming winter.

Marshal Ivan K. Kozlov was sixty-seven, two years older than the statutory retirement age, but in the Soviet Union, as everywhere else, those who made the rules never deemed they should apply to *them*. At the beginning of the year he had succeeded the veteran Marshal Akhromeyev, to the surprise of most in the military hierarchy. The two men were as unlike as chalk and cheese. Where Akhromeyev had been a small, stick-thin intellectual, Kozlov was a big, bluff, white-haired giant, a soldier's soldier, son, grandson, and nephew of soldiers. Although only the third-ranking First Deputy Chief before his promotion, he had jumped the two men ahead of him, who had slipped quietly into retirement. No one had any doubts as to why he had gone to the top; from 1987 to 1989 he had quietly and expertly supervised the Soviet withdrawal from Afghanistan, an exercise that had been achieved without any scandals, major defeats, or (most important of all) publicized loss of national face, even though the wolves of Allah had been snapping at the Russian heels all the way to the Salang Pass. The operation had brought him great credit in Moscow, bringing him to the personal attention of the General Secretary himself.

But while he had done his duty, and earned his marshal's baton, he had also made himself a private vow: Never again would he lead his beloved Soviet Army in retreat—and despite the fulsome PR exercise, Afghanistan had been a defeat. It was the prospect of another looming defeat that caused the bleakness of his mood as he stared out through the double glass at the horizontal drifts of tiny ice particles that snapped periodically past the window.

The key to his mood lay in a report lying on his desk, a report he had commissioned himself from one of the brightest of his own protégés, a young major general whom he had brought to the General Staff with him from Kabul. Kaminsky was an academic, a deep thinker who was also a genius at organization, and the marshal had given him the second-top slot in the logistics field. Like all experienced combat men, Kozlov knew better than most that battles are not won by courage or sacrifice or even clever generals; they are won by having the right gear in the right place at the right time and plenty of it.

He still recalled with bitterness how, as an eighteen-year-old trooper, he had watched the superbly equipped German blitzkrieg roll through the defenses of the Motherland as the Red Army, bled white by Stalin's purges of 1938 and equipped with antiques, had tried to stem the tide. His own father had died trying to hold an impossible position at Smolensk, fighting back with bolt-action rifles against Guderian's growling panzer regiments. Next time, he swore, they would have the right equipment and plenty of it. He had devoted much of his military career to that concept and now he headed the five services of the U.S.S.R.: the Army, Navy, Air Force, Strategic Rocket Forces, and Air Defense of the Homeland. And they all faced possible future defeat because of a three-hundred-page report lying on his desk.

He had read it twice, through the night in his spartan apartment off Kutuzovsky Prospekt and again this morning in his office, where he had arrived at 7:00 A.M. and taken the phone off the hook. Now he turned from the window, strode back to his great desk at the head of the T-shaped conference table, and turned to the last few pages of the report again.

SUMMARY. The point therefore is not that the planet is forecast to run out of oil in the next twenty to thirty years; it is that the Soviet Union definitely *will* run out of oil in the next seven or eight. The key to this fact lies in the table of Proved Reserves earlier in the report and particularly in the column of figures called the R/P ratio. The Reserves-to-Production ratio is achieved by taking the annual production of an oil-producing nation and dividing that figure into the known reserves of that nation, usually expressed in billions of barrels.

Figures at the end of 1985—Western figures, I am afraid, because we still have to rely on Western information to find out just what is going on in Siberia, despite my intimate contacts with our oil industry—show that in that year we produced 61 billion barrels of crude, giving us fourteen years of extractable reserves— assuming production at the same figure over the period. But that is optimistic, since our production and therefore use-up of reserves has been forced to increase since that time. Today our reserves stand at between seven and eight years.

The reason for the increase in demand lies in two areas. One is the increase in industrial production, mainly in the area of consumer goods, demanded by the Politburo since the introduction of the new economic reforms; the other lies in the gas-guzzling inefficiency of those industries, not only the traditional ones but even the new ones. Our manufacturing industry overall is hugely energy-inefficient and in many areas the use of obsolete machinery has an add-on effect. For example, a Russian car weighs three times as much as its American equivalent—not, as published, because of our bitter winters, but because our steel plants cannot produce sufficiently fine-gauge sheet metal. Thus more oil-produced electrical energy is needed for the production of the car than in the West, and it uses more gasoline when it hits the road.

ALTERNATIVES. Nuclear reactors used to produce 11 percent of the U.S.S.R.'s electricity, and our planners had counted on nuclear plants producing 20 percent or more by the year 2000. Until Chernobyl. Unfortunately, 40 percent of our nuclear capacity was generated by plants using the same design as Chernobyl. Since then, most have been shut down for "modifications"—it is extremely unlikely they will in fact reopen—and others scheduled for construction have been decommissioned. As a result, our nuclear production in percentage terms, instead of being in double figures, is down to 7 and dropping.

We have the largest reserves of natural gas in the world, but the problem is that the gas is mainly located in the extremity of Siberia, and simply to get it out of the ground is not enough. We need, and do not have, a vast infrastructure of pipelines and grids to get it from Siberia to our cities, factories, and generating stations.

You may recall that in the early seventies, when oil prices after the Yom Kippur war were hiked sky-high, we offered to supply Western Europe with long-term natural gas by pipeline. This would have enabled us to afford the supply grid we needed through the front-end financing the Europeans were ready to put up. But because America would not be benefitting, the U.S.A. killed the initiative by threatening a wide range of commercial sanctions on anyone who cooperated with us, and the project died. Today, since the so-called "thaw," such a scheme would probably be politically acceptable, but at the moment oil prices in the West are low and they have no need of our gas. By the time the global run-out of oil has hiked the Western price back to a level where they could use our gas, it will be far too late for the U.S.S.R.

Thus neither of the feasible alternatives will work in practice. Natural gas and nuclear energy will not come to our rescue. The overwhelming majority of our industries and those of our partners who rely on us for energy are indissolubly tied to oil-based fuels and feedstocks.

THE ALLIES. A brief aside to mention our allies in Central Europe, the states Western propagandists refer to as our "satellites." Although their joint production—mainly from the small Romanian field at Ploeşti—amounts to 2 billion barrels a year, this is a drop in the ocean compared to their needs. The rest comes from us, and is one of the ties that holds them in our camp. To relieve the demands on us we have, it is true, sanctioned a few barter deals between them and the Middle East. But if they were ever to achieve total independence from us in oil, and thus dependence on the West, it would surely be a matter of time, and a short time, before East Germany, Poland, Czechoslovakia, Hungary, and even Romania slipped into the grasp of the capitalist camp. Not to mention Cuba.

CONCLUSION. . . .

Marshal Kozlov looked up and checked the wall clock. Eleven o'clock. The ceremony out at the airport would be about to begin. He had chosen not to go. He had no intention of dancing attendance on Americans. He stretched, rose, and walked back to the window carrying the Kaminsky oil report with him. It was still classified Top Secret and Kozlov knew now he would have to continue to give it that designation. It was far too explosive to be bandied about the General Staff building.

In an earlier age any staff officer who had written as candidly as Kaminsky would have measured his career in microns, but Ivan Kozlov, though a diehard traditionalist in almost every area, had never penalized frankness. It was about the only thing he appreciated in the General Secretary; even though he could not abide the man's newfangled ideas for giving television sets to the peasants and washing machines to housewives, he had to admit you could speak your mind to Mikhail Gorbachev without getting a one-way ticket to Yakutsk.

The report had come as a shock to him. He had known things in the economy were not working any better since the introduction of *perestroika*—the restructuring—than before, but as a soldier he had spent his life locked into the military hierarchy, and the military had always had first call on resources, materiel, and technology, enabling them to occupy the only area in Soviet life where quality control could be practiced. The fact that civilians' hair dryers were lethal and their shoes leaked was not his problem. And now here was a crisis from which not even the military could be exempt. He knew the sting in the tail came in the report's conclusion. Standing by the window he resumed reading.

CONCLUSION. The prospects that face us are only four and they are all extremely bleak.

1. We can continue our own oil production at present levels in the certainty that we are going to run out in eight years maximum, and then enter the global oil market as a buyer. We would do so at the worst possible moment, just as global oil prices start their remorseless and inevitable climb to impossible levels. To purchase under these conditions even part of our oil needs would use up our entire reserves of hard currency and Siberian gold and diamond earnings.

Nor could we ease our position with barter deals. Over 55 percent of the world's oil lies in five Middle East countries whose domestic requirements are tiny in relation to their resources, and it is they who will soon rule the roost again. Unfortunately, apart from arms and some raw materials, our Soviet goods have no attraction for the Middle East, so we will not get barter deals for our oil needs. We will have to pay in cold hard cash, and we cannot.

Finally there is the strategic hazard of being dependent on any outside source for our oil, and even more so when one considers the character and historical behavior of the five Middle East states involved.

2. We could repair and update our existing oil production facilities to achieve a higher efficiency and thus lower our consumption without loss of benefit. Our production facilities are obsolete, in general disrepair, and our recovery potential from major reservoirs constantly damaged through excessive daily extraction. We would have to redesign all our extraction fields, refineries, and pipe infrastructure to spin out our oil for an extra decade. We would have to start now, and the resources needed would be astronomical.

3. We could put all our effort into correcting and updating our offshore oil-drilling technology. The Arctic is our most promising area for finding new oil, but the extraction problems are far more formidable even than those in Siberia. No wellhead-to-user pipe infrastructure exists at all and even the exploration program has slipped five years behind schedule. Again, the resources needed would be simply huge.

4. We could return to natural gas, of which, as stated, we have the largest reserves in the world, virtually limitless. But we would have to invest further massive resources in extraction, technology, skilled manpower, pipe infrastructure, and the conversion of hundreds of thousands of plants to gas usage.

Finally, the question must arise: Where would such resources as mentioned in Options 2, 3, and 4 come from? Given the necessity of using our foreign currency to import grain to feed our people, and the Politburo's commitment to spending the rest for imported high technology, the resources would apparently have to be found internally. And given the Politburo's further commitment to industrial modernization, their obvious temptation might be to look at the area of military appropriations.

I have the honor to remain, Comrade Marshal,
Pyotr V. Kaminsky, Major General

Marshal Kozlov swore quietly, closed the dossier, and stared down at the street. The ice flurries had stopped but the wind was still bitter; he could see the tiny pedestrians eight floors down holding their *shapka*s tight on their heads, earmuffs down, heads bent, as they hurried along Frunze Street.

It had been almost forty-five years since, as a twenty-two-year-old lieutenant of Motor/Rifles, he had stormed into Berlin under Chuikov and had climbed to the roof of Hitler's chancellery to tear down the last swastika flag fluttering there. There was even a picture of him doing it in several history books. Since then he had fought his way up through the ranks, step by step, serving in Hungary during the 1956 revolt, on the Ussuri River border with China, on garrison duty in East Germany, then back to Far Eastern Command at Khabarovsk, High Command South at Baku, and thence to the General Staff. He had paid his dues: He had endured the freezing nights in far-off outposts of the empire; he had divorced one wife who refused to follow him, and buried another who died in the Far East. He had seen a daughter married to a mining engineer, not a soldier as he had hoped, and watched a son refuse to join him in the Army. He had spent those forty-five years watching the Soviet Army grow into what he deemed to be the finest fighting force on the planet, dedicated to the defense of the *Rodina*, the Motherland, and the destruction of her enemies.

Like many a traditionalist he believed that one day those weapons that the toiling masses had worked to provide him and his men would have to be used, and he was damned if any set of circumstances or of men would stultify his beloved Army while he was in charge. He was utterly loyal to the Party—he would not have been where he was had he not been—but if anyone, even the men who now led the Party, thought they could strike billions of rubles off the military budget, then he might have to restructure his loyalty to those men.

The more he thought about the concluding pages of the report in his hand, the more he thought that Kaminsky, smart though he was, had overlooked a possible fifth option. If the Soviet Union could take political control of a ready-made source of ample raw crude oil, a piece of territory presently outside her own borders ... if she could import in exclusivity that crude oil at a price she could afford, i.e., dictate ... and do so before her own oil ran out ...

He laid the report on the conference table and crossed the room to the global map that covered half the wall opposite the windows. He studied it carefully as the minutes ticked away to noon. And always his eye fell on one piece of land. Finally he crossed to the desk, reconnected the intercom, and called his ADC.

"Ask Major General Zemskov to come and see me—now," he said.

He sat in the high-backed chair behind his desk, picked up the TV remote control, and activated the set on its stand to the left of his desk. Channel One swam into focus, the promised live news broadcast from Vnukovo, the VIP airport outside Moscow.

United States Air Force One stood fully fueled and ready to roll. She was the new Boeing 747 that had superseded the old and time-expired 707's earlier in the year, and she could get from Moscow back to Washington in one hop, which the old 707's could never do. Men of the 89th Military Airlift Wing, which guards and maintains the President's Wing at Andrews Air Force Base, stood around the aircraft just in case any overenthusiastic Russian tried to get close enough to attach something to it or have a peek inside. But the Russians were behaving like perfect gentlemen and had been throughout the three-day visit.

Some yards away from the tip of the airplane's wing was a podium, dominated by a raised lectern in its center. At the lectern stood the General Secretary of the Communist Party of the Soviet Union, Mikhail Sergeevich Gorbachev, bringing his valedictory address to a close. At his side, hatless, his iron-gray hair ruffled by the bitter breeze, sat his visitor, John J. Cormack, President of the United States of America. Ranged on either side of both were the twelve other members of the Politburo.

Drawn up in front of the podium was an honor guard of the Militia, the civil police from the Interior Ministry, the MVD; and another drawn from the Border Guards Directorate of the KGB. In an attempt to add the common touch, two hundred engineers, technicians, and members of the airport staff formed a crowd on the fourth side of the hollow square. But the focal point for the speaker was the battery of TV cameras, still photographers, and press placed between the two honor guards. For this was a momentous occasion.

Shortly after his inauguration the previous January, John Cormack, surprise winner of the preceding November's election, had indicated he would like to meet the Soviet leader and would be prepared to fly to Moscow to do so. Mikhail Gorbachev had not been slow to agree and to his gratification had found over the previous three days that this tall, astringent, but basically humane American academic appeared to be a man—to borrow Mrs. Thatcher's phrase—"with whom he could do business."

So he had taken a gamble, against the advice of his security and ideology advisers. He had acceded to the President's personal request that he, the American, be permitted to address the Soviet Union on live television without submitting his script for approval. Virtually no Soviet television is "live"; almost everything shown is carefully edited, prepared, vetted, and finally passed as fit for consumption.

Before agreeing to Cormack's strange request, Mikhail Gorbachev had consulted with the State Television experts. They had been as surprised as he, but pointed out that, first, the American would be understood by only a tiny fraction of Soviet citizens until the translation came through (and that could be sanitized if he went too far) and, second, that the American's speech could be held on an eight- or ten-second loop so that transmission (both sound and vision) would actually take place a few seconds after delivery; and if he really went too far, there could be a sudden breakdown in transmission. Finally it was agreed that if the General Secretary wished to effect such a breakdown, he had but to scratch his chin with a forefinger and the technicians would do the rest. This could not apply to the three American TV crews or the BBC from Britain, but that would not matter, as their material would never reach the Soviet people.

Ending his oration with an expression of good will toward the American people and his abiding hope for peace between the U.S.A. and the U.S.S.R., Mikhail Gorbachev turned toward his guest. John Cormack rose. The Russian gestured to the lectern and the microphone and made way, seating himself to one side of the center spot. The President stepped behind the microphone. He had no notes in view. He just lifted his head, stared straight at the eye of the Soviet TV camera, and began to speak.

"Men, women, and children of the U.S.S.R., listen to me."

In his office Marshal Kozlov jerked forward in his chair, staring intently at the screen. On the podium Mikhail Gorbachev's eyebrows flickered once before he regained his composure. In a booth behind the Soviet camera a young man who could pass for a Harvard graduate put his hand over a microphone and muttered a question to a senior civil servant beside him, who shook his head. For John Cormack was not speaking in English at all; he was speaking in fluent Russian.

Although not a Russian speaker, he had before coming to the U.S.S.R. memorized in the privacy of his bedroom in the White House a five-hundred-word speech in Russian, rehearsing himself through tapes and speech-coaching until he could deliver the speech with total fluency and perfect accent while not understanding a word of the language. Even for a former Ivy League professor it was a remarkable feat.

"Fifty years ago this, your country, your beloved Motherland, was invaded in war. Your menfolk fought and died as soldiers or lived like wolves in their own forests. Your women and children dwelt in cellars and fed off scraps. Millions perished. Your land was devastated. Although this never happened to my country, I give you my word I can understand how much you must hate and fear war.

"For forty-five years we both, Russians and Americans, have built up walls between ourselves, convincing ourselves that the other would be the next aggressor. And we have built up mountains—mountains of steel, of guns, of tanks, of ships and planes and bombs. And the walls of lies have been built ever higher to justify the mountains of steel. There are those who say we need these weapons because one day they will be needed so that we can destroy each other.

"*Noh, ya skazhu: mi po-idyom drugim putyom.*"

There was an almost audible gasp from the audience at Vnukovo. In saying "But I say, we will/must go another way," President Cormack had borrowed a phrase from Lenin known to every schoolchild in the U.S.S.R. In Russian the word *put* means a road, path, way, or course to be followed. He then continued the play on words by reverting to the meaning of "road."

"I refer to the road of gradual disarmament and of peace. We have only one planet to live on, and a beautiful planet. We can either live on it together or die on it together."

The door of Marshal Kozlov's office opened quietly and then closed. An officer in his early fifties, another Kozlov protégé and the ace of his planning staff, stood by the door and silently watched the screen in the corner. The American President was finishing.

"It will not be an easy road. There will be rocks and holes. But at its end lies peace with security for both of us. For if we each have enough weapons to defend ourselves, but not enough to attack each other, and if each one knows this and is allowed to verify it, then we could pass on to our children and grandchildren a world that is truly free of that awful fear that we have known these past fifty years. If you will walk down that road with me, then I on behalf of the people of America will walk it with you. And on this, Mikhail Sergeevich, I give you my hand."

President Cormack turned to Secretary Gorbachev and held out his right hand. Although himself an expert at public relations, the Russian had no choice but to rise and extend his hand. Then, with a broad grin, he bear-hugged the American with his left arm.

The Russians are a people capable of great paranoia and xenophobia but also capable of great emotionalism. It was the airport workers who broke the silence first. There was an outbreak of ardent clapping, then the cheering started, and in a few seconds the fur *shapka*s started flying through the air as the civilians, normally drilled to perfection, went out of control. The Militiamen came next; gripping their rifles with their left hands in the at-ease position, they started waving their red-banded gray caps by the peak as they cheered.

The KGB troops glanced at their commander beside the podium: General Vladimir Kryuchkov, Chairman of the KGB. Uncertain what to do as the Politburo stood up, he, too, rose to clap with the rest. The Border Guards took this as a cue (wrongly, as it turned out) and followed the Militiamen in cheering. Somewhere across five time zones, 80 million Soviet men and women were doing something similar.

"*Churt vashmi . . .*" Marshal Kozlov reached for the remote control and snapped off the TV set.

"Our beloved General Secretary," murmured Major General Zemskov smoothly. The marshal nodded grimly several times. First the dire forebodings of the Kaminsky report, and now this. He rose, came around his desk, and took the report off the table.

"You are to take this, and you are to read it," he said. "It is classified Top Secret and it stays that way. There are only two copies in existence and I retain the other one. You are to pay particular attention to what Kaminsky says in his Conclusion."

Zemskov nodded. He judged from the marshal's grim demeanor that there was more to it than reading a report. He had been a mere colonel two years before, when, on a visit to a Command Post exercise in East Germany, Marshal Kozlov had noticed him.

The exercise had involved maneuvers between the GSFG, the Group of Soviet Forces Germany, on the one hand and the East Germans' National People's Army on the other. The Germans had been pretending to be the invading Americans, and in previous instances had mauled their Soviet brothers-in-arms. This time the Russians had run rings around them, and the planning had all been due to Zemskov. As soon as he arrived in the top job at Frunze Street, Marshal Kozlov had sent for the brilliant planner and attached him to his own staff. Now he led the younger man to the wall map.

"When you have finished, you will prepare what appears to be a Special Contingency Plan. In truth this SCP will be a minutely detailed plan, down to the last man, gun, and bullet, for the military invasion and occupation of a foreign country. It may take up to twelve months."

Major General Zemskov raised his eyebrows.

"Surely not so long, Comrade Marshal. I have at my disposal—"

"You have at your disposal nothing but your own eyes, hands, and brain. You will consult no one else, confer with no one else. Every piece of information you need will be obtained by a subterfuge. You will work alone, without support. It will take months and there will be just one copy at the end."

"I see. And the country . . . ?"

The marshal tapped the map. "Here. One day this land must belong to us."

The Pan-Global Building in Houston, capital city of the American oil industry and, some say, of the world's oil business, was the headquarters of the Pan-Global Oil Corporation, the twenty-eighth-largest oil company in the United States and ninth-largest in Houston. With total assets of $3.25 billion, Pan-Global was topped only by Shell, Tenneco, Conoco, Enron, Coastal, Texas Eastern, Transco, and Pennzoil. But in one way it was different from all the others: It was still owned and controlled by its veteran founder. There were stockholders and board members, but the founder retained the control and no one could trammel his power within his own corporation.

Twelve hours after Marshal Kozlov had briefed his planning officer, and eight time zones to the west of Moscow, Cyrus V. Miller stood at the ceiling-to-floor plate-glass window of his penthouse office suite and stared toward the west. Four miles away, through the haze of a late November afternoon, the Transco Tower stared back. Cyrus Miller stood a while longer, then walked back across the deep-pile carpet to his desk and buried himself again in the report that lay on it.

Forty years earlier, when he had begun to prosper, Miller had learned that information was power. To know what was going on and, more important, what was going to happen gave a man more power than political office or even money. That was when he had initiated within his growing corporation a Research and Statistics Division, staffing it with the brightest and sharpest of the analysts from his country's universities. With the coming of the computer age he had stacked his R and S Division with the latest data banks, in which was stored a vast compendium of information about the oil industry and other industries, commercial needs, national economic performance, market trends, scientific advances, and people—hundreds of thousands of people from every walk of life who might, by some conceivable chance, one day be useful to him.

The report before him came from Dixon, a young graduate of Texas State with a penetrating intellect, whom he had hired a decade earlier and who had grown with the company. For all that he paid him, Miller mused, the analyst was not seeking to reassure him with the document on his desk. But he appreciated that. He went back for the fifth time to Dixon's conclusion.

The bottom line is that the Free World is simply running out of oil. At the moment this remains unperceived by the broad mass of the American people, due to successive governments' determination to maintain the fiction that the present "cheap oil" situation can continue in perpetuity.

The proof of the "running-out" claim lies in the table of global oil reserves enclosed earlier. Out of forty-one oil-producing nations today, only ten have known reserves beyond the thirty-year mark. Even this picture is optimistic. Those thirty years assume continued production at present levels. The fact is that consumption, and therefore extraction, is increasing in any event, and as the short-reserve producers will run out first, the extraction from the remainder will increase to make up the shortfall. Twenty years would be a safer period to assume run-out in all but ten producing nations.

There is simply no way that alternative energy sources can or will come to the rescue in time. For the next three decades it is going to be oil or economic death for the Free World.

The American position is heading fast for catastrophe. During the period when the controlling OPEC nations hiked the crude price from $2 a barrel to $40, the U.S. government sensibly gave every incentive to our oil industry to explore, discover, extract, and refine the maximum possible from domestic resources. Since the self-destruction of OPEC and the Saudi production hike of 1985, Washington has bathed in artificially cheap oil from the Middle East, leaving the domestic industry to wither on the vine. This shortsightedness is going to produce a terrible harvest.

The American response to cheap oil has been increased demand, higher crude and product imports, and shrinking domestic production, a total cutback in exploration, wholesale refinery closings, and an unemployment slump worse than 1932. Even if we started a crash program *now*, with massive investment, and large-scale federal incentives, it would take ten years to rebuild the pool of skills, mobilize the machinery, and execute the efforts needed to bring our now-total reliance on the Middle East back to manageable proportions. So far there is no indication that Washington intends to encourage any such resurgence in national American oil production.

There are three reasons for this—all of them wrong:

(a) New American oil would cost $20 a barrel to *find*, whereas Saudi/Kuwaiti oil costs 10–15 cents a barrel to produce and $16 a barrel for us to buy. It is assumed this will continue in perpetuity. It won't.

(b) It is assumed the Arabs and especially the Saudis will go on buying astronomical quantities of U.S. arms, technology, goods, and services for their own social and defense infrastructure, and thus keep on recycling their petrodollars with us. They won't. Their infrastructure is virtually complete, they cannot even think of anything else to spend the dollars on, and their recent (1986 and 1988) Tornado fighter deals with Britain have pushed us into second place as arms suppliers.

(c) It is assumed that the monarchs who rule the Mideastern kingdoms and sultanates are good and loyal allies who would never turn on us and hike the prices back up again, and who will stay in power forever. Their blatant blackmail of America from 1973 through 1985 shows where their hearts lie; and in an area as unstable as the Middle East *any* regime can fall from power before the end of the week.

Cyrus Miller glared at the paper. He did not like what he read but he knew it was true. As a domestic producer and refiner of crude oil he had suffered cruelly in the previous four years, and no amount of lobbying in Washington by the oil industry had persuaded Congress to grant oil leases on the Arctic National Wildlife Range in Alaska, the country's most promising discovery prospect for new oil. He loathed Washington.

He glanced at his watch. Half past four. He pressed a switch on his desk console and across the room a teak panel glided silently sideways to reveal a 26-inch color TV screen. He selected the CNN news channel and caught the headline story of the day.

Air Force One hung over the touchdown area at Andrews Base outside Washington, seemingly suspended in the sky until its seeking wheels gently found the waiting tarmac and it was back on American soil. As it slowed and then turned to taxi back toward the airport buildings, the image was replaced by the face of the gabbling newscaster relating again the story of the presidential speech just before the departure from Moscow twelve hours earlier.

As if to prove the newscaster's narration, the CNN production team, with ten minutes to wait until the Boeing came to rest, re-screened the speech President Cormack had made in Russian, with English-language subtitles, the shots of the roaring and cheering airport workers and Militiamen and the image of Mikhail Gorbachev embracing the American leader in an emotional bear hug. Cyrus Miller's fog-gray eyes did not blink, hiding even in the privacy of his office his hatred for the New England patrician who had unexpectedly stormed into the lead and the presidency twelve months earlier and was now moving further toward detente with Russia than even Reagan had dared to do. As President Cormack appeared in the doorway of Air Force One and the strains of "Hail to the Chief" struck up, Miller contemptuously hit the *off* button.

"Commie-loving bastard," he growled, and returned to Dixon's report.

In fact, the twenty-year deadline for oil run-out by all but ten of the world's forty-one producers is irrelevant. The price hikes will start in ten years or less. A recent Harvard University report predicted a price in excess of $50 a barrel (in 1989 dollars) before 1999 as against $16 a barrel today. The report was suppressed, but erred on the side of optimism. The prospect of the effect on the American public of such prices is nightmarish. What will Americans do when told to pay $2 a gallon for gasoline? How will farmers react when told they cannot feed their hogs or harvest their grain or even heat their houses through the bitter winters? We are facing social revolution here.

Even *if* Washington should authorize a massive revitalization of the U.S. oil-producing effort, we still have only five years of reserves at existing consumption levels. Europe is in even worse shape; apart from tiny Norway (one of the ten countries with thirty-plus years of reserves, but based on very small offshore production) Europe has three years of reserves. The countries of the Pacific Basin rely entirely on imported oil and have huge hard-currency surpluses. The result? Mexico, Venezuela, and Libya apart, we shall all be looking to the same source of supply: the six producers of the Middle East.

Iran, Iraq, Abu Dhabi, and the Neutral Zone have oil, but two are bigger than the rest of the eight put together: Saudi Arabia and neighboring Kuwait—and Saudi will be the key to OPEC. Today producing 170 billion barrels a year, 25 percent of the *world*'s oil production, rising in ten years to 50 percent as the thirty-one others run out one by one, *and* with over a hundred years of reserves, Saudi Arabia will control the world's oil price, and control America.

At predicted oil-price rises, America will by 1995 have an import bill of $450 million a day—all payable to Saudi Arabia and her adjunct Kuwait. Which means the Middle East suppliers will probably own the very U.S. industries whose needs they are supplying. America, despite her advancement, technology, living standard, and military might, will be economically, financially, strategically, and thus politically dependent on a small, backward, semi-nomadic, corrupt, and capricious nation that she cannot control.

Cyrus Miller closed the report, leaned back, and stared at the ceiling. If anyone had had the nerve to tell him to his face that he stemmed from the ultra-right in American political thought, he would have denied it with vehemence. Though a traditional Republican voter, he had never taken much interest in politics in his seventy-seven years except as they affected the oil industry. His political party, so far as he was concerned, was patriotism. Miller loved his adopted state of Texas and his country of birth with an intensity that sometimes seemed to choke him.

What he failed to realize was that it was an America much of his own devising, a White Anglo-Saxon Protestant America of traditional values and raw chauvinism. Not, he assured the Almighty during his several-times-daily prayers, that he had anything against Jews, Catholics, Hispanics, or nigras—did he not employ eight Spanish-speaking maids in the mansion at his ranch in the hill country outside Austin, not to mention several blacks in the gardens?—so long as they knew and kept their place.

He stared at the ceiling and tried to think of a name. The name of a man whom he had met about two years back at an oil convention in Dallas, a man who told him he lived and worked in Saudi Arabia. They'd had only a short conversation, but the man had impressed him. He could see him in his mind's eye; at just under six feet a mite shorter than Miller, compact, taut like a tensed spring, quiet, watchful, thoughtful, a man with enormous experience of the Middle East. He had walked with a limp, leaning on a silver-topped cane, and he had something to do with computers. The more he thought, the more Miller remembered. They had discussed computers, the merits of his Honeywells, and the man had favored IBMs. After several minutes Miller called in another member of his research staff and dictated his recollections.

"Find out who he is," he commanded.

It was already dark on the southern coast of Spain, the coast they call the Costa del Sol. Although well out of the tourist season, the whole coast from Málaga the hundred miles to Gibraltar was lit by a glittering chain of lights, which from the mountains behind the coast would have looked like a fiery snake twisting and turning its way through Torremolinos, Mijas, Fuengirola, Marbella, Estepona, Puerto Duquesa, and on to La Linea and the Rock. Headlights from cars and trucks flickered constantly on the Málaga–Cadiz highway running along the flatland between the hills and the beaches.

In the mountains behind the coast near the western end, between Estepona and Puerto Duquesa, lies the wine-growing district of south Andalusia, producing not the sherries of Jerez to the west but a rich, strong red wine. The center of this area is the small town of Manilva, just five miles inland from the coast but already having a panoramic view of the sea to the south. Manilva is surrounded by a cluster of small villages, almost hamlets, where live the people who till the slopes and tend the vines.

In one of them, Alcántara del Rio, the men were coming home from the fields, tired and aching after a long day's work. The grape harvest was long home, but the vines had to be pruned and set back before the coming winter and the work was hard on the back and shoulders. So, before going to their scattered homes, most of the men stopped by the village's single cantina for a glass and a chance to talk.

Alcántara del Rio boasted little but peace and quiet. It had a small white-painted church presided over by an old priest as decrepit as his incumbency, serving out his time saying mass for the women and children while regretting that the male members of his flock on a Sunday morning preferred the bar. The children went to school in Manilva. Apart from four dozen whitewashed cottages, there was just the Bar Antonio, now thronged with vineyard workers. Some worked for cooperatives based miles away; others owned their plots, worked hard, and made a modest living depending on the crop and the price offered by the buyers in the cities.

The tall man came in last, nodded a greeting to the others, and took his habitual chair in the corner. He was taller by several inches than the others, rangy, in his mid-forties, with a craggy face and humorous eyes. Some of the peasants called him "Señor," but Antonio, as he bustled over with a carafe of wine and a glass, was more familiar.

"*Muy bueno, amigo. ¿Va bien?*"

"*Hola, Tonio,*" said the big man easily. "*Si, va bien.*"

He turned as a burst of music came from the television set mounted above the bar. It was the evening news on TVE and the men fell silent to catch the day's headlines. The newscaster came first, describing briefly the departure from Moscow of President Cormack de los Estados Unidos. The image switched to Vnukovo, and the U.S. President moved in front of the microphone and began to speak. The Spanish TV had no subtitles but a voice-over translation into Spanish instead. The men in the bar listened intently. As John Cormack finished and held out his hand to Gorbachev, the camera (it was the BBC crew, covering for all the European stations) panned over the cheering airport workers, then the Militiamen, then the KGB troops. The Spanish newscaster came back on the screen. Antonio turned to the tall man.

"*Es un buen hombre, Señor Cormack,*" he said, smiling broadly and clapping the tall man on the back in congratulation, as if his customer had some part-ownership of the man from the White House.

"*Si.*" The tall man nodded thoughtfully. "*Es un buen hombre.*"

Cyrus V. Miller had not been born to his present riches. He had come from poor farming stock in Colorado and, as a boy, had seen his father's dirt farm bought out by a mining company and devastated by its machinery. Resolving that if one could not beat them one ought to join them, the youth had worked his way through the Colorado School of Mines in Golden, emerging in 1933 with a degree and the clothes he wore. During his studies he had become fascinated more by oil than by rocks and headed south for Texas. It was still the days of the wildcatters, when leases were unfettered by environmental impact statements and ecological worries.

In 1936 he had spotted a cheap lease relinquished by Texaco, and calculated they had been digging in the wrong place. He persuaded a tool pusher with his own rig to join him, and sweet-talked a bank into taking the farm-in rights against a loan. The oil field supply house took more rights for the rest of the equipment he needed, and three months later the well came in—big. He bought out the tool pusher, leased his own rigs, and acquired other leases. With the outbreak of war in 1941 they all went on stream with maximum production and he was rich. But he wanted more, and just as he had seen the coming war in 1939, he spotted something in 1944 that aroused his interest. A Britisher called Frank Whittle had invented an airplane engine with no propeller and potentially enormous power. He wondered what fuel it used.

In 1945 he discovered that Boeing/Lockheed had acquired the rights to Whittle's jet engine, and its fuel was not high-octane gasoline at all, but a low-grade kerosene. Sinking most of his funds into a down-market low-technology refinery in California, he approached Boeing/Lockheed, who coincidentally were becoming tired of the condescending arrogance of the major oil companies in their quest for the new fuel. Miller offered them his refinery, and together they developed the new Aviation Turbine Fuel—AVTUR. Miller's low-tech refinery was just the asset to produce AVTUR, and as the first samples came off the production line the Korean War started. With the Sabre jet fighters taking on the Chinese MiGs, the jet age had arrived. Pan-Global went into orbit and Miller returned to Texas.

He also married. Maybelle was tiny compared to her husband, but it was she who ruled his home and him through thirty years of marriage, and he doted on her. There were no children—she deemed she was too small and delicate to bear children—and he accepted this, happy to grant her any wish she could devise. When she died in 1980 he was totally inconsolable. Then he discovered God. He did not take to organized religion, just God. He began to talk to the Almighty and discovered that the Lord talked back to him, advising him personally on how best he might increase his wealth and serve Texas and the United States. It escaped his attention that the divine advice was always what he wished to hear, and that the Creator happily shared all his own chauvinism, prejudices, and bigotries. He continued as always to avoid the cartoonist's stereotype of the Texan, preferring to remain a nonsmoker, modest drinker, chaste, conservative in dress and speech, eternally courteous, and one who abominated foul language.

His intercom buzzed softly.

"The man whose name you wanted, Mr. Miller? When you met him he worked for IBM in Saudi Arabia. IBM confirms it must be the same man. He quit them and is now a free-lance consultant. His name is Easterhouse—Colonel Robert Easterhouse."

"Find him," said Miller. "Send for him. No matter what it costs. Bring him to me."

CHAPTER TWO

Marshal Kozlov sat impassively behind his desk and studied the four men who flanked the stem of the T-shaped conference table. All four were reading the Top Secret folders in front of them; all four were men he knew he could trust—had to trust, for his career, and maybe more, was on the line.

To his immediate left was the Deputy Chief of Staff (South), who worked with him here in Moscow but had overall charge of the southern quarter of the U.S.S.R. with its teeming Moslem republics and its borders with Romania, Turkey, Iran, and Afghanistan. Beyond him was the chief of High Command South at Baku, who had flown to Moscow believing he was coming for routine staff conferences. But there was nothing routine about this one. Before coming to Moscow seven years earlier as First Deputy, Kozlov himself had commanded at Baku, and the man who now sat reading Plan Suvorov owed his promotion to Kozlov's influence.

Across from these two sat the other pair, also engrossed. Nearest to the marshal was a man whose loyalty and involvement would be paramount if Suvorov was ever to succeed: the Deputy Head of the GRU, the Soviet armed forces' intelligence branch. Constantly at loggerheads with its bigger rival, the KGB, the GRU was responsible for all military intelligence at home and abroad, counterintelligence, and internal security within the armed forces. More important for Plan Suvorov, the GRU controlled the Special Forces, the Spetsnaz, whose involvement at the start of Suvorov—if it ever went ahead—would be crucial. It was the Spetsnaz who in the winter of 1979 had flown into Kabul airport, stormed the presidential palace, assassinated the Afghan president, and installed the Soviet puppet Babrak Karmal, who had promptly issued a back-dated appeal to Soviet forces to enter the country and quell the "disturbances."

Kozlov had chosen the Deputy because the head of the GRU was an old KGB man foisted on the General Staff, and no one had any doubt that he constantly scuttled back to his pals in the KGB with any tidbit he could gather to the detriment of the High Command. The GRU man had driven across Moscow from the GRU building just north of the Central Airfield.

Beyond the GRU man sat another, who had come from his headquarters in the northern suburbs and whose men would be vital for Suvorov—the Deputy Commander of the Vozdushna Desantniki Voist or Air Assault Force, the paratroopers of the VDV who would have to drop onto a dozen cities named in Suvorov and secure them for the following air bridge.

There was no need at this point to bring in the Air Defense of the Homeland, the Voiska PVO, since the U.S.S.R. was not about to be invaded; nor the Strategic Rockets Forces, since rockets would not be necessary. As for Motor/Rifles, Artillery, and Armor, the High Command South had enough for the job.

The GRU man finished the file and looked up. He seemed about to speak but the marshal raised a hand and they both sat silent until the other three had finished. The session had started three hours earlier, when all four had read a shortened version of Kaminsky's original oil report. The grimness with which they had noted its conclusions and forecasts was underscored by the fact that in the intervening twelve months several of those forecasts had come true.

There *were* already cutbacks in oil allocations; some maneuvers had had to be "rescheduled"—canceled—through lack of gasoline. The promised nuclear power plants had *not* reopened, the Siberian fields were still producing little more than usual, and the Arctic exploration was still a shambles for lack of technology, skilled manpower, and funds. *Glasnost* and *perestroika* and press conferences and exhortations from the Politburo were all very well, but making Russia efficient was going to take a lot more than that.

After a brief discussion of the oil report, Kozlov had handed out four files, one to each. This was Plan Suvorov, prepared over nine months since the previous November by Major General Zemskov. The marshal had sat on Suvorov for a further three months, until he estimated the situation south of their borders had reached a point likely to make his subordinate officers more susceptible to the boldness of the plan. Now they had finished and looked up expectantly. None wanted to be the first to speak.

"All right," said Marshal Kozlov carefully. "Comments?"

"Well," ventured the Deputy Chief of Staff, "it would certainly give us a source of crude oil sufficient to bring us well into the first half of the next century."

"That is the end game," said Kozlov. "What about feasibility?" He glanced at the man from High Command South.

"The invasion and the conquest—no problem," said the four-star general from Baku. "The plan is brilliant from that point of view. Initial resistance could be crushed easily enough. How we'd rule the bastards after that . . . They're crazies, of course. . . . We'd have to use extremely harsh measures."

"That could be arranged," said Kozlov smoothly.

"We'd have to use ethnic Russian troops," said the paratrooper. "*We* use them anyway, with Ukrainians. I think we all know we couldn't trust our divisions from the Moslem republics to do the job."

There was a growl of assent. The GRU man looked up.

"I sometimes wonder if we can any longer use the Moslem divisions for anything. Which is another reason I like Plan Suvorov. It would enable us to stop the spread of Islamic Fundamentalism seeping into our southern republics. Wipe out the source. My people in the South report that in the event of war we should probably not rely on our Moslem divisions to fight at all."

The general from Baku did not even dispute it.

"Bloody wogs," he growled. "They're getting worse all the time. Instead of defending the south, I'm spending half my time quelling religious riots in Tashkent, Samarkand, and Ashkhabad. I'd love to hit the bloody Party of Allah right at home."

"So," summed up Marshal Kozlov, "we have three plusses. It's feasible because of the long and exposed border and the chaos down there, it would get us our oil for half a century, and we could shaft the Fundamentalist preachers once and for all. Anything against . . . ?"

"What about Western reaction?" asked the paratrooper general. "The Americans could trigger World War Three over this."

"I don't think so," countered the GRU man, who had more experience of the West than any of them, having studied it for years. "American politicians are deeply subject to public opinion, and for most Americans today anything that happens to the Iranians can't be bad enough. That's how the broad masses of Americans see it."

All four men knew the recent history of Iran well enough. After the death of the Ayatollah Khomeini and an interregnum of bitter political infighting in Teheran, the succession had passed to the bloodstained Islamic judge Khalkhali, last seen gloating over American bodies recovered from the desert after the abortive attempt to rescue the hostages of the U.S. embassy.

Khalkhali had sought to protect his fragile ascendancy by instigating another reign of terror inside Iran, using the dreaded Patrols of Blood, the Gasht-e-Sarallah. Finally, as the most violent of these Revolutionary Guards threatened to go out of his control, he exported them abroad to conduct a series of terrorist atrocities against American citizens and assets across the Middle East and Europe, a campaign that had occupied most of the previous six months.

By the time the five Soviet soldiers were meeting to consider the invasion and occupation of Iran, Khalkhali was hated by the population of Iran, who had finally had enough of Holy Terror, and by the West.

"I think," resumed the GRU man, "that if we hanged Khalkhali, the American public would donate the rope. Washington might be outraged if we went in, but the congressmen and senators would hear the word from back home and advise the President to back off. And don't forget we're supposed to be buddy-buddies with the Yankees these days."

There was a rumble of amusement from around the table, in which Kozlov joined.

"Then where's the opposition going to come from?" he asked.

"I believe," said the general of the GRU, "that it wouldn't come from Washington, if we presented America with a *fait accompli*. But I think it will come from Novaya Ploshchad; the man from Stavropol will turn it down flat."

Novaya Ploshchad, or New Square, is the Moscow home of the Central Committee building, and the mention of Stavropol was a not-too-flattering reference to the General Secretary, Mikhail Gorbachev, who came from there.

The five soldiers nodded gloomily. The GRU man pressed his point.

"We all know that ever since that damned Cormack became the great Russian pop star at Vnukovo twelve months ago, teams from both Defense Ministries have been working out details for a big arms cutback treaty. Gorbachev flies to America in two weeks to try and clinch it, so he can liberate enough resources to develop our domestic oil industry. So long as he believes he can get our oil by that route, why should he shaft his beloved treaty with Cormack by giving us the green light to invade Iran?"

"And if he gets his treaty, will the Central Committee ratify it?" asked the general from Baku.

"He owns the Central Committee now," said Kozlov. "These last two years, almost all the opposition has been pruned away."

It was on that pessimistic but resigned note that the conference ended. The copies of Plan Suvorov were collected and locked in the marshal's safe, and the generals returned to their postings, prepared to stay silent, to watch and to wait.

Two weeks later Cyrus Miller also found himself in conference, although with a single man, a friend and colleague of many years. He and Melville Scanlon went back to the Korean War, when the young Scanlon was a feisty entrepreneur out of Galveston with his meager assets sunk in a few small tankers.

Miller had had a contract to supply and deliver his new jet fuel to the U.S. Air Force, delivery to be effected to the dockside in Japan where the Navy tankers would take it over and run it to beleaguered South Korea. He gave Scanlon the contract and the man had done wonders, running his rust-buckets around through the Panama Canal, picking up the AVTUR in California, and shipping it across the Pacific. By using the same ships to bring in crude and feedstock from Texas before changing cargoes and heading for Japan, Scanlon had kept his ships in freight all the way and Miller had got ample feedstock to convert into AVTUR. Three tanker crews had gone down in the Pacific but no questions were asked, and both men had made a great deal of money before Miller was eventually obliged to license his know-how to the majors.

Scanlon had gone on to become a bulk petroleum commodity broker and shipper, buying and transporting consignments of crude all over the world, mainly out of the Persian Gulf to America. After 1981, Scanlon had taken a pasting when the Saudis insisted that all their cargoes out of the Gulf should be carried in Arab-flag ships, a policy they were really able to enforce only in the movement of participation crude—i.e., that bit which belonged to the producing country rather than the producing oil company.

But it had been precisely the participation crude that Scanlon had been carrying across to America for the Saudis, and he had been squeezed out, forced to sell or lease his tankers to the Saudis and Kuwaitis at unattractive prices. He had survived, but he had no love for Saudi Arabia. Still, he had some tankers left which plied the route from the Gulf to the United States, mainly carrying Aramco crude, which managed to escape the Arab-flag-only demand.

Miller was standing at his favorite window staring down at the sprawl of Houston beneath him. It gave him a godlike feeling to be so high above the rest of humanity. On the other side of the room Scanlon leaned back in his leather club chair and tapped the Dixon oil report, which he had just finished. Like Miller, he knew that Gulf crude had just hit $20 a barrel.

"I agree with you, old friend. There is no way the U.S. of A. should ever become dependent for its very life on these bastards. What the hell does Washington think it's up to? They blind up there?"

"There'll be no help from Washington, Mel," said Miller calmly. "You want to change things in this life, you better do it yourself. We've all learned that the hard way."

Mel Scanlon produced a handkerchief and mopped his brow. Despite the air conditioning in the office, he always had a tendency to sweat. Unlike Miller he favored the traditional Texan rig—Stetson hat, bolo tie, Navajo tie clasp and belt buckle, and high-heeled boots. The pity was he hardly had the figure of a cattleman, being short and portly; but behind his good-ole-boy image he concealed an astute brain.

"Don't see how you can change the location of these vast reserves," he huffed. "The Hasa oil fields are in Saudi Arabia, and that's a fact."

"No, not their geographic location. But the political control of them," said Miller, "and therefore the ability to dictate the price of Saudi and thus world oil."

"*Political* control? You mean to another bunch of Ay-rabs?"

"No, to us," said Miller. "To the United States of America. If we're to survive, we have to control the price of world oil, pegging it at a price we can afford, and that means controlling the government in Riyadh. This nightmare of being at the beck and call of a bunch of goatherds has gone on long enough. It's got to be changed and Washington won't do it. But this might."

He picked up a sheaf of papers from his desk, neatly bound between stiff paper covers that bore no label. Scanlon's face puckered.

"Not another report, Cy," he protested.

"Read it," urged Miller. "Improve your mind."

Scanlon sighed and flicked open the file. The title page read simply:

THE DESTRUCTION AND FALL OF THE HOUSE OF SA'UD

"Holy shit," said Scanlon.

"No," said Miller calmly. "Holy Terror. Read on."

Islam: The religion of Islam was established through the teachings of the Prophet Mohammed around A.D. 622 and today encompasses between 800 million and 1 billion people. Unlike Christianity it has no consecrated priests; its religious leaders are laymen respected for their moral or intellectual qualities. The doctrines of Mohammed are laid down in the Koran.

Sects: Ninety percent of Moslems are of the Sunni (orthodox) branch. The most important minority is the Shi'ah (partisan) sect. The crucial difference is that the Sunnis follow the recorded statements of the Prophet, known as the Hadith (traditions), while the Shi'ites follow and accord divine infallibility to whoever is their current leader, or Imam. The strongholds of Shi'ism are Iran (93 percent) and Iraq (55 percent). Six percent of Saudi Arabians are Shi'ites, a persecuted, hate-filled minority whose leader is in hiding and who work mainly around the Hasa oil fields.

Fundamentalism: While Sunni fundamentalists *do* exist, the true home of fundamentalism is within the Shi'ah sect. This sect-within-a-sect predicates absolute adherence to the Koran as interpreted by the late Ayatollah Khomeini, who has not been replaced.

Hezb'Allah: Within Iran, the true and ultimate fundamentalist creed is contained within the army of fanatics who style themselves the Party of God, or Hezb'Allah. Elsewhere, fundamentalists operate under different names, but for the purposes of this report, Hezb'Allah will do.

Aims and Creeds: The basic philosophy is that *all* of Islam should be brought back to, and eventually all the world brought to, the submission to the will of Allah interpreted by and demanded by Khomeini. On that road there are a number of prerequisites, three of which are of interest: All existing Moslem governments are illegitimate because they are not founded on unconditional submission to Allah—i.e., Khomeini; any coexistence between Hezb'Allah and a secular Moslem government is inconceivable; it is the divine duty of Hezb'Allah to punish with death all wrongdoers against Islam throughout the world, but especially heretics within Islam.

Methods: The Hezb'Allah has long decreed that in accomplishing this last aim there shall be no mercy, no compassion, no pity, no restraint, and no flinching—even to the point of self-martyrdom. They call this Holy Terror.

Proposal: To inspire, rally, activate, organize, and assist the Shi'ah zealots to massacre the six hundred leading and controlling members of the House of Sa'ud, thus destroying the dynasty and with it the government in Riyadh, which would then be replaced by a princeling prepared to accept an ongoing American military occupation of the Hasa fields and peg the price of crude at a level "suggested" by the U.S.A.

"Who the hell wrote this?" asked Scanlon as he put down the report, of which he had read only the first half.

"A man I've been using as a consultant these past twelve months," said Miller. "Do you want to meet him?"

"He's here?"

"Outside. He arrived ten minutes ago."

"Sure," said Scanlon. "Let's take a look at this maniac."

"In a moment," said Miller.

The Cormack family, long before Professor John Cormack left academe to enter politics as a congressman from the state of Connecticut, had always had a summer vacation home on the island of Nantucket. He had come there first as a young teacher with his new bride thirty years earlier, before Nantucket became fashionable like Martha's Vineyard and Cape Cod, and had been entranced by the clean-air simplicity of life there.

Lying due east of Martha's Vineyard, off the Massachusetts coast, Nantucket then had its traditional fishing village, its Indian burial ground, its bracing winds and golden beaches, a few vacation homes, and not much else. Land was available and the young couple had scrimped and saved to purchase a four-acre plot at Shawkemo, along the strand from Children's Beach and on the edge of the near-landlocked lagoon called simply the Harbor. There John Cormack had built his frame house, clad in overlapping weathered-gray boards, with wooden shingles on the roof and rough-hewn furniture, hooked rugs, and patchwork quilts inside.

Later there was more money, and improvements were made and some extensions added. When he first came to the White House and said he wished to spend his vacations at Nantucket, a minor hurricane descended on the old home. Experts arrived from Washington, looked in horror at the lack of space, the lack of security, of communications. . . . They came back and said yes, Mr. President, that would be fine; they would just have to build quarters for a hundred Secret Service men, fix a helicopter pad, several cottages for visitors, secretaries, and household staff—there was no way Myra Cormack could continue to make the beds herself—oh, and maybe a satellite dish or two for the communications people. . . . President Cormack had called the whole thing off.

Then, that November, he had taken a gamble with the man from Moscow, inviting Mikhail Gorbachev up to Nantucket for a long weekend. And the Russian had loved it.

His KGB heavies had been as distraught as the Secret Service men, but both leaders were adamant. The two men, wrapped against the knifing wind off Nantucket Sound (the Russian had brought a sable fur *shapka* for the American), took long walks along the beaches while KGB and Secret Service men plodded after them, others hid in the sere grass and muttered into communicators, a helicopter clawed its way through the winds above them, and a Coast Guard cutter pitched and plunged offshore.

No one tried to kill anybody. The two men strolled into Nantucket town unannounced and the fishermen at Straight Wharf showed them their fresh-caught lobsters and scallops. Gorbachev admired the catch and twinkled and beamed, and then they had a beer together at a dockside bar and walked back to Shawkemo, looking side by side like a bulldog and a stork.

At night, after steamed lobsters in the frame house, the defense experts from each side joined them and the interpreters, and they worked out the last points of principle and drafted their communiqué.

On Tuesday the press was allowed in—there had always been a token force pooling pictures and words, for after all this *was* America, but on Tuesday the massed battalions arrived. At noon the two men emerged onto the wooden veranda and the President read the communiqué. It announced the firm intention to put before the Central Committee and the Senate a wide-ranging and radical agreement to cut back conventional forces across the board and across the world. There were still some verification problems to be ironed out, a job for the technicians, and the specific details of what types of weaponry and how much were to be decommissioned, mothballed, scrapped, or aborted would be announced later. President Cormack spoke of peace with honor, peace with security, and peace with good will. Secretary Gorbachev nodded vigorously as the translation came through. No one mentioned then, though the press did later and at great length, that with the U.S. budget deficit, the Soviet economic chaos, and a looming oil crisis, neither superpower could finally afford a continuing arms race.

Two thousand miles away in Houston, Cyrus V. Miller switched off the television and stared at Scanlon.

"That man is going to strip us naked," he said with quiet venom. "That man is dangerous. That man is a traitor."

He recovered himself and strode to the desk intercom.

"Louise, would you send in Colonel Easterhouse now, please."

Someone once said: All men dream, but they are most dangerous who dream with their eyes open. Colonel Robert Easterhouse sat in the elegant reception room atop the Pan-Global Building and stared at the window and the panoramic view of Houston. But his pale-blue eyes saw the vaulted sky and ocher sands of the Nejd and he dreamed of controlling the income from the Hasa oil fields for the benefit of America and all mankind.

Born in 1945, he was three when his father accepted a teaching job at the American University in Beirut. The Lebanese capital had been a paradise in those days, elegant, cosmopolitan, rich, and safe. He had attended an Arab school for a while, had French and Arab playmates; by the time the family returned to Idaho he was thirteen and trilingual in English, French, and Arabic.

Back in America the youth had found his schoolmates shallow, frivolous, and stunningly ignorant, obsessed by rock 'n' roll and a young singer called Presley. They mocked his tales of swaying cedars, Crusader forts, and the plumes of the Druse campfires drifting through the Chouf mountain passes. So he was driven to books, and none more than *The Seven Pillars of Wisdom* by Lawrence of Arabia. At eighteen, forsaking college and the girls back home, he volunteered for the 82nd Airborne. He was still at boot camp when Kennedy died.

For ten years he had been a paratrooper, with three tours in Vietnam, coming out with the last forces in 1973. Men can acquire fast promotion when casualties are high and he was the 82nd's youngest colonel when he was crippled, not in war but in a stupid accident. It had been a training drop in the desert; the DZ was supposed to be flat and sandy, the winds a breeze at five knots. As usual the brass had got it wrong. The wind was thirty-plus at ground level; the men were smashed into rocks and gullies. Three dead, twenty-seven injured.

The X-ray plates later showed the bones in Easterhouse's left leg

like a box of matches scattered on black velvet. He watched the embarrassing scuttle of the last U.S. forces out of the embassy in Saigon—
Bunker's bunker, as he knew it from the Tet offensive—on a hospital TV
in 1975. While in the hospital he chanced on a book about computers and
realized that these machines were the road to power: a way to correct
the madnesses of the world and bring order and sanity to chaos and
anarchy, if properly used.

Quitting the military, he went to college and majored in computer
science, joined Honeywell for three years, and moved to IBM. It was
1981, the petrodollar power of the Saudis was at its peak, Aramco had
hired IBM to construct for them foolproof computer systems to monitor
production, flow, exportation, and above all royalty dues throughout
their monopoly operation in Saudi Arabia. With fluent Arabic and
a genius for computers, Easterhouse was a natural. He spent five
years protecting Aramco's interests in Saudi, coming to specialize in
computer-monitored security systems against fraud and theft. In 1986,
with the collapse of the OPEC cartel, the power shifted back to the
consumers; and the Saudis felt exposed. They head-hunted the limping
computer genius who spoke their language and knew their customs,
paying him a fortune to go free-lance and work for them instead of IBM
and Aramco.

He knew the country and its history like a native. Even as a boy he
had thrilled to the written tales of the Founder, the dispossessed no-
madic Sheikh Abdal Aziz al Sa'ud, sweeping out of the desert to storm
the Musmak Fortress at Riyadh and begin his march to power. He had
marveled at the astuteness of Abdal Aziz as he spent thirty years con-
quering the thirty-seven tribes of the interior, uniting the Nejd to the
Hejaz to the Hadhramaut, marrying the daughters of his vanquished
enemies and binding the tribes into a nation—or the semblance of one.

Then Easterhouse saw the reality, and admiration turned to disillu-
sion, contempt, and loathing. His job with IBM had involved preventing
and detecting computer fraud in systems devised by unworldly whiz
kids from the States, monitoring the translation of operational oil production into accounting language and ultimately bank balances, creating foolproof systems that could also be integrated with the Saudi
treasury setup. It was the profligacy and the dizzying corruption that
turned his basically puritan spirit to a conviction that one day he would
become the instrument that would sweep away the result of a freak
accident of fate which had given such huge wealth and power to such a
people; it would be he who would restore order and correct the mad

imbalances of the Middle East, so that this God-given gift of oil would be used first for the service of the Free World and then for all the peoples of the world.

He could have used his skills to skim a vast fortune for himself from the oil revenues, as the princes did, but his morality forbade him. So to fulfill his dream he would need the support of powerful men, backup, funding. And then he had been summoned by Cyrus Miller to bring down the corrupt edifice and deliver it to America. Now, all he had to do was persuade these barbarian Texans that he was their man.

"Colonel Easterhouse?" He was interrupted by the honeyed tones of Louise. "Mr. Miller will see you now, sir."

He rose, leaned on his cane for a few seconds till the pain eased, then followed her into Miller's office. He greeted Miller respectfully and was introduced to Scanlon. Miller came straight to the point.

"Colonel, I would like my friend and colleague here to be convinced, as I am, of the feasibility of your concept. I respect his judgment and would like him to be involved with us."

Scanlon appreciated the compliment. Easterhouse spotted that it was a lie. Miller did not respect Scanlon's judgment, but they would both need Scanlon's ships, covertly used to import the needed weaponry for the coup d'état.

"You read my report, sir?" Easterhouse asked Scanlon.

"That bit about the Hez-Boll-Ah guys, yes. Heavy stuff, lot of funny names. How do you think you can use them to bring down the monarchy? And more important, deliver the Hasa oil fields to America?"

"Mr. Scanlon, you cannot control the Hasa oil fields and direct their product to America unless you first control the government in Riyadh, hundreds of miles away. That government must be changed into a puppet regime, wholly ruled by its American advisers. America cannot topple the House of Sa'ud openly—Arab reaction would be impossible. My plan is to provoke a small group of Shi'ah Fundamentalists, dedicated to Holy Terror, to carry out the act. The idea that Khomeinists have come to control the Saudi peninsula would send waves of panic throughout the entire Arab world. From Oman in the south, up through the Emirates to Kuwait, from Syria, Iraq, Jordan, Lebanon, Egypt, and Israel would come immediately overt or covert pleas to America to intervene to save them all from Holy Terror.

"Because I have been setting up a computerized Saudi internal security system for two years, I am aware that such a group of Holy

Terror fanatics exists, headed by an Imam who regards the King, his group of brothers—the inner Mafia known as the Al-Fahd—and the entire family of three thousand princelings who make up the dynasty, with pathological loathing. The Imam has publicly denounced them all as the Whores of Islam, Defilers of the Holy Places of Mecca and Medina. He has had to go into hiding, but I can keep him safe until we need him by erasing all news of his whereabouts from the central computer. Also, I have a contact with him—a disenchanted member of the Mutawain, the ubiquitous and hated Religious Police."

"But what's the point in handing over Saudi Arabia to these yoyos?" demanded Scanlon. "With Saudi's pending income of three hundred million U.S. dollars a day—hell, they'd wreak absolute havoc."

"Precisely. Which the Arab world itself could not tolerate. Every state in the area excepting Iran would appeal to America to intervene. Washington would be under massive pressure to fly the Rapid Deployment Force into its prepared base in Oman, on the Musandam Peninsula, and thence into Riyadh, the capital, and Dhahran and Bahrein, to secure the oil fields before they could be destroyed forever. Then we'd have to stay to prevent its ever happening again."

"And this Imam guy," asked Scanlon. "What happens to him?"

"He dies," said Easterhouse calmly, "to be replaced by the one princeling of the House who was not present at the massacre, because he was abducted to my house in time to avoid it. I know him well—he's Western educated, pro-American, weak, vacillating, and a drunk. But he will legitimize the other Arab appeals by one of his own, by radio from our embassy in Riyadh. As the sole surviving member of the dynasty, he can appeal for America to intervene to restore legitimacy. Then he'll be our man forever."

Scanlon thought it over. He reverted to type.

"What's in it for us? I don't mean the U.S.A. I mean *us!*"

Miller intervened. He knew Scanlon and how he would react.

"Mel, if this prince rules in Riyadh and is advised every waking moment of the day by the colonel here, we are looking at the breaking of the Aramco monopoly. We are looking at new contracts, shipping, importing, refining. And guess who's at the head of the line?"

Scanlon nodded his assent. "When do you plan to schedule this . . . event?"

"You may know that the storming of the Musmak Fortress was in January 1902; the declaration of the new kingdom was in 1932," said Easterhouse. "Fifteen months from now, in the spring of 1992, the King and his court will celebrate the ninetieth anniversary of the first and the diamond jubilee of the kingdom. They are planning a vast billion-dollar jamboree before a world audience. The new covered stadium is being built. I am in charge of all its computer-governed security systems—gates, doors, windows, air conditioning. A week before the great night there will be a full dress rehearsal attended by the leading six hundred members of the House of Sa'ud, drawn from every corner of the world. That is when I will arrange for the Holy Terrorists to strike. The doors will be computer-locked with them inside; the five hundred soldiers of the Royal Guard will be issued defective ammunition, imported, along with the submachine carbines needed by the Hezb'Allah to do the job, in your ships."

"And when it's over?" asked Scanlon.

"When it's over, Mr. Scanlon, there will be no House of Sa'ud left. Nor of the terrorists. The stadium will catch fire and the cameras will continue rolling until meltdown. Then the new ayatollah, the self-styled Living Imam, inheritor of the spirit and soul of Khomeini, will go on television and announce his plans to the world, which has just seen what happened in the stadium. That, I'm certain, will start the appeals to Washington."

"Colonel," said Cyrus Miller, "how much funding will you need?"

"To begin advance planning immediately, one million dollars. Later, two million for foreign purchases and hard-currency bribes. Inside Saudi Arabia—nothing. I can obtain a fund of local riyals amounting to several billion to cover all internal purchasing and palm-greasing."

Miller nodded. The strange visionary was asking peanuts for what he intended to do.

"I will see that you get it, Colonel. Now, would you mind waiting outside for a little while? I'd like you to come and have dinner at my house when I'm done."

As Colonel Easterhouse turned to go he paused in the doorway.

"There is, or might be, one problem. The only ungovernable factor I can perceive. President Cormack seems to be a man dedicated to peace and, from what I observed at Nantucket, now dedicated to a new treaty with the Kremlin. That treaty would probably not survive our takeover of the Saudi peninsula. Such a man might even refuse to send in the Rapid Deployment Force."

When he had gone, Scanlon swore, drawing a frown from Miller.

"He could be right, you know, Cy. God, if only Odell were in the White House."

Although personally chosen by Cormack as his running mate, Vice

President Michael Odell was also a Texan, a businessman, a self-made millionaire, and much farther to the right than Cormack. Miller, possessed by unusual passion, turned and gripped Scanlon by the shoulders.

"Mel, I have prayed to the Lord over that man—many, many times. And I asked for a sign. And with this colonel and what he just said, He has given me that sign. Cormack has got to go."

Just north of the gambling capital of Las Vegas in Nevada lies the huge sprawl of Nellis Air Force Range, where gambling is definitely not on the agenda. For the 11,274-acre base broods over the United States' most secret weapons-testing range, the Tonopah Test Range, where any stray private aircraft penetrating its 3,012,770 acres of test-ground during a test is likely to be given one warning and then shot down.

It was here, on a bright crisp morning in December 1990, that two groups of men disembarked from a convoy of limousines to witness the first testing and demonstration of a revolutionary new weapon. The first group comprised the manufacturers of the multi-launch rocket vehicle, which was the base of the system, and they were accompanied by men from the two associated corporations who had built the rockets and the electronics/avionics programs incorporated in the weapon. Like most modern hardware, Despot, the ultimate tank-destroyer, was not a simple device but involved a net of complex systems that in this case had come from three separate corporations.

Peter Cobb was chief executive officer and major shareholder in Zodiac AFV, Inc., a company specializing in armored fighting vehicles—hence the initials in its name. For him personally, and for his company, which had developed Despot at their own expense over seven years, everything hung on the weapon's being accepted and bought by the Pentagon. He had little doubt; Despot was years ahead of Boeing's Pave Tiger system and the newer Tacit Rainbow. He knew it responded completely to an abiding concern of NATO planners—isolating the first wave of any Soviet tank attack across the central German plain from the second wave.

His colleagues were Lionel Moir of Pasadena Avionics in California, who had built the Kestrel and Goshawk components, and Ben Salkind of ECK Industries, Inc., in the Silicon Valley near Palo Alto, California. These men also had crucial personal as well as corporate stakes in the adoption of Despot by the Pentagon. ECK Industries had a slice of the prototype-stage B2 Stealth bomber for the Air Force, but this was an assured project.

The Pentagon team arrived two hours later, when everything was set up. There were twelve of them, including two generals, and they comprised the technical group whose recommendation would be vital to the Pentagon decision. When they were all seated under the awning in front of the battery of TV screens, the test began.

Moir started with a surprise. He invited the audience to swivel in their seats and survey the nearby desert. It was flat, empty. They were puzzled. Moir pressed a button on his console. Barely yards away the desert began to erupt. A great metal claw emerged, reached forward, and pulled. Out of the sand where it had buried itself, immune to hunting fighter planes and downward-looking radar, came the Despot. A great block of gray steel on wheels and tracks, windowless, independent, self-contained, proof against direct hit by all but a heavy artillery shell or large bomb, proof against nuclear, gas, and germ attack, it hauled itself out of its self-dug grave and went to work.

The four men inside started the engines that powered the systems, drew back the steel screens that covered the reinforced glass portholes, and pushed out their radar dish to warn them of incoming attack, and their sensor antennae to help them guide their missiles. The Pentagon team was impressed.

"We will assume," said Cobb, "that the first wave of Soviet tanks has crossed the Elbe River into West Germany by several existing bridges and a variety of military bridges thrown up during the night. NATO forces are engaging the first wave. We have enough to cope. But the much bigger second wave of Russian tanks is emerging from their cover in the East German forests and heading for the Elbe. These will make the breakthrough and head for the French border. The Despots, deployed and buried in a north-south line through Germany, have their orders. Find, identify, and destroy."

He pressed another button and a hatch opened at the top of the AFV. From it, on a ramp, emerged a pencil-slim rocket. Twenty inches in diameter, an eight-foot tube. It ignited its tiny rocket motor and soared away into the pale-blue sky where, being pale blue itself, it disappeared from view. The men returned to their screens, where a high-definition TV camera was tracking the Kestrel. At 150 feet its high-bypass turbofan jet engine ignited, the rocket died and dropped away, short stubby wings sprouted from its sides, and tail fins gave it guidance. The miniature rocket began to fly like an airplane, and still it climbed away down the range. Moir pointed to a large radar screen. The sweep arm circled the disk but no responding image glowed into light.

"The Kestrel is made entirely of Fiberglas," intoned Moir proudly. "Its engine is made of ceramic derivatives, heat-resistant but nonreflective to radar. With a little 'stealth' technology thrown in, you will see it is totally invisible—to eye or machine. It has the radar signature of a strawberry finch. Less. A bird can be radar-detected by the flapping of its wings. Kestrel doesn't flap, and this radar is far more sophisticated than anything the Soviets have got."

In war the Kestrel, a deep-penetration vehicle, would penetrate two hundred to five hundred miles behind enemy lines. In this test it reached operating altitude at fifteen thousand feet, hauled in at one hundred miles downrange, and began to circle slowly, giving it ten hours of endurance at one hundred knots. It also began to look down electronically. Its range of sensors came into play. Like a hunting bird it scanned the terrain beneath, covering a circle of land seventy miles in diameter.

Its infrared scanners did the hunting; then it interrogated with millimeter-band radar.

"It is programmed to strike only if the target is emitting heat, is made of steel, and is moving," said Moir. "Target must emit enough heat to be a tank, not a car, a truck, or a train. It won't hit a bonfire, a heated house, or a parked vehicle, because they aren't moving. It won't hit angle-reflectors for the same reason, or brick, timber, or rubber, because they are not steel. Now look at the target area on this screen, gentlemen."

They turned to the giant screen whose image was being piped to them from the TV camera a hundred miles away. A large area had been fitted out like a Hollywood set. There were artificial trees, wooden shacks, parked vans, trucks, and cars. There were rubber tanks, which now began to crawl, pulled by unseen wires. There were bonfires, gasoline-ignited, which blazed into flame. Then a single real tank began to move, radio-controlled. At fifteen thousand feet the Kestrel spotted it at once and reacted.

"Gentlemen, here is the new revolution, of which we are justly proud. In former systems the hunter threw itself downward on the target, destroying itself and all that expensive technology. Very cost-inefficient. Kestrel doesn't do that; it calls up a Goshawk. Watch the Despot."

The audience swiveled again, in time to catch the flicker of the rocket of the yard-long Goshawk missile that now obeyed the Kestrel's call and headed for the target on command. Salkind took up the commentary.

"The Goshawk will scream up to one hundred thousand feet, keel over, and head back down. As it passes the Kestrel, the remotely piloted vehicle will pass on final target information to the Goshawk. Kestrel's onboard computer will give the target's position when the Goshawk hits zero feet, to the nearest eighteen inches. Goshawk will hit within that circle. It's coming down now."

Amid all the houses, shacks, trucks, vans, cars, bonfires, angle-reflectors dug into the sand of the target area; amid the decoy rubber tanks, the steel tank (an old Abrams Mark One) rumbled forward as to war. There was a sudden flicker and the Abrams seemed to have been punched by a massive fist. Almost in slow motion it flattened out, its sides burst outward, its gun jerked upward to point accusingly at the sky, and it burst into a fireball. Under the awning there was a collective letting-out of breath.

"How much ordnance do you have in the nose of that Goshawk?" asked one of the generals.

"None, General," said Salkind. "Goshawk is like a smart rock. It's coming down at close to ten thousand miles per hour. Apart from its receiver for getting information from Kestrel and its tiny radar for following instructions to the target for the last fifteen thousand feet, it has no technology. That's why it's so cheap. But the effect of ten kilograms of tungsten-tipped steel at that speed hitting a tank is like . . . well, like firing an air-gun pellet onto the back of a cockroach at point-blank range. That tank just stopped the equivalent of two Amtrak locomotives at a hundred miles per hour. It was just flattened."

The test continued for another two hours. The manufacturers proved they could reprogram the Kestrel in flight; if they told it to go for steel structures with water on each side and land at each end, it would take out bridges. If they changed the hunting profile, it would strike at trains, barges, or moving columns of trucks. So long as they were moving. Stationary, except for bridges Kestrel did not know if an object was a steel truck or a small steel shed. But its sensors could penetrate rain, cloud, snow, hail, sleet, fog, and darkness.

The groups broke up in mid-afternoon, and the Pentagon committee prepared to board its limousines for Nellis and the flight to Washington.

One of the generals held out his hand to the manufacturers.

"As a tank man," he said, "I have never seen anything so frightening in my life. It has my vote. It will worry Frunze Street sick. To be hunted by men is bad enough; to be hunted like that by a goddam robot—hell, what a nightmare!"

It was one of the civilians who had the last word.

"Gentlemen, it's brilliant. The best RPV deep-strike tank-buster system in the world. But I have to say, if this new Nantucket Treaty goes through, it looks like we'll never order it."

Cobb, Moir, and Salkind realized as they shared a car back to Las Vegas that Nantucket was facing them, along with thousands of others in the military-industrial complex, with utter corporate and personal ruin.

On the eve of Christmas there was no work in Alcántara del Rio but much drinking was done and it went on until late. When Antonio finally closed his little bar it was past midnight. Some of his customers lived right there in the village; others drove or walked back to their scattered cottages spread across the hillsides around the villages. Which was why José Francisco, called Pablo, was lurching happily along the track past the house of the tall foreigner, feeling no pain save a slight bursting of the bladder. Finding he could go no farther without relief, he turned to the rubble wall of the yard in which was parked the battered SEAT Terra mini-jeep, unzipped his fly, and devoted himself to enjoyment of man's second greatest single pleasure.

Above his head the tall man slept, and again he dreamed the awful dream that had brought him to these parts. He was drenched in sweat as he went through it all for the hundredth time. Still asleep, he opened his mouth and screamed, "No...o...o...o!"

Down below, Pablo leaped a foot clear in the air and fell back in the road, soaking his Sunday-best trousers. Then he was up and running, his urine sloshing down his legs, his zipper still undone, his organ receiving an unaccustomed breath of fresh air. If the big, rangy foreigner was going to get violent, then he, José Francisco Echevarría, by the grace of God, was not going to stick around. He was polite, all right, and spoke good Spanish, but there was something strange about that man.

In the middle of the following January a young freshman came cycling down St. Giles Street in the ancient British city of Oxford, bent upon meeting his new tutor and enjoying his first full day at Balliol College. He wore thick corduroy trousers and a down parka against the cold, but over it he had insisted on wearing the black academic gown of an undergraduate at Oxford University. It flapped in the wind. Later he would learn that most undergraduates did not wear them unless eating in hall, but as a newcomer he was very proud of it. He would have preferred to live in college, but his family had rented him a large house just off the Woodstock Road. He passed the Martyrs' Memorial and entered Magdalen Street.

Behind him, unperceived, a plain sedan came to a halt. There were three men in it, two in the front and one in the back. The third man leaned forward.

"Magdalen Street is restricted access. Not for cars. You'll have to continue on foot."

The man in the front passenger seat swore softly and slipped to the pavement. At a fast walk he glided through the crowd, intent on the cycling figure ahead of him. Directed by the man in the back, the car swerved right into Beaumont Street, then left into Gloucester Street and another left down George Street. It stopped, having reached the bottom end of Magdalen, just as the cyclist emerged. The freshman dismounted a few yards into Broad Street, across the junction, so the car did not move. The third man came out of Magdalen, flushed from the icy wind, glanced around, spotted the car, and rejoined them.

"Damn city," he remarked. "All one-way streets and no-entry areas."

The man in the back chuckled.

"That's why the students use bicycles. Maybe we should."

"Just keep watching," said the driver without humor. The man beside him fell silent and adjusted the gun under his left arm.

The student had dismounted and was staring down at a cross made of cobblestones in the middle of Broad Street. He had learned from his guidebook that on this spot in 1555 two bishops, Latimer and Ridley, had been burned alive on the orders of Catholic Queen Mary. As the flames took hold, Bishop Latimer called across to his fellow martyr: "Be of good comfort, Master Ridley, and play the man. We shall this day light such a candle by God's grace in England as I trust shall never be put out."

He meant the candle of the Protestant faith, but what Bishop Ridley replied is not recorded, since he was burning brightly at the time. A year later, on the same spot in 1556, Archbishop Cranmer followed them to death. The flames from the pyre had scorched the door of Balliol College a few yards away. Later that door was taken down and rehung at the entrance to the Inner Quadrangle, where the scorch marks are plainly visible today.

"Hello," said a voice by the student's side and he glanced down. He was tall and gangly; she, short with dark bright eyes and plump as a partridge. "I'm Jenny. I think we're sharing the same tutor."

The twenty-one-year-old freshman, attending Oxford on a junior-year-abroad program after two years at Yale, grinned.

"Hi. I'm Simon."

They walked across to the arched entrance to the college, the young man pushing his bicycle. He had been there the day before to meet the master, but that had been by car. Halfway through the arch they were confronted by the amiable but implacable figure of Tim Ward-Barber.

"New to the college, are we, sir?" he asked.

"Er, yes," said Simon. "First day, I guess."

"Very well then, let us learn the first rule of life here. Never, under any circumstances, drunk, drugged, or half-asleep, do we ever push, carry, or ride our bicycles through the arch into the quadrangle. Sir. Prop it against the wall with the others, if you please."

In universities there are chancellors, principals, masters, wardens, deans, bursars, professors, readers, fellows, and others in a variety of pecking orders. But a college's head porter is definitely Senior League. As a former NCO in the 16/5th Lancers, Tim had coped with a few squaddies in his time.

When Simon and Jenny came back he nodded benignly and told them: "You're with Dr. Keen, I believe. Corner of the quadrangle, up the stairs to the top."

When they reached the cluttered room at the top of the stairs of their tutor in medieval history and introduced themselves, Jenny called him "Professor" and Simon called him "Sir." Dr. Keen beamed at them over his glasses.

"Now," he said merrily, "there are two things and only two that I do not allow. One is wasting your time and mine; the other is calling me 'sir.' 'Dr. Keen' will do nicely. Then we'll graduate to 'Maurice.' By the way, Jenny, I'm not a professor either. Professors have chairs, and as you see I do not; at least not one in good repair."

He gestured happily at the collection of semi-collapsed upholstery and bade his students be comfortable. Simon sank his frame into a legless Queen Anne chair that left him three inches off the floor, and together they began to consider Jan Hus and the Hussite revolution in medieval Bohemia. Simon grinned. He knew he was going to enjoy Oxford.

It was purely coincidence that Cyrus Miller found himself a fortnight later sitting next to Peter Cobb at a fund-raising dinner in Austin,

Texas. He loathed such dinners and normally avoided them; this one was for a local politician, and Miller knew the value of leaving markers around the political world, to be called in later when he needed a favor. He was prepared to ignore the man next to him, who was not in the oil business, until Cobb let slip the name of his corporation and therefore his visceral opposition to the Nantucket Treaty and the man behind it, John Cormack.

"That goddam treaty has got to be stopped," said Cobb. "Somehow the Senate has got to be persuaded to refuse to ratify it."

The news of the day had been that the treaty was in the last stages of drafting, would be signed by the respective ambassadors in Washington and Moscow in April, ratified by the Central Committee in Moscow in October after the summer recess, and put before the Senate before year's end.

"Do you think the Senate *will* turn it down?" asked Miller carefully. The defense contractor looked gloomily into his fifth glass.

"Nope," he said. "Fact is, arms cutbacks are always popular among the voters, and despite the odds, Cormack has the charisma and the popularity to push it through by his own personality. I can't stand the guy, but that's a fact."

Miller admired the defeated man's realism.

"Do you know the terms of the treaty yet?" he asked.

"Enough," said Cobb. "They're fixing to slice tens of billions off the defense appropriations. Both sides of the Iron Curtain. There's talk of forty percent—bilateral, of course."

"Are there many more who think like you?" asked Miller.

Cobb was too drunk to follow the line of the questioning. "Just about the whole defense industry," he snarled. "We're looking at wholesale closings and total personal and corporate losses here."

"Mmmm. It's too bad Michael Odell is not our President," mused Miller. The man from Zodiac, Inc., gave a harsh laugh.

"Oh, what a dream. Yes, he'll be opposed to cutbacks. But that won't help us much. He'll stay Veep and Cormack will stay President."

"Will he now?" asked Miller quietly.

In the last week of the month, Cobb, Moir, and Salkind met Scanlon and Miller for a private dinner at Miller's invitation in a suite of cloistered luxury at the Remington Hotel in Houston. Over brandy and coffee Miller guided their thoughts to the notion of John Cormack's continued occupation of the Oval Office.

"He has to go," Miller intoned. The others nodded agreement.

"I'll have no truck with assassination," said Salkind hurriedly. "In any case, remember Kennedy. The effect of his death was to push through Congress every piece of civil rights legislation he couldn't get through himself. Totally counterproductive, if that was the point of the hit. And it was Johnson, of all people, who got it all into law."

"I agree," said Miller. "That course of action is inconceivable. But there must be a way of forcing his resignation."

"Name one," challenged Moir. "How the hell can anyone bring that about? The man's fireproof. There are no scandals in back of him. The caucus assured themselves of that before they asked him to step in."

"There must be something," said Miller. "Some Achilles' heel. We have the determination; we have the contacts; we have the financing. We need a planner."

"What about your man, the colonel?" asked Scanlon.

Miller shook his head. "He would still regard any U.S. President as his Commander in Chief. No, another man . . . out there somewhere . . ."

What he was thinking of, and what he intended to hunt down, was a renegade, subtle, ruthless, intelligent, and loyal only to money.

CHAPTER THREE

March 1991 Thirty miles west of Oklahoma City lies the federal penitentiary called El Reno, more officially known as a "federal corrections institution." Less formally, it is one of the toughest prisons in America—in criminal slang, a hard pen. At dawn on a chill morning in the middle of March a small door opened in the frame of its forbidding main gate and a man emerged.

He was of medium height, overweight, prison-pale, broke, and very bitter. He stared about him, saw little (there was little to see), turned toward the city, and began to walk. Above his head, unseen eyes in the guard towers watched him with small interest, then looked away. Other eyes from a parked car watched him far more intently. The stretch limousine was parked a discreet distance from the main gate, far enough for its license plate to be out of vision. The man staring through the rear window of the car put down his binoculars and muttered, "He's heading this way."

Ten minutes later the fat man passed the car, glanced at it, and walked on. But he was a pro, and already his alarm antennae were activated. He was a hundred yards beyond the car when its engine purred into life and it drew up beside him. A young man got out, clean-cut, athletic, pleasant-looking.

"Mr. Moss?"

"Who wants to know?"

"My employer, sir. He wishes to offer you an interview."

"No name, I suppose," said the fat man.

The other smiled. "Not yet. But we do have a warm car, a private airplane, and mean you no harm. Let's face it, Mr. Moss, do you have any place else to go?"

Moss thought. The car and the man did not smell of the Company—the CIA—or of the Bureau—the FBI—his sworn enemies. And no, he had no place else to go. He climbed into the back seat of the car, the young man got in beside him, and the limo headed not toward Oklahoma City but to Wiley Post Airport to the northwest.

In 1966, at the age of twenty-five, Irving Moss had been a junior provincial officer (a GS 12) with the CIA, fresh out of the States and working in Vietnam with the CIA-run Phoenix program. Those were the years when the Special Forces, the Green Berets, had been steadily handing over their hitherto rather successful hearts-and-minds program in the Mekong Delta to the South Vietnamese Army, who proceeded to handle the notion of actually *persuading* the peasants not to cooperate with the Viet Cong with considerably less skill and humanity. The Phoenix people had to liaise with the ARVN, while the Green Berets switched more and more to search-and-destroy missions, often bringing back Viet Cong prisoners or suspects for interrogation by the ARVN under the aegis of the Phoenix people. That was when Moss discovered both his secret taste and his true talent.

As a youth he had been puzzled and depressed by his own lack of sexuality, and recalled with unappeased bitterness the mockery he had suffered in his teenage years. He had also been bemused—the fifties were an age of relative innocence among teenagers—to observe that he could become immediately aroused by the sound of a human scream. For such a man the discreet and unquestioning jungles of Vietnam were an Aladdin's cave of pleasure. Alone with his rear-echelon Vietnamese unit, he had been able to appoint himself the chief interrogator of suspects, aided by a couple of like-minded South Vietnamese corporals.

It had been, for him, a beautiful three years, which ended one day in 1969 when a tall, craggy young Green Beret sergeant had unexpectedly walked out of the jungle, his left arm dripping blood, sent back by his officer to get medication. The young warrior had gazed for a few seconds upon Moss's work, turned without a word, and crashed a haymaker of a right-hand punch onto the bridge of his nose. The medics at

Danang had done their best, but the bones of the septum were so shattered that Moss had to go to Japan for treatment. Even then, remedial surgery had left the bridge of his nose broadened and flattened, and the passages were so damaged that he still whistled and snuffled as he breathed, especially when excited.

He never saw the sergeant again, there had been no official report, and he had managed to cover his tracks and stay with the Agency. Until 1983. In that year, much promoted, he had been with the CIA buildup of the *contra* movement in Honduras, supervising a series of jungle camps along the border with Nicaragua from which the *contras*, many of them former servants of the ousted and unlovable dictator Somoza, had run sporadic missions across the border into the land they had once ruled. One day such a group had returned with a thirteen-year-old boy, not a Sandinista, just a peasant kid.

The interrogation had taken place in a clearing in the bush a quarter of a mile from the *contra* camp, but on the still tropical air the demented shrieks could be clearly heard in the camp. No one slept. In the small hours the sounds finally ceased. Moss walked back into the camp as if drugged, threw himself on his cot, and fell into a deep sleep. Two of the Nicaraguan section commanders quietly left camp, walked into the bush, and returned after twenty minutes to demand an interview with the commander. Colonel Rivas saw them in his tent, where he was writing up reports by the light of his hissing Petromax. The two guerrillas talked to him for several minutes.

"We can't work with this one," concluded the first. "We have talked to the boys. They agree, *Coronel*."

"*Es malsano*," added the other. "*Un animal*."

Colonel Rivas sighed. He had once been a member of Somoza's death squads, had dragged a few trade unionists and malcontents from their beds in his time. He had seen a few executions, even taken part. But children . . . He reached for his radio. A mutiny or mass defection he did not need. Just after dawn an American military helicopter clattered into his camp and disgorged a stocky, dark man who happened to be the newly appointed CIA Deputy Chief of Latin American Section, on a familiarization tour of his new bailiwick. Rivas escorted the American into the bush and they, too, came back after a few minutes.

When Irving Moss awoke it was because someone was kicking the legs of his frame cot. He looked up blearily to see a man in green fatigues looking down at him.

"Moss, you're out," said the man.

"Who the hell are you?" asked Moss. He was told.

"One of them," he sneered.

"Yep, one of them. And you're out. Out of Honduras and out of the Agency." He showed Moss a piece of paper.

"This doesn't come from Langley," Moss protested.

"No," said the man, "this comes from me. *I* come from Langley. Get your gear into that chopper."

Thirty minutes later Agent David Weintraub watched the helicopter lift away into the morning sky. At Tegucigalpa, Moss was met by the Chief of Station, who was coldly formal and personally saw him on a flight to Miami and Washington. He never even went back to Langley. He was met at Washington National, given his papers, and told to get lost. For five years, much in demand, he worked for a variety of less and less palatable Middle Eastern and Central American dictators, and then organized drug-runs for Noriega of Panama. A mistake. The U.S. Drug Enforcement Agency put him on a Top Target list.

He was passing through London's Heathrow Airport in 1988 when the deceptively courteous guardians of British law stepped in front of him and wondered if they might have a quiet word. The word concerned a concealed handgun in his suitcase. Normal extradition procedures went through at record speed and he was landed back on U.S. soil three weeks later. At his trial he drew three years. As a first offender he might well have drawn a soft penitentiary. But while he was awaiting sentence two men had a discreet lunch at Washington's exclusive Metropolitan Club.

One was the stocky man called Weintraub, now risen to the post of Assistant Deputy Director (Operations) of the CIA. The other was Oliver "Buck" Revell, a big former Marine flier and Executive Assistant Director (Investigations) with the FBI. He had also been a football player in his youth, but had not played long enough to get his brain mashed. There were some at the Hoover Building who suggested it still worked quite well. Waiting until Revell had finished his steak, Weintraub showed him a file and some pictures. Revell closed the file and said simply, "I see." Unaccountably, Moss served his time in El Reno, also housing some of the most vicious murderers, rapists, and extortionists currently under lock and key in America. When he came out he had a pathological loathing of the Agency, the Bureau, the British . . . and that was just for starters.

At Wiley Post Airport the limousine swept through the main gate on a nod and pulled up beside a waiting Learjet. Apart from its license plate number, which Moss at once memorized, it bore no logo. Within five minutes it was airborne, heading a whisker west of due south. Moss could tell the approximate direction from the morning sun. The direction, he knew, was toward Texas.

Just outside Austin is the beginning of what Texans call the hill country and it was here that the owner of Pan-Global had his country home, a twenty-thousand-acre spread in the foothills. The mansion faced southeast, with panoramic views across the great Texan plain toward faraway Galveston and the Gulf. Apart from a sufficiency of servants' quarters, guest bungalows, swimming pool, and shooting range, the estate also contained its own landing strip, and it was here the Learjet landed shortly before noon.

Moss was conducted to a jacaranda-framed bungalow, given half an hour to bathe and shave, then led to the mansion and into a cool, leather-upholstered study. Two minutes later he was confronted by a tall, white-haired old man.

"Mr. Moss?" said the man. "Mr. Irving Moss?"

"Yes, sir," said Moss. He smelt money, a lot of it.

"My name is Miller," said the man. "Cyrus V. Miller."

April The meeting was in the Cabinet Room, down the hall and past the private secretary's room from the Oval Office. Like most people, President John Cormack had been surprised by the comparative smallness of the Oval Office when he had first seen it. The Cabinet Room, with its great eight-sided table beneath Stuart's portrait of George Washington, gave more room to spread papers and lean on elbows.

That morning John Cormack had invited his inner Cabinet of close and trusted friends and advisers to consider the final draft of the Nantucket Treaty. The details were worked out, the verification procedures checked through; the experts had given their grudging concurrence—or not, in the case of two senior generals who retired and three Pentagon staffers who had chosen to resign—but Cormack wanted last comments from his special team.

He was sixty years old, at the peak of his intellectual and political powers, unashamedly enjoying the popularity and authority of an office he had never expected to hold. When the crisis had enveloped the Republican party in the summer of '88, the party caucus had looked around wildly for someone to step in and take over the candidacy. Their collective eye had fallen on this congressman from Connecticut, scion of a wealthy and patrician New England family who had chosen to leave his family wealth in a series of trust funds and become a professor at Cornell until turning to Connecticut politics in his late thirties.

On the liberal wing of his party, John Cormack had been a virtual unknown to the country at large. Intimates knew him as decisive, honest, and humane, and had assured the caucus he was clean as the driven snow. He was not known as a television personality—now an indispensable attribute of a candidate—but they picked him nevertheless. To the media he was a bore. And then in four months of barnstorming campaigning, the unknown had turned things around. Forsaking tradition, he looked into the camera's eye and gave straight answers to every question, supposedly a recipe for disaster. He offended some, but mainly on the right, and they had nowhere else to go with their votes anyway. And he had pleased many more. A Protestant with an Ulster name, he had insisted as a condition of his coming that he pick his own Vice President, and had chosen Michael Odell, a confirmed Irish American and a Catholic from Texas.

They were quite unalike. Odell was much farther to the right than Cormack and had been governor of his state. Cormack just happened to like and trust the gum-chewing man from Waco. Somehow the ticket had worked; the voters went, by a narrow margin, for the man the press (wrongly) liked to compare with Woodrow Wilson, America's last professor-President, and the running mate who bluntly told Dan Rather:

"Ah don't always agree with mah friend John Cormack but, hell, this is America and I'll flatten any man who says he doesn't have the right to speak his mind."

And it worked. The combination of the arrow-straight New Englander, with his powerful and persuasive delivery, and the deceptively folksy Southwesterner took the vital black, Hispanic, and Irish votes and won. Since taking office Cormack had deliberately involved Odell in decision-making at the highest level. Now they sat opposite each other to discuss a treaty Cormack knew Odell disliked profoundly. Flanking the President were four other intimates: Jim Donaldson, Secretary of State; Bill Walters, the Attorney General; Hubert Reed of the Treasury; and Morton Stannard of Defense.

On either side of Odell were Brad Johnson, a brilliant black man from Missouri who had lectured in defense studies at Cornell and was now National Security Adviser, and Lee Alexander, Director of the CIA, who had replaced Judge William Webster a few months into

Cormack's incumbency. Alexander was there because, if the Soviets intended to breach the treaty terms, America would need rapid knowledge through her satellites and intelligence community with their in-place assets on the ground.

As the eight men read the final terms, none was in any doubt that this was one of the most controversial agreements the United States would ever sign. Already there was vigorous opposition on the right and from the defense-oriented industries. Back in 1988, under Reagan, the Pentagon had agreed to cut $33 billion in planned expenditures to produce a defense budget total of $299 billion. For the fiscal years 1990 through 1994, the services were told to cut *planned* expenditures by $37.1 billion, $41.3 billion, $45.3 billion, and $50.7 billion respectively. But that would only have limited spending *growth*. The Nantucket Treaty foresaw big *decreases* in defense expenditures, and if the growth cuts had caused problems, Nantucket was going to cause a furor.

The difference was, as Cormack stressed repeatedly, that the previous growth cuts had not been planned against actual cuts by the U.S.S.R. In Nantucket, Moscow had agreed to slash its own forces to an unheard-of degree. Moreover, Cormack knew the superpowers had little choice. Ever since he came to power he and Secretary of the Treasury Reed had wrestled with America's spiraling budget and trade deficits. They were heading out of control, threatening to shatter the prosperity not just of the United States but of the entire West. He had latched onto his own experts' analyses that the U.S.S.R. was in the same position for different reasons, and put it to Mikhail Gorbachev straight: I need to cut back and you need to redivert. The Russian had taken care of the rest of the Warsaw Pact countries; Cormack had won over NATO—first the Germans, then the Italians, the smaller members, and finally the British. These, broadly, were the terms:

In land forces, the U.S.S.R. agreed to cut her standing army in East Germany—the potential invasion force westward across the central German plain—by half of her twenty-one combat divisions in all categories. They would be not disbanded but withdrawn back beyond the Polish-Soviet frontier and not brought west again. Over and above this, the U.S.S.R. would reduce the manpower of the entire Soviet Army by 40 percent.

"Comments?" asked the President. Stannard of Defense, who not unnaturally had the gravest reservations about the treaty—the press had already speculated about his resignation—looked up.

"For the Soviets this is the meat of the treaty, because their army is their senior service," he said, quoting directly from the Chairman of the Joint Chiefs of Staff but not admitting it. "For the man in the street it looks fantastic; the West Germans already think so. But it's not as good as it looks.

"For one thing, the U.S.S.R. cannot maintain one hundred and seventy-seven line divisions as at present without extensive use of her southern ethnic groups—I mean the Moslems—and we know they'd dearly love to disband the lot. For another, what really frightens our planners is not a rambling Soviet Army; it's an army half that size but professionalized. A small professional army is much more use than a large oafish one, which is what they've got."

"But if they're back inside the U.S.S.R.," countered Johnson, "they can't invade West Germany. Lee, if they shifted them back via Poland into East Germany, would we fail to spot it?"

"Nope," said the CIA chief with finality. "Apart from satellites, which can be fooled by covered trucks and trains, I believe we and the British have too many assets in Poland not to spot it. Hell, the East Germans don't want to become a war zone either. They'd probably tell us themselves."

"Okay, what do we give up?" asked Odell.

"Some troops, not a lot," Johnson replied. "The Soviets withdraw ten divisions at fifteen thousand men each. We have three hundred and twenty-six thousand personnel in Western Europe. We cut to below three hundred thousand for the first time since 1945. At twenty-five thousand of us against a hundred and fifty thousand of them, it's still good: six to one, and we were looking at four to one."

"Yes," objected Stannard, "but we also have to agree not to activate our two new heavy divisions, one armored and one mechanized infantry."

"Cost savings, Hubert?" asked the President mildly. He tended to let others talk, listen carefully, make a few succinct and usually penetrating comments, and then decide. The Treasury Secretary supported Nantucket. It would make balancing his books a lot easier.

"Three-point-five billion the armored division, three-point-four billion the infantry," he said. "But these are just start-up costs. After that, we save three hundred million dollars a year in running costs by not having them. And now that Despot is canceled, another seventeen billion dollars for the projected three hundred units of Despot."

"But Despot is the best tank-busting system in the world," protested Stannard. "Hell, we need it."

"To kill tanks that have been withdrawn east of Brest-Litovsk?"

asked Johnson. "If they halve their tanks in East Germany, we can cope with what we've got, the A-ten aircraft and the ground-based tank-buster units. Plus, we can build more static defenses with part of the savings. That's allowed under the treaty."

"The Europeans like it," said Donaldson of State mildly. "They don't have to reduce manpower, but they do see ten to eleven Soviet divisions disappearing in front of their eyes. It seems to me we win on the ground."

"Let's consider the sea battle," suggested Cormack.

The Soviet Union had agreed to destroy, under supervision, half its submarine fleet; all its nuclear-powered subs in classes Hotel, Echo, and November, and all the diesel-electric Juliets, Foxtrots, Whiskeys, Romeos, and Zulus. But as Stannard was quick to point out, its old nuclear subs were already archaic and unsafe, constantly leaking neutrons and gamma rays, and the others scheduled to go were of old designs. After that the Russians could concentrate their resources and best men in the Sierra, Mike, and Akula classes, much better technically and therefore more dangerous.

Still, he conceded, 158 submarines were a lot of metal, and America's Anti-Submarine Warfare targets would be drastically reduced, simplifying the job of getting the convoys to Europe if the balloon ever did go up.

Finally, Moscow had agreed to scrap the first of its four Kiev-class aircraft carriers, and build no more—a minor concession, as they were already proving too expensive to support.

The United States was allowed to keep the newly commissioned carriers *Abraham Lincoln* and *George Washington*, but would scrap the *Midway* and the *Coral Sea* (destined to go anyway, but delayed to be included in the treaty) plus the next-oldest, the *Forrestal* and the *Saratoga*, plus their air wings. These air wings, once deactivated, would take three to four years to bring back to combat readiness.

"The Russians will say they've eliminated eighteen percent of our ability to strike at the Motherland," groused Stannard, "and all they've given up are a hundred and fifty-eight subs that were bitches to maintain anyway."

But the Cabinet, seeing savings of a minimum $20 billion a year, half in personnel and half in hardware, approved the navy side of the treaty, Odell and Stannard opposing. The key came in the air. Cormack knew that for Gorbachev it was the clincher. On balance, America won out on land and water, since she did not intend to be the aggressor; she just wanted to make sure the U.S.S.R. could not be. But unlike Stannard and Odell, Cormack and Donaldson knew that many Soviet citizens genuinely believed the West would one day hurl itself at the *Rodina*, and that included their leaders.

Under Nantucket, the West would discontinue the American TFX fighter, or F-18, and the European multi-role combat fighter for Italy, West Germany, Spain, and Britain, a joint project; Moscow would stop further work on the MiG–31. She would also scrap the Blackjack, the Tupolev version of the American B-1 bomber, and 50 percent of her air-tanker assets, massively reducing the strategic air threat to the West.

"How do we know they won't build the Backfire somewhere else?" asked Odell.

"We'll have official inspectors stationed in the Tupolev factory," Cormack pointed out. "They can hardly start up a new Tupolev factory somewhere else. Right, Lee?"

"Right, Mr. President," said the Director of Central Intelligence. He paused. "Also, we have assets in the key staff at Tupolev."

"Ah," said Donaldson, impressed. "As a diplomat, I don't want to know." There were several grins. Donaldson was known to be very straitlaced.

The stinger for America in the air section of the Nantucket Treaty was that she had to abandon the B–2 Stealth bomber, an airplane of revolutionary potential, since it was constructed to pass unnoticed through any radar detection screen and deliver its nuclear bombs as and where it wished. It frightened the Russian very badly. For Mikhail Gorbachev it was the one concession from the States that would get Nantucket through ratification. It would also obviate the need to spend a *minimum* 300 billion rubles rebuilding from the ground up the Air Defense of the Homeland system, the vaunted Voiska PVO that was supposed to detect any impending attack on the Motherland. *That* was the money he wanted to divert to new factories, technology, and oil.

For America, Stealth was a $40 billion project, so cancellation would mean a big saving, but at the cost of fifty thousand defense-industry jobs.

"Maybe we should just go on as we are and bankrupt the bastards," suggested Odell.

"Michael," said Cormack gently, "then they'd have to go to war."

After twelve hours the Cabinet approved Nantucket and the wearisome business started of trying to convince the Senate, industry, finance, the media, and the people that it was right. A hundred billion dollars had been cut from the Defense budget.

May　　　　　By the middle of May the five men who had dined at the Remington Hotel the previous January had constituted themselves the Alamo Group at Miller's suggestion, in memory of those who in 1836 had fought for the independence of Texas at the Alamo against the Mexican forces of General Santa Anna. The project to topple the Kingdom of Sa'ud they had named Plan Bowie, after Colonel Jim Bowie, who had died at the Alamo. The destabilization of President Cormack by a paid-for whispering campaign through lobbies, the media, the people, and the Congress, bore the name Plan Crockett, after Davy Crockett, the pioneer and Indian fighter who also died there. Now they met to consider the report of Irving Moss to wound John Cormack to the point where he would be susceptible to calls for him to step down and depart. Plan Travis, for the man who had commanded at the Alamo.

"There are parts of this that make me squirm," said Moir, tapping his copy.

"Me too," said Salkind. "The last four pages. Do we have to go that far?"

"Gentlemen, friends," rumbled Miller. "I fully appreciate your concern, your aversion even. I ask you only to consider the stakes. Not only we but all America stands in mortal peril. You have seen the terms proposed by the Judas in the White House to strip our land of its defenses and to propitiate the Antichrist in Moscow. That man must go before he destroys this our beloved country and brings us all to ruin. You especially, who now face bankruptcy. And I am assured by Mr. Moss here that, regarding the last few pages, it will never come to that. Cormack will go before that is necesssary."

Irving Moss sat in a white suit at the end of the table, silent. There were parts of his plan that he had not put in the report, things he could mention only in privacy to Miller. He breathed through his mouth to avoid the low whistling caused by his damaged nose.

Miller suddenly startled them all. "Friends, let us seek the guidance of Him who understands all things. Let us pray together."

Ben Salkind shot a rapid glance at Peter Cobb, who raised his eyebrows. Melville Scanlon's face was expressionless. Cyrus Miller placed both hands flat on the table, closed his eyes, and raised his face to the ceiling. He was not a man for bowing his head, even when addressing the Almighty. They were, after all, close confidants.

"Lord," intoned the oil tycoon, "hear us, we pray You. Hear us true and loyal sons of this glorious land, which is of Your creation and which

You have vouchsafed to our safekeeping. Guide our hands. Uphold our hearts. Teach us to have the courage to go through with the task that lies before us and which, we are sure, has Your blessing. Help us to save this, Your chosen country, and these, Your chosen people."

He went on in this vein for several minutes, then was silent for several more. When he lowered his face and surveyed the five men with him, his eyes burned with the conviction of those who truly have no doubt.

"Gentlemen, He has spoken. He is with us in our endeavors. We must go forward, not back, for our country and our God."

The other five had little choice but to nod their assent. An hour later Irving Moss talked privately with Miller in his study. There were, he made plain, two components that were vital but which he, Moss, could not arrange. One was a piece of high-complexity Soviet technology; the other was a secret source within the innermost councils of the White House. He explained why. Miller nodded thoughtfully.

"I will see to both," he said. "You have your budget and the down payment on your fee. Proceed with the plan without delay."

June   Colonel Easterhouse was received by Miller in the first week of June. He had been busy in Saudi Arabia but the summons was unequivocal, so he flew from Jiddah to New York via London and connected straight to Houston. A car met him on schedule, drove him to the private William P. Hobby Airport southeast of the city, and the Learjet brought him to the ranch, which he had not seen before. His progress report was optimistic and well received.

He was able to say that his go-between in the Religious Police had been enthusiastic when approached with the notion of a change of government in Riyadh, and had made contact with the fugitive Imam of the Shi'ah Fundamentalists when the man's secret hiding place had been revealed to him by Easterhouse. The fact that the Imam had not been betrayed proved that the Religious Police zealot was trustworthy.

The Imam had heard out the proposal—made to him on a no-name basis, since he would never have accepted that a Christian like Easterhouse should become an instrument of Allah's will—and was reported to be equally enthusiastic.

"The point is, Mr. Miller, the Hezb'Allah fanatics have so far not attempted to seize the obvious plum of Saudi Arabia, preferring to try to defeat and annex Iraq first, in which they have failed. The reason for their patience is that they feared, rightly, that seeking to topple the

House of Sa'ud would provoke a fierce reaction from the hitherto vacillating U.S.A. They have always believed Saudi Arabia would fall to them at the right moment. The Imam appears to accept that next spring—the Diamond Jubilee jamboree is now definitely slated for April—will be Allah's choice of the right moment."

During the jamboree, huge delegations from all the thirty-seven major tribes of the country would converge on Riyadh to pay homage to the royal house. Among these would be the tribes from the Hasa region, the oil-field workers who were mainly of the Shi'ah sect. Hidden in their midst would be the two hundred chosen assassins of the Imam, unarmed until their submachine carbines and ammunition, covertly imported in one of Scanlon's tankers, had been distributed among them.

Easterhouse was finally able to report that a senior Egyptian officer—the Egyptian Military Adviser Group played a crucial role at all technical levels of the Saudi Army—had agreed that if his country, with its teeming millions and shortage of money, was given access to Saudi oil after the coup, he would ensure the reissue of defective ammunition to the Royal Guard, who would then be helpless to defend their masters. Miller nodded thoughtfully.

"You have done well, Colonel," he said, then changed the subject. "Tell me, what would Soviet reaction be to this American takeover of Saudi Arabia?"

"Extreme perturbation, I would imagine," said the colonel.

"Enough to put an end to the Nantucket Treaty, of which we now know the full terms?" asked Miller.

"I would have thought so," said Easterhouse.

"Which group inside the Soviet Union would have most reason to dislike the treaty and all its terms, and wish to see it destroyed?"

"The General Staff," said the colonel without hesitation. "Their position in the U.S.S.R. is like that of our Joint Chiefs of Staff and the defense industry rolled into one. The treaty will cut their power, their prestige, their budget, and their numbers by forty percent. I can't see them welcoming that."

"Strange allies," mused Miller. "Is there any way of getting in discreet contact?"

"I . . . have certain acquaintances," said Easterhouse carefully.

"I want you to use them," said Miller. "Just say there are powerful interests in the U.S.A. who view the Nantucket Treaty with as little favor as they, and believe it might be aborted from the American end, and would like to confer."

· · ·

The kingdom of Jordan is not particularly pro-Soviet, but King Hussein has long had to tread a delicate path to stay on his throne in Amman, and has occasionally bought Soviet weaponry, though his Hashemite Arab Legion is mainly Western-armed. Still, there exists a thirty-man Soviet Military Advisory Team in Amman, headed by the defense attaché at the Russian embassy. Easterhouse, once attending the desert testing of some Soviet hardware east of Aqaba on behalf of his Saudi patrons, had met the man. Passing through Amman on his way back, Easterhouse stopped over.

The defense attaché, Colonel Kutuzov, whom Easterhouse was convinced was from the GRU, was still in place and they had a private dinner. The American was stunned by the speed of the reaction. Two weeks later he was contacted in Riyadh to be told that certain gentlemen would be happy to meet his "friends" in circumstances of great discretion. A fat package of travel instructions was given to him, which he couriered unopened to Houston.

<u>July</u>   Of all the Communist countries, Yugoslavia is the most relaxed in the matter of tourism, so much so that entry visas may be acquired with little formality right on arrival at Belgrade airport. In mid-July five men flew into Belgrade on the same day but from different directions and on different flights. They came by scheduled airlines out of Amsterdam, Rome, Vienna, London, and Frankfurt. As all were American passport holders, none had needed visas for any of those cities either. All applied for and received visas at Belgrade for a week's harmless tourism—one in the mid-morning, two in the lunch hour and two in the afternoon. All told the interviewing visa officers they had come to hunt boar and stag from the famous Karadjordjevo hunting lodge, a converted fortress on the Danube much favored by wealthy Westerners. Each of the five claimed, as he was issued his visa, that en route to the hunting lodge he would be spending one night at the super-luxury Hotel Petrovaradin at Novi Sad, eighty kilometers northwest of Belgrade. And each took a taxi to that hotel.

The visa officers' shift changed in the lunch hour, so only one came under the eye of Officer Pavlic, who happened to be a covert asset in the pay of the Soviet KGB. Two hours after Pavlic checked off duty, a routine report from him arrived on the desk of the Soviet *rezident* in his office at the embassy in central Belgrade.

Pavel Kerkorian was not at his best; he had had a late night—not entirely in the course of duty but his wife was fat and constantly complaining, while he found some of these flaxen Bosnian girls irresistible—and a heavy lunch, definitely in the course of duty, with a hard-drinking member of the Yugoslav Central Committee whom he hoped to recruit. He almost put Pavlic's report on one side. Americans were pouring into Yugoslavia nowadays—to check them all out would be impossible. But there was something about the name. Not the surname—that was common enough—but where had he seen the first name Cyrus before?

He found it again an hour later right in his office; a back number of *Forbes* magazine had carried an article on Cyrus V. Miller. By such flukes are destinies sometimes decided. It did not make sense, and the wiry Armenian KGB major liked things to make sense. Why would a man of nearly eighty, known to be pathologically anti-Communist, come hunting boar in Yugoslavia by scheduled airlines when he was rich enough to hunt anything he wanted in North America and travel by private jet? He summoned two of his staff, youngsters fresh in from Moscow, and hoped they wouldn't make a mess of it. (As he had remarked to his CIA opposite number at a cocktail party recently, you just can't get good help nowadays. The CIA man had agreed completely.)

Kerkorian's young agents spoke Serbo-Croatian, but he still advised them to rely on their driver, a Yugoslav who knew his way around. They checked back that evening from a phone booth in the Petrovaradin Hotel, which made the major spit because the Yugoslavs certainly had it tapped. He told them to go somewhere else.

He was just about to go home when they checked in again, this time from a humble inn a few miles from Novi Sad. There was not one American, but five, they said. They might have met at the hotel, but seemed to know each other. Money had changed hands at the reception desk and they had copies of the first three pages of each American's passport. The five were due to be picked up in the morning in a minibus and taken to some hunting lodge, said the gumshoes, and what should we do now?

"Stay there," said Kerkorian. "Yes, all night. I want to know where they go and who they see."

Serve them right, he thought as he went home. These youngsters have it too easy nowadays. It was probably nothing, but it would give the sprogs a bit of experience.

At noon the next day they were back, tired, unshaven, but triumphant. What they had to say left Kerkorian stunned. A mini-van had duly arrived and taken the five Americans on board. The guide was in plain clothes but looked decidedly military—and Russian. Instead of heading for the hunting lodge, the bus had taken the five Americans back toward Belgrade, then ducked straight into Batajnica Air Base. They had not shown their passports at the main gate—the guide had produced five passes from his own inside pocket and got them through the barrier.

Kerkorian knew Batajnica; it was a big Yugoslav air base twenty kilometers northwest of Belgrade, definitely not on the sightseeing schedule of American tourists. Among other things it hosted a constant stream of Soviet military transports bringing in resupplies for the enormous Soviet Military Adviser Group in Yugoslavia. That meant there was a team of Russian engineers inside the base, and one of them worked for him. The man was in cargo control. Ten hours later Kerkorian sent a "blitz" report to Yazenevo, headquarters of the KGB's First Chief Directorate, the external espionage arm. It went directly to the desk of the Deputy Head of the FCD, General Vadim Kirpichenko, who made a number of inquiries internal to the U.S.S.R. and sent an expanded report right up to his chairman, General Kryuchkov.

What Kerkorian had reported was that the five Americans had all been escorted straight from the minibus into an Antonov 42 jet transport which had just arrived with cargo from Odessa and at once headed back there. A later report from the Belgrade *rezident* announced that the Americans had returned the same way twenty-four hours later, spent a second night at the Petrovaradin Hotel, and then left Yugoslavia altogether, without hunting a single boar. Kerkorian was commended for his vigilance.

August   The heat hung over the Costa del Sol like a blanket. Down on the beaches the million tourists were turning themselves over and over like steaks on a griddle, oiling and basting courageously as they tried to acquire a deep mahogany tan in their two precious weeks and too often simply achieving lobster-red. The sky was such a pale blue it was almost white, and even the usual breeze off the sea had sagged to a zephyr.

To the west the great molar of the Rock of Gibraltar jutted into the heat haze, shimmering at its range of fifteen miles; the pale slopes of the concrete rain-catchment system built by the Royal Engineers to feed the underground cisterns stuck out like a leprous scar on the flank of the rock.

In the hills behind Casares beach the air was a mite cooler but not much; relief really came only at dawn and just before sunset, so the vineyard workers of Alcántara del Rio were rising at four in the morning to put in six hours before the sun drove them into the shade. After lunch they would snooze through the traditional Spanish siesta behind their thick, cool, lime-washed walls until five, then put in more labor till the light faded around eight.

Under the sun the grapes ripened and became fat. The harvest would not come yet, but it would be good this year. In his bar Antonio brought the carafe of wine to the foreigner as usual and beamed.

"¿Sera bien, la cosecha?" he asked.

"Yes," said the tall man with a smile. "This year the harvest will be very good. We shall all be able to pay our bar bills."

Antonio roared with laughter. Everyone knew the foreigner owned his own land outright and always paid cash on the spot.

Two weeks later Mikhail Sergeevich Gorbachev was in no mood to joke. Though often a genial man, with a reputation for a good sense of humor and a light touch with subordinates, he could also show a hair-trigger temper, as when preached at by Westerners over civil rights issues or when he felt badly let down by a subordinate. He sat at his desk on the seventh and top floor of the Central Committee Building in Novaya Ploshchad and stared angrily at the reports spread all over the table.

It's a long narrow room, sixty feet by twenty, with the General Secretary's desk at the end opposite the door. He sits with his back to the wall, all the windows onto the square being ranged to his left behind their net curtains and buff velour drapes. Running down the center of the room is the habitual conference table, of which the desk formed the head of the letter T.

Unlike many of his predecessors, he had preferred a light and airy decor; the table is of pale beech, like his desk, and surrounded by upright but comfortable chairs, eight on each side. It was on this table he had spread the reports collected by his friend and colleague, the Foreign Minister Eduard Shevardnadze, whose plea had brought him unwillingly back from his seaside holiday at Yalta in the Crimea. He would, he thought savagely, have preferred to be splashing in the sea with his granddaughter Aksaina than sitting in Moscow reading this sort of trash.

It had been more than six years since that freezing March day in 1985 when Chernenko had finally dropped off his perch and he had been raised with almost bewildering speed—even though he had schemed and prepared for it—into the top slot. Six years he had sought to take the country he loved by the scruff of the neck and hurl it into the last decade of the twentieth century in a state fit to face, match, and triumph on equal terms over the capitalist West.

Like all devoted Russians he was half admiring and wholly resentful of the West; of her prosperity, her financial power, her almost contemptuous self-assurance. Unlike most Russians he had for years not been prepared to accept that things could never change in his homeland, that corruption, laziness, bureaucracy, and lethargy were part of the system, always had been and always would be. Even as a young man he had known he had the energy and the dynamism to change things, given the chance. That had been his mainspring, his driving force, through all those years of study and party work in Stavropol, the conviction that one day he would get his chance.

For six years he had had the chance, and realized even *he* had underestimated the opposition and the inertia. The first years had been touch-and-go; he had walked a very fine tightrope indeed, almost come to grief a dozen times.

The cleansing of the Party had come first, cutting out the die-hards and the deadwood—well, almost all of them. Now he knew he ruled the Politburo and the Central Committee; knew his appointees controlled the scattered Party secretaryships throughout the republics of the Union, shared his conviction that the U.S.S.R. could really compete with the West only if she was economically strong. That was why most of his reforms dealt with economic and not moral matters.

As a dedicated Communist he already believed his country had moral superiority—there was for him no need to prove it. But he was not fool enough to deceive himself over the economic strengths of the two camps. Now with the oil crisis, of which he was perfectly well aware, he needed massive resources to pump into Siberia and the Arctic, and that meant cutting back somewhere else. Which led to Nantucket and his unavoidable head-to-head with his own military establishment.

The three pillars of power were the Party, the Army, and the KGB, and he knew no one could take on two at the same time. It was bad enough to be at loggerheads with his generals; to be back-stabbed by the KGB was intolerable. The reports on his table, culled by the Foreign Minister from the Western media and translated, he did not need, least of all when American public opinion might still cause the Senate to reject the Nantucket Treaty and insist on the building and deployment of the (for Russia) disastrous Stealth bomber.

Personally he had no particular sympathy with Jews who wanted to quit the Motherland that had given them everything. There was nothing un-Russian in Mikhail Gorbachev so far as turds and dissidents were concerned. But what angered him was that what had been done was deliberate, no accident, and he knew who was behind it. He still resented the vicious video tape attacking his wife's London spending spree years before and circulated on the Moscow circuit. He knew who had been behind that too. The same people. The predecessor of the one who had been summoned and whom he now awaited.

There was a knock on the door to the right of the bookcase at the far end of the room. His private secretary popped his head in and simply nodded. Gorbachev raised a hand to indicate "wait a minute."

He returned to his desk and sat down behind the spare, clear top with its three telephones and cream onyx pen set. Then he nodded. The secretary swung the door wide open.

"The Comrade Chairman, Comrade General Secretary," the young man announced, then withdrew.

He was in full uniform—he would be, of course—and Gorbachev let him walk the full length of the room without salutation. Then he rose and gestured at the spread-out papers.

General Vladimir Kryuchkov, Chairman of the KGB, had been a close friend, protégé, and like-thinker of his own predecessor, the die-hard ultraconservative Viktor Chebrikov. The General Secretary had secured the ouster of Chebrikov in the great purge he had conducted in the fall of 1988, thus ridding himself of his last powerful opponent on the Politburo. But he had had no choice but to appoint the First Deputy Chairman, Kryuchkov, as successor. One ouster was enough; two would have been a massacre. There are limits, even in Moscow.

Kryuchkov glanced at the papers and raised an eyebrow. Bastard, thought Gorbachev.

"There was no need to beat the shit out of them on camera," said Gorbachev, as usual coming to the nub without preamble. "Six Western TV camera units, eight radio reporters, and twenty newspaper and magazine hacks, half of them American. We got less coverage for the Olympics in '84."

Kryuchkov raised an eyebrow. "The Jews were conducting an illegal demonstration, my dear Mikhail Sergeevich. Personally, I was on vacation at the time. But my officers in the Second Chief Directorate acted properly, I believe. These people refused to disperse when commanded and my men used the usual methods."

"It was on the street. That's a Militia matter."

"These people are subversives. They were spreading anti-Soviet propaganda. Look at the placards. That's a KGB matter."

"And the full turnout of foreign press?"

The KGB chief shrugged. "These weasels get everywhere."

Yes, if they are rung up and tipped off, thought Gorbachev. He wondered whether this might be the issue over which he could secure the ouster of Kryuchkov, and dismissed it. It would take the full Politburo to fire the Chairman of the KGB, and never for beating up a bunch of Jews. Still, he was angry and prepared to speak his mind. He did so for five minutes. Kryuchkov's mouth tightened in silence. He did not appreciate being ticked off by the younger but senior man. Gorbachev had come around the desk; the two men were of the same height, short and stocky. Gorbachev's eye contact was, as usual, unflinching. That was when Kryuchkov made a mistake.

He had in his pocket a report from the KGB's man in Belgrade, amplified with some stunning information gleaned by Kirpichenko at the First Chief Directorate. It was certainly important enough to bring to the General Secretary himself. Screw it, thought the bitter KGB chief; he can wait. And so the Belgrade report was suppressed.

September   Irving Moss had established himself in London, but before leaving Houston he had agreed on a personal code with Cyrus Miller. He knew that the monitors of the National Security Agency at Fort Meade constantly scanned the ether, intercepting billions of words in foreign telephone calls, and that banks of computers sifted them for nuggets of interest. Not to mention the British GCHQ people, the Russians, and just about anyone else nowadays who could rustle up a listening post. But the volume of commercial traffic is so vast that unless something sticks out as suspicious, it will probably pass. Moss's code was based on lists of salad produce prices, passing between sunny Texas and gloomy London. He took down the list of prices off the telephone, cut out the words, retained the numbers, and according to the date of the calendar, deciphered them from a one-time pad of which only he and Cyrus Miller had copies.

That month he learned three things: that the piece of Soviet technology he needed was in the last stages of preparation and would be delivered within a fortnight; that the source he had asked for in the White House was in place, bought and paid for; and that he should now go ahead with Plan Travis on schedule. He burned the sheets and grinned. His fee was based on planning, activation, and success. Now he could claim the second installment.

October   There are eight weeks in the autumn term at Oxford University, and since scholars seek to abide by the precepts of logic, they are called First Week, Second Week, Third Week, and so on. A number of activities take place after the end of term—mainly athletic, theatrical, and debating events—in Ninth Week. And quite a few students appear before the start of term, either to prepare their studies, get settled in, or start training, in the period called Nought Week.

On October 2, the first day of Nought Week, there was a scattering of early birds in Vincent's Club, a bar and haunt of undergraduate athletes, among them the tall thin student called Simon, preparing for his third and last term at Oxford under the year-abroad program. He was hailed by a cheerful voice from behind.

"Hallo, young Simon. Back early?"

It was Air Commodore John De'Ath, Bursar of Jesus College and senior treasurer of the Athletics Club, which included the cross-country team.

Simon grinned. "Yes, sir."

"Going to get the fat of the summer vacation off, are we?" The retired Air Force officer smiled. He tapped the student's nonexistent stomach. "Good man. You're our main hope to knock seven bells out of Cambridge in December in London."

Everyone knew that Oxford's great sporting rival was Cambridge University, the needle match in any sporting contest.

"I'm looking to start a series of morning runs and get back in shape, sir," said Simon.

He did indeed begin a series of punishing early-morning runs, starting at five miles and pushing up to twelve as the week progressed. On the morning of Wednesday the 9th he set off as usual by bicycle from his house off the Woodstock Road in the southern part of Summertown in north Oxford, and pedaled for the town center. He skirted the Martyr's Memorial and Saint Mary Magdalen Church, turned left into Broad Street, past the doors of his own college, Balliol, and on down Holywell and Longwall to join the High Street. A final left turn brought him to the railings outside Magdalen College.

Here he dismounted, chained his bike to the railing for safety, and began to run. Over Magdalen Bridge across the Cherwell and down St. Clement's at the Plain. Now he was heading due east. At six-thirty in the morning the sun would soon rise ahead of him and he had a straight four-mile run to get clear of the last suburbs of Oxford.

He pounded through New Headington to cross the dual-carriageway Ring Road on the steel bridge leading to Shotover Hill. There were no other runners to join him. He was almost alone. At the end of Old Road he hit the incline of the hill and felt the pain of the long-distance runner. His sinewy legs drove him on up the hill and out into Shotover Plain. Here the paved road ran out and he was on the track, deeply potholed and with water from the overnight rain lying in the ruts. He swerved to the grass verge, delighting in the springy comfort of the grass underfoot, through the pain barrier, exulting in the freedom of the run.

Behind him the unmarked sedan emerged from the trees of the hill, ran out of pavement, and began to jolt through the potholes. The men inside knew the route and were sick of it. Five hundred yards of track, lined with gray boulders, to the reservoir, then back to blacktop road for the downhill glide to Wheatley village via the hamlet of Little-worth.

A hundred yards short of the reservoir the track narrowed and a giant ash tree overhung the lane. It was here the van was parked, drawn well onto the verge. It was a well-used green Ford Transit bearing on its side the logo BARLOW'S ORCHARD PRODUCE. Nothing unusual about it. In early October, Barlow vans were all over the county delivering the sweet apples of Oxfordshire to the greengrocers. Anyone looking at the back of the van—invisible to the men in the car, for the van was facing them—would have seen stacked apple crates. That same person would not have realized the crates were really two cunning paintings stuck to the inside of the twin windows.

The van had had a puncture, front offside tire. A man crouched beside it with a wrench, seeking to free the wheel which was raised on a jack. He bowed over his work. The youth called Simon was on the verge across the rutted track from the van and he kept running.

As he passed the front end of the van two things happened with bewildering speed. The rear doors flew open and two men, identical in black track suits and ski masks, leaped out, hurled themselves on the startled runner, and bore him to the ground. The man with the wrench turned and straightened up. Beneath his slouch hat he, too, was masked, and the wrench was not a wrench but a Czech Skorpion submachine gun. Without a pause he opened fire and raked the windshield of the sedan sixty feet away.

The man behind the wheel died instantly, hit in the face. The car swerved and stalled as he died. The man in the back seat reacted like a cat, opening his door, bailing out, rolling twice, and coming up in the "fire" position. He got off two shots with his short-nosed Smith & Wesson 9mm. The first was wide by a foot, the second ten feet short, for as he fired it the continuing burst from the Skorpion hit him in the chest. He never stood a chance.

The man in the passenger seat got free of the car a second after the man in the back. The passenger door was wide open and he was trying to fire through the open window at the machine gunner when three slugs punched straight through the fabric and hit him in the stomach, bowling him backwards. In five more seconds the gunman was back beside the driver of the van; the other two had hurled the student into the rear of the Transit and slammed the doors, the van had rolled off its jack, done a fast-reverse into the entrance of the reservoir, hauled a three-point turn, and was headed back down the lane toward Wheatley.

The Secret Service agent was dying, but he had a lot of courage. Inch by agonizing inch he pulled himself back to the open car door, scrabbled for the microphone beneath the dash, and croaked out his last message. He did not bother with call signs or codes or radio procedure; he was too far gone. By the time help came five minutes later, he was dead. What he said was: "Help . . . we need help here. Someone has just kidnapped Simon Cormack."

CHAPTER FOUR

I n the wake of the dying American
Secret Service man's radio call
many things began to happen exceedingly fast and at a rising tempo.
The snatch of the President's only son had taken place at 7:05 A.M. The
radio call was logged at 7:07. Although the caller was using a dedicated
waveband, he was speaking in clear. It was fortunate no unauthorized
person was listening to police frequencies at that hour. The call was
heard in three places.

At the rented house off the Woodstock Road were the other ten
men of the Secret Service team tasked to guard the President's son
during his year at Oxford. Eight were still abed, but two were up, including the night-watch officer, who was listening on the dedicated frequency.

The Director of the Secret Service, Creighton Burbank, had from
the outset protested that the President's son should not be studying
abroad at all during the incumbency. He had been overruled by President Cormack, who saw no good reason to deprive his son of his longed-
for chance to spend a year at Oxford. Swallowing his objections,
Burbank had asked for a fifty-man team at Oxford.

Again, John Cormack had yielded to his son's pleading—"Give me
a break, Dad, I'll look like an exhibit at a cattle show with fifty goons all

around me"—and they had settled on a team of twelve. The American embassy in London had rented a large detached villa in north Oxford, collaborated for months with the British authorities, and engaged three thoroughly vetted British staff: a male gardener, a cook, and a woman for the cleaning and laundry. The aim had been to give Simon Cormack a chance at a perfectly normal enjoyment of his student days.

The team had always had a minimum of eight men on duty, four on weekend furlough. The duty men had made four pairs: three shifts to cover the twenty-four-hour day at the house, and two men to escort Simon everywhere when away from Woodstock Road. The men had threatened to resign if they were not allowed their weapons, and the British had a standing rule that no foreigners carried sidearms on British soil. A typical compromise was evolved: Out of the house, an armed British sergeant of the Special Branch would be in the car. Technically the Americans would be operating under his auspices and could have guns. It was a fiction, but the Special Branch men, being local to Oxfordshire, were useful guides, and relations had become very friendly. It was the British sergeant who had come out of the rear seat of the ambushed car and tried to use his two-inch Smith & Wesson before being gunned down on Shotover Plain.

Within seconds of receiving the dying man's call at the Woodstock Road house, the rest of the team threw themselves into two other cars and raced toward Shotover Plain. The route of the run was clearly marked and they all knew it. The night-watch officer remained behind in the house with one other man, and he made two fast telephone calls. One was to Creighton Burbank in Washington, fast asleep at that hour of the morning, five hours behind London; the other was to the legal counselor at the U.S. embassy in London, caught shaving at his St. John's Wood home.

The legal counselor at an American embassy is always the FBI representative, and in London that is an important post. The liaison between the law enforcement agencies of the two countries is constant. Patrick Seymour had taken over from Darrell Mills two years earlier, got on well with the British, and enjoyed the job. His immediate reaction was to go very pale and put in a scrambled call to Donald Edmonds, Director of the FBI, catching him fast asleep at his Chevy Chase residence.

The second listener to the radio call was a patrol car of the Thames Valley Police, the force covering the old counties of Oxfordshire, Berkshire, and Buckinghamshire. Although the American team with their

Special Branch escort were always in close on Simon Cormack, the TVP made a policy of having one of their cars no more than a mile away on a "first call" basis. The patrol car was tuned to the dedicated frequency, was cruising through Headington at the time, and covered the missing mile in fifty seconds. Some would later say the sergeant and driver in it should have passed the ambush site and tried to overtake the escaping van. Hindsight; with three bodies on the Shotover track, they stopped to see if they could render assistance and/or get some kind of a description. It was too late for either.

The third listening post was the Thames Valley Police headquarters in the village of Kidlington. Woman Police Constable Janet Wren was due to go off duty after the night shift at 7:30 and was yawning when the croaking voice with the American accent crackled into her headset. She was so stunned she thought for a fleeting second it might be a joke. Then she consulted a checklist and hit a series of keys on the computer to her left. At once her screen flashed up a series of instructions, which the badly frightened woman began to follow to the letter.

After lengthy collaboration a year earlier between the Thames Valley Police Authority, Scotland Yard, the British Home Office, the U.S. embassy, and the Secret Service, the joint protection operation around Simon Cormack had been tagged Operation Yankee Doodle. The routines had been computerized, as had the procedures to be followed in any of a variety of contingencies—such as the President's son being in a bar brawl, a street fight, a road accident, a political demonstration, being taken ill, or wishing to spend time away from Oxford in another country. WPC Wren had activated the Kidnap code and the computer was answering back.

Within minutes the duty officer of the watch was by her side, pale with worry and starting a series of phone calls. One was to the Chief Superintendent of the Criminal Investigation Department (CID) who took it on himself to bring in his colleague, the Superintendent heading TVP's Special Branch (SB). The man at Kidlington also called the Assistant Chief Constable (Operations), who was attacking two boiled eggs when the call came to his home. He listened intently and rapped out a series of orders and questions.

"Where, exactly?"

"Shotover Plain, sir," said Kidlington. "Delta Bravo is at the scene. They've turned back a private car coming from Wheatley, two other runners, and a lady with a dog from the Oxford end. Both the Americans are dead; so is Sergeant Dunn."

"Jesus," breathed the ACC Ops. This was going to be the biggest flap of his career, and as head of Operations, the sharp end of police work, it was up to him to get it right. No near misses. Not acceptable. He went into overdrive.

"Get a minimum fifty uniformed men there fast. Posts, mallets, and ribbons. I want it sealed off—now. Every SOCO we've got. And roadblocks. That's a two-ended track, isn't it? Did they get away through the Oxford end?"

"Delta Bravo says not," replied the man at headquarters. "We don't know the time lapse between the attack and the American's call. But if it was short, Delta Bravo was on the road at Headington and says no one passed them coming from Shotover. The tire tracks will tell us—it's muddy there."

"Concentrate the roadblocks north through south on the eastern side," said the ACC. "Leave the Chief Constable to me. My car's on its way?"

"Should be outside now," said Kidlington.

It was. The ACC glanced through his sitting-room window and saw his car, normally due forty minutes later, pulling up. "Who's already on their way?" he asked.

"CID, SB, SOCOs, and now uniformed," said Kidlington.

"Get every detective off every case and put them on the knocker," said the ACC. "I'll go straight to Shotover."

"Range of roadblocks?" queried the watch officer at headquarters. The ACC thought. Roadblocks are easier said than done. The Home Counties, all very historic and heavily populated, have a maze of country lanes, secondary roads, and tracks running between the towns, villages, and hamlets that make up the countryside. Cast the net too wide and the number of minor roads would multiply to hundreds; cast it too narrow and the distance the kidnappers had to cover to escape the net would shrink.

"Edge of Oxfordshire," snapped the ACC. He hung up, then called his ultimate superior, the Chief Constable. In any British county force the day-to-day anti-crime policing goes to the ACC Ops. The Chief Constable may or may not have a background in police work, but his task concerns policy, morale, the public image, and liaison with London. The ACC glanced at his watch as he made the call: 7:31 A.M.

The Chief Constable of the Thames Valley lived in a handsome converted rectory in the village of Bletchingdon. He strode from his breakfast room to the study, wiping marmalade from his mouth, to take the call. When he heard the news he forgot about breakfast. There were going to be many disturbed mornings that ninth day of October.

"I see," he said as the details so far sank in. "Yes, carry on. I'll . . . call London."

On his study desk were several telephones. One was a designated and very private line to the office of the Assistant Secretary of the F.4 Division in the Home Office, Britain's Interior Ministry, which rules the Metropolitan and County Police forces. At that hour the civil servant was not at his office, but the call was patched through to his home in Fulham, London. The bureaucrat let out an unwonted oath, made two phone calls, and headed straight for the big white building in Queen Anne's Gate, running off Victoria Street, that housed his ministry.

One of his calls was to the duty officer at F.4 Division, requiring his desk to be cleared of all other matters and his entire staff to be brought in from their homes at once. He did not say why. He still did not know how many people were aware of the Shotover Plain massacre, but as a good civil servant he was not about to add to that number if he could help it.

The other call he could not help. It was to the Permanent Undersecretary, senior civil servant for the entire Home Office. Fortunately both men lived inside London, rather than miles away in the outer suburbs, and met at the ministry building at 7:51. Sir Harry Marriott, the Conservative government's Home Secretary and their Minister, joined them at 8:04 and was briefed. His immediate reaction was to put in a call to 10 Downing Street and insist on speaking to Mrs. Thatcher herself.

The call was taken by her private secretary—there are innumerable "secretaries" in Whitehall, the seat of the British administration: Some are really Ministers; some, senior civil servants; some, personal aides; and a few do secretarial work. Charles Powell was in the second-last group. He knew that his Prime Minister, in her adjacent private study, had been working for an hour already, polishing off reams of paperwork before most of her colleagues were out of pajamas. It was her custom. Powell also knew that Sir Harry was one of her closest colleagues and intimates. He checked with her briefly and she took the call without delay.

"Prime Minister, I have to see you. Now. I have to come 'round without delay."

Margaret Thatcher frowned. The hour and the tone were unusual.

"Then come, Harry," she said.

"Three minutes," said the voice on the phone. Sir Harry Marriott replaced the receiver. Down below, his car was waiting for the five hundred-yard drive. It was 8:11 A.M.

The kidnappers were four in number. The gunman, who now sat in the passenger seat, stuffed the Skorpion down between his feet and pulled off his woolen ski mask. Beneath it he still wore a wig and a moustache. He pulled on a pair of heavy-framed spectacles with no glass in them. Beside him was the driver, the leader of the team; he, too, had a wig, and a false beard as well. Both disguises were temporary, because they had to drive several miles looking natural.

In the rear the other two subdued a violently fighting Simon Cormack. Not a problem. One of the men was huge and simply smothered the young American in a bear hug while the lean and wiry one applied an ether pad. The van bounced off the track from the reservoir and settled down as it found the blacktop lane toward Wheatley, and the sounds from the rear ceased as the U.S. President's son slumped unconscious.

It was downhill through Littleworth, with its scattering of cottages, and then straight into Wheatley. They passed an electric milk van delivering the traditional breakfast pint of fresh milk, and a hundred yards later the van driver had a brief image of a newspaper delivery boy glancing at them. Out of Wheatley they joined the main A.40 highway into Oxford, turned back toward the city for five hundred yards, then turned right onto the B.4027 minor road through the villages of Forest Hill and Stanton St. John.

The van drove at normal speed through both villages, over the crossroads by New Inn Farm, and on toward Islip. But a mile after New Inn, just beyond Fox Covert, it pulled toward a farm gate on the left. The man beside the driver leaped out, used a key to undo the padlock on the gate—they had replaced the farmer's padlock with their own ten hours earlier—and the van rolled into the track. Within ten yards it had reached the semi-ruined timber barn behind its stand of trees which the kidnappers had reconnoitered two weeks earlier. It was 7:16 A.M.

The daylight was brightening and the four men worked fast. The gunman hauled open the barn doors and drove out the big Volvo sedan that had been parked there only since midnight. The green van drove in and the driver descended, bringing with him the Skorpion and two woolen masks. He checked the front of the van to make sure nothing was left, then slammed the door. The other two men bailed out of the rear doors, hefted the form of Simon Cormack, and placed it in the Volvo's capacious trunk, already fitted with ample air holes. All four men stripped off their oversized black track suits to reveal respectable business suits, shirts, and ties. They retained their wigs, moustaches, and glasses. The bundled clothing went into the trunk with Simon, the Skorpion on the floor of the Volvo's back seat under a blanket.

The van driver and team leader took the wheel of the Volvo and waited. The lean man from the back placed the charges in the van and the giant closed the barn doors. Both got into the back of the Volvo, which now cruised to the gate leading to the road. The gunman closed it behind the car, recovered the padlock, and replaced the farmer's rusted chain. It had been cut through but now hung realistically enough. The Volvo had left tracks in the mud, but that could not be helped. They were standard tires and would soon be changed. The gunman climbed in beside the driver, and the Volvo headed north. It was 7:22 A.M. The ACC Ops was just saying "Jesus."

The kidnappers drove northwest straight through Islip village and cut into the arrow-straight A.421, taking a ninety-degree right turn toward Bicester. They drove through this pleasant market town in northeast Oxfordshire at a steady pace and along the A.421 toward the county town of Buckingham. Just outside Bicester a big police Range Rover loomed up behind them. One of the men in the back muttered a warning and reached down for the Skorpion. The driver snapped at him to sit still and continued at a legal speed. A hundred yards on, a sign said WELCOME TO BUCKINGHAMSHIRE. The county line. At the sign the Range Rover slowed, slewed across the road, and began unloading steel barriers. The Volvo kept motoring and soon disappeared. It was 8:05. In London, Sir Harry Marriott was picking up the phone to Downing Street.

The British Prime Minister happens to be an extremely humane person, much more so than her five immediate male predecessors. Although able to stay cooler than any of them under extreme pressure, she is far from immune to tears. Sir Harry would later tell his wife that when he broke the news her eyes filled; she covered her face with her hands and whispered, "Oh, dear God. Poor man."

"Here we were," Sir Harry would tell Debbie, "facing the biggest bloody crisis with the Yanks since Suez, and her first thought was for the father. Not the son, mind you—the father."

Sir Harry had no children and had not been in office in January 1982, so, unlike the retired Cabinet Secretary Robert Armstrong, who would not have been surprised, he had not witnessed Margaret Thatcher's anguish when her son Mark had gone missing on the Dakar Rally in the Algerian desert. Then, in the privacy of the night, she had cried from that pure and very special pain felt by a parent whose child is in danger. Mark Thatcher had been found alive by a patrol after six days.

When she raised her head she had recovered; she pressed a button on her intercom.

"Charlie, I want you to put through a personal call to President Cormack. From me. Tell the White House it is urgent and cannot wait. Yes, of *course* I know what time it is in Washington."

"There is the American ambassador, via the Foreign Secretary," ventured Sir Harry Marriott. "He could . . . perhaps . . ."

"No, I will do it myself," insisted the Prime Minister. "You will please form the COBRA, Harry. Reports every hour on the hour, please."

There is nothing particularly hot about the so-called hotline between Downing Street and the White House. It is in fact a dedicated telephone link, via satellite, but with unbreakable scramblers fitted at both ends to ensure privacy. A hotline link normally takes about five minutes to set up. Margaret Thatcher pushed her papers to one side, stared out of the bulletproof windows of her private office, and waited.

Shotover Plain was crawling, literally, with activity. The two men of the patrol car Delta Bravo knew enough to keep everyone else off the area and to walk extremely carefully even as they examined the three bodies for signs of life. When they saw none, they left the bodies alone. Investigations can all too easily be ruined at the outset because someone walked all over evidence that would have been treasures to the forensic people, or a big foot pushed a spent cartridge into the mud, wiping off any fingerprints it might still have contained.

The uniformed men had cordoned off the area, the whole track from Littleworth down the hill to the east along to the steel bridge crossing the Ring Road between Shotover and Oxford City. Within this area the SOCOs, scene-of-crime officers, looked for anything and everything. They found that the British SB sergeant had fired twice; a metal detector got one slug out of the mud in front of him—he had slumped forward on his knees, firing as he went down. They could not find the other slug. It might have hit one of the kidnappers, they would report. (It hadn't, but they did not know that.)

There were the spent cases from the Skorpion, twenty-eight of them, all in the same pool; each was photographed where it lay, picked up with tweezers, and bagged for the lab boys. One American was still slumped behind the wheel of the car; the other lay where he had died beside the passenger door, his bloodied hands over the three holes in his belly, the hand mike swinging free. Everything was photographed from every angle before anything was moved. The bodies went to the Radcliffe Infirmary while a Home Office pathologist sped down from London.

The tracks in the mud were of special interest: the smear where Simon Cormack had crashed down with two men on top of him, the prints of the kidnappers' shoes—they would turn out to be from ultra-common running shoes and untraceable—and the tire tracks from the getaway vehicle, quickly identified as some kind of van. And there was the jack, brand-new and purchasable from any of the Unipart chain of stores. Like the Skorpion 9mm cartridges, it would turn out to bear no prints.

There were thirty detectives seeking witnesses—wearisome but vital work that yielded some first descriptions. Two hundred yards east of the reservoir on the lane into Littleworth were two cottages. The lady in one, brewing up tea, had heard "some popping noises" down the lane about seven o'clock but had seen nothing. A man in Littleworth had seen a green van go by just after seven, heading toward Wheatley. The detectives would find the newspaper delivery boy and the milk-van driver just before nine, the boy at school, the milkman having breakfast.

He was the best witness. Medium-green, battered Ford Transit with the Barlow's logo on the side. The marketing manager at Barlow confirmed they had had no vans in that area at that hour. All were accounted for. The police had their getaway vehicle; an all-points alert went out. No reason; just find it. No one connected it with a burning barn on the Islip road—yet.

Other detectives were around the house in Summertown, knocking on doors in Woodstock Road and its vicinity. Had anyone seen parked cars, vans, other vehicles? Anyone seen observing the house down the street? They followed the route of Simon's run right into the center of Oxford and out the other side. About twenty people reported they *had* seen the young runner being tailed by men in a car, but it always turned out to be the Secret Service car.

By nine o'clock the ACC Ops was getting the familiar feeling: There would be no rapid windup now, no lucky breaks, no quick catch. They were away, whoever they were. The Chief Constable, in full uniform, joined him at Shotover Plain and watched the teams at work.

"London seems to want to take over," said the Chief Constable.

The ACC grunted. It was a snub, but also the removal of a hellish responsibility. The inquiry into the past would be tough enough, but to fail in the future . . .

"Whitehall seems to feel they may have quit our patch, don't you see. The powers might want the Met. to be in charge. Any press?"

The ACC shook his head. "Not yet, sir. But it won't stay quiet for long. Too big."

He did not know that the lady walking her dog who had been shooed away from the scene by the men of Delta Bravo at 7:16 had seen two of the three bodies, had run home badly frightened, and told her husband. Or that he was a printer on the *Oxford Mail*. Although a technician, he thought he ought to mention it to the duty editor when he arrived.

The call from Downing Street was taken by the senior duty officer in the Communications Center of the White House, situated in the subground level of the West Wing, right next to the Situation Room. It was logged at 3:34 A.M. Washington time. Hearing who it was, the SDO bravely agreed to call the senior ranking Secret Service agent of the shift, at his post over in the Mansion.

The Secret Service man was patrolling the Center Hall at the time, quite close to the family quarters on the second floor. He responded when the phone at his desk opposite the First Family's gilded elevator trilled discreetly.

"She wants what?" he whispered into the receiver. "Do those Brits know what time it is over here?"

He listened a while longer. He could not recall when last someone had awakened a President at that hour. Must have happened, he thought, in case of war, say. Maybe that was what this was about. He could be in for one bad time from Burbank if he got it wrong. On the other hand . . . the British Prime Minister herself . . .

"I'll hang up now, call you back," he told the Communications Room. London was told the President was being roused; they should hang on. They did.

The Secret Service guard, whose name was Lepinsky, went through the double doors into the West Sitting Hall and faced the door to the Cormacks's bedroom on his left. He paused, took a deep breath, and knocked gently. No reply. He tried the handle. Unlocked. With, as he saw it, his career up for grabs, he entered. In the large double bed he could make out two sleeping forms, guessed the President would be nearer the window. He tiptoed around the bed, identified the maroon cotton pajama top, and shook the President's shoulder.

"Mr. President, sir. Would you wake up, sir, please?"

John Cormack came awake, identified the man standing timorously over him, glanced at his wife, and did not put on the light.

"What time is it, Mr. Lepinsky?"

"Just after half past three, sir. I'm sorry about this . . . Er, Mr. President, the British Prime Minister is on the line. She says it cannot wait. I'm sorry about this, sir."

John Cormack thought for a moment, then swung his legs out of the bed—gently, so as not to wake Myra. Lepinsky handed him a nearby robe. After nearly three years in power Cormack knew the British Prime Minister well enough. He had twice seen her in England—the second time on a two-hour stopover on his return from Vnukovo—and she had been twice to the States. They were both decisive people; they got on well. If it was she, it had to be important. He would catch up on sleep later.

"Return to the Center Hall, Mr. Lepinsky," he whispered. "Don't worry. You have done well. I'll take the call in my study."

The President's study is sandwiched between the master bedroom and the Yellow Oval Room, which is under the central rotunda. Like the bedroom, its windows look out over the lawn toward Pennsylvania Avenue. He closed the communicating door, put on the light, blinked several times, seated himself at his desk, and lifted the phone. She was on the line in ten seconds.

"Has anyone else been in touch with you yet?"

Something seemed to punch him in the stomach.

"No . . . no one. Why?"

"I believe Mr. Edmonds and Mr. Burbank must know by now," she said. "I'm sorry to have to be the first . . ."

Then she told him. He held the phone very tightly and stared at the curtains, not seeing them. His mouth went dry and he could not swallow. He heard the phrases: everything, but everything being done . . . Scotland Yard's best teams . . . no escape . . . He said yes, and thank you, and put the phone down. It was like being punched hard in the chest. He thought of Myra, still asleep. He would have to tell her. It would hit her very hard.

"Oh, Simon," he whispered. "Simon, my boy."

He knew he could not handle this himself. He needed a friend who could step in while he looked after Myra. After several minutes he called the operator, kept his voice very steady.

"Get me Vice President Odell, please. Yes, now."

In his residence at the Naval Observatory, Michael Odell was roused the same way, by a Secret Service man. The telephoned summons was unequivocal and unexplained. Please come straight to the Executive Mansion. Second floor. The study. Now, Michael, now, please.

Odell heard the phone go dead, replaced his own, scratched his head, and peeled the wrapper off a stick of spearmint gum. It helped him concentrate. He called for his car and went to the closet for his clothes. A widower, Odell slept alone, so there was no one to disturb. Ten minutes later, in slacks, shoes, and a sweater over his shirt, he was in the back of the stretch limousine, staring at the clipped back of the Navy driver's head or the lights of nighttime Washington until the illuminated mass of the White House came into view. He avoided the South Portico and the South Entrance and entered the ground-floor corridor by the door at its western end. He told his driver to wait; he would not be long. He was wrong. The time was 4:07 A.M.

Crisis management at the top level in Britain falls to a hastily convened committee whose membership varies according to the nature of the crisis. But its place of meeting rarely changes. The chosen conference hall is almost always the Cabinet Office Briefing Room, a quiet air-conditioned chamber two floors below ground level, under the Cabinet Office adjacent to Downing Street. From the initials these committees are known as COBRA.

It had taken Sir Harry Marriott and his staff just over an hour to get the "bodies," as he called his cast list, out of their homes, off their commuter trains, or from their scattered offices and into the Cabinet Office. He took the chair at 9:56 A.M.

The kidnapping was clearly a crime and a matter for the police, which came under the Home Office. But in this case there were many further ramifications. Apart from the Home Office, there was a Minister of State from the Foreign Office, which would try to maintain relationships with the State Department in Washington and thus the White House. Furthermore, if Simon Cormack had been spirited to Europe, their involvement would be vital at a political level. Answering to the Foreign Office was the Secret Intelligence Service, MI-6—"the Firm"—and their input would concern the possibility of foreign terrorist groups being involved. Their man had come across the river from Century House and would report back to the Chief.

Also coming under the Home Office, separate from the police, was the Security Service, MI-5, the counterintelligence arm with more than a passing interest in terrorism as it affected Britain internally. Their man had come from Curzon Street in Mayfair, where files on likely candidates were already being vetted by the score and a number of "sleepers" contacted to answer a particularly burning question: who?

There was a senior civil servant from the Defence Ministry, in charge of the Special Air Service regiment at Hereford. In the event that Simon Cormack and his abductors were located quickly and a siege situation developed, the SAS might well be needed for hostage recovery, one of their arcane specialities. No one needed to be told that already the troop on permanent half-hour standby—in this case, according to the rotation, Seven Troop, the free-fall men of B Squadron—had quietly moved up to Amber Alert, ten minutes, and their backup moved from two-hour standby to sixty minutes.

There was a man from the Ministry of Transport, controlling Britain's ports and airports. Liaising with the Coastguards and Customs, his department would operate a blanket port-watch, for a prime concern now was to keep Simon Cormack inside the country in case the kidnappers had other ideas. He had already spoken to the Department of Trade and Industry, who had made plain that to examine every single sealed and bonded freight container heading out of the country was quite literally impossible. Still, any private airplane, yacht or cruiser, fishing smack, camper, or motor home heading out with a large crate on board, or someone on a stretcher or simply drugged and insensible, would find a Customs officer or Coastguard taking more than a passing interest.

The key man, however, sat at Sir Harry's right: Nigel Cramer.

Unlike Britain's provincial county constabularies and police authorities, London's police force—the Metropolitan Police, known as "the Met."—is headed not by a chief constable but by a commissioner and is the largest force in the country. The commissioner, in this case Sir Peter Imbert, is assisted in his task by four assistant commissioners, each in charge of one of the four departments. Second of these is Specialist Operations, or S.O.

S.O. Department has thirteen branches, One through Fourteen, excluding Five, which, for no known reason, does not exist. Among the thirteen are the Covert Squad, Serious Crimes Squad, Flying Squad, Fraud Squad, and Regional Crimes Squad. And the Special Branch (counterintelligence), the Criminal Intelligence Branch (S.O. 11), and the Anti-Terrorist Branch (S.O. 13).

The man designated by Sir Peter Imbert to represent the Met. on the COBRA committee was the Deputy Assistant Commissioner, S.O. Department, Nigel Cramer. Cramer would report in two directions: upward, to his Assistant Commissioner and the Commissioner himself; sideways, to the COBRA committee. Toward him would flow the input from the official investigating officer, the I.O., who in turn would be using all the branches and squads of the department, as appropriate.

It takes a political decision to superimpose the Met. on a provincial force, but the Prime Minister had already taken that decision, justified by the suspicion that Simon Cormack might well by now be out of the Thames Valley area; and Sir Harry Marriott had just informed the Chief Constable of that decision. Cramer's men were already on the outskirts of Oxford.

There were two non-British invited to sit with the COBRA. One was Patrick Seymour, the FBI man at the American embassy; the other was Lou Collins, the London-based liaison officer of the CIA. Their inclusion was more than just courtesy; they were there so they could keep their own organizations aware of the level of effort being put in at London to solve the outrage, and maybe to contribute any nuggets their own people might unearth.

Sir Harry opened the meeting with a brief report of what was known so far. The abduction was just three hours old. At this point he felt it necessary to make two assumptions. One was that Simon Cormack had been driven away from Shotover Plain and was by now sequestered in a secret place; the second was that the perpetrators were terrorists of some kind who had not yet made any form of contact with the authorities.

The man from Secret Intelligence volunteered that his people were trying to contact a variety of penetration agents inside known European terrorist groups in an attempt to identify the group behind the snatch. It would take some days.

"These penetration agents lead very dangerous lives," he added. "We can't just ring them up and ask for Jimmy. Covert meetings will take place in various places over the next week to see if we can get a lead."

The Security Service man added that his department was doing the same with home-grown groups who might be involved, or know something. He doubted that the perpetrators were local. Apart from the I.R.A. and the INLA—both Irish—the British Isles had its fair share of weirdos, but the level of ruthless professionalism shown at Shotover Plain seemed to exclude the usual noisy malcontents. Still, his own penetration agents would also be activated.

Nigel Cramer reported that the first clues were likely to come from forensic examination or a chance witness not yet interviewed.

"We know the van used," he said. "A green-painted, far-from-new Ford Transit, bearing on both sides the familiar logo—in Oxfordshire—of the Barlow fruit company. It was seen heading east through Wheatley, away from the scene of the crime, about five minutes after the attack. And it was not a Barlow van—that is confirmed. The witness did not note the registration number. Obviously, a major search is on for anyone else who saw that van, its direction of travel, or the men in the front seat. Apparently there were two—just vague shadows behind the glass—but the milkman believes one had a beard.

"On forensics, we have a car jack, perfect tire prints from the van—the Thames Valley people established exactly where it stood—and a collection of spent brass casings, apparently from a submachine carbine. They are going to the Army experts at Fort Halstead. Ditto the slugs when they come out of the bodies of the two Secret Service men and Sergeant Dunn of the Oxford Special Branch. Fort Halstead will tell us exactly, but at first glance they look like Warsaw Pact ordnance. Almost every European terrorist group except the I.R.A. uses East Bloc weaponry.

"The forensic people at Oxford are good, but I'm still bringing every piece of evidence back to our own labs at Fulham. Thames Valley will continue to look for witnesses.

"So, gentlemen, we have four lines of enquiry. The getaway van, witnesses at or near the scene, the evidence they left behind, and—another for the Thames Valley people—a search for anyone seen observing the house off the Woodstock Road. Apparently"—he glanced at the two Americans—"Simon Cormack made the same run over the same ground each morning at the same hour for several days."

At that point the phone rang. It was for Cramer. He took the call, asked several questions, listened for some minutes, then came back to the table.

"I've appointed Commander Peter Williams, head of S.O. 13, the Anti-Terrorist Branch, the official investigating officer. That was he. We think we have the van."

The owner of Whitehill Farm, close to Fox Covert on the Islip road, had called the fire brigade at 8:10 after seeing smoke and flames rising from a near-derelict timber barn he owned. It was situated in a meadow close to the road but five hundred yards from his farmhouse and he seldom visited it. The Oxford Fire Brigade had responded, but too late to save the barn. The farmer had been standing helplessly by and had watched the flames consume the timber structure, bringing down first the roof and then the walls.

As the firemen were damping down the debris, they observed what appeared to be the gutted wreck of a van underneath the charred timbers. That was at 8:41. The farmer was adamant there had not been a vehicle stored in the barn. Fearing there might have been people—gypsies, tinkers, even campers—inside the van, the firemen stayed on to pull the timbers away. They peered inside the van when they could get near to it, but saw no evidence of bodies. But it was definitely the wreck of a Ford Transit.

On returning to the Brigade headquarters, a smart leading officer heard on the radio that the Thames Valley Police were looking for a Transit, believed to have participated in "an offense involving firearms" earlier that morning. He had rung Kidlington.

"I'm afraid it's gutted," said Cramer. "Tires probably burnt out, fingerprints erased. Still, engine block and chassis numbers will not be affected. My Vehicles Section people are on their way. If there's anything—and I do mean anything—left, we'll get it."

Vehicles Section at Scotland Yard comes under the Serious Crimes Squad, part of S.O. Department.

The COBRA stayed in session, but some of its leading participants left to get on with other matters, handing over to subordinates who would report if there was a break. The chair was taken by a junior Minister from the Home Office.

In a perfect world, which it never is, Nigel Cramer would have preferred to keep the press out of things, for a while at least. By 11:00 A.M. Clive Empson of the *Oxford Mail* was at Kidlington asking about reports of a shooting and killing on Shotover Plain just about sunrise. Three things then surprised him. One was that he was soon taken to a detective chief superintendent, who asked him where he had got this report. He refused to say. The second was that there was an air of genuine fear among the junior officers at the Thames Valley Police headquarters. The third was that he was given no help at all. For a double shooting—the print technician's wife had seen only two bodies—the police would normally be asking for press cooperation and issuing a statement, not to mention holding a press conference.

Driving back to Oxford, Empson mulled things over. A "natural causes" would go to the city morgue. But a shooting would mean the more sophisticated facilities of the Radcliffe Infirmary. By chance he was having a rather agreeable affair with a nurse at the Radcliffe; she was not in the "bodies" section, but she might know someone who was.

By the lunch hour he had been told there was a big flap going on at the Radcliffe. There were three bodies in the morgue; two were apparently American and one was a British policeman. There was a forensic pathologist all the way from London, and someone from the American embassy. That puzzled him.

Servicemen from nearby Upper Heyford base would bring uniformed USAF to the Infirmary; American tourists on a slab might bring someone from the embassy; but why would Kidlington not say so? He thought of Simon Cormack, widely known to be a student these past nine months, and went to Balliol College. Here he met a pretty Welsh student called Jenny.

She confirmed that Simon Cormack had not come to tutorials that day but took it lightly. He was probably knocking himself out with all that cross-country running. Running? "Yes, he's the main hope to beat Cambridge in December. Goes for brutal training runs every morning. Usually on Shotover Plain."

Clive Empson thought he had been kicked in the belly. Accustomed to the idea of spending his life covering affairs for the *Oxford Mail*, he suddenly saw the bright lights of Fleet Street, London, beckoning. He almost got it right, but he assumed Simon Cormack had been shot. That was the report he filed to a major London newspaper in the late afternoon. It had the effect of forcing the government to make a statement.

Washington insiders will sometimes, in complete privacy, admit to British friends that they would give their right arms for the British governmental system.

The British system is fairly simple. The Queen is the head of state and she stays in place. The head of government is the Prime Minister, who is always the leader of the party that wins the general election. This has two advantages. The nation's chief executive cannot be at loggerheads with a majority from the opposing political party in Parliament (which facilitates necessary, though not always popular, legislation) and the incoming Prime Minister after an election victory is almost always a skilled and experienced politician at the national level, and probably a former Cabinet Minister in a previous administration. The experience, the know-how, the awareness of how things happen and how to make them happen, are always there.

In London there is a third advantage. Behind the politicians stands an array of senior civil servants who probably served the previous administration, the one before that, and the one before that. With a hundred years of experience at the top between a dozen of them, these "mandarins" are of vital help to the new winners. They know what happened last time and why; they keep the records; they know where the land mines are situated.

In Washington the outgoing incumbent takes almost everything with him—the experience, the advisers, and the records—or, at any rate, those that some congenial colonel has not shredded. The incoming man starts cold, often with experience in government only at the state level, bringing his own team of advisers, who may come in "cold turkey," just as he does, not quite sure which are the footballs and which the land mines. It accounts for quite a few Washington reputations soon walking around with a permanent limp.

Thus when a stunned Vice President Odell left the Mansion and crossed to the West Wing at 5:05 that October morning, he realized that he was not entirely certain what to do or whom to ask.

"I cannot handle this thing alone, Michael," the President had told him. "I will try to carry on the duties of the President. I retain the Oval Office. But I cannot chair the Crisis Management Committee. I am too involved, in any case. . . . Get him back for me, Michael. Get my son back for me."

Odell was a much more emotional man than John Cormack. He had never seen his wry, dry, academic friend so distraught, nor ever thought to. He had embraced his President and sworn it would be done. Cormack had returned to the bedroom where the White House physician was administering sedation to a weeping First Lady.

Odell now sat in the center chair at the Cabinet Room table, ordered coffee, and started to make phone calls himself. The snatch had taken place in Britain; that was abroad; he would need the Secretary of State. He called Jim Donaldson and woke him up. He did not tell him why, just to come straight to the Cabinet Room. Donaldson protested. He would be there at nine.

"Jim, get your butt in here *now*. It's an emergency. And don't call the President to check. He can't take your call, and he's asked me to handle it."

While he had been governor of Texas, Michael Odell had always considered foreign affairs a closed book. But he had been in Washington, and Vice President, long enough to have had numberless briefings on foreign affairs issues and to have learned a lot. Those who fell for the deliberately folksy image he liked to cultivate did Odell an injustice, often to their later regret. Michael Odell had not gained the trust and respect of a man like John Cormack because he was a fool. In fact, he was very smart indeed.

He called Bill Walters, the Attorney General, political chief of the FBI. Walters was up and dressed, having taken a call from Don Edmonds, Director of the Bureau. Walters knew already.

"I'm on my way, Michael," he said. "I want Don Edmonds on hand as well. We're going to need the Bureau's expertise here. Also, Don's man in London is keeping him posted on an hourly basis. We need up-to-date reports. Okay?"

"That's great," said Odell with relief. "Bring Edmonds."

When the full group was present by 6:00 A.M., it also included Hubert Reed of Treasury (responsible for the Secret Service); Morton Stannard of Defense; Brad Johnson, the National Security Adviser; and Lee Alexander, Director of Central Intelligence. Waiting and available in addition to Don Edmonds were Creighton Burbank of the Secret Service, and the Deputy Director for Operations of the CIA.

Lee Alexander was aware that although he was DCI, he was a political appointee, not a career intelligence officer. The man who headed up the entire operational area of the Agency was the DDO, David Weintraub. He waited outside with the others.

Don Edmonds had also brought one of his top men. Under the Director of the FBI come three executive assistant directors, heading respectively Law Enforcement Services, Administration, and Investigations. Within Investigations were three divisions—Intelligence, International Liaison (from which came Patrick Seymour in London), and Criminal Investigations Division. The EAD for Investigations, Buck Revell, was away sick, so Edmonds had brought the assistant director in charge of the CID, Philip Kelly.

"We'd better have them all in," suggested Brad Johnson. "As of now, they know more than we do."

Everyone concurred. Later the experts would form the Crisis Management Group, meeting in the Situation Room downstairs, next to the Communications Center, for convenience and privacy. Later still, the Cabinet men would join them there, when the telephoto lenses on the press cameras began to peer through the windows of the Cabinet Room and across the Rose Garden.

First they heard from Creighton Burbank, an angry man who blamed the British squarely for the disaster. He gave them everything he had learned from his own team in Summertown, a report that covered everything up to the runner's departure from Woodstock Road that morning, and what his men had later seen and learned at Shotover Plain.

"I've got two men dead," he snapped, "two widows and three orphans to see. And all because those bastards can't run a security operation. I wish it to go on record, gentlemen, that my service repeatedly asked that Simon Cormack not spend a year abroad, and that we needed fifty men in there, not a dozen."

"Okay, you were right," said Odell placatingly.

Don Edmonds had just taken a long call from the FBI man in London, Patrick Seymour. He filled them in on everything else he had learned right up to the close of the first COBRA meeting under the Cabinet Office, which had just ended.

"Just what happens in a kidnap case?" asked Hubert Reed mildly.

Of all President Cormack's senior advisers in the room, Reed was the one generally deemed to be least likely to cope with the tough political infighting habitually associated with power in Washington.

He was a short man whose air of diffidence, even defenselessness, was accentuated by owllike eyeglasses. He had inherited wealth, and had started on Wall Street as a pension-fund manager with a major brokerage house. A sound nose for investments had made him a leading financier by his early fifties, and he had in previous years managed the Cormack family trusts—which was how the two men met and became friends.

It was Reed's genius for finance that had caused John Cormack to invite him to Washington, where, at Treasury, he had managed to hold America's spiraling budget deficit within some limits. So long as the matter at hand was finance, Hubert Reed was at home; only when he was made privy to some of the "hard" operations of the Drug Enforcement Agency or the Secret Service, both subagencies of the Treasury Department, did he become thoroughly uncomfortable.

Don Edmonds glanced at Philip Kelly for an answer to Reed's question. Kelly was the crime expert in the room.

"Normally, unless the abductors and their hideout can be quickly established, you wait until they make contact and demand a ransom. After that, you try to negotiate the return of the victim. Investigations continue, of course, to try to locate the whereabouts of the criminals. If that fails, it's down to negotiation."

"In this case, by whom?" asked Stannard.

There was silence. America has some of the most sophisticated alarm systems in the world. Her scientists have developed infrared sensors that can detect body heat from several miles above the earth's surface; there are noise sensors that can hear a mouse breathe at a mile; there are movement and light sensors to pick up a cigarette stub from inner space. But no system in the entire arsenal can match the CYA sensor system that operates in Washington. It had already been in action for two hours and now was headed for peak performance.

"We need a presence over there," urged Walters. "We can't just leave this entirely to the British. We have to be seen to be doing something, something positive, something to get that boy back."

"Hell, yes," exploded Odell. "We can say they lost the boy, even though the Secret Service insisted that the British police take a back seat." Burbank glared at him. "We have the leverage. We can insist we participate in their investigation."

"We can hardly send a Washington Police Department team in to take over from Scotland Yard on their real estate," Attorney General Walters pointed out.

"Well, what about the negotiation, then?" asked Brad Johnson. There was still silence from the professionals. By his insistence, Johnson was blatantly infringing the rules of Cover Your Ass.

Odell spoke, to mask the hesitation of them all. "If it comes to negotiation," he asked, "who is the best hostage-recovery negotiator in the world?"

"Out at Quantico," ventured Kelly, "we have the Bureau's Behavioral Science Group. They handle our kidnap negotiations here in America. They're the best we have over here."

"I said, who's the best in the world?" repeated the Vice President.

"The most consistently successful hostage-recovery negotiator in the world," remarked Weintraub quietly, "is a man called Quinn. I know him—knew him once, at any rate."

Ten pairs of eyes swiveled toward the CIA man.

"Background him," commanded Odell.

"He's American," said Weintraub. "After leaving the Army he joined an insurance company in Hartford. After two years they sent him to head their Paris operation, covering all their clients in Europe. He married, had a daughter. His French wife and child were killed in an expressway accident outside Orleans. He hit the bottle, Hartford fired him, he pulled himself back together, and he went to work for a firm of Lloyd's underwriters in London, a firm specializing in personal security and, thus, hostage negotiation.

"So far as I recall, he spent ten years with them—1978 through '88. Then he retired. Till then he had handled personally—or, where there was a language problem, advised on—over a dozen successful hostage recoveries all over Europe. As you know, Europe is the kidnap capital of the developed world. I believe he speaks three languages outside of English, and he knows Britain and Europe like the back of his hand."

"Is he the man for us?" asked Odell. "Could he handle this for the U.S.?"

Weintraub shrugged. "You asked who was the best in the world, Mr. Vice President," he pointed out. There were nods of relief around the table.

"Where is he now?" asked Odell.

"I believe he retired to the South of Spain, sir. We'll have it all on file back at Langley."

"Go get him, Mr. Weintraub," said Odell. "Get him back here, this Mr. Quinn. No matter what it takes."

At 7:00 P.M. that evening the first news hit the TV screens like an exploding bomb. On TVE a gabbling newscaster told a stunned Spanish public of the events of that morning outside the city of Oxford. The men around the bar at Antonio's in Alcántara del Rio watched in silence. Antonio brought the tall man a complimentary glass of the house wine.

"*Mala cosa,*" he said sympathetically. The tall man did not take his eyes from the screen.

"*No es mi asunto,*" he said, puzzlingly. It is not my affair.

David Weintraub took off from Andrews Air Force Base outside Washington at 10:00 A.M. Washington time in a USAF VC20A, the military version of the Gulfstream Three. She crossed the Atlantic direct, cruising at 43,000 feet and making 483 mph, in seven and a half hours, with a helpful tail wind.

With six hours' time difference, it was 11:30 P.M. when the DDO, CIA, landed at Rota, the U.S. Navy air base across the bay from Cadiz, Andalusia. He transferred at once to a waiting Navy SH2F Sea Sprite helicopter, which lifted away toward the east before he was even seated. The rendezvous was the wide, flat beach called Casares, and here the young staffer who had driven down from Madrid was waiting for him with a car from the Madrid Station. Sneed was a brash, bright young man fresh out of CIA training school at Camp Peary, Virginia, and seeking to impress the DDO. Weintraub sighed.

They drove carefully through Manilva, operative Sneed twice asking directions, and found Alcántara del Rio just after midnight. The whitewashed *casita* out of town was harder, but a helpful peasant pointed the way.

The limousine eased to a halt and Sneed killed the engine. They got out, surveyed the darkened cottage, and Sneed tried the door. It was on the latch. They walked straight into the wide, cool ground-floor sitting area. By the moonlight Weintraub could make out a man's room: cowhide rugs over quarry tiles, easy chairs, an old refectory table of Spanish oak, a wall of books.

Sneed began poking about looking for a light switch. Weintraub noticed the three oil lamps and knew he was wasting his time. There would be a diesel generator out back to give electricity for cooking and bathing, probably shut off at sundown. Sneed was still clattering about. Weintraub took a step forward. He felt the needle tip of the knife just below the lobe of his right ear, and froze. The man had come down the tiled stair from the bedroom without a sound.

"Been a long time since Son Tay, Quinn," said Weintraub in a low voice. The knife point moved away from his jugular.

"What's that, sir?" asked Sneed cheerfully from the other end of the room. A shadow moved over the tiles, a match flared, and the oil lamp on the table gave a warm glow to the room. Sneed jumped a foot. Major Kerkorian in Belgrade would have loved him.

"Tiring journey," said Weintraub. "Mind if I sit?"

Quinn was in a cotton wraparound from the waist down, like a sarong from the Orient. Bare to the waist, lean, work-hardened. Sneed's mouth fell open at the scars.

"I'm out of it, David," said Quinn. He seated himself at the refectory table, at the opposite end from the DDO. "I'm retired."

He pushed a tumbler and the earthenware pitcher of red wine toward Weintraub, who poured a glass, drank, and nodded with appreciation. A rough red wine. It would never see the tables of the rich. A peasant's and a soldier's wine.

"Please, Quinn."

Sneed was amazed. DDOs did not say "please." They gave orders.

"I'm not coming," said Quinn. Sneed came into the light glow, his jacket hanging free. He allowed it to swing to show the butt of the piece he carried in a hip holster. Quinn did not even look at him. He stared at Weintraub.

"Who is this asshole?" he inquired mildly.

"Sneed," said Weintraub firmly, "go check the tires."

Sneed went outside. Weintraub sighed.

"Quinn, the business at Taormina. The little girl. We know. It wasn't your fault."

"Can't you understand? I'm out. It's over. No more. You've wasted your journey. Get someone else."

"There is no one else. The Brits have people, good people. Washington says we need an American. In-house, we don't have anyone to match you when it comes to Europe."

"Washington wants to protect its ass," snapped Quinn. "They always do. They need a fall guy in case it goes wrong."

"Yeah, maybe," admitted Weintraub. "But one last time, Quinn. Not for Washington, not for the establishment, not even for the boy. For the parents. They need the best. I told the committee you're it."

Quinn stared around the room, studying his few but treasured possessions as if he might not see them again.

"I have a price," he said at last.

"Name it," said the DDO simply.

"Bring my grapes in. Bring in the harvest."

They walked outside ten minutes later, Quinn hefting a gunnysack, dressed in dark trousers, sneakers on bare feet, a shirt. Sneed held open the car door. Quinn took the front passenger seat; Weintraub, the wheel.

"You stay here," he said to Sneed. "Bring in his grapes."

"Do *what*?" Sneed gasped.

"You heard. Go down to the village in the morning, rent some labor, and bring in the man's grape harvest. I'll tell Madrid Head of Station it's okay."

He used a hand communicator to summon the Sea Sprite, which was hovering over Casares beach when they arrived. They climbed aboard and wheeled away through the velvety darkness toward Rota and Washington.

CHAPTER FIVE

David Weintraub was away from Washington for just twenty hours. On the eight-hour flight from Rota to Andrews, he gained six hours in time zones, landing at the Maryland headquarters of the 89th Military Airlift Wing at 4:00 A.M. In the intervening period two governments, in Washington and London, had been virtually under siege.

There are few more awesome sights than the combined forces of the world's media when they have completely lost any last vestige of restraint. The appetite is insatiable; the methodology, brutal.

Airplanes bound out of the United States for London, or any British airport, were choked from the flight-deck doors to the toilets, as every American news outlet worth the name sent a team to the British capital. On arrival they went berserk; there were minute-by-minute deadlines to meet and nothing to say. London had agreed with the White House to stick with the original terse statement. Of course it was nowhere near enough.

Reporters and TV teams staked out the detached house off the Woodstock Road as if its doors might open to reveal the missing youth. The doors remained firmly closed as the Secret Service team, on orders from Creighton Burbank, packed every last item and prepared to leave.

The Oxford city coroner, using his powers under Section Twenty of the Coroners Amendment Act, released the bodies of the two dead Secret Service agents as soon as the Home Office pathologist had finished with them. Technically they were released to Ambassador Aloysius Fairweather on behalf of next of kin; in fact they were escorted by a senior member of the embassy staff to the USAF base at nearby Upper Heyford, where an honor guard saw the caskets aboard a transport for Andrews Air Force Base, accompanied by the other ten agents, who had nearly been mobbed for statements when they left the house in Summertown.

They returned to the States, to be met by Creighton Burbank and to begin the long inquiry into what had gone wrong. There was nothing left for them to do in England.

Even when the Oxford house had been closed down, a small and forlorn group of reporters waited outside it lest something, anything, happen there. Others pursued, throughout the university city, anyone who had ever known Simon Cormack—tutors, fellow students, college staff, barmen, athletes. Two other American students at Oxford, albeit at different colleges, had to go into hiding. The mother of one, traced in America, was kind enough to say she was bringing her boy home at once to the safety of downtown Miami. It made a paragraph and got her a spot on a local quiz show.

The body of Sergeant Dunn was released to his family, and the Thames Valley Police prepared for a funeral with full honors.

All the forensic evidence was brought east to London. The military hardware went to the Royal Armoured Research and Development Establishment at Fort Halstead, outside Sevenoaks in Kent, where the ammunition from the Skorpion was quickly identified, underlining the chance of European terrorists' being involved. This was not made public.

The other evidence went to the Metropolitan Police laboratory in Fulham, London. That meant blades of crumpled grass with blood smears on them, pieces of mud, casts of tire tracks, the jack, footprints, the slugs taken from the three dead bodies, and the fragments of glass from the shattered windshield of the shadowing car. Before nightfall of the first day, Shotover Plain looked as if it had been vacuum-cleaned.

The car itself went on a flatbed truck to the Vehicles Section of the Serious Crimes Squad, but of much more interest was the Ford Transit van recovered from the torched barn. Experts crawled all over the charred timbers of the barn until they emerged as black as the soot. The farmer's rusted and severed chain was removed from the gate as if it were made of eggshell, but the only outcome was a report that it had been sheared by a standard bolt-cutter. A bigger clue was the track of the sedan that had driven out of the field after the switch-over.

The gutted Transit van came to London in a crate and was slowly taken to pieces. Its license plates were false but the criminals had taken pains; the plates would have belonged to a van of that year of manufacture.

The van had been worked on—serviced and tuned by a skilled mechanic; that at least they could tell. Someone had tried to abrade the chassis and engine numbers, using a tungsten-carbide angle-grinder, obtainable from tool stores anywhere and slotted into a power drill. Not good enough. These numbers are die-stamped into the metal, so spectroscopic examination brought out the numbers from the deeper imprint inside the metal.

The central vehicle computer at Swansea came up with the original registration number and the last known owner. The computer said he lived in Nottingham. The address was visited; he had moved. No forwarding address. An all-points went out for the man—very quietly.

Nigel Cramer reported to the COBRA committee every hour on the hour and his listeners reported back to their various departments. Langley authorized Lou Collins, their man in London, to admit they, too, were raising all and any penetration agents they might have inside the European terrorist groups. There were quite a few. Counterintelligence and antiterrorist services in each of the countries hosting such groups were also offering any help they could. The hunt was becoming very heavy indeed, but there was no big break—yet.

And the abductors had not been in contact. From the time of the first news break, phone lines had been jammed; to Kidlington, to Scotland Yard, the American embassy in Grosvenor Square, any government office. Extra telephone staff had to be drafted. One had to say that for them—the British public was really trying to help. Every call was checked out; almost all other criminal investigations went on the back burner. Among the thousands of calls came the freaks, the weirdos, the hoaxers, the optimists, the hopeful, the helpful, and the simply certifiable.

The first filter was the line of switchboard operators; then the thousands of police constables who listened carefully and agreed the cigar-shaped object in the sky might be very important and would be drawn to the attention of the Prime Minister herself. The final cull came from the senior police officers who interviewed the real "possibles." These included two more early morning drivers who had seen the green van between Wheatley and Stanton St. John. But it all ran out at the barn.

Nigel Cramer had cracked a few cases in his time; he had come up from beat constable, switched to detective work, and been in it thirty years. He knew that criminals left tracks; every time you touch something, you leave a tiny trace behind. A good copper could find that trace, especially with modern technology, if he looked hard enough. It just took time, which was what he did not have. He had known some high-pressure cases, but nothing like this.

He also knew that despite all the technology in the world the successful detective was usually the lucky detective. There was almost always one break in a case that was due to luck—good luck for the detective, bad for the criminal. If it went the other way, the criminal could still get away. Still, you could make your own luck, and he told his scattered teams to overlook nothing, absolutely nothing, however crazy or futile it might seem. But after twenty-four hours he began to think, like his Thames Valley colleague, that this was not going to be a quickie. They had got away clean, and to find them would be just plain slog.

And there was the other factor—the hostage. That he was the President's son was a political matter, not a police one. The gardener's boy was still a human life. Hunting men with a sack of stolen money, or a murder behind them, you just went for the target. In a hostage case the chase had to be very quiet. Spook the kidnappers badly enough, and despite their investment of time and money in the crime, they could still cut and run, leaving a dead hostage behind them. This he reported to a somber committee just before midnight, London time. An hour later in Spain, David Weintraub was taking a glass of wine with Quinn. Cramer, the British cop, knew nothing of this. Yet.

Scotland Yard will admit in private that it has better relations with Britain's press than sometimes appears. On small matters they often irritate each other, but when the issue is really serious the editors and proprietors, in the face of a serious plea, usually accede and use restraint. *Serious* means where human life or national security is in jeopardy. That is why some kidnap cases have been handled with no publicity at all, even though the editors have known most of the details.

In this case, because of a sharp-nosed young reporter in Oxford, the fox was already out and running; there was little the British press could do to exercise restraint. But Sir Peter Imbert, the Commissioner, personally met eight proprietors, twenty editors, and the chiefs of the two television networks and twelve radio stations. He argued that whatever the foreign press might print or say, there was a good chance the kidnappers, holed up somewhere in Britain, would be listening to British radio, watching British TV, and reading British newspapers. He asked for no crazy stories to the effect that the police were closing in on them and that a storming of their fortress was imminent. That was exactly the sort of story to panic them into killing their hostage and fleeing. He got his agreement.

It was the small hours of the morning in London. Far to the south a VC20A was gliding over the darkened Azores, destination Washington.

In fact the kidnappers *were* holed up. Passing through Buckingham the previous morning, the Volvo had intersected the M.1 motorway east of Milton Keynes and turned south toward London, joining at that hour the great torrent of steel rolling toward the capital, becoming lost among the juggernaut trucks and the commuters heading south from their Buckinghamshire, Bedfordshire, and Hertfordshire homes. North of London the Volvo had pulled onto the M.25, the great orbital motorway that rings the capital at a range of about twenty-five miles from the city center. From the M.25 the arterial routes linking the provinces to London spread out like the spokes of a wheel.

The Volvo had eventually taken one of these spokes and, before 10:00 A.M., slid into the garage of a detached house on a tree-lined avenue a mile from the center of a small town not forty miles in a direct line from Scotland Yard. The house was well chosen; not so isolated as to excite interest in its purchase, not too close to prying neighbors. Two miles before the Volvo reached it, the team leader ordered the other three to slide down and crouch out of sight below window level. The two in the back, one on top of the other, pulled a blanket over themselves. Anyone watching would have seen a single man in a business suit and a beard driving through his gate and into his garage.

The garage opened with an automatic garage-door opener operated from the car and closed the same way. Only when it was closed did the leader allow his henchmen to surface and climb out. The garage was joined to the house, reached through a communicating door.

All four men changed back to their black track suits and black woolen ski masks before they opened the trunk. Simon Cormack was groggy, with unfocused vision, and he screwed his eyes tight against the flashlight that blinded him. Before he could adjust, a hood of black serge was thrown over his head. He saw nothing of his abductors.

He was led through the door into the house and down the stairs to the basement. It had been prepared; clean, white, concrete floor, recessed ceiling light behind shatterproof glass, a steel-frame bed screwed to the floor, toilet bucket with plastic lid. There was a peephole in the door; the shutter was on the outside, as were two steel bolts.

The men were not brutal; they just hefted the youth onto the bed and the giant held him still while one of the others slipped a steel handcuff around one ankle, not tight enough to cause gangrene but so as to ensure that no foot would ever slip through it. The other cuff was locked tight. Through it went a ten-foot steel chain, which was then padlocked to itself. The other end of the chain was already padlocked around one leg of the bed. Then they left him. They never said a word to him and never would.

He waited half an hour before he dared take the hood off. He did not know if they were still there, though he had heard a door close and the rasp of sliding bolts. His hands were free, but he took the hood off very slowly. There were no blows, no shouts. At last it was off. He blinked against the light, then adjusted and stared around. His memory was hazy. He recalled running on soft springy grass, a green van, a man changing a tire; two black-clad figures coming at him, a searing roar of gunfire, the impact, the feeling of weight on top of him, and grass in his mouth.

He remembered the open van doors, trying to shout, flailing limbs, the mattresses inside the van, the big man holding him down, something sweet and aromatic across his mouth, and then nothing. Until now. Until this. Then it hit him. With the realization came the fear. And the loneliness, the utter isolation.

He tried to be brave, but tears of fear welled up and trickled down. "Oh, Dad," he whispered. "Dad, I'm sorry. Help me."

If Whitehall was having problems from the tidal wave of telephone calls and press inquiries, the pressure on the White House was trebled. The first statement on the affair out of London had been issued at 7:00 P.M. London time and the White House had been warned an hour before that it would have to come. But that was only 2:00 P.M. Washington time, and the American media reaction had been frenzied.

Craig Lipton, the White House press secretary, had spent an hour in the Cabinet Room with the committee, being briefed on what to say. The trouble was, there was so little. The fact of the abduction could be confirmed, along with the death of two accompanying Secret Service men. Plus the fact that the President's son was a fine athlete, specializing in cross-country running, and had been on a training run at the time.

It would not help, of course. There is no hindsight as brilliantly perceptive as that of an outraged journalist. Creighton Burbank, while agreeing he would not actually criticize the President nor blame Simon himself, made plain he was not having his Secret Service crucified for falling down on protection when he had specifically asked for more men. A compromise was worked out that would fool no one.

Jim Donaldson pointed out that, as Secretary of State, he still had to maintain relations with London and in any case angry friction between the two capitals would not help and might do real harm; he insisted Lipton stress that a British police sergeant had been murdered as well. This was agreed, though the White House press corps eventually took little notice.

Lipton faced a baying press just after 4:00 P.M. and made his statement. He was on live TV and radio. The moment he finished, the uproar started. He pleaded he could answer no further questions. A victim in the Roman Colosseum might as well have told the lions he was really only a very thin Christian. The uproar increased. Many questions were drowned out but some came through to 100 million Americans, sowing the seeds. Did the White House blame the British? Er, well, no . . . Why not? Were they not in charge of security over there? Well, yes, but . . . Did the White House blame the Secret Service then? Not exactly . . . Why were there only two men guarding the son of the President? What was he doing running almost alone in an isolated area? Was it true Creighton Burbank had offered his resignation? Had the kidnappers communicated yet? To that one he could gratefully answer no, but he was already being goaded into exceeding his brief. That was the point. Reporters can smell a spokesman-on-the-run like a Limburger cheese.

Lipton finally retreated behind the scene, bathed in sweat and determined to go back to Grand Rapids. The glamour of work in the White House was wearing off fast. The newscasters and editorial writers would say what they wanted, regardless of his answers to questions. By nightfall the press tone was becoming markedly hostile to Britain.

Up at the British embassy on Massachusetts Avenue the press attaché, who had also heard of CYA, made a statement. While expressing his country's dismay and shock at what had happened, he slipped in two points. That the Thames Valley Police had taken a very low-profile role specifically at American request, and that Sergeant Dunn was the only one who had got off two shots at the abductors, giving his life in doing so. It was not what was wanted, but it made a paragraph. It also made a watching Creighton Burbank snarl with anger. Both men knew that the low-profile request, indeed insistence, had come from Simon Cormack via his father, but could not say so.

The Crisis Management Group, the professionals, met through the day in the basement Situation Room, monitoring the information flow out of COBRA in London and reporting upstairs as and when necessary. The National Security Agency had stepped up its monitoring of all telephone communications into and out of Britain in case the kidnappers made a call via satellite. The FBI's behavioral scientists at Quantico had come up with a list of psycho-portraits of previous kidnappers and a menu of things the Cormack kidnappers might or might not do, along with lists of do's and don'ts for the Anglo-American authorities. Quantico firmly expected to be called in and flown to London en masse, and were perplexed at the delay, although none of them had ever operated in Europe.

In the Cabinet Room the committee was living on nerves, coffee, and antacid tablets. This was the first major crisis of the incumbency and the middle-aged politicians were learning the hard way the first rule of crisis management: It is going to cost a lot of sleep, so get what you can while you can. Having risen at 4:00 A.M., the Cabinet members were still awake at midnight.

At that hour the VC20A was over the Atlantic, well west of the Azores, three and a half hours short of landfall and four hours short of touchdown. In the spacious rear compartment the two veterans, Weintraub and Quinn, were catching some sleep. Also sleeping, farther back, was the three-man crew who had flown the jet to Spain; the "slip" crew brought her home.

The men in the Cabinet Room browsed over the dossier on the man called Quinn, gouged out of the files at Langley, with additions from the Pentagon. Born on a farm in Delaware, it said; lost his mother at age ten; now aged forty-six. Joined the infantry at age eighteen in 1963, transferred two years later to the Special Forces and went to Vietnam four months after. Spent five years there.

"He never seems to use his first name," complained Hubert Reed. "Says here even his intimates call him Quinn. Just Quinn. Odd."

"He *is* odd," observed Bill Walters, who had read further along. "It also says here he hates violence."

"Nothing odd about that," replied Jim Donaldson. "*I* hate violence."

Unlike his predecessor at State, George Shultz, who had occasionally been known to give vent to a four-letter word, Jim Donaldson was a man of unrelieved primness, a characteristic that had often made him the unappreciative butt of Michael Odell's leg-pulling jokes.

Thin and angular, even taller than John Cormack, he resembled a flamingo en route to a funeral, and was never seen without his three-piece charcoal-gray suit, gold-fob watch chain, and stiff white collar. Odell deliberately made mention of bodily functions whenever he wished to twit the astringent New Hampshire lawyer, and at each mention Donaldson's narrow nose would wrinkle in distaste. His attitude to violence was similar to his distaste for crudeness.

"Yes," rejoined Walters, "but you haven't read page eighteen."

Donaldson did so, as did Michael Odell. The Vice President whistled.

"He did *that*?" he queried. "They should have given the guy the Congressional Medal."

"You need witnesses for the Congressional Medal," Walters pointed out. "As you see, only two men survived that encounter on the Mekong, and Quinn brought the other one forty miles on his back. Then the man died of wounds at Danang USMC Military Hospital."

"Still," said Hubert Reed cheerfully, "he managed a Silver Star, two Bronze, and five Purple Hearts." As if getting wounded was fun if they gave you more ribbons.

"With the campaign medals, that guy must have four rows," mused Odell. "It doesn't say how he and Weintraub met."

It didn't. Weintraub was now fifty-four, eight years older than Quinn. He had joined the CIA at age twenty-four, just out of college in 1961, gone through his training at the Farm—the nickname for Camp Peary on the York River in Virginia—and gone to Vietnam as a GS-12 provincial officer in 1965, about the time the young Green Beret called Quinn arrived from Fort Bragg.

Through 1961 and 1962 ten A-teams of the U.S. Special Forces had been deployed in Darlac Province, building strategic and fortified villages with the peasants, using the "oil-spot" theory developed by the British in beating the Communist guerrillas in Malaya: to deny the terrorists local support, supplies, food, safe-houses, information, and money. The Americans called it the hearts-and-minds policy. Under the Special Forces guidance, it was working.

In 1963, Lyndon Johnson came to power. The Army argued that Special Forces should be returned from CIA control to theirs. They won. It marked the end of hearts-and-minds, though it took another two years to collapse. Weintraub and Quinn met in those two years. The CIA man was concerned with gathering information on the Viet Cong, which he did by skill and cunning, abhorring the methods of men like Irving Moss (whom he did not encounter, since they were in different parts of Vietnam), even though he knew such methods were sometimes used in the Phoenix program, of which he was a part.

The Special Forces were increasingly taken away from their village program to be sent on search-and-destroy missions in the deepest jungle. The two men met in a bar over a beer; Quinn was twenty-one and had been out there a year; Weintraub was twenty-nine and also had a year in 'Nam behind him. They found common cause in a shared belief that the Army High Command was not going to win that kind of war just by throwing ordnance at it. Weintraub found he very much liked the fearless young soldier. Self-educated he might be; he had a first-rate brain and had taught himself fluent Vietnamese, a rarity among the military. They stayed in touch. The last time Weintraub had seen Quinn was during the run up to Son Tay.

"Says here the guy was at Son Tay," said Michael Odell. "Son of a gun."

"With a record like that, I wonder why he never made officer," said Morton Stannard. "The Pentagon has some people with the same kind of decorations out of 'Nam, but they got themselves commissioned at the first opportunity."

David Weintraub could have told them, but he was still sixty minutes short of touchdown. After taking back control of the Special Forces, the orthodox military—who hated S.F. because they could not understand it—slowly ran down the S.F. role over the six years to 1970, handing over more and more of the hearts-and-minds program, as well as the search-and-destroy missions, to the South Vietnamese ARVN—with dire results.

Still, the Green Berets kept going, trying to bring the fight to the Viet Cong through stealth and guile rather than mass bombing and defoliation, which simply fed the VC with recruits. There were projects like Omega, Sigma, Delta, and Blackjack. Quinn was in Delta, commanded by "Charging Charlie" Beckwith who would later, in 1977, set up the Delta Force at Fort Bragg and plead with Quinn to return from Paris to the Army.

The trouble with Quinn was that he thought orders were requests. Sometimes he did not agree with them. And he preferred to operate alone. Neither behavior constituted a good recommendation for a commission. He made corporal after six months, sergeant after ten. Then back to private, then sergeant, then private . . . His career was like a yo-yo.

"I figure we have the answer to your question, Morton," said Odell, "right here. The business after Son Tay." He chuckled. "The guy busted a general's jaw."

The 5th Special Forces Group finally pulled out of Vietnam on December 31, 1970, three years before the full-scale military withdrawal that included Colonel Easterhouse, and five years before the embarrassing evacuation, via the embassy roof, of the last Americans in the country. Son Tay was in November 1970.

Reports had come in of a number of American prisoners of war being located at the Son Tay prison, twenty-four miles from Hanoi. It was decided the Special Forces should go in and bring them out. It was an operation of complexity and daring. The fifty-eight volunteers came from Fort Bragg, North Carolina, via Eglin Air Force Base in Florida, for jungle training. All save one: they needed a fluent Vietnamese speaker. Weintraub, who was in the affair on the intelligence side, said he knew one. Quinn joined the rest of the group in Thailand, and they flew in together.

The operation was commanded by Colonel Arthur "Bull" Simons, but the spearhead group that went right into the prison compound came under Captain Dick Meadows. Quinn was with them. He established from a stunned North Vietnamese guard within seconds of landing that the Americans had been moved—two weeks earlier. The S.F. soldiers came out intact, with a few flesh wounds.

Back at base, Quinn berated Weintraub for the lousy intelligence. The CIA man protested that the spooks knew the Americans had been taken away, and had told the commanding general so. Quinn walked into the officers' club, strode up to the bar, and broke the general's jaw. It was hushed up, of course. A good defense lawyer can make such a mess of a career over a thing like that. Quinn was busted to private—again— and flew home with the rest. He resigned a week later and went into insurance.

"The man's a rebel," said the Secretary of State with distaste as he closed the file. "He's a loner, a maverick, and a violent one at that. I think we may have made a mistake here."

"He also has an unmatched record of hostage negotiation," pointed out the Attorney General. "It says he can use skill and subtlety when dealing with kidnappers. Fourteen successful recoveries in Ireland,

France, Holland, Germany, and Italy. Either done by him, or with him advising."

"All we want," said Odell, "is for him to get Simon Cormack back home in one piece. It doesn't matter to me if he punches generals or screws sheep."

"Please," begged Donaldson. "By the way, I've forgotten. Why did he quit?"

"He retired," said Brad Johnson. "Something about a little girl being killed in Sicily three years back. Took his severance pay, cashed in his life insurance policies, and bought himself a spread in the South of Spain."

An aide from the Communications Center put his head around the door. It was 4:00 A.M., twenty-four hours since they had all been roused.

"The DDO and his companion have just landed at Andrews," he said.

"Get them in here without delay," ordered Odell, "and get the DCI, the Director of the FBI, and Mr. Kelly up here as well, by the time they arrive."

Quinn still wore the clothes in which he had left Spain. Because of the cold he had pulled on a sweater from his gunnysack. His near-black trousers, part of his only suit, were adequate for attending mass in Alcántara del Rio, for in the villages of Andalusia, people still wear black for mass. But they were badly rumpled. The sweater had seen better days and he wore three days of stubble.

Despite their lack of sleep, the committee members looked in better shape. Relays of fresh laundry, pressed shirts, and suits had been ferried in from their distant homes; washroom facilities were right next door. Weintraub had not stopped the car between Andrews and the White House; Quinn looked like a reject from the Hole-in-the-Wall Gang.

Weintraub walked in first, stood aside for Quinn, and closed the door. The Washington officials stared at Quinn in silence.

The tall man walked without a word to the chair at the end of the table, sat down without invitation, and said, "I'm Quinn."

Vice President Odell cleared his throat.

"Mr. Quinn, we have asked you here because we are considering asking you to take on the task of negotiating the safe return of Simon Cormack."

Quinn nodded. He assumed he had not been brought this distance to discuss football.

"You have an update on the situation in London?" he asked.

It was a relief to the committee to have a practical matter brought up so early. Brad Johnson pushed a teletype printout down the table to Quinn, who studied it in silence.

"Coffee, Mr. Quinn?" asked Hubert Reed. Treasury Secretaries did not normally serve coffee, but he rose and went to the urn that now stood on a table against the wall. A lot of coffee had been drunk.

"Black," said Quinn, reading. "They haven't been in touch yet?"

There was no need to ask who "they" were.

"No," said Odell. "Total silence. Of course there have been hundreds of hoax calls. Some in Britain. We've logged seventeen hundred in Washington alone. The crazies are having a field day."

Quinn went on reading. On the flight, Weintraub had given him the entire background. He was just coming up to date with developments since. There were precious few.

"Mr. Quinn, would you have any idea who might have done this?" asked Donaldson.

Quinn looked up.

"Gentlemen, there are four kinds of kidnapper. Only four. The best from our point of view would be amateurs. They plan badly. If they succeed in the snatch, they leave traces. They can usually be located. They have little nerve, which can be dangerous. Usually the hostage-recovery teams move in, outwit them, and get the hostage back unharmed. But these weren't amateurs."

There was no argument. He had their attention.

"Worst of all are the maniacs—people like the Manson gang. Unapproachable, illogical. They want nothing material; they kill for fun. The good news is, these people don't smell like maniacs. The preparations were meticulous, the training precise."

"And the other two kinds?" asked Bill Walters.

"Of the other two, the worse are the fanatics, political or religious. Their demands are sometimes impossible to meet—literally. They seek glory, publicity—that above all. They have a Cause. Some will die for it; all will kill for it. We may think their Cause is lunatic. They don't. And they are not stupid—just filled with hate for the Establishment and therefore their victim, who comes from it. They kill as a gesture, not in self-defense."

"Who is the fourth type?" asked Morton Stannard.

"The professional criminal," said Quinn without hesitation. "They want money—that's the easy part. They have made a big investment, now locked up in the hostage. They won't easily destroy that investment."

"And *these* people?" asked Odell.

"Whoever they are, they suffer from one great disadvantage, which may work out to be good or bad for us. The guerrillas of Central and South America, the Mafia in Sicily, the Camorra in Calabria, the mountain men of Sardinia, or the Hezb'Allah in South Beirut—all operate within a safe, native environment. They don't have to kill because they are not in a hurry. They can hold out forever. These people are holed up in Britain of all places; a very hostile environment—for them. So the strain is on them already. They will want to make their deal quickly and get away, which is good. But they may be spooked by the fear of imminent discovery, and cut and run. Leaving a body behind them, which is bad."

"Would you negotiate with them?" asked Reed.

"If possible. If they get in touch, someone has to."

"It sticks in my craw to pay money to scum like these," said Philip Kelly of the FBI's Criminal Investigations Division. People come to the Bureau from a variety of backgrounds; Kelly's route was via the New York Police Department.

"Do professional criminals show more mercy than fanatics?" asked Brad Johnson.

"No kidnappers show mercy," said Quinn shortly. "It's the filthiest crime in the book. Just hope for greed."

Michael Odell looked around at his colleagues. There was a series of slow nods.

"Mr. Quinn, *will* you attempt to negotiate this boy's release?"

"Assuming the abductors get in touch, yes. There are conditions."

"Of course. Name them."

"I don't work for the U.S. government. I have its cooperation in all things, but I work for the parents. Just them."

"Agreed."

"I operate out of London, not here. It's too far away. I have no profile at all, no publicity, nothing. I get my own apartment, the phone lines I need. And I get primacy in the negotiation process—that needs clearing with London. I don't need a feud with Scotland Yard."

Odell glanced at the Secretary of State.

"I think we can prevail on the British government to concede that," said Donaldson. "They have primacy in the criminal investigation, which will continue in parallel with any direct negotiation. Anything else?"

"I operate my own way, make my own decisions how to handle these people. There may have to be money exchanged. It's made available. My job is to get the boy returned. That's all. After he's free you can hunt them down to the ends of the earth."

"Oh, we will," said Kelly with quiet menace.

"Money is not the problem," said Hubert Reed. "You may understand there is no financial limit to what we'll pay."

Quinn kept silent, though he realized that telling the kidnappers that would be the worst route to go.

"I want no crowding, no bird-dogging, no private initiatives. And before I leave, I want to see President Cormack. In private."

"This is the President of the United States you're talking about," said Lee Alexander of the CIA.

"He's also the father of the hostage," said Quinn. "There are things I need to know about Simon Cormack that only he can tell me."

"He's terribly distressed," said Odell. "Can't you spare him that?"

"My experience is that fathers often want to talk to someone, even a stranger. Maybe especially a stranger. Trust me."

Even as he said it, Quinn knew there was no hope of that. Odell sighed.

"I'll see what I can do. Jim, would you clear it with London? Tell them Quinn is coming. Tell them this is what we want. Someone has to get him some fresh clothes. Mr. Quinn, would you care to use the washroom down the hall to freshen up? I'll call the President. What's the fastest way to London?"

"The Concorde out of Dulles in three hours," said Weintraub without hesitation.

"Hold space on it," said Odell, and rose. They all did.

Nigel Cramer had news for the COBRA committee under Whitehall at 10:00 A.M. The Driver and Vehicle Licencing Centre in Swansea had come up with a lead. A man with the same name as the missing former owner of the Transit van had purchased and registered another van, a Sherpa, a month earlier. There was now an address, in Leicester. Commander Williams, the head of S.O. 13 and the official investigating officer, was on his way there by police helicopter. If the man no longer owned it, he must have sold it to somebody. It had never been reported stolen.

After the conference Sir Harry Marriott took Cramer to one side.

"Washington wants to handle the negotiations, if there are any," he said. "They're sending their own man over."

"Home Secretary, I must insist that the Met has primacy in all areas," said Cramer. "I want to use two men from Criminal Intelligence Branch as negotiators. This is not American territory."

"I'm sorry," said Sir Harry. "I have to overrule you on this one. I've cleared it with Downing Street. If they want it that way, the view is we have to let them have it."

Cramer was affronted, but he had made his protest. The loss of his primacy in negotiation simply made him more determined than ever to end the abduction by finding the kidnappers through police detective work.

"May I ask who their man is, Home Secretary?"

"Apparently he's called Quinn."

"Quinn?"

"Yes. Have you heard of him?"

"Certainly, Home Secretary. He used to work for a firm in Lloyd's. I thought he'd retired."

"Well, Washington tells us he's back. Is he any good?"

"Extremely good. Excellent record in five countries, including Ireland years ago. I met him on that one. The victim was a British citizen, a businessman snatched by some renegade I.R.A. men."

Privately, Cramer was relieved. He had feared some behavioral theorist who would be amazed to find that the British drove on the left.

"Splendid," said Sir Harry. "Then I think we should concede the point with good grace. Our complete cooperation, all right?"

The Home Secretary, who had also heard of CYA—though he would have pronounced and spelled the last word "arse"—was not displeased by Washington's demand. After all, if anything went wrong . . .

Quinn was shown into the private study on the second floor of the Executive Mansion an hour after leaving the Cabinet Room. Odell had led him personally, not via the holly and box hedges of the Rose Garden, but through the basement corridor that emerged to a set of stairs giving onto the Mansion's ground-floor corridor. Long Tom cameras were now ranged on the garden from half a mile away.

President Cormack was fully dressed in a dark suit, but he looked pale and tired, the lines of strain showing around his mouth, smudges of insomnia beneath his eyes. He shook hands and nodded at the Vice President, who withdrew.

Gesturing Quinn to a chair, he took his own seat behind his desk. A defense mechanism, creating a barrier, not wanting to unbend. He was about to speak when Quinn got in first.

"How is Mrs. Cormack?"

Not "the First Lady." Just Mrs. Cormack, his wife. He was startled.

"Oh, she's sleeping. It has been a terrible shock. She's under sedation." He paused. "You have been through this before, Mr. Quinn."

"Many times, sir."

"Well, as you see, behind the pomp and the circumstance is just a man, a very worried man."

"Yes, sir. I know. Tell me about Simon, please."

"Simon? What about him?"

"What he is like. How he will react to . . . to this. Why did you have him so late in life?"

There was no one in the White House who would have dared ask that. John Cormack looked across the desk. He was tall himself, but this man matched him at six feet two inches. Neat gray suit, striped tie, white shirt—all borrowed, though he did not know that. Clean-shaven, deeply suntanned. A craggy face, calm gray eyes, an impression of strength and patience.

"So late? Well, I don't know. I married when I was thirty; Myra was twenty-one. I was a young professor then. We thought we would start a family in two or three years. But it didn't happen. We waited. The doctors said there was no reason . . . Then, after ten years of marriage, Simon came. I was forty by then, Myra thirty-one. There was only ever the one child . . . just Simon."

"You love him very much, don't you?"

President Cormack stared at Quinn in surprise. The question was so unexpected. He knew Odell was completely estranged from his own two grown-up offspring, but it had never occurred to him how much he loved his only son. He rose, came around the desk, and seated himself on the edge of an upright chair, much closer to Quinn.

"Mr. Quinn, he is the sun and the moon to me—to us both. Get him back for us."

"Tell me about his childhood, when he was very young."

The President jumped up.

"I have a picture," he said triumphantly. He walked to a cabinet and returned with a framed snapshot. It showed a sturdy toddler of four or five, in swim trunks on a beach, holding a pail and shovel. A proud father was crouched behind him, grinning.

"That was taken at Nantucket in '75. I had just been elected congressman from New Haven."

"Tell me about Nantucket," said Quinn gently.

President Cormack talked for an hour. It seemed to help him. When Quinn rose to leave, Cormack scribbled a number on a pad and handed it to Quinn.

"This is my private number. Very few people have it. It will reach me directly, night or day." He held out his hand. "Good luck, Mr. Quinn. God go with you." He was trying to control himself. Quinn nodded and left quickly. He had seen it before, the effect, the dreadful effect.

While Quinn was still in the washroom, Philip Kelly had driven back to the J. Edgar Hoover Building, where he knew his Deputy Assistant Director, CID, would be waiting for him. He and Kevin Brown had a lot in common, which was why he had pressed for Brown's appointment.

When he entered his office his deputy was there, reading Quinn's file. Kelly nodded toward it as he took his seat.

"So, that's our hotshot. What do you think?"

"He was brave enough in combat," conceded Brown. "Otherwise a smartass. About the only thing I like about the guy is his name."

"Well," said Kelly, "they've put him in there over the Bureau's head. Don Edmonds didn't object. Maybe he figures if it all turns out badly . . . Still and all, the sleazeballs who did this thing have contravened at least three U.S. statutes. The Bureau still has jurisdiction, even though it happened on British territory. And I don't want this yo-yo operating out on his own with no supervision, no matter who says so."

"Right," agreed Brown.

"The Bureau's man in London, Patrick Seymour—do you know him?"

"Know of him," grunted Brown. "Hear he's very pally with the Brits. Maybe too much so."

Kevin Brown had come out of the Boston police force, an Irishman like Kelly, whose admiration for Britain and the British could be written on the back of a postage stamp with room left over. Not that he was soft on the I.R.A.; he had pulled in two arms dealers trading with the I.R.A., who would have gone to jail but for the courts.

He was an old-style law-enforcement officer who had no truck with criminals of any ilk. He also remembered as a small boy in the slums of Boston listening wide-eyed to his grandmother's tales of people dying with mouths green from grass-eating during the famine of 1848, and of the hangings and the shootings of 1916. He thought of Ireland, a place he had never visited, as a land of mists and gentle green hills, enlivened by the fiddle and the chaunter, where poets like Yeats and O'Faolain wandered and composed. He knew Dublin was full of friendly bars where peaceable folk sat over a stout in front of peat fires, immersed in the works of Joyce and O'Casey.

He had been told that Dublin had the worst teenage drug problem in Europe but knew it was just London's propaganda. He had heard Irish Prime Ministers on American soil pleading for no more money to be sent to the I.R.A. Well, people were entitled to their views. And he had his. Being a crime-buster did not require him to like the people he saw as the timeless persecutors of the land of his forefathers. Across the desk, Kelly came to a decision.

"Seymour is close to Buck Revell, but Revell's away sick. The Director has put me in charge of this from the Bureau's point of view. And I don't want this Quinn getting out of hand. I want you to get together a good team and take the midday flight and get over there. You'll be behind the Concorde by a few hours, but no matter. Base yourself at the embassy—I'll tell Seymour you're in charge, just for the emergency."

Brown rose, pleased.

"One more thing, Kevin. I want one special agent in close on Quinn. All the time, day and night. If that guy burps, we want to know."

"I know just the one," said Brown grimly. "A good operative, tenacious and clever. Also personable. Agent Sam Somerville. I'll do the briefing myself. Now."

Out at Langley, David Weintraub was wondering when he would ever sleep again. During his absence the work had piled up in a mountain. Much of it had to do with the files on all the known terrorist groups in Europe—latest updates, penetration agents inside the groups, known locations of the leading members, possible incursions into Britain over the previous forty days . . . the list of headings alone was almost endless. So it was the Chief of the European Section who briefed Duncan McCrea.

"You'll meet Lou Collins from our embassy," he said, "but he'll be keeping us posted from outside the inner circle. We have to have somebody close in on this man Quinn. We need to identify those abductors and I wouldn't be displeased if we could do it before the Brits. And especially before the Bureau. Okay, the British are pals, but I'd like this one for the Agency. If the abductors are foreigners, that gives us an edge; we have better files on foreigners than the Bureau, maybe than the Brits. If Quinn gets any smell, any instinct about them, and lets anything slip, you pass it on to us."

Operative McCrea was awestruck. A GS-12 with ten years in the Agency since recruitment abroad—his father had been a businessman in Central America—he had had two foreign postings but never London. The responsibility was enormous, but matched by the opportunity.

"You can rely on m-m-me, sir."

Quinn had insisted that no one known to the media accompany him to Dulles International Airport. He had left the White House in a plain compact car, driven by his escort, an officer of the Secret Service in plain clothes. Quinn had ducked into the back seat, down near the floor, as they passed the knot of press grouped at Alexander Hamilton Place at the extreme east end of the White House complex and farthest away from the West Wing. The press glanced at the car, saw nothing of importance, and took no notice.

At Dulles, Quinn checked in with his escort, who refused to leave him until he actually walked onto the Concorde and who raised eyebrows by flashing his White House ID card to get past passport control. He did at least serve one purpose; Quinn went to the duty-free shop and bought a number of items: toiletries, shirts, ties, underwear, socks, shoes, a raincoat, a valise, and a small tape recorder with a dozen batteries and spools. When the time came to pay he jerked a thumb at the Secret Service man.

"My friend here will pay by credit card," he said.

The limpet detached himself at the door of the Concorde. The British stewardess showed Quinn to his seat near the front, giving him no more attention than anyone else. He settled into his aisle seat. A few moments later someone took the aisle seat across the way. He glanced across. Blond, short shining hair, about thirty-five, a good, strong face. The heels were a smidgen too flat, the suit a mite too severe for the figure beneath.

The Concorde swung into line, paused, trembled, and then hurled herself down the runway. The bird-of-prey nose lifted, the claws of the rear wheels lost contact, the ground below tilted forty-five degrees, and Washington dropped quickly away.

There was something else. Two tiny holes in her lapel, the sort of holes that might be made by a safety pin. The sort of safety pin that might hold an ID card. He leaned across.

"Which department are you from?"

She looked startled. "I beg your pardon?"

"The Bureau. Which department in the Bureau are you from?"

She had the grace to blush. She bit her lip and thought it over. Well, it had to come sooner or later.

"I'm sorry, Mr. Quinn. My name's Somerville. Agent Sam Somerville. I've been told . . ."

"It's all right, Miss Sam Somerville. I know what you've been told."

The no-smoking lights flicked off. The addicts in the rear lit up. A stewardess approached, dispensing glasses of champagne. The businessman in the window seat to Quinn's left took the last one. She turned to go. Quinn stopped her, apologized, took her silver salver, whipped away the doily that covered it, and held up the tray. In the reflection he surveyed the rows behind him. It took seven seconds. Then he thanked the puzzled stewardess and gave her back the tray.

"When the seat-belt lights go off, you'd better tell that young sprig from Langley in Row Twenty-one to get his butt up here," he said to Agent Somerville. Five minutes later she returned with the young man from the rear. He was flushed and apologetic, pushing back his floppy blond hair and managing a boy-next-door grin.

"I'm sorry, Mr. Quinn. I didn't mean to intrude. It's just that they told me . . ."

"Yes, I know. Take a seat." Quinn gestured to a vacant seat one row forward. "Someone as badly troubled by cigarette smoke stands out, sitting back there."

"Oh." The young man was subdued, did as he was told.

Quinn glanced out. The Concorde wheeled over the New England coast, preparing to go supersonic. Not yet out of America and the promises were being broken already. It was 10:15 Eastern Daylight time and 3:15 P.M. in London, and three hours to Heathrow.

CHAPTER SIX

Simon Cormack spent the first twenty-four hours of his captivity in total isolation. Experts would know this was part of the softening-up process, a long opportunity for the hostage to dwell upon his isolation and his helplessness. Also a chance for hunger and tiredness to set in. A hostage full of pep, prepared to argue and complain, or even plan some kind of escape, simply makes problems for his abductors. A victim reduced to hopelessness and pathetic gratitude for small mercies is much easier to handle.

At 10:00 A.M. of the second day, about the time Quinn strode into the Cabinet Room in Washington, Simon was in a fitful doze when he heard the click of the peephole in the cellar door. Looking at it, he could make out a single eye watching him; his bed was exactly opposite the door and even when his ten-foot chain was fully extended he could never be out of view from the peephole.

After several seconds he heard the rasp of two bolts being drawn back. The door opened three inches and a black-gloved hand came around the edge. It gripped a white card with a message written with a marker pen in block capitals:

YOU HEAR THREE KNOCKS YOU PUT ON THE HOOD.
UNDERSTAND? ACKNOWLEDGE.

He waited for several seconds, unsure what to do. The card waggled impatiently.

"Yes," he said, "I understand. Three knocks on that door and I put on the hood."

The card was withdrawn and replaced by another. The second card said:

TWO KNOCKS YOU CAN TAKE THE HOOD OFF AGAIN.
ANY TRICKS—YOU DIE.

"I understand that," he called toward the door. The card was withdrawn. The door closed. After several seconds there were three loud knocks. Obediently the youth reached for the thick black cowl hood, which lay on the end of his bed. He pulled it over his head and even down to his shoulders, placed his hands on his knees, and waited, trembling. Through the thickness of the material he heard nothing, just sensed that someone in soft shoes had entered the cellar.

In fact the kidnapper who came in was still dressed in black from head to foot, complete with ski mask, only his eyes visible, despite Simon Cormack's inability to see a thing. These were the leader's instructions. The man placed something near the bed and withdrew. Under his hood Simon heard the door close, the rasp of bolts, then two clear knocks. Slowly he pulled off the hood. On the floor lay a plastic tray. It bore a plastic plate, knife, fork, and tumbler. On the plate were sausages, baked beans, bacon, and a hunk of bread. The tumbler held water.

He was ravenous, having eaten nothing since the dinner of the night before his run, and without thinking called "Thank you" at the door. As he said it he could have kicked himself. He should not be thanking these bastards. He did not realize in his innocence that the Stockholm syndrome was beginning to take effect: that strange empathy that builds up from a victim to his persecutors, so that the victim turns his rage against the authorities who allowed it all to happen, rather than against the abductors.

He ate every last scrap of food, drank the water slowly and with deep satisfaction, and fell asleep. An hour later the signals were repeated, the process was reversed, and the tray disappeared. Simon used the bucket for the fourth time, then lay back on the bed and thought of home, and what they might be doing for him.

As he lay there Commander Williams returned from Leicester to London and reported to Deputy A. C. Cramer at the latter's office in

New Scotland Yard. Conveniently, the Yard, headquarters of the Met., is only four hundred yards from the Cabinet Office.

The former owner of the Ford Transit had been in Leicester police station under guard, a frightened and, as it turned out, innocent man. He protested that his Transit van had been neither stolen nor sold; it had been written off in a crash two months earlier. As he was moving to a new home at the time, he had forgotten to inform the Licencing Centre at Swansea.

Step by step Commander Williams had checked out the story. The man, a jobbing builder, had been picking up two marble fireplaces from a dealer in south London. Swerving around a corner near the demolition site from which the fireplaces had been stripped, he had an argument with a steam shovel. The steam shovel won. The Transit van, then still its original blue, had to be written off completely. Although visible damage had been small, and mainly concentrated in the radiator area, the chassis had been twisted out of alignment.

He had returned to Nottingham alone. His insurance company had examined the Transit in the yard of a local recovery firm, pronounced it unmendable, but declined to pay him because his coverage was not comprehensive and he was at fault for hitting the steam shovel. Much aggrieved, he had accepted £20 for the wreck, by telephone from the recovery firm, and had never returned to London.

"Someone put it back on the road," said Williams.

"Good," said Cramer. "That means they're 'bent.' It checks. The lab boys said someone had worked on the chassis with a welder. Also the green paint had been laid over the maker's blue cellulose finish. A rough spray job. Find out who did it and who they sold it to."

"I'm going down to Balham," said Williams. "The crash-recovery firm is based there."

Cramer went back to his work. He had a mountain of it, coming in from a dozen different teams. The forensic reports were almost all in and were brilliant as far as they went. The trouble was, that was not far enough. The slugs taken from the bodies matched the bullet cases from the Skorpion, not surprisingly. No further witnesses had come forward from the Oxford area. The abductors had left no fingerprints, or any other traces except car tire tracks. The van tracks were useless—they had the van, albeit fire-gutted. No one had seen anyone near the barn. The sedan tire tracks leading from the barn had been identified by make and model, but would fit half a million sedans.

A dozen county forces were quietly checking with real estate agents for a property leased over the past six months with enough space and privacy to suit the kidnappers. The Met. was doing the same inside London, in case the criminals were holed up right in the capital itself. That meant thousands of house rentals to be checked out. Cash deals were top of the list, and there were still hundreds of those. Already a dozen discreet little love nests, two rented by national celebrities, had come to light.

Underworld informants, the "grasses," were being leaned on to see if they had heard whispers of a team of known villains preparing a big one, or of "slags" and "faces" (slang for known criminals) suddenly disappearing from their haunts. The underworld was being turned over in a big way but had come up with nothing so far.

Cramer had a pile of reports of "sightings" of Simon Cormack which ranged from the plausible through the possible to the lunatic, and they were all being checked out. There was another pile of transcripts of phoned-in messages from people claiming to be holding the U.S. President's son. Again, some were crazy, and some sounded promising. Each of the latter callers had been treated seriously and begged to stay in touch. But Cramer had a gut feeling that the real kidnappers were still maintaining silence, allowing the authorities to sweat. It would be the skillful thing to do.

A special room in the basement was already set aside and a skilled team of men from the Criminal Intelligence Branch, the negotiators used in British kidnappings, sat waiting for the big one, meanwhile talking patiently and calmly to the hoaxers. Several of the latter had already been caught and would be charged in due course.

Nigel Cramer walked to the window and looked down. The sidewalk on Victoria Street was awash with reporters—he had to avoid them every time he left for Whitehall by driving straight through, sealed into his car with windows firmly closed. And still they howled through the glass for a tidbit of information. The Met.'s press office was being driven crazy.

He checked his watch and sighed. If the kidnappers held on a few more hours, the American, Quinn, would presumably take over. He did not like having been overruled on that one. He had read the Quinn file, loaned to him by Lou Collins of the CIA, and he had had two hours with the Chief Executive Officer of the Lloyd's underwriting firm that had employed Quinn and his strange but effective talents for ten years. What he had learned left him with mixed feelings. The man was good, but unorthodox. No police force likes to work with a maverick, however talented. He would not be going out to Heathrow to meet Quinn, he decided. He would see him later and introduce him to the two chief inspectors who would sit at his side and advise him throughout the negotiation—if there ever was one. It was time to go back to Whitehall and brief the COBRA—on precious little. No, this was definitely not going to be a "quickie."

The Concorde had picked up a jetstream at 60,000 feet and rode into London fifteen minutes ahead of schedule at 6:00 P.M. Quinn hefted his small valise and headed down the tunnel toward the arrivals area with Somerville and McCrea in tow. A few yards into the tunnel two quiet gray men in gray suits waited patiently. One stepped forward.

"Mr. Quinn?" he said quietly. Quinn nodded. The man did not flash an identity card, American-style; he just assumed that his manner and bearing would indicate he represented the authorities. "We were expecting you, sir. If you would just care to come with me . . . My colleague will carry your case."

Without waiting for objections he glided down the tunnel, turned away from the stream of passengers at the entrance to the main corridor and soon into a small office that bore simply a number on the door. The bigger man, with ex-NCO stamped all over him, nodded amiably at Quinn and took his valise. In the office the quiet man flipped quickly through Quinn's passport, and those of "your assistants," produced a stamp from his side pocket, stamped all three, and said "Welcome to London, Mr. Quinn."

They left the office by another door, down some steps to a waiting car. But if Quinn thought he was going straight into London, he was wrong. They drove to the VIP suite. Quinn stepped inside and stared bleakly about him. Low-profile, he had said. No-profile. There were representatives from the American embassy, the British Home Office, Scotland Yard, the Foreign Office, the CIA, the FBI, and, for all he knew, McDonald's and Coca-Cola. It took twenty minutes.

The motorcade into London was worse. He rode up front in an American limousine half a block long with a pennant on the nose. Two motorcycle outriders cleared a path through the early evening traffic. Behind came Lou Collins, giving a ride—and a briefing—to his CIA colleague Duncan McCrea. Two cars back was Patrick Seymour, doing the same for Sam Somerville. The British in their Rovers, Jaguars, and Granadas tagged along.

They swept along the M.4 motorway toward London, pulled onto the North Circular, and down the Finchley Road. Just after Lords roundabout, the lead car swerved into Regent's Park, followed the

Outer Circle for a while, and swept into a formal entrance, past two security guards who saluted.

Quinn had spent the drive gazing out at the lights of a city he knew as well as any in the world, better than most, and maintained silence until at last even the self-important Minister/counselor lapsed into quiet. As the cars headed toward the illuminated portico of a palatial mansion, Quinn spoke. Snapped, really. He leaned forward—it was a long way—and barked into the driver's ear.

"*Stop the car.*"

The driver, an American Marine, was so surprised he did exactly that, fast. The car behind was not so smart. There was a tinkling of glass from taillights and headlights. Farther down the line the Home Office driver, to avoid a collision, drove into the rhododendron bushes. The cavalcade made like a concertina and stopped. Quinn stepped out and stared at the mansion. A man was standing on the top step of the portico.

"Where are we?" asked Quinn. He knew perfectly well. The diplomat scuttled out of the rear seat behind him. They had warned him about Quinn. He had not believed them. Other figures from down the column were moving up to join them.

"Winfield House, Mr. Quinn. That's Ambassador Fairweather waiting to greet you. It's all set up: You have a suite of rooms—it's all been arranged."

"Unarrange it," said Quinn. He opened the trunk of the limousine, grabbed his valise, and started to walk down the driveway.

"Where are you going, Mr. Quinn?" wailed the diplomat.

"Back to Spain," called Quinn.

Lou Collins was in front of him. He had spoken with David Weintraub on the enciphered link while the Concorde was airborne.

"He's a strange bastard," the DDO had said, "but give him what he wants."

"We have an apartment," Collins said quietly. "Very private, very discreet. We sometimes use it for first debriefing Soviet bloc defectors. Other times for visiting guys from Langley. The DDO stays there."

"Address," said Quinn. Collins gave it to him. A back street in Kensington. Quinn nodded his thanks and kept walking. On the Outer Circle a taxi was cruising by. Quinn hailed it, gave instructions, and disappeared.

It took fifteen minutes to sort out the tangle in the driveway. Eventually Lou Collins took McCrea and Somerville in his own car and drove them to Kensington.

Quinn paid off the cab and surveyed the apartment block. They were going to bug him anyway; at least with a Company flat the hardware would be installed, saving a lot of lame excuses and redecorating. The number he needed was on the third floor. When he rang the bell it was answered by a burly, low-level Company man. The caretaker.

"Who are you?" he asked.

"I'm in," said Quinn, walking past him. "You're out." He walked through the apartment, checking the sitting room, the master bedroom, and the two smaller ones. The caretaker was frantically on the phone; they patched him through to Lou Collins in his car, and the man subsided. Grumpily he packed his things. Collins and the two bird dogs arrived three minutes after Quinn, who had selected the principal bedroom as his own. Patrick Seymour followed Collins. Quinn surveyed the four of them.

"These two have to live with me?" he asked, nodding at Special Agent Somerville and GS-12 McCrea.

"Look, be reasonable, Quinn," said Collins. "This is the President's son we're trying to recover. Everyone wants to know what's going on. They just won't be satisfied with less. The powers-that-be just aren't going to let you live here like a monk, telling them nothing."

Quinn thought it over.

"All right. What can you two do apart from snooping?"

"We could be useful, Mr. Quinn," said McCrea pleadingly. "Go and fetch things—help out."

With his floppy hair, constant shy smile, and air of diffidence, he seemed much younger than his thirty-four years, more like a college kid than a CIA operative. Sam Somerville took up the theme.

"I'm a good cook," she said. "Now that you've deep-sixed the Residence and all its staff, you're going to have to have someone who can cook. Being where we are, it would be a spook anyway."

For the first time since they had met him, Quinn grinned. Somerville thought it transformed his otherwise enigmatic face.

"All right," he said to Collins and Seymour. "You're going to bug every room and phone call anyway. You two take the remaining bedrooms."

The young agents went down the hall.

"But that's it," he told Collins and Seymour. "No more guests. I need to speak to the British police. Who's in charge?"

"Deputy Assistant Commissioner Cramer. Nigel Cramer. Number two man in Specialist Operations Department. Know him?"

"Rings a bell," said Quinn.

At that moment a bell did ring—the telephone. Collins took it, listened, and covered the mouthpiece.

"This is Cramer," he said. "At Winfield House. He went there to liaise with you, just heard the news. Wants to come here. Okay?"

Quinn nodded. Collins spoke to Cramer and asked him to come 'round. He arrived in an unmarked police car twenty minutes later.

"Mr. Quinn? Nigel Cramer. We met once, briefly."

He stepped into the apartment warily. He had not known about its existence as a Company safe-house, but he did now. He also knew the CIA would vacate it when this affair was over and take another one.

Quinn recalled Cramer when he saw the face.

"Ireland, years back. The Don Tidey affair. You were head of Anti-Terrorist Branch then."

"S.O. 13, yes. You've a good memory, Mr. Quinn. I think we need to talk."

Quinn led Cramer into the sitting room, sat him down, took a chair opposite, and gestured around the room with his hand to indicate it was certainly bugged. Lou Collins might be a nice guy, but no spook is ever *that* nice. The British policeman nodded gravely. He realized he was effectively on American territory, in the heart of his own capital city, but what he had to say would be fully reported by him to the COBRA.

"Let me, as you say in America, level with you, Mr. Quinn. The Metropolitan Police have been granted full primacy in the investigation into this crime. Your government has agreed to that. So far we have not had a big break, but it's early days and we are working flat-out."

Quinn nodded. He had worked in bugged rooms before, many times, and spoken on tapped phone lines. It was always an effort to keep conversation normal. He realized Cramer was speaking for the record, hence the pedantry.

"We asked for primacy in the negotiation process and were overruled at Washington's request. I have to accept that. I don't have to like it. I have also been instructed to give you every cooperation the Met. and the entire range of our government's departments can offer. And that you will get. You have my word on it."

"I'm very grateful for that, Mr. Cramer," said Quinn. He knew it sounded terribly stilted, but somewhere the spools were turning.

"What exactly is it you want?"

"Background first. The last update I read was in Washington . . ." Quinn checked his watch—8:00 P.M. in London. "Over seven hours ago. Have the kidnappers made contact yet?"

"So far as we are aware, no," said Cramer. "There have been calls, of course. Some obvious hoaxes, some not so obvious, a dozen really plausible. To the last, we asked for some element of proof they were really holding Simon Cormack—"

"How?" asked Quinn.

"A question to be answered. Something from his nine months at Oxford that it would be hard to discover. No one called back with a right answer."

"Forty-eight hours is not unusual waiting time for the first contact," said Quinn.

"Agreed," said Cramer. "They may communicate by mail, with a letter or a tape recording, in which case the package may be on its way. Or by phone. If it's the former, we'll bring them 'round here, though I will want our forensic people to have first crack at the paper, envelope, wrappings, and letter for any prints, saliva, or other traces. Fair, I think? You have no laboratory facilities here."

"Perfectly fair," said Quinn.

"But if the first contact is by phone, how do you want to handle it, Mr. Quinn?"

Quinn spelled out his requirements. A public announcement on the *News at Ten* program, requiring anyone holding Simon Cormack to contact the American embassy and only the embassy on any of a series of given numbers. A line of switchboard operators in the embassy basement to filter out the obvious phonies and patch the serious possibilities through to him at the apartment.

Cramer looked up at Collins and Seymour, who nodded. They would set up the embassy first-filter multiline switchboard within the next hour and a half, in time for the newscast. Quinn went on.

"Your Telecom people can trace every call as it comes into the embassy, maybe make a few arrests of hoaxers stupid enough not to use a public phone booth or who stay on the line too long. I don't think the real kidnappers will be that dumb."

"Agreed," said Cramer. "So far, they're smarter than that."

"The patch-through must be without a cutoff, and just to one of the phones in this flat. There are three, right?"

Collins nodded. One was a direct line to his office, which was in the embassy building anyway.

"Use that one," said Quinn. "When I've established contact with the real kidnappers, assuming I do, I want to give them a new number, a designated line that reaches me and only me."

"I'll get you a flash line within ninety minutes," said Cramer, "a number that has never been used before. We'll have to tap it, of course, but you won't hear a sound on the line. Finally, I'd like to have two detective chief inspectors living in here with you, Mr. Quinn. They're good and experienced. One man can't stay awake twenty-four hours a day."

"I'm sorry, no," said Quinn.

"They could be of great help," Cramer persisted. "If the kidnappers are British, there will be the question of regional accents, slang words, hints of strain or desperation in the voice at the other end, tiny traces only another Britisher could spot. They wouldn't say anything, just listen."

"They can listen at the exchange," said Quinn. "You will be recording everything anyway. Run it past the speech experts, add your own comments on how lousily I'm doing, and come knock on the door here with the results. But I work alone."

Cramer's mouth tightened slightly. But he had his orders. He rose to leave. Quinn rose too.

"Let me see you to your car," he said. They all knew what that meant—the stairs were not bugged. At the door Quinn jerked his head at Seymour and Collins to stay behind. Reluctantly they did so. On the stairs he murmured in Cramer's ear.

"I know you don't like it this way. I'm not very happy about it myself. Try to trust me. I'm not about to lose this boy if I can help it. You'll hear every damn syllable on the phone. My own people will even hear me on the can. It's like a Radio Shack in there."

"All right, Mr. Quinn. You'll get everything I can offer you. That's a promise."

"One last thing . . ." They had reached the pavement; the police car waited. "Don't spook them. If they phone, or stay on the line a mite too long, no squad cars roaring up to the phone booth . . ."

"We do know that, Mr. Quinn. But we'll have to have plainclothes men heading for the source of the phone call. They'll be very discreet, just about invisible. But if we just spot the car number . . . get a physical description . . . that could shorten the whole thing to a couple of days."

"Don't get seen," warned Quinn. "The man in the phone booth will be under horrendous pressure. Neither of us wants contact to cease. That would probably mean they've cut and run for the tall timber, leaving a body behind them."

Cramer nodded, shook hands, and climbed into his car.

Thirty minutes later the engineers arrived, none in Telecom uniform, all offering Telecom identification cards. Quinn nodded amiably, knowing they came from MI-5, the Security Service, and they set to work. They were good and they were fast. Most of the work was being done in the Kensington exchange, anyway.

One of the engineers, with the base off the sitting-room telephone, raised an eyebrow a fraction. Quinn pretended not to notice. Trying to insert a bug, the man had found one in there already. Orders are orders; he slotted his own in beside the American one, establishing a new and miniature Anglo-American relationship. By 9:30 P.M. Quinn had his flash line, the ultraprivate line to which he would pass the real kidnapper if he ever spoke to the man. The second line was patched through permanently to the embassy switchboard, for incoming "possibles." The third was left for outgoing calls.

More work was going on in the basement at the embassy in Grosvenor Square. Ten lines already existed and they were all taken over. Ten young women, some American, some British, sat and waited.

The third operation was in the Kensington exchange, where the police set up an office to monitor incoming calls heading for Quinn's flash line. As Kensington was one of the new electronic exchanges, tracing would be fast, eight to ten seconds. On their way out of the exchange, the flash-line calls would have two more taps, one to the MI-5 communications center in Cork Street, Mayfair, the other to the U.S. embassy basement which, after the isolation of the kidnapper, would change from a switchboard to a listening post.

Thirty seconds after the British group left, Lou Collins's American engineer arrived to remove all the newly installed British bugs and tune their own. Thus, when Quinn spoke other than on the telephone, only his fellow Americans would be listening. "Nice try," remarked Seymour to his MI-5 colleague a week later over a drink in Brooks's Club.

At 10:00 P.M. ITN newscaster Sandy Gall stared into the camera as the booming chimes of the Big Ben theme died away, and made the announcement to the kidnappers. The numbers to call stayed on the screen throughout the update on the Simon Cormack kidnapping, which had little to say but said it anyway.

In the sitting room of a quiet house forty miles from London, four silent and tense men watched the broadcast. The leader rapidly translated into French for two of them. In fact one was Belgian, the other Corsican. The fourth needed no translation. His spoken English was good but heavily accented with the Afrikaner tones of his native South Africa.

The two from Europe spoke no English at all, and the leader had forbidden all of them to stray from the house until the affair was over. He alone left and returned, always out of the attached garage, always in the Volvo sedan, which now had new tires and license plates—the original and legitimate plates. He never left without his wig, beard, moustache, and tinted glasses. During his absences the others were instructed to stay out of sight, not even appearing at the windows and certainly not answering the door.

As the newscast changed to the Middle East situation, one of the Europeans asked a question. The leader shook his head.

"Demain," he replied, "tomorrow morning."

More than two hundred calls came to the embassy basement that night. Each was handled carefully and courteously, but only seven were passed through to Quinn. He took each with a cheerful friendliness, addressing the caller as "friend" or "pal," explaining that regretfully "his people" simply had to go through the tiresome formality of establishing that the caller really *had* Simon Cormack, and carefully asking them to get the answer to a simple question and call him back. No one called back. In a break between 3:00 A.M. and sunrise he catnapped for four hours.

Through the night, Sam Somerville and Duncan McCrea stayed with him. Sam commented on his laid-back performance on the phone.

"It hasn't even begun yet," he said quietly. But the strain had. The two younger people were feeling it already.

Just after midnight, having caught the noon plane from Washington, Kevin Brown and a picked team of eight FBI agents flew into Heathrow. Forewarned, an exasperated Patrick Seymour was there to greet them. He gave the senior officer an update on the situation to 11:00 P.M., when he had left for the airport. That included the installation of Quinn in his chosen aerie as opposed to Winfield House, and the telephone-intercept situation.

"Knew he was a smartass," growled Brown when told of the tangle in the Winfield House driveway. "We've got to sit on this bastard or he'll be into every kind of trick. Let's get to the embassy. We'll sleep on cots right there in the basement. If that yo-yo farts, I want to hear it, loud and clear."

Inwardly, Seymour groaned. He had heard of Kevin Brown and could have done without the visit. Now, he thought, it was going to be worse than he had feared. When they reached the embassy at 1:30 A.M., the 106th phony call was coming in.

. . .

Other people were getting little sleep that night. Two of them were Commander Williams of S.O. 13 and a man called Sidney Sykes. They spent the hours of darkness confronting each other in the interview room of Wandsworth police station in south London. A second officer present was the head of the Vehicles Section of the Serious Crimes Squad, whose men had traced Sykes.

As far as a small-time crook like Sykes was concerned, the two men across the plain table were very heavy pressure indeed and by the end of the first hour he was a badly frightened man. After that things got worse.

The Vehicles Section, following a description given by the jobbing builder in Leicester, had traced the recovery firm that had removed the wrecked Transit from its lethal embrace with the steam shovel. Once it was established that the vehicle had a twisted chassis and was a write-off, the recovery company offered it back to its owner. As the charge for bringing it on a flat-bed to Leicester was greater than its value, he had declined. The recovery team had sold it to Sykes as scrap, for he ran a car-wrecking yard in Wandsworth. The Vehicles Section rummage crews had spent the day turning over that yard.

They found a barrel three-quarters full of dirty black sump oil, whose murky depths had yielded twenty-four car license plates, twelve perfectly matched pairs, all made up in the Sykes yard and all as genuine as a three-pound note. A recess beneath the floorboards of Sykes's shabby office had given up a wad of thirty vehicle registration documents, all pertaining to cars and vans that had ceased to exist except on paper.

Sykes's racket was to acquire crash vehicles written off by their insurers, tell the owner that he, Sykes, would inform Swansea the vehicle had ceased to exist except as a mass of scrap, and then inform Swansea of exactly the opposite—that he had bought the vehicle from its previous owner. The Swansea computer would then log that "fact." If the car really was a write-off, Sykes was simply buying the legitimate paperwork, which could then be applied to a working vehicle of similar make and type, the working vehicle having been stolen from some parking lot by one of Sykes's light-fingered associates. With new plates to match the registration document of the write-off, the stolen car could then be resold. The final touch was to abrade the original chassis and engine block numbers, etch in new ones, and smear on enough grease and dirt to fool the ordinary customer. Of course this would not fool the police, but as all such deals were in cash, Sykes could later deny he had ever seen the offending car, let alone sold it.

A variation on the racket was to take a van like the Transit, in good shape apart from its twisted chassis, cut out the distorted section, bridge the gap with a length of girder, and put it back on the road. Illegal and dangerous, but such cars and vans could probably run for several thousand more miles before falling apart.

Confronted by the statements of the Leicester builder, the recovery firm that had sold him the Transit as scrap for £20, and the imprints of the old, real chassis and engine numbers; and informed what deed the truck had been used for, Sykes realized he was in very deep trouble indeed, and came clean.

The man who had bought the Transit, he recalled after racking his memory, had been wandering around the yard one day six weeks back, and on being questioned had said he was looking for a low-priced van. By chance, Sykes had just finished recycling the chassis of the blue Transit and spraying it green. It had left his yard within the hour for £300 cash. He had never seen the man again. The fifteen £20 notes were long gone.

"Description?" asked Commander Williams.

"I'm trying, I'm trying," pleaded Sykes.

"Do that," said Williams. "It will make the rest of your life so much easier."

Medium height, medium build. Late forties. Rough face and manner. Not a posh voice, and not a Londoner by birth. Ginger hair—could have been a wig, but a good one. Anyway, he wore a hat, despite the heat of late August. Moustache, darker than the hair—could have been a stick-on, but a good one. And tinted glasses. Not sunglasses, just blue-tinted, with horn frames.

The three men spent two more hours with the police artist. Commander Williams brought the picture back to Scotland Yard just before the breakfast hour and showed it to Nigel Cramer. He took it to the COBRA committee at nine that morning. The trouble was, the picture could have been anyone. And there the trail ran out.

"We know the van was worked on by another and better mechanic after Sykes," Cramer told the committee. "And a sign painter created the Barlow fruit company logo on each side. It must have been stored somewhere, a garage with welding facilities. But if we issue a public appeal, the kidnappers will see it and could lose their nerve, cut and run, and leave Simon Cormack dead."

It was agreed to issue the description to every police station in the country, but not to bring in the press and the public.

Andrew "Andy" Laing spent the night poring over the records of bank transactions, becoming more and more puzzled, until just before dawn his bemusement gave way to the growing certainty that he was right and there was no other explanation.

Andy Laing was the head of the Credit and Marketing team in the Jiddah branch of the Saudi Arabian Investment Bank, an institution established by the Saudi government to handle most of the astronomical sums of money that washed around those parts.

Although Saudi-owned and with a mainly Saudi board of directors, the SAIB was principally staffed by foreign contract officers, and the biggest single contributor of staff was New York's Rockman-Queens Bank, from which Laing had been seconded.

He was young, keen, conscientious, and ambitious, eager to make a good career in banking and enjoying his term in Saudi Arabia. The pay was better than in New York, he had an attractive apartment, several girlfriends among the large expatriate community in Jiddah, was not worried by the no-liquor restrictions, and got on with his colleagues.

Although the Riyadh branch was the head office of SAIB, the busiest branch was in Jiddah, the business and commercial capital of Saudi Arabia. Normally, Laing would have left the crenellated white building—looking more like a Foreign Legion fort than a bank—and walked up the street to the Hyatt Regency for a drink before six o'clock the previous evening. But he had two more files to close, and rather than leave them till the next morning, he stayed on for an extra hour.

So he was still at his desk when the old Arab messenger wheeled 'round the cart stacked with printout sheets torn from the bank's computer, leaving the appropriate sheets in each executive's office for attention the next day. These sheets bore the records of the day's transactions undertaken by the bank's several departments. Patiently the old man placed a sheaf of printouts on Laing's desk, bobbed his head, and withdrew. Laing called a cheerful *"Shukran"* after him—he prided himself on being courteous to the Saudi menial staff—and went on working.

When he had finished he glanced at the papers by his side and uttered a sound of annoyance. He had been given the wrong papers. The ones beside him were the in-and-out records of deposits and withdrawals from all the major accounts lodged with the bank. These were the business of the Operations manager, not Credit and Marketing. He took them and strolled down the corridor to the empty office of the Ops manager, Mr. Amin, his colleague from Pakistan.

As he did so he glanced at the sheets and something caught his attention. He stopped, turned back, and began to go through the records page by page. On each the same pattern emerged. He switched on his computer and asked it to go back into the records of two client accounts. Always the same pattern.

By the small hours of the morning he was certain there could be no doubt. What he was looking at had to be a major fraud. The coincidences were just too bizarre. He replaced the printouts on the desk of Mr. Amin and resolved to fly to Riyadh at the first opportunity for a personal interview with his fellow American, the general manager, Steve Pyle.

As Laing was going home through the darkened streets of Jiddah, eight time zones to the west the White House committee was listening to Dr. Nicholas Armitage, an experienced psychiatrist who had just come across to the West Wing from the Executive Mansion.

"Gentlemen, so far I have to tell you that the shock has affected the First Lady to a greater degree than the President. She is still taking medication under the supervision of her physician. The President has, no doubt, the tougher temperament, though I'm afraid the strain is already beginning to become noticeable, and the telltale signs of post-abduction parental trauma are beginning to show in him too."

"What signs, Doctor?" asked Odell without ceremony. The psychiatrist—who did not like to be interrupted, and never was when he lectured students—cleared his throat.

"You have to understand that in these cases the mother acceptably has the release of tears, even hysteria. The male parent often suffers in a greater way, experiencing, apart from the normal anxiety for the abducted child, a profound sense of guilt, of self-blame, of conviction that he was responsible in some way, should have done more, should have taken more precautions, should have been more careful."

"That's not logical," protested Morton Stannard.

"We're not talking about logic here," said the doctor. "We're talking about the symptoms of trauma, made worse by the fact the President was—is—extremely close to his son, loves him very deeply indeed. Add to that the feeling of helplessness, the inability to do anything. So far, of course, with no contact from the kidnappers, he does not even know if the boy is alive or dead. It's still early, of course, but it won't get better."

"These kidnappings can go on for weeks," said Jim Donaldson. "This man is our Chief Executive. What changes can we expect?"

"The strain will be eased slightly when and if the first contact is made and proof obtained that Simon is still alive," said Dr. Armitage. "But the relief will not last long. As time drags on, the deterioration will deepen. There will be stress at a very high level, leading to irritability. There will be insomnia—that can be helped with medication. Finally there will be listlessness in matters concerning the father's profession—"

"In this case running the damn country," said Odell.

". . . and lack of concentration, loss of memory in matters of government. In a word, gentlemen, half or more of the President's mind until further notice will be devoted to thinking about his son, and a further part to concern for his wife. In some cases, even after the successful release of a child kidnap victim, it has been the parents who needed months, even years, of post-trauma therapy."

"In other words," said Attorney General Bill Walters, "we have half a President, maybe less."

"Oh, come now," Treasury Secretary Reed interjected. "This country has had Presidents on the operating table, wholly incapacitated in the hospital, before now. We must just take over, run things as he would wish, disturb our friend as little as possible."

His optimism evoked little matching response. Brad Johnson rose.

"Why the hell won't those bastards get in touch?" he asked. "It's been nearly forty-eight hours."

"At least we have our negotiator set up and waiting for their first call," said Reed.

"And we have a strong presence in London," added Walters. "Mr. Brown and his team from the Bureau arrived two hours ago."

"What the hell are the British police doing?" muttered Stannard. "Why can't they find those bastards?"

"We have to remember it's been only forty-eight hours—not even," observed Secretary of State Donaldson. "Britain's not as big as the U.S., but with fifty-four million people there are a lot of places to hide. You recall how long the Symbionese Liberation Army kept Patty Hearst, with the whole FBI hunting them? Months."

"Let's face it, gentlemen," drawled Odell, "the problem is, there's nothing more we can do."

That *was* the problem; there was nothing anybody could do.

. . .

The boy they were talking about was getting through his second night of captivity. Though he did not know it, there was someone on duty in the corridor outside his cell throughout the night. The cellar of the suburban house might be made of poured concrete, but if he decided to scream and shout, the abductors were quite prepared to subdue him and gag him. He made no such mistake. Resolving to quell his fear and behave with as much dignity as possible, he did two dozen push-ups and toe-touching calisthenics, while a skeptical eye watched through the peephole. He had no wristwatch—he had been running without one on—and was losing track of time. The light burned constantly but at what he judged to be around midnight—he was two hours off—he curled up on the bed, drew the thin blanket over his head to shut out most of the light, and slept. As he did so, the last dozen of the hoax calls were coming in at his country's embassy forty miles away in Grosvenor Square.

Kevin Brown and his eight-strong team did not feel like sleep. Jet-lagged from the flight across the Atlantic, their body clocks were still on Washington time, five hours earlier than London.

Brown insisted that Seymour and Collins show him around the basement telephone exchange and listening post at the embassy, where in an office at the end of the complex, American engineers—the British had not been given access—had set up wall speakers to bring in the sounds recorded by the various bugs in the Kensington apartment.

"There are two taps in the sitting room," explained Collins reluctantly. He saw no reason why he should explain Company techniques to the man from the Bureau, but he had his orders, and the Kensington apartment was "burned" from an operational point of view anyway.

"If a senior officer from Langley was using the place as a base, they would of course be deactivated. But if we were debriefing a Soviet there, we find invisible bugs less inhibiting than having a tape recorder turning away on the table. The sitting room would be the main debriefing area. But there are two more in the master bedroom—Quinn's sleeping in there, but not at the moment, as you will hear—and others in the remaining two bedrooms and the kitchen.

"Out of respect for Miss Somerville and our own man McCrea, we have deactivated the two smaller bedrooms. But if Quinn went into one of them to talk confidentially, we could reactivate them by switching here and here."

Collins indicated two switches on the master console.

Brown asked, "In any case, if he talked to either of them out of range of any speakers, we would expect them to report back to us, right?"

Collins and Seymour nodded.

"That's what they're there for," added Seymour.

"Then we have three telephones in there," Collins went on. "One is the new flash line. Quinn will use that only when he is convinced he is talking to the genuine abductors, and for no other purpose at all. All conversations on that line will be intercepted in the Kensington exchange by the British and piped through on this speaker here. Second, he has a direct patch-through from this room, which he is using now to talk to one of the callers we believe to be a hoaxer, but maybe not. That connection also passes through the Kensington exchange. And there is the third line, an ordinary outgoing and incoming line, also on intercept but probably not to be used unless he wants to call out."

"You mean the British are listening to all this as well?" asked Brown dourly.

"Only the phone lines," said Seymour. "We have to have their cooperation on telephones—they own the exchanges. Besides, they could have a good input on voice patterns, speech defects, regional accents. And of course the call-tracing has got to be done by them, right out of the Kensington exchange. We don't have an untappable line from the apartment to this basement."

Collins coughed.

"Yes, we do," he said, "but it only works for the room bugs. We have two apartments in that building. All the stuff on all the room bugs is fed on internal wires down to our second and smaller apartment in the basement. I have a man down there now. In the basement the speech is scrambled, transmitted on ultrashort-wave radio up here, received, descrambled, and piped down here."

"You radio it for just a mile?" asked Brown.

"Sir, my Agency gets on very well with the British. But no secret service in the world will ever pipe classified information through the land lines running under a city they do not control."

Brown enjoyed that. "So the Brits can hear the phone conversations but not the room talk."

He was wrong, actually. Once MI-5 knew of the Kensington apartment, that the two Metropolitan chief inspectors were not being allowed to live in, and that their own bugs had been removed, they calculated there must be a second American apartment in there to relay

Soviet debriefings to CIA Control somewhere else. Within an hour the apartment-building records had pinpointed the small bed-sitter in the basement. By midnight a team of plumbers had found the connecter wires running through the central heating system, and did an intercept from a ground-floor apartment, whose tenant was courteously urged to take a brief vacation and thus assist Her Majesty. By sunrise everyone was listening to everyone.

Collins's ELINT—electronic intelligence—man at the console lifted the headset off his ears.

"Quinn's just finished with the caller," he said. "Now they'll talk among themselves. You want to hear, sir?"

"Sure," said Brown.

The engineer threw the conversation in the sitting room in Kensington from headset to wall mike. Quinn's voice came through the speaker.

". . . would be fine. Thanks, Sam. Milk and sugar."

"Do you think he'll call back, Mr. Quinn?" That was McCrea.

"Nope. Plausible, but he didn't smell right." Quinn.

The men in the embassy basement turned to go. Cots had been set up in a number of nearby offices. Brown intended to stay on the job at all times. He designated two of his eight men to take the night watch. It was 2:30 A.M.

The same conversations, on the phone and in the sitting room, had been heard and logged in the MI-5 communications center in Cork Street. In the Kensington telephone exchange the police heard only the telephone call, traced it within eight seconds to a phone booth in nearby Paddington, and dispatched a plainclothes officer from Paddington Green police station, two hundred yards from the booth. He arrested an old man with a history of mental illness.

At 9:00 A.M. on the third day, one of the women in Grosvenor Square took another call. The voice was English, rough, curt.

"Put me through to the negotiator."

The girl went pale. No one had used that word before. She kept her voice honeyed.

"Putting you through, sir."

Quinn had the receiver in his hand at half a ring. The girl's voice was a rapid whisper.

"Someone asking for the negotiator. Just that."

Half a second later the connection was made. Quinn's deep, reassuring voice came through the speakers.

"Hi there, pal. You wanted to speak to me?"

"You want Simon Cormack back, it's going to cost you. A lot. Now listen to me—"

"No, friend, you listen to me. I've had a dozen hoax calls already today. You can understand how many crazies there are in this world, right? So do me a favor—just a simple question . . ."

In Kensington the tracers got a "lock" in eight seconds. Hitchin, Hertfordshire . . . a public booth in . . . the railway station. Cramer got it at the Yard ten seconds later; Hitchin police station was slower to get in gear. Their man set off in a car thirty seconds later, was dropped two corners from the station a minute thereafter, and came ambling around the corner toward the booths 141 seconds after the call began. Too late. The man had spent thirty seconds on the line and was by then three streets away, lost in the morning throng.

McCrea stared at Quinn in amazement.

"You hung up on him," he said.

"Had to," said Quinn laconically. "By the time I had finished we were out of time."

"If you'd kept him on the line," said Sam Somerville, "the police might have caught him."

"If he's the man, I want to give him confidence, not a bad fright—yet," said Quinn, and lapsed into silence. He seemed completely relaxed; his two companions were strung out with tension, staring at the phone as if it might ring again. Quinn knew the man could not possibly get back to another phone booth for a couple of hours. He had learned long ago in combat: If you cannot do anything but wait, relax.

In Grosvenor Square, Kevin Brown had been awakened by one of his men and hustled into the listening post in time to hear the end of Quinn's conversation.

". . . is the name of that book? You answer me that and call me right back. I'll be waiting, pal. Bye now."

Collins and Seymour joined him, and all three listened to the playback.

Then they switched to wall speaker and heard Sam Somerville make her point.

"Right," growled Brown.

They heard Quinn's reply.

"Asshole," said Brown. "Another couple of minutes and they could have caught that bastard."

"They get one," pointed out Seymour. "The others still have the boy."

"So get the one and persuade him to reveal the hideout," said Brown. He smacked one beefy fist into the palm of his other hand.

"They probably have a deadline. It's something we use if a member of one of our networks gets taken. If he doesn't show back at the hideout in, say, ninety minutes, allowing for traffic, the others know he's been taken. They waste the kid and vaporize."

"Look, sir, these men have nothing to lose," added Seymour, to Brown's irritation. "Even if they walk in and hand Simon back, they're going to do life anyway. They killed two Secret Service men and a British cop."

"That Quinn just better know what he's doing," said Brown as he walked out.

There were three loud knocks on the door of Simon Cormack's cellar prison at 10:15. He pulled on his hood. When he took it off, a card was propped against the wall by the door.

WHEN YOU WERE A KID ON HOLIDAY AT NANTUCKET,
YOUR AUNT EMILY USED TO READ TO YOU FROM HER
FAVOURITE BOOK. WHICH BOOK WAS IT?

He stared at the card. A wave of relief swept over him. Someone was in contact. Someone had spoken to his father in Washington. Someone was out there trying to get him back. He tried to fight back the tears, but they kept welling up into his eyes. Someone was watching through the peephole. He snuffled; he had no handkerchief. He thought back to Aunt Emily, his father's elder sister, prim in her high-necked cotton dresses, taking him for walks along the beach, sitting him on a tussock and reading about little animals who talked and acted like humans. He sniffed again and shouted the answer at the peephole. It closed. The door opened a fraction; a black-gloved hand came around the corner and withdrew the card.

The man with the gruff voice came through again at 1:30 P.M. The patch-through from the embassy was immediate. The call was traced in eleven seconds—to a booth in a shopping mall at Milton Keynes, Buckinghamshire. By the time a plainclothes officer from the Milton Keynes force reached the booth and looked around, the caller had been gone for ninety seconds. On the line he had wasted no time.

"The book," he rasped. "Called *The Wind in the Willows.*"

"Okay, friend, you're the man I've been waiting to speak to. Now take this number, get off the line, and call me from a fresh booth. It's a line that reaches me, and me only. Three-seven-oh; zero-zero-four-zero. Please stay in touch. Bye now."

Again he replaced the receiver. This time he raised his head and addressed the wall.

"Collins, you can tell Washington we have our man. Simon is alive. They want to talk. You can dismantle the telephone exchange in the embassy."

They heard it all right. They all heard it. Collins used his encoded flash line to Weintraub in Langley, and he told Odell, who told the President. Within minutes the switchboard operators in Grosvenor Square were being sent away. There was one last call, a plaintive, whining voice.

"We are the Proletarian Liberation Army. We are holding Simon Cormack. Unless America destroys all her nuclear weapons—"

The switchboard girl's voice was like running molasses.

"Honeychild," she said, "go screw yourself."

"You did it again," said McCrea. "You hung up on him."

"He has a point," said Sam. "These people can be unbalanced. Couldn't that kind of treatment annoy him to the point of hurting Simon Cormack?"

"Possible," said Quinn. "But I hope I'm right, and I think I am. Doesn't sound like political terrorists. I'm praying he's just a professional killer."

They were aghast.

"What's so good about a professional killer?" asked Sam.

"Not a lot," admitted Quinn, who seemed strangely relieved. "But a professional only works for money. And so far he doesn't have any."

CHAPTER SEVEN

The kidnapper did not call back until six that evening. In the interim Sam Somerville and Duncan McCrea stared at the flash-line telephone almost without cease, praying that whoever he was, the man would call back and not sever communication.

Quinn alone seemed to have the ability to relax. He lay on the sitting-room sofa, stretched out with his shoes off, reading a book. The *Anabasis* by Xenophon, Sam reported quietly from the phone in her room. He had brought it from Spain.

"Never heard of it," grumbled Brown in the basement of the embassy.

"It's about military tactics," volunteered Seymour helpfully, "by a Greek general."

Brown grunted. He knew they were members of NATO but that was about it.

The British police were far busier. Two telephone booths, one in Hitchin, a small and pretty provincial town at the northern tip of Hertfordshire, the other in the great new-town sprawl of Milton Keynes, were visited by quiet men from Scotland Yard and dusted for fingerprints. There were dozens, but though they did not know it, none belonged to the kidnapper, who had worn flesh-colored surgical gloves.

Discreet inquiries were made in the vicinity of both booths to discover if any witness might have seen the booths being used at the specific moments that the calls were made. No one had noticed, not to a matter of seconds. Both booths were in banks of three or four, all in constant use. Besides, both places had been crowded at the time. Cramer grunted.

"He's using the daily rush hours. Morning and lunch."

The tapes of the caller's voice were taken to a professor of philology, an expert in speech patterns and the origins of accents, but Quinn had done most of the talking and the academic shook his head.

"He's using several layers of paper tissue or a thin cloth over the mouthpiece of the phone," he said. "Crude, but fairly effective. It won't fool the speech-pattern oscillators, but I, like the machines, need more material to discern patterns."

Commander Williams promised to bring him more material when the man phoned again. During the day, six houses went quietly under surveillance. One was in London, the other five in the Home Counties. All were rented properties, all six-month leases. By nightfall two had been cleared: a French bank official in one, married with two children, working quite legitimately for the London branch of the Société Générale; and in the other, a German professor doing research work at the British Museum.

By the end of the week the other four would also be cleared, but the property market was producing more "possibles" in a constant stream. They would all be checked out.

"If the criminals have actually bought a property," Cramer told the COBRA committee, "or borrowed one from a bona fide homeowner, I'm afraid it becomes impossible. In the latter case there would be no trace at all; in the former the volume of house purchases in the Southeast in any one year would simply swamp our resources for months on end."

Privately Nigel Cramer favored Quinn's argument (which he had heard on tape) that the caller sounded more like a professional criminal than a political terrorist. Still, the run-through of both kinds of lawbreaker went on and would do so until the end of the case. Even if the abductors *were* underworld criminals, they might have acquired their Czech machine pistol from a terrorist group. The two worlds sometimes met and did business.

If the British police were overwhelmed with work, the problem for the American team in the basement of the embassy was idleness. Kevin Brown paced the long room like a caged lion. Four of his men were on their cots, the other four watching the light that would flash on when the single dedicated phone in the Kensington apartment, whose number the kidnapper now had, was used. The light flashed at two minutes after six.

To everyone's amazement, Quinn let it ring four times. Then he answered, getting in the first words.

"Hi, there. Glad you called."

"Like I said, you want Simon Cormack back alive, it's going to cost you." Same voice, deep, gruff, throaty, and muffled by paper tissues.

"Okay, let's talk," said Quinn in a friendly tone. "My name's Quinn. Just Quinn. Can you give me a name?"

"Get stuffed."

"Come on, not the real one. We're not fools, either of us. Any name. Just so I can say 'Hi there, Smith, or Jones—'"

"Zack," said the voice.

"Z-A-C-K? You got it. Listen, Zack, you've got to keep these calls to twenty seconds, right? I'm not a magician. The spooks are listening and tracing. Call me back in a couple of hours and we'll talk again. Okay?"

"Yeah," said Zack, and put the phone down.

The Kensington exchange wizards had got their "lock" in seven seconds. Another public phone booth, in the town center of Great Dunmow, county of Essex, nine miles west of the M.11 motorway from London to Cambridge. Like the other two towns, north of London. A small town with a small police station. The plainclothes officer reached the bank of three booths eighty seconds after the phone was hung up. Too late. At that hour, with the shops closing and the pubs open, there was a swirl of people but no one looking furtive, or wearing a ginger wig, moustache, and tinted glasses. Zack had chosen the third daily rush hour, early evening, dusk but not yet dark, for in the dark, phone booths are illuminated inside.

In the embassy basement Kevin Brown exploded.

"Who the hell side does Quinn think he's on?" he asked. "He's treating that bastard like the flavor of the month."

His four agents nodded in unison.

In Kensington, Sam Somerville and Duncan McCrea asked much the same question. Quinn just lay back on the couch, shrugged, and returned to his book. Unlike the newcomers, he knew he had two things to do: try to get into the mind of the man on the other end of the line, and try to gain his confidence.

He suspected already that Zack was no fool. So far, at any rate, he had made few mistakes, or he would have been caught by now. So he must know his calls would be monitored and traced. Quinn had told him nothing he did not know already. Volunteering the advice that would keep Zack safe and at large would teach Zack nothing he wouldn't be doing anyway, without instruction.

Quinn was just bridge-building, repugnant though the task was, laying down the first bricks in a relationship with a killer that, he hoped, would cause the man almost involuntarily to believe that Quinn and he shared a common goal—an exchange—and that the authorities were really the bad guys.

From his years in England, Quinn knew that to British ears the American accent can appear the friendliest tone in the world. Something about the drawl. More amiable than the clipped British voice. He had accentuated his drawl a mite beyond its usual level. It was vital not to give Zack the impression he was putting him down or making a mockery of him in any way. Also vital to let nothing slip as to how much he loathed the man who was crucifying a father and a mother three thousand miles away. He was so persuasive he fooled Kevin Brown.

But not Cramer.

"I wish he'd keep the bastard talking a while longer," said Commander Williams. "One of our country colleagues might get a look at him, or his car."

Cramer shook his head.

"Not yet," he said. "Our problem is, these detective constables in the smaller county stations are not trained agents when it comes to shadowing people. Quinn will try to extend the speaking periods later and hope Zack doesn't notice."

Zack did not call that evening; not until the following morning.

Andy Laing took the day off and flew by an internal Saudia commuter flight to Riyadh, where he sought and was given a meeting with the general manager, Steve Pyle.

The office block of SAIB in the Saudi capital was a far cry from the Foreign Legion fort building in Jiddah. The bank had really spent some money here, constructing a tower of buff-colored marble, sandstone, and polished granite. Laing crossed the vast central atrium at ground-floor level, the only sound the clack of his heels on the marble and the splash of the cooling fountains.

Even in mid-October it was fiercely hot outside, but the atrium was like a garden in spring. After a thirty-minute wait he was shown into the office of the general manager on the top floor, a suite so lush that even the president of Rockman-Queens, on a stopover visit six months earlier, had found it more luxurious than his own New York penthouse quarters.

Steve Pyle was a big, bluff executive who prided himself on his paternal handling of his younger staff of all nationalities. His slightly flushed complexion indicated that though the Kingdom of Saudi Arabia might be "dry" down at street level, his own cocktail cabinet lacked for nothing.

He greeted Laing with geniality but some surprise.

"Mr. Al-Haroun didn't warn me you were coming, Andy," he said. "I'd have had a car meet you at the airport."

Mr. Al-Haroun was the manager at Jiddah, Laing's Saudi boss.

"I didn't tell him, sir. I just took a day's leave. I think we have a problem down there and I wanted to bring it to your attention."

"Andy, Andy, my name's Steve, right? Glad you came. So what's the problem?"

Laing had not brought the printouts with him; if anyone at Jiddah was involved in the scam, taking them would have given the game away. But he had copious notes. He spent an hour explaining to Pyle what he had found.

"It can't be coincidence, Steve," he argued. "There is no way these figures can be explained except as major bank fraud."

Steve Pyle's geniality had dropped away as Laing explained his predicament. They had been sitting in the deep club chairs of Spanish leather that were grouped around the low beaten-brass coffee table. Pyle rose and walked to the smoked-glass wall, which gave a spectacular view over the desert for many miles around. Finally he turned and walked back to the table. His broad smile was back, his hand outstretched.

"Andy, you are a very observant young man. Very bright. And loyal. I appreciate that. I appreciate your coming to me with this . . . problem." He escorted Laing to the door. "Now I want you to leave this with me. Think nothing more about it. I'll handle this one personally. Believe me, you're going to go a long way."

Andy Laing left the bank building and headed back to Jiddah aglow with self-righteousness. He had done the proper thing. The GM would put a stop to the swindle.

When he had left, Steve Pyle drummed his fingers on his desk top for several minutes, then made a single phone call.

■　■　■

Zack's fourth call, and second on the flash line, was at quarter to nine in the morning. It was traced to Royston, on the northern border of Hertfordshire, where that county abuts Cambridge. The police officer who got there two minutes later was ninety seconds adrift. And there were no fingerprints.

"Quinn, let's keep it short. I want five million dollars, and fast. Small denominations, used bills."

"Jeez, Zack, that's a hell of a lot. You know how much that *weighs*?"

A pause. Zack was bemused by the unexpectedness of the reference to the money's weight.

"That's it, Quinn. Don't argue. Any tricks and we can always send you a couple of fingers to straighten you out."

In Kensington, McCrea gagged and skittered away to the bathroom. He hit a coffee table on the way.

"Who's with you?" snarled Zack.

"A spook," said Quinn. "You know the way it is. These assholes are not going to leave me alone, now are they?"

"I meant what I said."

"Come on, Zack, there's no need for that. We're both pros. Right? Let's keep it like that, eh? We do what we have to do, nothing more or less. Now time's up. Get off the line."

"Just get the money, Quinn."

"I have to deal with the father on this one. Call me back in twenty-four hours. By the way, how is the kid?"

"Fine. So far." Zack cut the call and left the booth. He had been online for thirty-one seconds. Quinn replaced the receiver. McCrea came back into the room.

"If you ever do that again," said Quinn softly, "I will have you both out of here instantly, and screw the Agency and the Bureau."

McCrea was so apologetic he looked ready to cry.

In the basement of the embassy Brown looked at Collins.

"Your man fouled up," he said. "What was that bang on the line anyway?"

Without waiting for an answer he picked up the direct line from the basement to the apartment. Sam Somerville took it and explained about the threat of severed fingers, and McCrea's knee hitting the coffee table.

When she put the phone down, Quinn asked, "Who was that?"

"Mr. Brown," she said formally. "Mr. Kevin Brown."

"Who's he?" asked Quinn. Sam glanced nervously at the walls.

"The Deputy Assistant Director of the C.I. Division at the Bureau," she said formally, knowing Brown was listening.

Quinn made a gesture of exasperation. Sam shrugged.

There was a conference at noon, in the apartment. The feeling was that Zack would not phone back until the next morning, allowing the Americans to think over his demand.

Kevin Brown came, with Collins and Seymour. So did Nigel Cramer, who brought Commander Williams. Quinn had met all but Brown and Williams.

"You can tell Zack that Washington agrees," said Brown. "It came through twenty minutes ago. I hate it myself, but it's been agreed. Five million dollars."

"But I don't agree," said Quinn.

Brown stared at him as if unable to believe his ears.

"Oh, you don't agree, Quinn. *You* don't agree. The government of the U.S.A. agrees, but Mr. Quinn doesn't agree. May we ask why?"

"Because it is highly dangerous to agree to a kidnapper's first demand," said Quinn quietly. "Do that, and he thinks he should have asked for more. A man who thinks that, thinks he has been fooled in some way. If he's a psychopath, that makes him angry. He has no one on whom to vent that anger but the hostage."

"You think Zack is a psychopath?" asked Seymour.

"Maybe. Maybe not," said Quinn. "But one of his sidekicks may be. Even if Zack's the one in charge—and he may not be—psychos can go out of control."

"Then what do you advise?" asked Collins. Brown snorted.

"It's still early days," said Quinn. "Simon Cormack's best chance of surviving unhurt lies in the kidnappers' believing two things: that they have finally screwed out of the family the absolute maximum they can pay; and that they will see that money only if they produce Simon alive and unharmed. They won't come to those conclusions in a few seconds. On top of that, the police may yet get a break and find them."

"I agree with Mr. Quinn," said Cramer. "It may take a couple of weeks. It sounds harsh, but it's better than a rushed and botched case resulting in an error of judgment and a dead boy."

"Any more time you can give me I'd appreciate," said Commander Williams.

"So what do I tell Washington?" demanded Brown.

"You tell them," said Quinn calmly, "that they asked me to negotiate Simon's return, and I am trying to do that. If they want to pull me off the case, that's fine. They just have to tell the President that."

Collins coughed. Seymour stared at the floor. The meeting ended.

When Zack phoned again, Quinn was apologetic.

"Look, I tried to get through to President Cormack personally. No way. The man's under sedation much of the time. I mean, he's going through hell—"

"So cut it short and get me the money," snapped Zack.

"I tried, I swear to God. Look, five million is over the top. He doesn't have that kind of cash—it's all tied up in blind trust funds that will take weeks to unlock. The word is, I can get you nine hundred thousand dollars, and I can get it fast—"

"Naff off," snarled the voice on the phone. "You Yanks can get it from somewhere else. I can wait."

"Yeah, sure, I know," said Quinn earnestly. "You're safe. The fuzz are getting nowhere, that's for sure—so far. If you could just come down a bit . . . The boy all right?"

"Yeah."

Quinn could tell Zack was thinking.

"I have to ask this, Zack. Those bastards in back of me are leaning real hard. Ask the boy what his pet dog's name was—the one he had from a toddler up through the age of ten. Just so we know he's okay. Won't cost you anything. Helps me a lot."

"Four million," snapped Zack. "And that's bloody it."

The phone cut off. The call had come from St. Neots, a town in the south of Cambridge, just east of the county line with Bedfordshire. No one was spotted leaving the booth, one of a row outside the main post office.

"What are you doing?" asked Sam curiously.

"Putting the pressure on," said Quinn, and would explain no more.

What Quinn had realized days before was that in this case he had one good ace not always available to negotiators. Bandits in the mountains of Sardinia or Central America could hold out for months or years if they wished. No army sweep, no police patrol would ever find them in those hills riddled with caves and undergrowth. Their only real hazard might be from helicopters, but that was it.

In the densely populated southeast corner of England, Zack and his men were in law-abiding—that is, hostile—territory. The longer they hid, the greater by the law of averages the chance of their being identified and located. So the pressure on *them* would be to settle and clear out. The trick would be to get them to think they had won, had got the best deal they could, and had no need to kill the hostage as they fled.

Quinn was counting on the rest of Zack's team—the police knew from the ambush site that there were at least four in the gang—being confined to the hideout. They would get impatient, claustrophobic, eventually urging their leader to settle up and be done with it, precisely the same argument Quinn would be using. Assailed from both sides, Zack would be tempted to take what he could get and seek escape. But that would not happen until the pressure on the kidnappers had built up a lot more.

Quinn had deliberately sown two seeds in Zack's mind: that Quinn was the good guy, trying to do his best for a fast deal and being obstructed by the Establishment—he recalled the face of Kevin Brown and wondered if that was wholly a lie—and that Zack was quite safe . . . so far. Meaning the opposite. The more Zack's sleep was disturbed by nightmares of a police breakthrough, the better.

The professor of linguistics had now decided that Zack was almost certainly in his mid-forties to early fifties, and probably the leader of the gang. There was no hesitation to indicate he would have to consult someone else before agreeing to terms. He was born of working-class people, did not have a very good formal education, and almost certainly stemmed from the Birmingham area. But his native accent had been muted over the years by long periods away from Birmingham, possibly abroad.

A psychiatrist tried to build up a portrait of the man. He was certainly under strain, and it was growing as the conversations were prolonged. His animosity toward Quinn was decreasing with the passage of time. He was accustomed to violence—there had been no hesitation or qualm in his voice when he mentioned the severing of Simon Cormack's fingers. On the other hand he was logical and shrewd, wary but not afraid. A dangerous man but not crazy. Not a psycho and not "political."

These reports went to Nigel Cramer, who reported all to the COBRA committee. Copies went at once to Washington, straight to the White House committee. Other copies came to the Kensington apartment. Quinn read them, and when he was finished, so did Sam.

"What I don't understand," she said as she put down the last page, "is why they picked Simon Cormack. The President comes from a wealthy family, but there must be other rich kids walking around England."

Quinn, who had worked that one out while sitting watching a TV screen in a bar in Spain, glanced at her but said nothing. She waited for an answer but got none. That annoyed her. It also intrigued her. She found as the days passed that she was becoming very intrigued by Quinn.

.   .   .

On the seventh day after the kidnap and the fourth since Zack had made his first call, the CIA and the British SIS took their penetration agents throughout the network of European terrorist organizations off the job. There had been no news of the procurement of a Skorpion machine pistol from these sources, and the view had faded that political terrorists were involved. Among groups investigated had been the I.R.A. and the INLA, both Irish, and in both of which the CIA and SIS each had sleepers whose identity they were not going to reveal to each other; the German Red Army Faction, successor to Baader-Meinhof; the Italian Red Brigades; the French Action Directe; the Spanish/Basque ETA; and the Belgian CCC. There were smaller and even weirder groups, but these had been thought too small to have mounted the Cormack operation.

The next day Zack was back. The call came from a bank of booths in a service station on the M.11 motorway just south of Cambridge and was locked and identified in eight seconds, but it took seven minutes to get a plainclothes officer there. In the swirling mass of cars and people passing through, it was a false hope that Zack would still be there.

"The dog," he said curtly. "Its name was Mister Spot."

"Thanks, Zack," said Quinn. "Just keep the kid okay and we'll conclude our business sooner than you know. And I have news: Mr. Cormack's financial people can raise one-point-two million dollars after all, spot cash and fast. Go for it, Zack."

"Get stuffed," barked the voice on the phone. But he was in a hurry; time was running out. He dropped his demand to $3 million. And the phone went dead.

"Why don't you settle for it, Quinn?" asked Sam. She was sitting on the edge of her chair; Quinn had stood up, ready to go to the bathroom. He always washed, bathed, dressed, used the bathroom, and ate just after a call from Zack. He knew there would be no further contact for a while.

"It's not a question just of money," said Quinn as he headed out of the room. "Zack's not ready yet. He'd start raising the demand again, thinking he was being cheated. I want him undermined a bit more yet; I want more pressure on him."

"What about the pressure on Simon Cormack?" Sam called down the corridor. Quinn paused and came back to the door.

"Yeah," he said soberly, "and on his mother and father. I haven't forgotten. But in these cases the criminals have to believe, truly believe, that the show is over. Otherwise they get angry and hurt the hostage. I've seen it before. It really is better slow and easy than rushing around like the cavalry. If you can't crack it in forty-eight hours with a quick arrest, it comes to a war of attrition, the kidnapper's nerve against the negotiator's. If he gets nothing, he gets mad; if he gets too much too quickly, he reckons he blew it and his pals will tell him the same. So he gets mad. And that's bad for the hostage."

His words were heard on tape a few minutes later by Nigel Cramer, who nodded in agreement. In two cases he had been involved in, the same experience had been gone through. In one the hostage was recovered alive and well; in the other he had been liquidated by an angry and resentful psychopath.

The words were heard live in the basement beneath the American embassy.

"Crap," said Brown. "He has a deal, for God's sake. He should get the boy back now. Then I want to go after those sleazeballs myself."

"If they get away, leave it to the Met.," advised Seymour. "They'll find 'em."

"Yeah, and a British court will give them life in a soft pen. You know what life means over here? Fourteen years with time off. Bullshit. You hear this, mister: No one, but no one, does this to the son of my President and gets away with it. One day this is going to become a Bureau matter, the way it should have been from the start. And I'm going to handle it—Boston rules."

Nigel Cramer came around to the apartment personally that night. His news was no news. Four hundred people had been quietly interviewed, nearly five hundred "sightings" checked out, one hundred and sixty more houses and apartments discreetly surveyed. No breakthrough.

Birmingham CID had gone back into their records for fifty years looking for criminals with a known record of violence who might have left the city long ago. Eight possibles had come up and all had been investigated and cleared; either dead, in prison, or identifiably somewhere else.

Among one of Scotland Yard's resources, little known to the public, is the voice bank. With modern technology, human voices can be broken down to a series of peaks and lows, representing the way a speaker inhales, exhales, uses tone and pitch, forms his words, and delivers them. The trace-pattern on the oscillograph is like a fingerprint; it can be matched and, if there is a sample on file, identified.

Often unknown to themselves, many criminals have tapes of their voices in the voice bank: obscene callers, anonymous informants, and others who have been arrested and taped in the interview room. Zack's voice simply did not show up.

The forensic leads had also fizzled out. The spent cartridge cases, lead slugs, footprints, and tire tracks lay dormant in the police laboratories and refused to give up any more secrets.

"In a radius of fifty miles outside London, including the capital, there are eight million dwelling units," said Cramer. "Plus dry drains, warehouses, vaults, crypts, tunnels, catacombs, and abandoned buildings. We once had a murderer and rapist called the Black Panther, who practically lived in a series of abandoned mines under a national park. He took his victims down there. We got him—eventually. Sorry, Mr. Quinn. We just go on looking."

By the eighth day the strain in the Kensington apartment was telling. It affected the younger people more; if Quinn was experiencing it, he showed little trace. He lay on his bed a lot, between calls and briefings, staring at the ceiling, trying to get inside the mind of Zack and thence to work out how to handle the next call. When should he go for a final step? How to arrange the exchange?

McCrea remained good-natured but was becoming tired. He had developed an almost doglike devotion to Quinn, always prepared to run an errand, make coffee, or do his share of chores around the flat.

On the ninth day Sam asked permission to go out shopping. Grudgingly Kevin Brown called up from Grosvenor Square and gave it. She left the apartment, her first time outside for almost a fortnight, took a cab to Knightsbridge, and spent a glorious four hours wandering through Harvey Nichols and Harrods. In Harrods she treated herself to an extravagant and handsome crocodile-skin handbag.

When she got back, both men admired it very much. She also had a present for each of them: a rolled-gold pen for McCrea and a cashmere sweater for Quinn. The young CIA operative was touchingly grateful; Quinn put on the sweater and cracked one of his rare but dazzling smiles. It was the only lighthearted moment the three of them spent in that Kensington apartment.

In Washington the same day, the crisis management committee listened grimly to Dr. Armitage. The President had made no public appearances since the kidnapping, which a sympathetic populace understood, but his behavior behind the scenes had the committee members very concerned.

"I am becoming increasingly worried about the President's

health," Dr. Armitage told the Vice President, National Security Adviser, four Cabinet Secretaries, and the Directors of the FBI and the CIA. "There have been periods of stress in government before, and always will be. But this is personal and much deeper. The human mind, let alone the body, is not equipped to tolerate these levels of anxiety for very long."

"How is he physically?" asked Bill Walters, the Attorney General.

"Extremely tired, needing medication to sleep at night if he sleeps at all. Aging visibly."

"And mentally?" asked Morton Stannard.

"You have seen him trying to handle the normal affairs of state," Armitage reminded them. They all nodded soberly. "To be blunt, he is losing his grip. His concentration is ebbing; his memory is often faulty."

Stannard nodded sympathetically but his eyes were hooded. A decade younger than Donaldson of State or Reed of Treasury, the Defense Secretary was a former international banker from New York, a cosmopolitan operator who had developed tastes for fine food, vintage wines, and French Impressionist art. During a stint with the World Bank he had established a reputation as a smooth and efficient negotiator, a hard man to convince—as Third World countries seeking overblown credits with small chance of repayment had discovered when they went away empty-handed.

He had made his mark at the Pentagon over the previous two years as a stickler for efficiency, committed to the notion that the American taxpayer should get a dollar's worth of defense for his tax dollar. He had made his enemies there, among the military brass and the lobbyists. But then came the Nantucket Treaty, which had changed a few allegiances across the Potomac. Stannard found himself siding with the defense contractors and the Joint Chiefs of Staff in opposing the sweeping cuts.

While Michael Odell had fought against Nantucket on gut feeling, Stannard's priorities were also concerned with the brokerage of power, and his opposition to the treaty had not been wholly on philosophical grounds. Still, when he had lost his case in the Cabinet, not a flicker of expression had crossed his face; and none did now as he listened to the account of his President's deterioration.

Not so Hubert Reed. "Poor man. God, poor man," he murmured.

"The added problem," concluded the psychiatrist, "is that he is not a demonstrative, emotional man. Not on the outside. Inside . . . of course, we all are. All normal people, anyway. But he bottles things up, won't scream or shout. The First Lady is different—she does not have the strains of office; she's more willing to accept medication. Even so, I think her condition is as bad, if not worse. This is her only child. And that's an added pressure on the President."

He left eight very worried men behind him when he returned to the Executive Mansion.

It was curiosity more than anything else that caused Andy Laing to stay on in his office two nights later, in the Jiddah branch of the Saudi Arabian Investment Bank, and consult his computer. What it showed stunned him.

The scam was still going on. There had been four further transactions since he had spoken to the general manager, who could have stopped it with a phone call. The rogue account was bloated with money, all diverted from Saudi public funds. Laing knew that peculation was no stranger to office-holding in Saudi Arabia, but these sums were huge, enough to finance a major commercial operation, or any other kind of operation.

He realized with a start of horror that Steve Pyle, a man he had respected, had to be involved. It would not be the first time a bank official had gone on the take. But it was still a shock. And to think he had gone with his findings straight to the culprit. He spent the rest of the night back at his apartment, bent over his portable typewriter. By chance his own hiring had taken place not in New York but in London, where he had been working for another American bank when the Rockman-Queens hired him.

London was also the base for European and Mideast operations of Rockman-Queens, the bank's biggest office outside New York, and it housed the chief Internal Accountant for Overseas Operations. Laing knew his duty; it was to this officer that he mailed his report, enclosing four printout sheets from the computer as evidence of his claim.

If he had been a bit smarter he would have sent the package by the ordinary mails. But they were slow and not always reliable. He dropped his package in the bank's courier bag, which normally would have gone direct from Jiddah to London. Normally. But since Laing's visit to Riyadh a week earlier, the general manager had caused all Jiddah inclusions in the bag to pass via Riyadh. The next day Steve Pyle flicked through the outgoing mail, abstracted the Laing report, sent the rest on its way, and read what Laing had to say very carefully. When he had finished, he picked up the phone and dialed a local number.

"Colonel Easterhouse, we have a problem here. I think we should meet."

. . .

On both sides of the Atlantic the media had said everything there was to say, then said it again and again, but still the words poured out. Experts of every kind, from professors of psychiatry to mediums, had offered their analyses and their advice to the authorities. Psychics had communed with the spirit world—on camera—and received a variety of messages, all contradictory. Offers to pay the ransom, whatever it was, had poured in from private individuals and wealthy foundations. The TV preachers had worked themselves into frenzies; vigils were mounted on church and cathedral steps.

The self-seekers had had a field day. Several hundred had offered themselves in place of Simon Cormack, secure in the knowledge that the transposition would never take place. On the tenth day after Zack's first call to Quinn in Kensington, a new note crept into some of the broadcasts being beamed to the American people.

A Texas-based evangelist, whose coffers had received a large and unexpected donation from an oil corporation, claimed he had had a vision of divine inspiration. The outrage against Simon Cormack, and thus against his father the President, and thus against the United States, had been perpetrated by the Communists. There was no doubt of it. The message from the divine was picked up by national news networks and used briefly. The first shots of Plan Crockett had been fired, the first seeds sown.

Divested of her tailored working suit, which she had not worn since the first night in the apartment, Special Agent Sam Somerville was a strikingly attractive woman. Twice in her career she had used her beauty to help close a case. On one occasion she had several times dated a senior official of the Pentagon, finally pretending to pass out from drink in his apartment. Fooled by her unconsciousness, the man had made a highly compromising phone call, which had proved he was fixing defense contracts on behalf of preferred manufacturers and taking a kickback from the profits that resulted.

On another case she had accepted a dinner date from a Mafia boss and while in his limousine secreted a bug deep in the upholstery. What the Bureau heard from the device gave them enough to arraign the man on several federal charges.

Kevin Brown had been well aware of this when he chose her as the Bureau's agent to bird-dog the negotiator the White House insisted on sending to London. He hoped Quinn would be as impressed as several other men had been and, thus weakened, would confide to Sam Somerville any inner thoughts or intentions that the microphones could not pick up.

What he had not counted on was the reverse occurring. On the eleventh evening in the Kensington apartment, the two met in the narrow corridor leading from the bathroom to the sitting room. There was hardly room to pass. On an impulse Sam Somerville reached up, put her arms 'round Quinn's neck, and kissed him. She had wanted to do that for a week. She was not disappointed or rebuffed, but somewhat surprised at the longing in the kiss that he returned.

The embrace lasted for several minutes, while McCrea, unaware, toiled over a frying pan in the kitchen beyond the sitting room. Quinn's hard brown hand stroked her gleaming blond hair. She felt waves of strain and exhaustion draining out of her.

"How much longer, Quinn?" she whispered.

"Not long," he murmured. "A few more days if all goes well—maybe a week."

When they returned to the sitting room and McCrea summoned them to eat, he did not notice a thing.

Colonel Easterhouse limped across the deep carpet of Steve Pyle's office and stared out of the window, the Laing report on the coffee table behind him. Pyle watched him with a worried expression.

"I fear that young man could do our country's interests here enormous harm," said Easterhouse softly. "Inadvertent, of course. I'm sure he's a conscientious young man. Nevertheless . . ."

Privately he was more worried than he gave out. His plan to arrange the massacre and destruction of the House of Sa'ud from the top down was in mid-stage and sensitive to disruption.

The Shi'ah fundamentalist Imam was in hiding, safe from the security police, since the entire file in the central security computer had been erased, wiping out all record of the man's known contacts, friends, supporters, and possible locations. The zealot from the Mutawain Religious Police kept up the contact. Among the Shi'ah, recruitment was progressing, the eager volunteers being told only that they were being prepared for an act of lasting glory in the service of the Imam and thus of Allah.

The new arena was being completed on schedule. Its huge doors, its windows, side exits, and ventilation system were all controlled by a central computer, programmed with a system of Easterhouse's devising. Plans for desert maneuvers to draw most of the regular Saudi Army away from the capital on the night of the dress rehearsal were well advanced. An Egyptian major general and two Palestinian military armorers were in his pay and prepared to substitute defective ammunition for the ordinary issue to the Royal Guard on the night in question.

His American Piccolo machine pistols, with their magazines and ammunition, were due by ship early in the new year, and arrangements were in place for their storage and preparation before issue to the Shi'ah. As he had promised Cyrus Miller, he needed U.S. dollars only for external purchases. Internal accounts could be settled in riyals.

That was not the story he had told Steve Pyle. The general manager of SAIB had heard of Easterhouse and his enviable influence with the royal family, and had been flattered to be asked to dinner two months earlier. When he had seen Easterhouse's beautifully forged CIA identification he had been massively impressed. To think that this man was no free-lance, but really worked for his own government and only he, Steve Pyle, knew it.

"There are rumors of a plan afoot to topple the royal house," Easterhouse had told him gravely. "We found out about it, and informed King Fahd. His Majesty has agreed to a joint effort between his security forces and the Company to unmask the culprits."

Pyle had ceased eating, his mouth open in amazement. And yet it was all perfectly feasible.

"As you know, money buys everything in this country, including information. That's what we need, and the regular Security Police funds cannot be diverted in case there are conspirators among the police. You know Prince Abdul?"

Pyle had nodded. The King's cousin, Minister of Public Works.

"He is the King's appointed liaison with me," said the colonel. "The Prince has agreed that the fresh funds we both need to penetrate the conspiracy shall come from his own budget. Needless to say, Washington at the highest level is desperately eager that nothing should happen to this most friendly of governments."

And thus the bank, in the form of a single and rather gullible officer, had agreed to participate in the creation of the fund. What Easterhouse had actually done was to hack into the Ministry of Public Works' accounting computer, which he had set up, with four fresh instructions.

One was to alert his own computer terminal every time the Ministry issued a draft in settlement of an invoice from a contractor. The sum of these invoices on a monthly basis was huge; in the Jiddah area the

Ministry was funding roads, schools, hospitals, deep-water ports, sports stadiums, bridges, overpasses, housing developments, and apartment blocks.

The second instruction was to add 10 percent to every settlement, but transfer that 10 percent into his own numbered account in the Jiddah branch of the SAIB. The third and fourth instructions were protective: If the Ministry ever asked for the total in its account at the SAIB, its own computer would give the total plus 10 percent. Finally, if questioned directly, it would deny all knowledge and erase its memory. So far the sum in Easterhouse's account was 4 billion riyals.

What Laing had noticed was the weird fact that every time the SAIB, on instructions from the Ministry, made a credit transfer to a contractor, a matching transfer of precisely 10 percent of that sum went from the Ministry's account to a numbered account in the same bank.

Easterhouse's swindle was just a variation of the Fourth Cash Register scam, and could only be uncovered by the full annual Ministry audit the following spring. (The fraud is based on the tale of the American bar owner who, though his bar was always full, became convinced his take was 25 percent less than it ought to be. He hired the best private detective, who took the room above the bar, bored a hole in the floor, and spent a week on his belly watching the bar below. Finally he reported: I'm sorry to have to say this, but your bar staff are honest people. Every dollar and dime that crosses that bar goes into one of your four cash registers. "What do you mean, four?" asked the bar owner. "I only installed three.")

"One does not wish any harm to this young man," said Easterhouse, "but if he is going to do this sort of thing, if he refuses to stay quiet, would it not be wise to transfer him back to London?"

"Not so easy. Why would he go without protest?" asked Pyle.

"Surely," said Easterhouse, "he believes this package to have reached London. If London summons him—or that is what you tell him—he will go like a lamb. All you have to tell London is that you wish him reassigned. Grounds: He is unsuitable here, has been rude to the staff and damaged the morale of his colleagues. His evidence is right here in your hands. If he makes the same allegations in London, he will merely prove your point."

Pyle was delighted. It covered every contingency.

Quinn knew enough to know there was probably not one bug but two in his bedroom. It took him an hour to find the first, another to trace the second. The big brass table lamp had a one-millimeter hole drilled in its base. There was no need for such a hole; the cord entered at the side of the base. The hole was right underneath. He chewed for several minutes on a stick of gum—one of several given him by Vice President Odell for the transatlantic crossing—and shoved the wad firmly into the aperture.

In the basement of the embassy the duty ELINT man at the console turned around after several minutes and called over an FBI man. Soon afterward, Brown and Collins were in the listening post.

"One of the bedroom bugs just went out," said the engineer. "The one in the base of the table lamp. Showing defective."

"Mechanical fault?" asked Collins. Despite the makers' claims, technology had a habit of fouling up at regular intervals.

"Could be," said the ELINT man. "No way of knowing. It seems to be alive. But its sound-level reception is batting zero."

"Could he have discovered it?" asked Brown. "Shoved something in it? He's a tricky son of a bitch."

"Could be," said the engineer. "Want we should go down there?"

"No," said Collins. "He never talks in the bedroom anyway. Just lies on his back and thinks. Anyway, we have the other, the one in the wall outlet."

That night, the twelfth since Zack's first call, Sam came to Quinn's room, at the opposite end of the apartment from where McCrea slept. The door uttered a click as it opened.

"What was that?" asked one of the FBI men sitting through the night watch beside the engineer. The technician shrugged.

"Quinn's bedroom. Door catch, window. Maybe he's going to the can. Needs some fresh air. No voices, see?"

Quinn was lying on his bed, silent in the near darkness, the streetlamps of Kensington giving a low light to the room. He was quite immobile, staring up at the ceiling, naked but for the sarong wrapped around his waist. When he heard the door click he turned his head. Sam stood in the entrance without a word. She, too, knew about the bugs. She knew her own room was not tapped, but it was right next to McCrea's.

Quinn swung his legs to the floor, knotted his sarong, and raised one finger to his lips in a gesture to keep silent. He left the bed without a sound, took his tape recorder from the bedside table, switched it on, and placed it by an electrical outlet in the baseboard six feet from the head of the bed.

Still without a sound he took the big club chair from the corner, upended it, and placed it over the tape recorder and against the wall, using pillows to stuff into the cracks where the arms of the club chair did not reach the wall.

The chair formed four sides of a hollow box, the other two sides being the floor and the wall. Inside the box was the tape recorder.

"We can talk now," he murmured.

"Don't want to," whispered Sam and held out her arms.

Quinn swept her up and carried her to the bed. She sat up for a second and slipped out of her silk nightgown. Quinn lay down beside her. Ten minutes later they became lovers.

In the embassy basement the engineer and two FBI men listened idly to the sound coming from the baseboard outlet two miles away.

"He's gone," said the engineer. The three listened to the steady, rhythmic breathing of a man fast asleep, recorded the previous night when Quinn had left the tape recorder on his pillow. Brown and Seymour wandered into the listening post. Nothing was expected that night; Zack had phoned during the six o'clock evening rush hour— Bedford railway station, no sighting possible.

"I do not understand," said Patrick Seymour, "how that man can sleep like that with the level of stress he's under. Me, I've been catnapping for two weeks and wonder if I'll ever sleep again. He must have piano wire for nerves."

The engineer yawned and nodded. Normally his work for the Company in Britain and Europe did not require much night work, certainly not back-to-back like this, night after night.

"Yeah, well I wish to hell I was doing what he's doing."

Brown turned without a word and returned to the office that had been converted into his quarters. He had been nearly fourteen days in this damn city, becoming more and more convinced the British police were getting nowhere and Quinn was just playing footsie with a rat who ought not to be counted among the human race. Well, Quinn and his British pals might be prepared to sit on their collective butts till hell froze over; *he* had run out of patience. He resolved to get his team around him in the morning and see if a little old-fashioned detective work could produce a lead. It would not be the first time a mighty police force had overlooked some tiny detail.

CHAPTER EIGHT

Quinn and Sam spent almost three hours in each other's arms, alternately making love and talking in low whispers. She did most of the talking, of herself and her career in the Bureau. She also warned Quinn of the abrasive Kevin Brown, who had chosen her for this mission and had established himself in London with a team of eight to "keep an eye on things."

She had fallen into a deep and dreamless sleep, the first time in a fortnight she had slept so well, when Quinn nudged her awake.

"It's only a three-hour tape," he whispered. "It's going to run out in fifteen minutes."

She kissed him again, slipped into her nightgown, and tiptoed back to her room. Quinn eased the armchair away from the wall, grunted a few times for the benefit of the wall microphone, switched off the tape recorder, rolled onto the bed, and genuinely went to sleep. The sounds recorded in Grosvenor Square were of a sleeping man shifting position, rolling over, and resuming his slumbers. The engineer and two FBI men glanced at the console, then back to their cards.

Zack called at half past nine. He seemed more brusque and hostile than on the previous day—a man whose nerves were beginning to fray, a man on whom the pressure was mounting and who had decided to exert some pressure of his own.

"All right, you bastard, now listen. No more sweet talk. I've had enough. I'll settle for your bloody two million dollars but that's the lot. You ask for one more thing and I'll send you a couple of fingers. I'll take a hammer and chisel to the little prick's right hand—see if Washington likes you after that."

"Zack, cool it," pleaded Quinn earnestly. "You've got it. You win. Last night I told them over there to screw it up to two million dollars or I'm out. Jesus, you think *you're* tired? I don't even sleep at all, in case you call."

Zack seemed pacified by the thought that there was someone with nerves more ragged than his own.

"One more thing," he growled. "Not money. Not in cash. You bastards would try to bug the suitcase. Diamonds. This is how . . ."

He talked for ten more seconds, then hung up. Quinn took no notes. He did not need to. It was all on tape. The call had been traced to one of a bank of three public booths in Saffron Walden, a market town in western Essex, just off the M.11 motorway from London to Cambridge. It took three minutes for a plainclothes policeman to wander past the booths, but all were empty. The caller had been swallowed in the crowds.

At the time, Andy Laing was having lunch in the executive canteen of the Jiddah branch of the SAIB. His companion was his friend and colleague the Pakistani operations manager, Mr. Amin.

"I am being very puzzled, my friend," said the young Pakistani. "What is going on?"

"I don't know," said Laing. "You tell me."

"You know the daily mail bag from here to London? I had an urgent letter for London, with some documents included. I need a quick reply. When will I get it? I ask myself. Why has it not come? I asked the mailroom why there is no reply. They tell me something very strange."

Laing put down his knife and fork.

"What is that, old pal?"

"They tell me all is delayed. All packages from here for London are being diverted to the Riyadh office for a day before they go forward."

Laing lost his appetite. There was a feeling in the pit of his stomach and it was not hunger.

"How long did they say this has been going on?"

"Since one week, I do believe."

Laing left the canteen for his office. There was a message on his desk from the branch manager, Mr. Al-Haroun. Mr. Pyle would like to see him in Riyadh without delay.

He made the mid-afternoon Saudia commuter flight. On the journey he could have kicked himself. Hindsight is all very well, but if only he had sent his London package by regular mail . . . He had addressed it to the chief accountant personally, and a letter so addressed, in his distinctive handwriting, would stand out a mile when the letters were spread across Steve Pyle's desk. He was shown into Steve Pyle's office just after the bank closed its doors for public business.

Nigel Cramer came around to see Quinn during the lunch hour, London time.

"You've closed your exchange at two million dollars," he said. Quinn nodded.

"My congratulations," said Cramer. "Thirteen days is fast for this sort of thing. By the way, my tame shrink has listened to this morning's call. He takes the view the man is serious, under a lot of pressure to get out."

"He'll have to take a few more days," said Quinn. "We all will. You heard him ask for diamonds instead of cash. They'll take time to put together. Any leads on their hideout?"

Cramer shook his head.

"I'm afraid not. Every last conceivable property rental has been checked out. Either they're not in residential quarters at all, or they've bought the damn thing. Or borrowed it."

"No chance of checking outright purchases?" asked Quinn.

"I'm afraid not. The volume of properties being bought and sold in southeast England is enormous. There are thousands and thousands owned by foreigners, foreign corporations, or companies whose nominees—lawyers, banks, et cetera—acted for them in the sale. Like this place, for example."

He got in a dig at Lou Collins and the CIA, who were listening.

"By the way, I talked with one of our men in the Hatton Garden district. He spoke to a contact in diamond trading. Whoever he is, your man knows his diamonds. Or one of his colleagues does. What he asked for is easily purchasable and easily disposable. And light. About a kilogram, perhaps a bit more. Have you thought about the exchange?"

"Of course," said Quinn. "I'd like to handle it myself. But I want no concealed bugs—they'll probably think of that. I don't think they'll bring Simon to the rendezvous, so he could still die if there were any tricks."

"Don't worry, Mr. Quinn. We'd obviously like to try and grab them, but I take your point. There'll be no tricks from us, no heroics."

"Thank you," said Quinn. He shook hands with the Scotland Yard man, who left to report progress to the one o'clock COBRA committee.

Kevin Brown had spent the morning secluded in his office beneath the embassy. When the stores opened he had sent out two of his men to buy him a list of items he needed: a very large-scale map of the area north of London, extending fifty miles in all directions; a matching sheet of clear plastic; map pins; wax pencils in different colors. He assembled his team of detectives and spread the plastic across the map.

"Okay, let's just look at these phone booths the rat has been using. Chuck, read them out one by one."

Chuck Moxon studied his list. "First call, Hitchin, county of Hertfordshire."

"Okay, we have Hitchin right . . . here." A pin was stuck in Hitchin.

Zack had made eight calls in thirteen days; the ninth was about to come in. One by one, pins were stuck in the site of each call. Just before ten o'clock one of the two FBI men in the listening post stuck his head around the door.

"He just called again. Threatening to cut off Simon's fingers with a chisel."

"Hot damn," swore Brown. "That fool Quinn's going to blow it away. I knew he would. Where'd the call come from?"

"Place called Saffron Walden," said the young man.

When the nine pins were in place, Brown joined up the perimeter of the area they bounded. It was a jagged shape, involving pieces of five counties. Then he took a ruler and joined the extremities to their opposites on the other side of the pattern. In the approximate center a web of crisscross lines appeared. To the southeast the extremity was Great Dunmow, Essex; to the north was St. Neots, Cambridgeshire; and to the west, Milton Keynes in Buckinghamshire.

"The densest area of the crossed lines lies right here," Brown pointed out with his fingertip, "just east of Biggleswade, county of Bedfordshire. No calls from that area at all. Why?"

"Too close to base?" ventured one of the men.

"Could be, boy, could be. Look, I want you to take these two country towns, Biggleswade and Sandy, the two closest to the geographic center of the web. Get up there and visit all the realtors who have offices in those towns. Make like you are prospective clients, looking to rent a secluded house to write a book or something. Listen to what they say—maybe some place that'll be free soon, maybe some place they could have let you have three months back but it went to someone else. You got it?"

They all nodded.

"Should we let Mr. Seymour know we're on our way?" asked Moxon. "I mean, maybe Scotland Yard has been in that area."

"You leave Mr. Seymour to me," said Brown reassuringly. "We get along just fine. And the bobbies may have been up there and they may just have overlooked something. Maybe so, maybe not. Let's just check it out."

Steve Pyle greeted Laing with an attempt at his usual geniality.

"I . . . ah . . . called you up here, Andy, because I just got a request from London that you go visit with them. Seems this could be the start of a career move for you."

"Sure," said Laing. "Would this request from London have anything to do with the package and report I sent them, which never arrived because it was intercepted right here in this office?"

Pyle dropped all semblance of bonhomie.

"All right. You're smart, maybe too smart. But you've been dabbling in things that don't concern you. I tried to warn you off, but no, you had to go playing private detective. Okay, now I'll level with you. *I'm* transferring you back to London. You don't fit in down here, Laing. I'm not happy with your work. You're going back. That's it. You have seven days to put your desk in order. Your ticket's been booked. Seven days from now."

Had he been older, more mature, Andy Laing would probably have played his cards more coolly. But he was angry that a man of Pyle's eminence in the bank could be ripping off client money for his own enrichment. And he had the naïveté of the young and eager, the conviction that Right would triumph. He turned at the door.

"Seven days? Time enough for you to fix things with London? No way. I'm going back all right, but I'm going back tomorrow."

He was in time for the last flight of the night back to Jiddah. When he got there he went straight to the bank. He kept his passport in the top drawer of his desk, along with any other valuable papers—burglaries of European-owned apartments in Jiddah are not unheard-of, and the bank was safer. At least, it was supposed to be. The passport was missing.

·　·　·

That night there was a stand-up row among the four kidnappers.

"Keep your bloody voices down," hissed Zack on several occasions. *"Baissez les voix, merde."*

He knew his men were running to the limit of their patience. It was always a risk, using this kind of human material. After the screaming adrenaline of the snatch outside Oxford, they had been penned up day and night in a single house, drinking beer from cans he had bought at motorway service stations, keeping out of sight all the time, hearing callers at the door ring and ring before finally going away without an answer. The nervous strain had been bad, and these were not men with the mental resources to immerse themselves in books or thought. The Corsican listened to his French-language pop programs all day, interspersed with news flashes. The South African whistled tunelessly for hours on end, and always the same tune, "Marie Marais." The Belgian watched the television, of which he could not understand a word. He liked the cartoons best.

The argument was over Zack's decision to close with the negotiator called Quinn and have done with the whole thing at $2 million ransom.

The Corsican objected, and because they both spoke French, the Belgian tended to agree with him. The South African was fed up, wanted to get home, and agreed with Zack. The main argument from the Corsican was that they could hold out forever. Zack knew this was not true, but he was aware he could have a very dangerous situation on his hands if he told them they were beginning to show cracks, and could not take more than another six days of numbing boredom and inactivity.

So he appeased them, placated them, told them they had done brilliantly and would all be very rich men in just a few more days. The thought of all that money calmed them down and they subsided. Zack was relieved it had ended without blows. Unlike the three men in the house, his problem was not boredom but stress. Every time he drove the big Volvo along the crowded motorways he knew that one random police check, one brush with another car, one moment of inattention, would have a blue-capped officer leaning in his window, wondering why he wore a wig and false moustache. His disguise would pass in a crowded street, but not at six inches' range.

Every time he went into one of those phone booths, he had a mental image of something going wrong, of a faster-than-usual trace, of a plain-clothes policeman being only a few yards away, taking the alarm on his personal radio and walking up to the phone booth. Zack carried a gun, and knew he would use it to get away. If he did, he would have to abandon the Volvo, always parked a few hundred yards away, and escape on foot. Some idiot member of the public might even try to tackle him. It was getting to the point that whenever he saw a policeman sauntering along the crowded streets he chose for his phone calls, his stomach turned over.

"Go give the kid his supper," he told the South African.

Simon Cormack had been fifteen days in his underground cell, and thirteen since he had answered the question about Aunt Emily and known that his father was trying to get him out. He realized now what solitary confinement must be like and wondered how people could survive months, even years of it. At least in the prisons he had heard of, inmates in solitary had writing materials, books, sometimes television, something to occupy the mind. He had nothing. But he was a tough boy and he determined not to go to pieces.

He exercised regularly, forcing himself to overcome the prisoner's lethargy, doing his push-ups ten times a day, jogging in place a dozen times. He still wore his same running shoes, socks, shorts, and T-shirt, and was aware he must smell awful. He used the toilet bucket carefully, so as not to soil the floor, and was grateful it was removed every second day.

The food was boring, mainly fried or cold, but it was enough. He had no razor, of course, so he sported a straggly beard and moustache. His hair had grown; he tried to comb it with his fingers. He had asked for, and eventually been given, a plastic bucket of cold water and a sponge. He never realized how grateful a man could be for the chance to wash. He had stripped naked, running his shorts halfway up the ankle-chain to keep them dry, and sponged himself from head to foot, scouring his skin with the sponge to try to keep clean. After it he felt transformed. But he tried no escape maneuvers. The chain was impossible to break; the door solid and bolted from the outside.

Between exercises he tried to keep his mind occupied in a number of ways: reciting every poem he could remember, pretending to dictate his autobiography to an invisible stenographer so that he could go over everything that had ever happened to him in his twenty-one years. And he thought of home, of New Haven and Nantucket and Yale and the White House. He thought of his mom and dad and how they were; he hoped they weren't worried about him, but expected they were. If only he could tell them he was all right, in good shape, considering . . .

There were three loud knocks on the cellar door. He reached for his black hood and put it on. Suppertime—or was it breakfast . . . ?

. . .

That same evening, but after Simon Cormack had fallen asleep, and
Sam Somerville lay in Quinn's arms while the tape recorder breathed
into the wall outlet, five time zones farther west, the White House committee met in the late evening. Apart from the usual Cabinet members
and department heads, Philip Kelly of the FBI and David Weintraub of
the CIA also attended.

They heard the tapes of Zack on the phone to Quinn, the rasping
tones of the British criminal and the reassuring drawl of the American
trying to appease him, as they had done almost every day for two
weeks.

When Zack had finished, Hubert Reed was pale with shock.

"My God," he said, "cold chisel and hammer. The man's an animal."

"We know that," said Odell. "But at least now we have an agreed
ransom. Two million dollars. In diamonds. Any objections?"

"Of course not," said Jim Donaldson. "This country will pay that
easily, for the President's son. I'm just surprised it's taken two weeks."

"Actually, that's pretty fast, or so I'm told," said Bill Walters. Don
Edmonds of the FBI nodded his agreement.

"We want to rehear the rest, the tapes from the apartment?" asked
the Vice President.

No one needed to.

"Mr. Edmonds, what about what Mr. Cramer, the Scotland Yard
man, told Quinn? Any comments from your people?"

Edmonds cast a sidelong glance at Philip Kelly, but answered for
the Bureau.

"Our people at Quantico agree with their British colleagues," he
said. "This Zack is at the end of his tether, wants to close it down, make
an exchange. The strain in his voice is coming through, hence the
threats most probably. They also agree with the analysts over there on
another thing. Which is that Quinn appears to have established some
kind of wary empathy with this animal Zack. It seems his efforts—
which are what has taken two weeks"—he glanced at Jim Donaldson as
he spoke—"to portray himself as the guy trying to help Zack, and all
the rest of us here and there as the bad guys making problems, has
worked. Zack has an element of trust for Quinn, but for no one else.
That may prove crucial at the safe-handover process. At least, that's
what the voice analysts and behavioral psychologists are saying."

"Lord, what a job, having to sweet-talk scum like that," observed
Jim Donaldson with distaste.

David Weintraub, who had been staring at the ceiling, cast an eye toward the Secretary of State. To keep these amateurs in their high office, he might have said but did not, he and his people sometimes had to deal with creatures just as nasty as Zack.

"Okay, gentlemen," said Odell, "we go with the deal. At last the ball is back with us in America, so let's make it fast. Personally I think this Quinn has done a pretty good job. If he can get the boy back safe and sound, we owe him. Now, diamonds. Where do we get them?"

"New York," said Weintraub, "diamond center of the country."

"Morton, you're from New York. Have you got any discreet contacts you could tap into fast?" Odell asked the ex-banker.

"Certainly," Stannard said. "When I was with Rockman-Queens we had a number of clients who were high in the diamond trade. Very discreet—they have to be. You want me to handle it? How about the money?"

"The President has insisted he will personally pay the ransom, won't have it any other way," said Odell. "But I don't see why he should be troubled by these details. Hubert, could the Treasury make a personal loan until the President can liquidate trust funds?"

"No problem," said Hubert Reed. "You'll have your money, Morton."

The committee rose. Odell had to see the President over at the Executive Mansion.

"Fast as you can, Morton," he said. "We want to be talking here in two to three days. Tops."

In fact, it would take another seven.

It was not until morning that Andy Laing could secure an interview with Mr. Al-Haroun, the branch manager. But he did not waste the night.

Mr. Al-Haroun, when confronted, was as gently apologetic as only a well-bred Arab can be when confronted by an angry Occidental. The matter gave him enormous regret, no doubt an unhappy situation whose solution lay in the lap of the all-merciful Allah; nothing would give him greater pleasure than to return to Mr. Laing his passport, which he had taken into nightly safekeeping only at the specific request of Mr. Pyle. He went to his safe and, with slim brown fingers, withdrew the blue United States passport and handed it back.

Laing was mollified, thanked him with the more formal and gracious *"Ashkurak,"* and withdrew. Only when he had returned to his own office did it occur to him to flick through the passport's pages.

In Saudi Arabia, foreigners not only need an entry visa, but an exit visa as well. His own, formerly valid without limit of time, had been canceled. The stamp of the Jiddah Immigration Control office was perfectly genuine. No doubt, he mused bitterly, Mr. Al-Haroun had a friend in that bureau. It was, after all, the local way of doing things.

Aware there was no going back, Andy Laing determined to scrap it out. He recalled something the Operations manager had once told him.

"Amin, my friend, did you not mention once that you had a relative in the Immigration Service here?" he asked him. Amin saw no trap in the question.

"Yes, indeed. A cousin."

"In which office is he based?"

"Ah, not here, my friend. He is in Dhahran."

Dhahran was not near Jiddah, on the Red Sea, but right across the country in the extreme east, on the Persian Gulf. In the late morning Andy Laing made a phone call to Mr. Zulfiqar Amin at his desk in Dhahran.

"This is Mr. Steven Pyle, General Manager of the Saudi Arabian Investment Bank," he said. "I have one of my officers conducting business in Dhahran at this moment. He will need to fly on urgent matters to Bahrein tonight. Unfortunately he tells me his exit visa is time-expired. You know how long these things can take through normal channels. . . . I was wondering, in view of your cousin being in such high esteem with us . . . You will find Mr. Laing a most generous man. . . ."

Using the lunch hour, Andy Laing returned to his apartment, packed his bags, and caught the 3:00 P.M. Saudia airline flight to Dhahran. Mr. Zulfiqar Amin was expecting him. The reissue of an exit visa took two hours and a thousand riyals.

Mr. Al-Haroun noticed the absence of the Credit and Marketing Manager around the time he took off for Dhahran. He checked the Jiddah airport, but only the international departures office. No trace of a Mr. Laing. Puzzled, he called Riyadh. Pyle asked if a block could be put on Laing's boarding any flight at all, even internal.

"I'm afraid, dear colleague, that cannot be arranged," said Mr. Al-Haroun, who hated to disappoint. "But I can ask my friend if he has left by any internal flight."

Laing was traced into Dhahran just at the moment he crossed the frontier on the causeway to the neighboring Emirate of Bahrein. From there he easily caught a British Airways flight on a stopover from Mauritius to London.

Unaware that Laing had obtained a new exit visa, Pyle waited till the following morning, then asked his bank staff in the Dhahran office to check around the city and find out what Laing was doing there. It took them three days and they came up with nothing.

Three days after the Secretary of Defense was charged by the Washington committee with obtaining the package of diamonds demanded by Zack, he reported back that the task was taking longer than foreseen. The money had been made available; that was not the problem.

"Look," he told his colleagues, "I know nothing about diamonds. But my contacts in the trade—I am using three, all very discreet and understanding men—tell me the number of stones involved is very substantial.

"This kidnapper has asked for uncut, rough melees—mixtures—of one fifth of a carat to half a carat, and of medium quality. Such stones, I am told, are worth between two hundred and fifty and three hundred dollars a carat. To be on the safe side they are calculating the base price of two-fifty. We are talking here about some eight thousand carats."

"And what's the problem?" asked Odell.

"Time," said Morton Stannard. "At a fifth of a carat per stone, that would be forty thousand stones. At half a carat, sixteen thousand stones. With a mixture of different weights, let's say twenty-five thousand stones. It's a lot to put together this fast. Three men are buying furiously, and trying not to make waves."

"What's the bottom line?" asked Brad Johnson. "When can they be ready for shipment?"

"Another day, maybe two," said the Defense Secretary.

"Stay on top of it, Morton," Odell ordered. "We have the deal. We can't keep this boy and his father waiting much longer."

"The moment they're in a bag, weighed and authenticated, you'll have them," said Stannard.

The following morning Kevin Brown took a private call in the embassy from one of his men.

"We may have hit paydirt, Chief," said the agent tersely.

"No more on an open line, boy. Get your ass in here fast. Tell me to my face."

The agent was in London by noon. What he had to say was more than interesting.

East of the towns of Biggleswade and Sandy, both of which lie on the A.1 highway from London to the north, the county of Bedfordshire butts up against Cambridgeshire. The area is intersected only by minor B-class roads and country lanes, contains no large towns, and is largely given over to agriculture. The county border area contains only a few villages, with old English names like Potton, Tadlow, Wrestlingworth, and Gamlingay.

Between two of these villages, off the beaten path, lay an old farm-house, partly ruined by fire but with one wing still furnished and habit-able, in a shallow valley and approached by a single track.

Two months earlier, the agent had discovered, the place had been rented by a small group of supposed "rustic freaks," who claimed they wanted to return to nature, live simply, and create artifacts in pottery and basket-weaving.

"The thing is," said the agent, "they had the money for the rental in cash. They don't seem to sell much pottery, but they can run two off-road Jeeps, which are parked undercover in the barns. And they mix with no one."

"What's the name of this place?" asked Brown.

"Green Meadow Farm."

"Okay, we have enough time if we don't hang around. Let's go take a look at Green Meadow Farm."

There were two hours of daylight left when Kevin Brown and the agent parked their car at the entrance to a farm lane and made the rest on foot. Guided by the agent, the pair approached with extreme caution, using the trees for cover, until they emerged from the tree line above the valley. From there they crawled the last ten yards to the edge of a rise and looked down into the valley. The farmhouse lay below them, its fire-gutted wing black in the autumn afternoon, a low gleam as from an oil lamp coming from one window of the other wing.

As they watched, a burly man came out of the farmhouse and crossed to one of the three barns. He spent ten minutes there, then returned to the house. Brown scanned the complex of farm buildings with powerful binoculars. Down the track to their left came a powerful Japanese off-road four-wheel-drive. It parked in front of the farm and a man climbed out. He gazed carefully around him, scanning the rim of the valley for movement. There was none.

"Damn," said Brown. "Ginger hair, eyeglasses."

The driver went into the farmhouse and emerged a few seconds later with the burly man. This time they had a big Rottweiler with them. The pair went to the same barn, spent ten minutes, and returned.

The burly man drove the Jeep into another barn and closed the doors.

"Rustic pottery, my ass," said Brown. "There's something or someone in that damn barn. Five will get you ten it's a young man."

They wriggled back into the line of trees. Dusk was descending.

"Take the blanket from the trunk," said Brown. "And stay here. Stake it out all night. I'll be back with the team before sunup—if there ever is any sun in this damn country."

Across the valley, stretched out along a branch in a giant oak, a man in camouflage uniform lay motionless. He, too, had powerful binoculars, with which he had noted the movements among the trees on the opposite side from his own position. As Kevin Brown and his agent slithered off the rim of the high ground and into the woodland, he drew a small radio from his pocket and spoke quietly and urgently for several seconds. It was October 28, nineteen days since Simon Cormack had been kidnapped and seventeen since Zack's first call to the Kensington apartment.

Zack called again that evening, burying himself in the hurrying crowds in the center of Luton.

"What the hell's going on, Quinn? It's been three bloody days."

"Hey, take it easy, Zack. It's the diamonds. You caught us by surprise, ole buddy. That kind of package takes a while to put together. I laid it on them over there in Washington—I mean, but hard. They're working on it as fast as they can, but hell, Zack, twenty-five thousand stones, all good, all untraceable—that takes a bit—"

"Yeah, well, just tell them they got two more days and then they get their boy back in a bag. Just tell 'em."

He hung up. The experts would later say his nerves were badly shot. He was reaching the point where he might be tempted to hurt the boy out of frustration or because he thought he was being tricked in some way.

Kevin Brown and his team were good and they were armed. They came in four pairs, from the only four directions from which the farm could be assailed. Two skirted the track, darting from cover to cover. The other three pairs came from the trees and down the sloping fields in complete silence. It was that hour just before dawn when the light is at its trickiest, when the spirits of the quarry are at their lowest, the hour of the hunter.

The surprise was total. Chuck Moxon and his partner took the suspect barn. Moxon snipped off the padlock; his partner went in on the roll, coming to his feet on the dusty floor inside the barn with his side-arm drawn. Apart from a petrol generator, something that looked like a kiln, and a bench with an array of chemistry glassware, there was no one there.

The six men, plus Brown, who took the farmhouse, fared better. Two pairs went in through windows, taking the glass and the frames as they went, came to their feet without a pause, and headed straight upstairs to the bedrooms.

Brown and the remaining pair went through the front door. The lock shattered with a single blow of the sledgehammer and they were in.

By the embers of the fire in the grate of the long kitchen, the burly man had been asleep in a chair. It was his job to keep watch through the night, but boredom and tiredness had taken over. At the crash from the front door he came out of his chair and reached for a .12-bore shotgun that lay on the pine table. He almost made it. The shout of "Freeze!" from the door and the sight of the big crew-cut man crouched over a Colt .45 aimed straight at his chest caused the burly one to stop. He spat and slowly raised both hands.

Upstairs the red-haired man was in bed with the only woman in the group. They both awoke as the windows and doors crashed in downstairs. The woman screamed. The man went for the bedroom door and met the first FBI man on the landing. The fighting was too close for firearms; the two men went down together in the darkness and wrestled until another American could discern which was which and hit the redhead hard with the butt of his Colt.

The fourth member of the farmhouse group was led blinking out of his bedroom a few seconds later, a thin, scrawny young man with lank hair. The FBI team all had flashlights in their belts. It took two more minutes to examine all the other bedrooms and establish that four people was the limit. Kevin Brown had them all brought to the kitchen, where lamps were lit. He surveyed them with loathing.

"Okay, where's the kid?" he asked. One of his men looked out the window.

"Chief, we have company."

About fifty men were descending into the valley and toward the farmhouse on all sides, all in kneeboots, all in blue, a dozen with Alsatians straining at the leash. In an outhouse the Rottweiler roared his rage at the intrusion. A white Range Rover with blue markings jolted up the track to stop ten yards from the broken door. A middle-aged man in blue, aglitter with silver buttons and insignia, descended, a braided peaked cap on his head. He walked into the lobby without a word, entered the kitchen, and gazed at the four prisoners.

"Okay, we hand it over to you now," said Brown. "He's here somewhere. And those sleazeballs know where."

"Exactly," asked the man in blue, "who are you?"

"Yes, of course." Kevin Brown produced his Bureau identification. The Englishman looked at it carefully and handed it back.

"See here," said Brown, "what we've done—"

"What you've done, Mr. Brown," said the Chief Constable of Bedfordshire with icy rage, "is to blow away the biggest drug bust this county was ever likely to have and now, I fear, never will have. These people are low-level minders and a chemist. The big fish and their consignment were expected any day. Now, would you please return to London?"

At that hour Steve Pyle was with Mr. Al-Haroun in the latter's office in Jiddah, having flown to the coast following a disturbing phone call.

"What exactly did he take?" he asked for the fourth time. Mr. Al-Haroun shrugged. These Americans were even worse than the Europeans, always in a hurry.

"Alas, I am not an expert in these machines," he said, "but my night watchman here reports . . ."

He turned to the Saudi night watchman, and rattled off a stream of Arabic. The man replied, holding out his arms to signify the extent of something.

"He says that the night I returned Mr. Laing his passport, duly altered, the young man spent most of the night in the computer room, and left before dawn with a large amount of computer printout. He returned for work at the normal hour without it."

Steve Pyle went back to Riyadh a very worried man. Helping his government and his country was one thing, but in an internal accounting inquiry, that would not show up. He asked for an urgent meeting with Colonel Easterhouse.

The Arabist listened to him calmly and nodded several times.

"You think he has reached London?" he asked.

"I don't know how he could have done it, but where the hell else could he be?"

"Mmmm. Could I have access to your central computer for a while?"

It took the colonel four hours at the console of the master computer in Riyadh. The job was not difficult, since he had all the access codes. By the time he had finished, all the computerized records had been erased and a new record created.

Nigel Cramer got a first telephone report from Bedford in mid-morning, long before the written record arrived. When he called Patrick Seymour at the embassy he was incandescent with anger. Brown and his team were still on the road south.

"Patrick, we've always had a damn good relationship, but this is outrageous. Who the hell does he think he is? Where the hell does he think he is?"

Seymour was in an impossible position. He had spent three years building on the excellent cooperation between the Bureau and the Yard which he had inherited from his predecessor, Darrell Mills. He had attended courses in England and arranged visits by senior Metropolitan officers to the Hoover Building to form those one-on-one relationships that in a crisis can cut through miles of red tape.

"What exactly was going on at the farm?" he asked. Cramer calmed down and told him. The Yard had had a tip months before that a big drug ring was setting up a new and major operation in England. After patient investigation the farm had been identified as the base. Covert Squad men from his own S.O. Department had mounted surveillance week after week, in liaison with the Bedford police. The man they wanted was a New Zealand-born heroin czar, sought in a dozen countries but slippery as an eel. The good news was, he was expected to show up with a large coke consignment for processing, cutting, and distributing; the bad news was, he would now not come near the place.

"I'm sorry, Patrick, but I'm going to have to ask the Home Secretary to have Washington send for him."

"Well, if you must, you must," said Seymour. As he put the phone down he thought: You go right ahead.

Cramer also had another task, even more urgent. That was to stop the story appearing in any publication, or on radio or TV. That morning he had to call on a lot of good will from the proprietors and editors of the media.

The Washington committee got Seymour's report at their first—7:00 A.M.—meeting of the day.

"Look, he got a first-class lead and he followed it up," protested Philip Kelly. Don Edmonds shot him a warning glance.

"He should have cooperated with Scotland Yard," said the Secretary of State. "What we don't need is to foul relations with the British authorities at this point. What the hell am I to say to Sir Harry Marriott when he asks for Brown's ouster?"

"Look," said Treasury Secretary Reed, "why not propose a compromise? Brown was overzealous and we're sorry. But we believe Quinn and the British will secure Simon Cormack's release momentarily. When that happens, we need a strong group to escort the boy home. Brown and his team should be given a few days' extension to accomplish that. Say, end of the week?"

Jim Donaldson nodded.

"Yes, Sir Harry might accept that. By the way, how is the President?"

"Bucking up," said Odell. "Almost optimistic. I told him an hour ago Quinn had secured further proof Simon was alive and apparently well—the sixth time Quinn's got the kidnappers to prove that. How about the diamonds, Morton?"

"Ready by sundown," said Stannard.

"Get a fast bird standing by and ready," said Vice President Odell. Stannard nodded and made a note.

Andy Laing finally got his interview with the internal accountant just after lunch that day. The man was a fellow-American and had been on a tour of European branches for the previous three days.

He listened soberly and with growing dismay to what the young bank officer from Jiddah had to say, and scanned the computer printouts across his desk with a practiced eye. When he had finished he leaned back in his chair, puffed out his cheeks, and exhaled noisily.

"Dear God, these are very serious accusations indeed. And yes, they appear to be substantiated. Where are you staying in London?"

"I still have an apartment in Chelsea," said Laing. "I've been there since I arrived. Luckily my tenants moved out two weeks back."

The accountant noted its address and phone number.

"I'm going to have to consult with the general manager here, maybe the president in New York. Before we face Steve Pyle with this. Stay close to the phone for a couple of days."

What neither of them knew was that the morning pouch from Riyadh contained a confidential letter from Steve Pyle to the London-based general manager for Overseas Operations.

. . .

The British press was as good as its word, but Radio Luxembourg is based in Paris and for French listeners the story of a first-class row between their Anglo-Saxon neighbors to the west is too good to miss.

Where the tip-off really came from could never be later established, except that it was a phone-in and anonymous. But the London office checked it out and confirmed that the sheer secrecy of the Bedford police gave credence to the story. It was a thin day and they ran it on the four o'clock news.

Hardly anybody in England heard it, but the Corsican did. He whistled in amazement and went to find Zack. The Englishman listened carefully, asked several supplementary questions in French, and went pale with anger.

Quinn knew already, and that was a saving grace because he had time to prepare an answer in the event Zack called. He did, just after 7:00 P.M. and in a towering rage.

"You lying bastard. You said there'd be no cowboy antics from the police or anyone else. You bloody lied to me—"

Quinn protested that he did not know what Zack was talking about—it would have been too phony to know all the details without a reminder. Zack told him in three angry sentences.

"But that was nothing to do with you," Quinn shouted back. "The Frogs got it wrong, as usual. It was a DEA drug-bust that went wrong. You know these Rambos from the Drug Enforcement Agency—they did it. They weren't looking for you—they were looking for cocaine. I had a Scotland Yard man here an hour ago and he was puking about it. For chrissake, Zack, you know the media. If you believe them, Simon's been sighted eight hundred different places and you've been caught fifty times."

It was plausible. Quinn counted on Zack's having spent three weeks reading miles of inaccurate nonsense in the tabloid papers and having a healthy contempt for the press. In a booth in Linslade bus depot, he calmed down. His phone time was running out.

"Better not be true, Quinn. Just better not," he said, and hung up.

Sam Somerville and Duncan McCrea were pale with fear by the time the call ended.

"Where are those damn diamonds?" asked Sam.

There was worse to come. Like most countries, Britain has a range of breakfast-hour radio programs, a mix of mindless chitchat from the show host, pop music, news flashes, and phone-in trivia. The news is up-to-the-minute snippets torn from the wire service printers, hastily rewritten by junior subeditors, and thrust under the disc jockey's nose. The pace of the programs is such that the careful checking and rechecking practiced by the investigative reporters of the Sunday "heavies" just does not take place.

When an American voice rang the busy news desk of City Radio's *Good Morning* show, the call was taken by a girl trainee who later tearfully admitted she had not thought to query the claim that the speaker was the press counselor from the U.S. embassy with a genuine news bulletin. It went on the air in the excited tones of the D.J. seventy seconds later.

Nigel Cramer did not hear it but his teenage daughter did.

"Dad," she called from the kitchen, "you going to catch them today?"

"Catch who?" said her father, pulling on his coat in the hall. His official car was at the curb.

"The kidnappers—you know."

"I doubt it. Why do you ask?"

"Says so on the radio."

Something hit Cramer hard in the stomach. He turned back from the door and into the kitchen. His daughter was buttering toast.

"What, exactly, did it say on the radio?" he asked in a very tight voice. She told him. That an exchange of the ransom for Simon Cormack would be set up within the day, and that the authorities were confident all the kidnappers would be caught in the process. Cramer ran out to his car, took the handset from the dashboard, and began to make a series of frantic calls as the car rolled.

It was too late. Zack had not heard the program, but the South African had.

CHAPTER NINE

The call from Zack was later than usual—10:20 A.M. If he had been angry the previous day over the matter of the raid on the Bedfordshire farm, he was by now almost hysterical with rage.

Nigel Cramer had had time to warn Quinn, speaking from his car as it sped toward Scotland Yard. When Quinn put down the phone, it was the first time Sam had seen him appear visibly shaken. He paced the apartment in silence; the other two sat and watched in fear. They had heard the gist of Cramer's call and sensed that it was all going to fail, somehow, somewhere.

Just waiting for the flash line to ring, not even knowing whether the kidnappers would have heard the radio show at all, or how they would react if they had, made Sam nauseous from stress. When the phone finally rang, Quinn answered it with his usual calm good humor. Zack did not even bother with preambles.

"Right, this time you've bloody blown it, you Yankee bastard. You take me for some kind of fool, do you? Well, you're the fool, mate. 'Cos you're going to look a right fool when you bury Simon Cormack's body."

Quinn's shock and amazement were convincingly feigned.

"Zack, what the hell are you talking about? What's gone wrong?"

"Don't give me that," screamed the kidnapper, his gruff voice rising. "If you didn't hear the news, then ask your police mates about it.

And don't pretend it was a lie—it came from your own sodding embassy."

Quinn persuaded Zack to tell him what he had heard, even though he knew. The telling caused Zack to calm down slightly; and his time was running out.

"Zack, it's a lie, a phony. Any exchange would be just you and me, pal. Alone and unarmed. No direction-finder devices, no tricks, no police, no soldiers. Your terms, your place, your time. That's the only way I'd have it."

"Yeah, well it's too late. Your people want a body, that's what they're going to get."

He was about to hang up. For the last time. Quinn knew if that happened it would be over. Days, weeks later, someone somewhere would enter a house or a flat, a cleaner, a caretaker, a real estate agent, and there he'd be. The President's only son, shot through the head, or strangled, half decomposed . . .

"Zack, please, stay there just a few more seconds."

Sweat was running off Quinn's face, the first time he had ever shown the massive strain inside himself these past twenty days. He knew just how close it was to disaster.

In the Kensington exchange a group of Telecom engineers and police officers stared at the monitors and listened to the rage coming down the line; at Cork Street, beneath the pavements of smart Mayfair, four men from MI-5 were rooted in their chairs, motionless as the anger poured out of the speaker into the room and the tape deck wound silently around and around.

Below the U.S. embassy in Grosvenor Square there were two ELINT engineers and three FBI agents, plus Lou Collins of the CIA and FBI representative Patrick Seymour. The news of the morning broadcast had brought them all to this place, anticipating something like what they were now hearing—which did not make it any better.

The fact that all the nation's radio stations, including City Radio, had spent two hours denouncing the hoax call of the breakfast hour was irrelevant. They all knew that; leaks can be repudiated for the rest of time—it changes nothing. As Hitler said, the big lie is the one they believe.

"Please Zack, let me get on to President Cormack personally. Just twenty-four hours more. After all this time, don't throw it away now. The President's got the authority to tell these assholes to get out of here and leave it to you and me. Just the two of us—we're the only ones who can be trusted to get it right. All I ask, after twenty days, is just one more. Twenty-four hours, Zack, give me just that."

There was a pause on the line. Somewhere along the streets of Aylesbury, Buckinghamshire, a young detective constable was moving casually toward the bank of phone booths.

"This time tomorrow," said Zack finally, and put the phone down. He quit the booth and had just turned the corner when the plainclothes policeman emerged from an alley and glanced at the bank of phone booths. All were empty. He had missed spotting Zack by eight seconds.

Quinn replaced the phone, walked to the long couch, lay on his back with his hands clasped behind his head, and stared at the ceiling.

"Mr. Quinn," said McCrea hesitantly. Despite repeated assurances that he could drop the "Mister," the shy young CIA man insisted on treating Quinn like his grade-school teacher.

"Shut up," said Quinn clearly. The crestfallen McCrea, who had been about to ask if Quinn wanted coffee, went to the kitchen and made it anyway. The third, the "ordinary," telephone rang. It was Cramer.

"Well, we all heard that," he said. "How are you feeling?"

"Beat," said Quinn. "Any news on the source of the broadcast?"

"Not yet," said Cramer. "The girl subeditor who took the call is still at Holborn police station. She swears it was an American voice, but what would she know? She swears the man made it sound convincingly official, knew what to say. You want a transcript of the broadcast?"

"Bit late now," said Quinn.

"What are you going to do?" asked Cramer.

"Pray a bit. I'll think of something."

"Good luck. I have to go 'round to Whitehall now. I'll stay in touch."

The embassy came next. Seymour. Congratulations on the way Quinn had handled it . . . If there's anything we can do . . . That's the trouble, thought Quinn. Someone is doing too damn much. But he did not say it.

He was halfway through his coffee when he swung his legs off the couch and picked up the phone to the embassy. It was answered at once in the basement. Seymour again.

"I want a patch-through on a secure line to Vice President Odell," he said, "and I want it now."

"Er, look, Quinn, Washington is being alerted about what just happened here. They'll have the tapes themselves momentarily. I figure we should let them hear what happened and discuss—"

"I speak with Michael Odell inside ten minutes, or I raise him on the open line," said Quinn carefully.

Seymour thought it over. The open line was insecure. NSA would pick up the call with their satellites; the British GCHQ would get it. So would the Russians. . . .

"I'll get to him and ask him to take your call," said Seymour.

Ten minutes later Michael Odell came on the line. It was 6:15 A.M. in Washington; he was still at his residence at the Naval Observatory. But he had been awakened half an hour earlier.

"Quinn, what the hell's going on over there? I just heard some horse shit about a hoax call to a radio show—"

"Mr. Vice President," said Quinn levelly, "have you a mirror nearby?"

There was a stunned pause.

"Yes, I guess so."

"If you look in it, you will see the nose on your face, right?"

"Look, what is this? Yeah, okay, I can see the nose on my face."

"As surely as what you are looking at, Simon Cormack is going to be murdered in twenty-four hours . . ."

He let the words sink in to the shocked man sitting on the edge of his bed in Washington.

" . . . unless . . ."

"Okay, Quinn, lay it on the line."

"Unless I have that package of diamonds, market value two million dollars, here in my hands by sunrise, London time, tomorrow. This call has been taped, for the record. Good day, Mr. Vice President."

He put the phone down. At the other end, for several minutes the Vice President of the United States of America used language that would have lost him the votes of the Moral Majority, had those good citizens had the opportunity to hear him. When he was done, he called the telephone operator.

"Get me Morton Stannard," he said. "At his home, wherever. Just *get him!*"

Andy Laing was surprised to be summoned back to the bank so quickly. The appointment was for 11:00 A.M. and he was there ten minutes early. When he was shown up, it was not to the office of the internal accountant, but to that of the general manager. The accountant was by the GM's side. The senior officer gestured Laing to a seat opposite his desk without a word. The man then rose, walked to the window, stared out for a while over the pinnacles of the City, turned and spoke. His tone was grave and frosty.

"Yesterday, Mr. Laing, you came to see my colleague here, having quit Saudi Arabia by whatever means you were able, and made serious allegations concerning the integrity of Mr. Steven Pyle."

Laing was worried. Mr. Laing? Where was "Andy"? They always first-named each other in the bank, part of the family atmosphere New York insisted on.

"And I brought a mass of computer printout to back up what I had found," he said carefully, but his stomach was churning. Something was wrong. The general manager waved dismissively at the mention of Laing's evidence.

"Yesterday I also received a long letter from Steve Pyle. Today I had a lengthy phone call. It is perfectly clear to me, and to the internal accountant here, that you are a rogue, Laing, and an embezzler."

Laing could not believe his ears. He shot a glance for support at the accountant. The man stared at the ceiling.

"I have the story," said the GM. "The full story. The *real* story."

In case Laing was unfamiliar with it, he told the young man what he now knew to be true. Laing had been embezzling money from a client's account, the Ministry of Public Works. Not a large amount in Saudi terms, but enough; one percent of every invoice paid out to contractors by the Ministry. Mr. Amin had unfortunately missed spotting the figures but Mr. Al-Haroun had seen the flaws and alerted Mr. Pyle.

The general manager at Riyadh, in an excess of loyalty, had tried to protect Laing's career by only insisting that every riyal be returned to the Ministry's account, something that had now been done.

Laing's response to this extraordinary solidarity from a colleague, and in outrage at losing his money, had been to spend the night in the Jiddah Branch falsifying the records to "prove" that a much larger sum had been embezzled with the cooperation of Steve Pyle himself.

"But the tape I brought back—" protested Laing.

"Forgeries, of course. We have the real records here. This morning I ordered our central computer here to hack into the Riyadh computer and do a check. The real records now lie there, on my desk. They show quite clearly what happened. The one percent you stole has been replaced. No other money is missing. The bank's reputation in Saudi Arabia has been saved, thank God—or, rather, thank Steve Pyle."

"But it's not true," protested Laing, too shrilly. "The skim Pyle and his unknown associate were perpetrating was *ten* percent of the Ministry accounts."

The GM looked stonily at Laing and then at the evidence fresh in from Riyadh.

"Al," he asked, "do you see any record of ten percent being skimmed?"

The accountant shook his head.

"That would be preposterous in any case," he said. "With such sums washing around, one percent might be hidden in a big Ministry in those parts. But never ten percent. The annual audit, due in April, would have uncovered the swindle. Then where would you have been? In a filthy Saudi jail cell forever. We do assume, do we not, that the Saudi Government will still be there next April?"

The GM gave a wintry smile. That was too obvious.

"No. I'm afraid," concluded the accountant, "that it's an open-and-shut case. Steve Pyle has not only done us all a favor, he has done you one, Mr. Laing. He's saved you from a long prison term."

"Which I believe you probably deserve," said the GM. "We can't inflict that in any case. And we don't relish the scandal. We supply contract officers to many Third World banks, and a scandal we do not need. But you, Mr. Laing, no longer constitute one of those bank officers. Your dismissal letter is in front of you. There will, of course, be no severance pay, and a reference is out of the question. Now please go."

Laing knew it was a sentence: never to work in banking ever again, anywhere in the world. Sixty seconds later he was on the pavement of Lombard Street.

In Washington, Morton Stannard had listened to the rage of Zack as the spools unwound on the conference table in the Situation Room.

The news out of London that an exchange was imminent, whether true or false, had galvanized a resurgence of press frenzy in Washington. Since before dawn the White House had been deluged with calls for information and once again the press secretary was at his wits' end.

When the tape finally ran out the eight members present were silent with shock.

"The diamonds," growled Odell. "You keep promising and promising. Where the hell are they?"

"They're ready," said Stannard promptly. "I apologize for my overoptimism earlier. I know nothing of such matters—I thought arranging such a consignment would take less time. But they are ready—just under twenty-five thousand mixed stones, all authentic and valued at just over two million dollars."

"Where are they?" asked Hubert Reed.

"In the safe of the head of the Pentagon office in New York, the office that handles our East Coast systems-purchasing. For obvious reasons, it's a very secure safe."

"What about shipment to London?" asked Brad Johnson. "I suggest we use one of our air bases in England. We don't need problems with the press at Heathrow, or anything like that."

"I am meeting in one hour with a senior Air Force expert," said Stannard. "He will advise how best to get the package there."

"We will need a Company car to meet them on arrival and get them to Quinn at the apartment," said Odell. "Lee, you arrange that. It's your apartment, after all."

"No problem," said Lee Alexander of the CIA.

"I'll have Lou Collins pick them up himself at the air base on touchdown."

"By dawn tomorrow, London time," said the Vice President. "In London, in Kensington, by dawn. We know the details of the exchange yet?"

"No," said the Director of the FBI. "No doubt Quinn will work out the details in conjunction with our people."

The U. S. Air Force proposed the use of a single-seat jet fighter to make the Atlantic crossing, an F-15 Eagle.

"It has the range if we fit it with FAST packs," the Air Force general told Morton Stannard at the Pentagon. "We must have the package delivered to the Air National Guard base at Trenton, New Jersey, no later than two P.M."

The pilot selected for the mission was an experienced lieutenant colonel with more than seven thousand flying hours on the F-15. Through the late morning the Eagle at Trenton was serviced as seldom before in her existence, and the FAST packs were fitted to each of the port and starboard air-intake trunks. These packs, despite their name, would not increase the Eagle's speed; the acronym stands for "fuel and sensor tactical," and they are really long-range extra fuel tanks.

Stripped down, the Eagle carries 23,000 pounds of fuel, giving her a ferry range of 2,878 miles; the extra 5,000 pounds in each FAST pack boost that to 3,450 miles.

In the navigation room Colonel Bowers studied his flight plan over a sandwich lunch. From Trenton to the USAF base at Upper Heyford outside the city of Oxford was 3,063 miles. The meteorology men told him the wind strengths at his chosen altitude of 50,000 feet, and he worked out that he would make it in 5.4 hours flying at Mach .95 and would still have 4,300 pounds of fuel remaining.

At 2:00 P.M. a big KC-135 tanker lifted off from Andrews Air Force Base outside Washington and headed for a midair rendezvous at 45,000 feet over the eastern seaboard with the Eagle.

At Trenton there was one last holdup. Colonel Bowers was in his flying suit by three o'clock, and ready to go, when the long black limousine from the Pentagon's New York bureau came through the main gate. A civilian official, accompanied by an Air Force general, handed over a plain flat attaché case and a slip of paper with the number of the combination lock.

Hardly had he done so when another unmarked limousine entered the base. There was a flustered conference on the tarmac between two groups of officials. Eventually the attaché case and the slip of paper were retrieved from Colonel Bowers and taken to the rear seat of one of the cars.

The attaché case was opened and its contents, a flat pack of black velvet, ten inches by twelve inches and three inches thick, was transferred to a new attaché case. This was the one that was handed to the impatient colonel.

Interceptor fighters are not accustomed to hauling freight, but a storage space had been prepared right beneath the pilot's seat, and it was here the attaché case was slotted. The colonel lifted off at 3:31 P.M.

He climbed rapidly to 45,000 feet, called up his tanker, and topped off his fuel tanks to begin the run for England with a full load. After fueling he nosed up to 50,000 feet, turned to his compass course for Upper Heyford, and boosted power to settle at Mach .95, just below the shudder zone that marks the sound barrier. He caught his expected westerly tailwind over Nantucket.

While the conference was still continuing on the tarmac at Trenton, a scheduled airlines jumbo jet had taken off from Kennedy for London Heathrow. In the business class section was a tall and clean-cut young man who had caught the flight after connecting from Houston. He worked for a major oil corporation there called Pan-Global and felt he was privileged to be entrusted by his employer, the proprietor himself, with such a discreet mission.

Not that he had the faintest idea of the contents of the envelope he carried within the breast pocket of the jacket he declined to hand over to the stewardess. Nor did he wish to know. He only knew it must contain documents of great corporate sensitivity, since it could not be mailed or faxed or sent by commercial courier pouch.

His instructions were clear; he had repeated them many times. He was to go to a certain address on a certain day—the following day—at a certain hour. He was not to ring the bell, just drop the envelope through the letter slot, then return to Heathrow Airport and Houston. Tiring but simple. Cocktails were being served, before dinner; he did not drink alcohol, so he gazed out the window.

Flying west to east on a winter's day, one meets the darkness quickly. After just two hours in the air he saw that the sky had turned a deep purple and the stars were clearly visible. As he watched he saw, high above his own aircraft, a small pinpoint of red fire moving through the band of stars, heading the same way as he. Though he did not know it, he was looking at the blazing jetpipe of Colonel Bowers's F-15 Eagle as both men raced on different missions toward the British capital, neither man knowing what it was he carried.

The colonel got there first. He touched down at Upper Heyford right on schedule at 1:55 A.M. local time, disturbing the sleep of the villagers beneath him as he made his final turn into the approach lights. The tower told him which way to taxi and he finally stopped in a bright ring of lights inside a hangar whose doors closed the moment he shut down his engines. When he opened the canopy the base commander approached with a civilian. It was the civilian who spoke.

"Colonel Bowers?"

"That's me, sir."

"You have a package for me?"

"I have an attaché case. Right under my seat."

He stretched stiffly, climbed out, and clambered down the steel ladder to the hangar floor. Helluva way to see England, he thought. The civilian went up the ladder and retrieved the attaché case. He held out his hand for the combination code. Ten minutes later Lou Collins was back in his Company limousine, heading toward London. He reached the Kensington apartment at ten minutes after four. The lights still burned; no one had slept. Quinn was in the sitting room drinking coffee.

Collins laid the attaché case on the low table, consulted the slip of paper, and tumbled the rollers. From the case he took the flat, near-square, velvet-wrapped package and handed it to Quinn.

"In your hands, by dawn," he said. Quinn hefted the pack in his hands. Just over a kilogram—about three pounds.

"You want to open it?" asked Collins.

"No need," said Quinn. "If they are glass, or paste, or any part of them are, or any one of them, someone will probably blow away Simon Cormack's life."

"They wouldn't do that," said Collins. "No, they're genuine all right. Do you think he'll call?"

"Just pray he does," said Quinn.

"And the exchange?"

"We'll have to arrange it today."

"How are you going to handle it, Quinn?"

"My way."

He went off to his room to take a bath and dress. For quite a lot of people the last day of October was going to be a very rough day indeed.

The young man from Houston landed at 6:45 A.M. London time and, with only a small suitcase of toiletries, moved quickly through customs and into the concourse of Number Three Building. He checked his watch and knew he had three hours to wait. Time to use the washroom, freshen up, have breakfast, and take a cab to the center of London's West End.

At 9:55 he presented himself at the door of the tall and impressive apartment house a block back from Great Portland Street in the Marble Arch district. He was five minutes early. He had been told to be exact. From across the street a man in a parked car watched him, but he did not know that. He strolled up and down for five minutes, then, on the dot of ten, dropped the fat envelope through the letter slot of the apartment house. There was no hall porter to pick it up. It lay there on the mat inside the door. Satisfied that he had done as he had been instructed, the young American walked back down to Bayswater Road and soon hailed a cab for Heathrow.

Hardly was he around the corner than the man in the parked car climbed out, crossed the road, and let himself into the apartment house. He lived there—had done for several weeks. His sojourn in the car was simply to assure himself that the messenger responded to the given description and had not been followed.

The man picked up the fallen envelope, took the lift to the eighth floor, let himself into his apartment, and slit open the envelope. He was satisfied as he read, and his breath came in snuffles, whistling through the distorted nasal passages as he breathed. Irving Moss now had what he believed would be his final instructions.

· · ·

In the Kensington apartment the morning ticked away in silence. The tension was almost tangible. In the telephone exchange, in Cork Street, in Grosvenor Square, the listeners sat hunched over their machines waiting for Quinn to say something or McCrea or Sam Somerville to open their mouths. There was silence on the speakers. Quinn had made it plain that if Zack did not call, it was over. The careful search for an abandoned house and a body would have to begin.

And Zack did not call.

At half past ten Irving Moss left his Marble Arch flat, took his rental car from its parking bay, and drove to Paddington Station. His beard, grown in Houston during the planning stages, had changed the shape of his face. His Canadian passport was beautifully forged and had brought him effortlessly into the Republic of Ireland and thence on the ferry to England. His driving license, also Canadian, had caused no problems in the renting of a compact car on long-term lease. He had lived quietly and unobtrusively for weeks behind Marble Arch, one of more than a million foreigners in the British capital.

He was a skilled enough agent to be able to drop into almost any city and disappear from view. London, in any case, he knew. He knew how things worked in London, where to go to obtain what he wanted or needed, had contacts with the underworld, was smart enough and experienced enough not to make mistakes of the kind that draw a visitor to the attention of the authorities.

His letter from Houston had been an update, filling in a range of details that it had not been possible to fit into coded messages to and from Houston in the form of price lists of market produce. There were also further instructions in the letter, but most interesting of all was the situation report from within the West Wing of the White House, notably the state of deterioration that President John Cormack had suffered these past three weeks.

Finally there was the ticket for the left-luggage office at Paddington Station, something that could only cross the Atlantic by hand. How it had got from London to Houston he did not know or want to know. He did not need to know. He knew how it had come back to London, to him, and now it was in his hand. At 11:00 A.M. he used it.

The British Rail staffer thought nothing of it. In the course of a day hundreds of packages, grips, and suitcases were consigned to his office for safekeeping, and hundreds more withdrawn. Only after being unclaimed for three months would a package be taken off the shelves and opened, for disposal if it could not be identified. The ticket presented that morning by the silent man in the medium-gray gabardine raincoat was just another ticket. He ranged along his shelves, found the numbered item, a small fiber suitcase, and handed it over. It was prepaid anyway. He would not remember the transaction by nightfall.

Moss took the case back to his apartment, forced the cheap locks, and examined the contents. They were all there, as he had been told they would be. He checked his watch. He had three hours before he need set off.

There was a house set in a quiet road on the outskirts of a commuter town not forty miles from the center of London. At a certain time he would drive past that house, as he did every second day, and the position of his driver's window—fully up, half lowered, or fully down—would convey to the watcher the thing he needed to know. This day, for the first time, the window would be in the fully down position. He slotted one of his locally acquired S&M videotapes—ultra hard core, but he knew where to go for his supplies—into his television and settled back to enjoy himself.

When Andy Laing left the bank he was almost in a state of shock. Few men go through the experience of seeing an entire career, worked on and nurtured through years of effort, scattered in small and irrecoverable pieces at their feet. The first reaction is incomprehension; the second, indecision.

Laing wandered aimlessly through the narrow streets and hidden courtyards that hide between the roaring traffic of the City of London, the capital's most ancient square mile and center of the country's commercial and banking world. He passed the walls of monasteries that once echoed to the chants of the Greyfriars, the Whitefriars, and the Blackfriars, past guildhalls where merchants had convened to discuss the business of the world when Henry VIII was executing his wives down the road at the Tower, past delicate little churches designed by Wren in the aftermath of the Great Fire of 1666.

The men who scurried past him, and the increasingly large number of attractive young women, were thinking of commodity prices, buying long or short, or a flicker of movement in the money markets that might be a trend or just a flicker. They used computers instead of quill pens, but the outcome of their labors was still what it had been for centuries: trade, the buying and selling of things that other people made. It was a world that had captured Andy Laing's imagination ten years before, when he was just finishing school, and it was a world he would never enter again.

He had a light lunch in a small sandwich bar off the street called Crutched Friars, where monks once hobbled with one leg bound behind them to cause pain for the greater glory of God, and he made up his mind what he would do.

He finished his coffee and took the underground back to his studio apartment in Beaufort Street, Chelsea, where he had prudently stored photocopies of the evidence he had brought out of Jiddah. When a man has nothing more to lose, he can become very dangerous. Laing decided to write it all down, from start to finish, to include copies of *his* print-outs, which he knew to be genuine, and to send a copy to every member of the bank's board of directors in New York. The membership of the board was public knowledge; their business addresses would be in the American *Who's Who*.

He saw no reason why he should suffer in silence. Let Steve Pyle do some worrying for a change, he thought. So he sent the general manager in Riyadh a personal letter telling him what he was going to do.

Zack finally rang at 1:20 P.M., the height of the lunchtime rush hour, while Laing was finishing his coffee, and Moss was entranced by a new child-abuse movie fresh in from Amsterdam. Zack was in one of a bank of four public booths set into the rear wall of Dunstable post office—as always, north of London.

Quinn had been dressed and ready since sunup, and that day there really was a sun to see, shining brightly out of a blue sky with only a hint of cool in the air. Whether he was feeling the cold neither McCrea nor Sam had thought to ask, but he had put on jeans, his new cashmere sweater over his shirt, and a zip-up leather jacket.

"Quinn, this is the last call—"

"Zack, old buddy, I am staring at a fruit bowl, a big bowl, and you know what? It's full to the damn brim with diamonds, glittering and gleaming away like they were alive. Let's deal, Zack. Let's deal now."

The mental image he had drawn stopped Zack in his tracks.

"Right," said the voice on the phone. "These are the instructions—"

"No, Zack. We do this my way or it all gets blown to Kingdom come. . . ."

In the Kensington exchange, in Cork Street and Grosvenor Square, there was stunned silence among the listeners. Either Quinn knew just what he was doing or he was going to provoke the kidnapper into putting down the phone. Quinn's voice went on without a pause.

"I may be a bastard, Zack, but I'm the only bastard in this whole damn mess you can trust and you're going to have to trust me. Got a pencil?"

"Yeah. Now listen, Quinn—"

"You listen, buddy. I want you to move to another booth and call me in forty seconds on this number. Three-seven-oh; one-two-oh-four. Now GO!"

The last word was a shout. Sam Somerville and Duncan McCrea would later tell the inquiry that they were as stunned as those listening on the line. Quinn slammed down the phone, grabbed the attaché case—the diamonds were still inside it, not in a fruit bowl—and ran out the sitting-room door. He turned as he went and roared, "Stay there!"

The surprise, the shout, the authority in his command, kept them pinned in their chairs for a vital five seconds. When they reached the apartment's front door they heard the key turn in the lock on the far side. Apparently it had been placed there in the predawn.

Quinn avoided the elevator and hit the stairs about the time McCrea's first shout came through the door, followed by a hefty kick at the lock. Among the listeners there was already a nascent chaos that would soon grow to pandemonium.

"What the hell's he doing?" whispered one policeman to another at the Kensington exchange, to be met by a shrug. Quinn was racing down the three flights of stairs to the lobby level. The inquiry would show that the American at the listening post in the basement apartment did not move because it was not his job to move. His job was to keep the stream of voices from inside the apartment above him recorded, encoded, radioed to Grosvenor Square for decoding and digestion by the listeners in the basement. So he stayed where he was.

Quinn crossed the lobby fifteen seconds after slamming down the phone. The British porter in his booth looked up, nodded, and went back to his copy of the *Daily Mirror*. Quinn pushed open the street door, which opened outward, closed it behind him, dropped a wooden wedge—which he had carved in the privacy of the toilet—under the sill and gave it a hard kick. Then he ran across the road, dodging the traffic.

"What do they mean, he's gone?" shouted Kevin Brown in the listening post at Grosvenor Square. He had been sitting there all morning, waiting, as they all were, British and Americans alike, for Zack's latest and maybe last call. At first the sounds coming from Kensington had been merely confusing; they heard the phone cut off, heard Quinn shout "Stay there!" at someone, then a series of bangs, confused shouts and cries from McCrea and Somerville, then a series of regular bangs, as if someone was kicking a door.

Sam Somerville had come back into the room, shouting at the bugs: "He's gone! Quinn's gone!" Brown's question could be heard in the listening post but not by Somerville. Frantically Brown scrambled for the phone that would connect him with his special agent in Kensington.

"Agent Somerville," he boomed when he heard her on the line, "get after him."

At that moment McCrea's fifth kick broke the lock on the apartment door. He raced for the stairs, followed by Sam. Both were in bedroom slippers.

The greengrocer's shop and delicatessen across the street from the apartment, whose number Quinn had obtained from the London telephone directory in the sitting-room cabinet, was called Bradshaw, after the man who had started it, but was now owned by an Indian gentleman called Mr. Patel. Quinn had watched him from across the street, tending his exterior fruit display or disappearing inside to attend to a customer.

Quinn hit the opposite pavement thirty-three seconds after ending his call from Zack. He dodged two pedestrians and came through the doorway into the food shop like a tornado. The telephone was on the cash desk, next to the register, behind which stood Mr. Patel.

"Those kids are stealing your oranges," said Quinn without ceremony. At that moment the phone rang. Torn between a telephone call and stolen oranges, Mr. Patel reacted like a good Gujarati and ran outside. Quinn picked up the receiver.

The Kensington exchange had reacted fast, and the inquiry would show they had done their best. But they lost several of the forty seconds through sheer surprise, then had a technical problem. Their lock was on the flash line in the apartment. Whenever a call came into that number, their electronic exchange could run back up the line to establish the source of the call. The number it came from would then be revealed by the computer to be such-and-such a booth in a certain place. Between six and ten seconds.

They already had a lock on the number Zack had used first, but when he changed booths, even though the kiosks were side by side in Dunstable, they lost him. Worse, he was now ringing another London number into which they were not tapped. The only saving grace was that the number Quinn had dictated on the line to Zack was still on the Kensington exchange. Still, the tracers had to start at the beginning, their call-finder mechanism racing frantically through the twenty thousand numbers on the exchange. They tapped into Mr. Patel's phone fifty-eight seconds after Quinn had dictated the number, then got a lock on the second number in Dunstable.

"Take this number, Zack," said Quinn without preamble.

"What the hell's going on?" snarled Zack.

"Nine-three-five; three-two-one-five," said Quinn remorselessly. "Got it?"

There was a pause as Zack scribbled.

"Now we'll do it ourselves, Zack. I've walked out on the lot of them. Just you and me; the diamonds against the boy. No tricks—my word on it. Call me on that number in sixty minutes, and ninety minutes if there's no reply first time. It's not on trace."

He put the phone down. In the exchange the listeners heard the words ". . .minutes, and ninety minutes if there's no reply first time. It's not on trace."

"Bastard's given him another number," said the engineer in Kensington to the two Metropolitan officers with him. One of them was already on the phone to the Yard.

Quinn came out of the shop to see Duncan McCrea across the road trying to push his way through the jammed street door. Sam was behind him, waving and gesticulating. The porter joined them, scratching his thinning hair. Two cars went down the street on the opposite side; on Quinn's side a motorcyclist was approaching. Quinn stepped into the road, right in the man's path, his arms raised, attaché case swinging from his left hand. The motorcyclist braked, swerved, skidded, and slithered to a stop.

"'Ere, wot on erf . . ."

Quinn gave him a disarming smile as he ducked around the handlebars. The short, hard kidney punch completed the job. As the youth in the crash helmet doubled over, Quinn hoisted him off his machine, swung his own right leg over it, engaged gear, and gunned the engine. He went off down the street just as McCrea's flailing hand missed his jacket by six inches.

McCrea stood in the street, dejected. Sam joined him. They looked at each other, then ran back into the apartment building. The fastest way to talk to Grosvenor Square was to get back to the third floor.

"Right, that's it," said Brown five minutes later, after listening to both McCrea and Somerville on the line from Kensington. "We find that bastard. That's the job."

Another phone rang. It was Nigel Cramer from Scotland Yard.

"Your negotiator has done a bunk," he said flatly. "Can you tell me how? I've tried the apartment—the usual number is engaged."

Brown told him in thirty seconds. Cramer grunted. He still resented the Green Meadow Farm affair, and always would, but events had now overtaken his desire to see Brown and the FBI team off his patch.

"Did your people get the number of that motorcycle?" he asked. "I can put out an all-points on it."

"Better than that," said Brown with satisfaction. "That attaché case he's carrying. It contains a direction finder."

"It *what*?"

"Built in, undetectable, state-of-the-art," said Brown. "We had it fitted out in the States, changed it for the case provided by the Pentagon just before takeoff last night."

"I see," said Cramer thoughtfully. "And the receiver?"

"Right here," said Brown. "Came in on the morning commercial flight at dawn. One of my boys went out to Heathrow to pick it up. Range two miles, so we have to move. I mean right now."

"This time, Mr. Brown, will you please stay in touch with the Met.'s squad cars? You do not make arrests in this City. I do. Your car has radio?"

"Sure."

"Stay on open line, please. We'll patch in on you and join you if you tell us where you are."

"No problem. You have my word on it."

The embassy limousine swept out of Grosvenor Square sixty seconds later. Chuck Moxon drove; his colleague beside him operated the D/F receiver, a small box like a miniature television set, save that on the screen in place of a picture was a single glowing dot. When the antenna now clipped to the metal rim above the passenger door heard the blip emitted from the D/F transmitter in Quinn's attaché case, a line would race out from the glowing dot to the perimeter of the screen. The car's driver would have to maneuver so that the line on the screen pointed dead ahead of his car's nose. He would then be following the direction finder. The device in the attaché case would be activated by remote control from inside the limousine.

They drove fast down Park Lane, through Knightsbridge, and into Kensington.

"Activate," said Brown. The operator depressed a switch. The screen did not respond.

"Keep activating every thirty seconds until we get lock-on," said Brown. "Chuck, start to sweep around Kensington."

Moxon took the Cromwell Road, then headed south down Gloucester Road toward Old Brompton Road. The antenna got a lock.

"He's behind us, heading north," said Moxon's colleague. "Range, about a mile and a quarter."

Thirty seconds later Moxon was back across the Cromwell Road, heading north up Exhibition Road toward Hyde Park.

"Dead ahead, running north," said the operator.

"Tell the boys in blue we have him," said Brown. Moxon informed the embassy by radio, and halfway up Edgware Road a Metropolitan Police Rover closed up behind them.

In the back with Brown were Collins and Seymour.

"Should have known," said Collins regretfully. "Should have spotted the time gap."

"What time gap?" asked Seymour.

"You recall that snarl-up in the Winfield House driveway three weeks back? Quinn set off fifteen minutes before me but arrived in Kensington three minutes ahead. I can't beat a London cabbie in rush-hour traffic. He paused somewhere, made some preparations."

"He couldn't have planned this three weeks ago," objected Seymour. "He didn't know how things would pan out."

"Didn't have to," said Collins. "You've read his file. Been in combat long enough to know about fallback positions in case things go wrong."

"He's pulled a right into St. John's Wood," said the operator.

At Lord's roundabout the police car came alongside, its window down.

"He's heading north up there," said Moxon, pointing up the Finchley Road. The two cars were joined by another squad car and headed north through Swiss Cottage, Hendon, and Mill Hill. The range decreased to three hundred yards and they scanned the traffic ahead for a tall man wearing no crash helmet, on a small motorcycle.

They went through Mill Hill Circus just a hundred yards behind the bleeper and up the slope to Five Ways Corner. Then they realized Quinn must have changed vehicles again. They passed two motorcyclists who emitted no bleep, and two powerful motorbikes overtook them, but the D/F finder they sought was still proceeding steadily ahead of them. When the bleep turned around Five Ways Corner onto the A.1 to Hertfordshire, they saw that their target was now an open-topped Volkswagen Golf GTi whose driver wore a thick fur hat to cover his head and ears.

The first thing Cyprian Fothergill recalled about the events of that day was that as he headed toward his charming little cottage in the countryside behind Borehamwood he was suddenly overtaken by a huge black car that swerved violently in front of him, forcing him to scream to a stop in a lay-by. Within seconds three big men, he would later tell his open-mouthed friends at the club, had leaped out, surrounded his car, and were pointing enormous guns at him. Then a police car pulled in behind, then another one, and four lovely bobbies got out and told the Americans—well they must have been Americans, and *huge*, they were—to put their guns away or be disarmed.

The next thing he knew—by this time he would have the undivided attention of the *entire* bar—one of the Americans tore his fur hat off and screamed "Okay, craphead, where is he?" while one of the bobbies reached into the open back seat and pulled out an attaché case that he had to spend an hour telling them he had never seen before.

The big gray-haired American, who seemed to be in charge of his party from the black car, grabbed the case from the bobby's hands, flicked the locks, and looked inside. It was empty. After all that, it was empty. Such a terrifying fuss over an empty case . . . Anyway, the Americans were swearing like troopers, using language that he, Cyprian, had never heard before and hoped never to hear again. Then in stepped the British sergeant, who was quite out of this world. . . .

At 2:25 P.M. Sergeant Kidd returned to his patrol car to answer the insistent calls coming through for him on the radio.

"Tango Alpha," he began.

"Tango Alpha, this is Deputy Assistant Commissioner Cramer. Who's that?"

"Sergeant Kidd, sir. F Division."

"What have you got, Sergeant?"

Kidd glanced across at the cornered Volkswagen, its terrified inhabitant, the three FBI men examining the empty attaché case, two more Yankees standing back and staring hopefully at the sky, and three of his colleagues trying to take statements.

"Bit of a mess, sir."

"Sergeant Kidd, listen carefully. Have you captured a very tall American who has just stolen two million dollars?"

"No, sir," said Kidd. "We've captured a very gay hairdresser who's just wet his pants."

"What do you mean . . . disappeared?" The cry, shout, or yell, in a variety of tones and accents, was within an hour echoing around a Kensington apartment, Scotland Yard, Whitehall, the Home Office, Downing Street, Grosvenor Square, and the West Wing of the White House. "He can't just disappear."

But he had.

CHAPTER TEN

Quinn had dropped the attaché case into the open back of the Golf only thirty seconds after swerving around the corner of the street containing the apartment house. When he had opened the case as Lou Collins presented it to him before dawn, he had not seen any direction-finding device, but did not expect to. Whoever had worked on the case in the laboratory would have been smarter than to leave any traces of the implant visible. Quinn had gambled on there being something inside the case to lead police and troops to whatever rendezvous he established with Zack.

Waiting at a traffic light, he had flicked open the locks, stuffed the package of diamonds inside his zipped leather jacket, and looked around. The Golf was standing next to him. The driver, muffled in his fur hat, had not noticed a thing.

Half a mile later Quinn abandoned the motorcycle; without the legally obligatory crash helmet, he was likely to attract the attention of a policeman. Outside the Brompton Oratory he hailed a cab, directed it to Marylebone, and paid it off in George Street, completing his journey on foot.

His pockets contained all he had been able to abstract from the apartment without attracting attention: his U. S. passport and driver's license—though these would soon be useless when the alert went out—a wad of British money from Sam's purse, his multibladed penknife, and a pair of pliers from the fuse cupboard. A chemist's shop in Marylebone High Street had yielded a pair of plain-glass spectacles with heavy horn rims; and a men's outfitters, a tweed hat and Burberry.

He made a number of further purchases at a confectioner's, a hardware shop, and a luggage store. He checked his watch: fifty-five minutes from the time he had replaced the phone in Mr. Patel's fruit store. He turned into Blandford Street and found the call box he sought on the corner of Chiltern Street, one of a bank of two. He took the second, whose number he had memorized three weeks earlier and dictated to Zack an hour before. It rang right on time.

Zack was wary, uncomprehending, and angry. "All right, you bastard, what the hell are you up to?"

In a few short sentences Quinn explained what he had done. Zack listened in silence.

"Are you leveling?" he asked. "'Cos if you ain't, that kid is still going to end up in a body bag."

"Look, Zack, I frankly don't give a shit whether they capture you or not. I have one concern and one only: to get that kid back to his family alive and well. And I have inside my jacket two million dollars' worth of raw diamonds I figure interest you. Now, I've thrown the bloodhounds off because they wouldn't stop interfering, trying to be smart. So, do you want to set up an exchange or not?"

"Time's up," said Zack. "I'm moving."

"This happens to be a public phone in Marylebone," said Quinn, "but you're right not to trust it. Call me, same number, this evening with the details. I'll come, alone, unarmed, with the stones, wherever. Because I'm on the lam, make it after dark. Say, eight o'clock."

"All right," growled Zack. "Be there."

It was the moment Sergeant Kidd took his car's radio mike to talk to Nigel Cramer. Minutes later every police station in the metropolitan area was receiving a description of a man and instructions for every beat officer to keep an eye open, to spot but not approach, to radio back to the police station, and tail the suspect but not intervene. There was no name appended to the all-points, nor a reason why the man was wanted.

Leaving the phone booth, Quinn walked back into Blandford Street and down to Blackwood's Hotel. It was one of those old established inns tucked away into the side streets of London that have somehow avoided being bought and sanitized by the big chains, an ivy-covered twenty-room place with paneling and bay windows and a fire blazing in the brick hearth of a reception area furnished in rugs over uneven boards. Quinn approached the pleasant-looking girl behind the desk.

"Hi, there," he said, with his widest grin.

She looked up and smiled back. Tall, stooping, tweed hat, Burberry, and calfskin grip—an all-American tourist.

"Good afternoon, sir. Can I help you?"

"Well, now, I hope so, miss. Yes, I surely do. You see, I just flew in from the States and I took your British Airways—my all-time favorite airline—and you know what they did? They lost my luggage. Yes, ma'am, sent it all the way to Frankfurt by mistake."

Her face puckered with concern.

"Now, see here, they're going to get it back for me, twenty-four hours tops. Only my problem is, all my package-tour details were in my small suitcase, and would you believe it, I cannot for the life of me recall where I am checked in. Spent an hour with that lady from the airline going over names of hotels in London—you know how many there are?—but no way can I recall it, not till my suitcase reaches me. So the bottom line is, I took a cab into town and the driver said this was a real nice place . . . er . . . would you by any chance have a room I could take for the night? By the way, I'm Harry Russell."

She was quite entranced. The tall man looked so bereft at the loss of his luggage, his inability to recall where he was supposed to be staying. She watched a lot of movies and thought he looked a bit like that gentleman who was always asking people to make his day, but he talked like the man with the funny bird-feather in his hat from *Dallas*. It never occurred to her not to believe him, or even to ask for identification. Blackwood's did not normally take guests with neither luggage nor reservation, but losing one's luggage, *and* forgetting one's hotel, and because of a British airline . . . She scanned the vacancy sheet; most of their guests were regulars up from the provinces, and a few permanent residents.

"There's just the one, Mr. Russell—a small one at the back, I'm afraid . . ."

"That will suit me just fine, young lady. Oh, I can pay cash—changed me some dollars right in the airport."

"Tomorrow morning, Mr. Russell." She reached for an old brass key. "Up the stairs, on the second floor."

Quinn went up the stairs with their uneven treads, found Number

Eleven, and let himself in. Small, clean, and comfortable. More than adequate. He stripped to his shorts, set the alarm clock he had bought in the hardware store for 6:00 P.M., and slept.

"Well, what on earth did he do it for?" asked the Home Secretary, Sir Harry Marriott. He had just heard the full story from Nigel Cramer in his office atop the Home Office building. He had had ten minutes on the telephone with Downing Street, and the lady resident there was not very pleased.

"I suspect he did not feel he could trust someone," said Cramer delicately.

"Not us, I hope," said the Minister. "We've done everything we can."

"No, not us," said Cramer. "He was moving close to an exchange with this man Zack. In a kidnap case, that is always the most dangerous phase. It has to be handled with extreme delicacy. After those two leaks of privy information on radio programs, one French and one British, he seems to feel he'd prefer to handle it himself. We can't allow that, of course. We have to find him, Home Secretary."

Cramer still smarted from having the primacy in the handling of the negotiation process removed from his control at all, and being confined to the investigation.

"Can't think how he escaped in the first place," complained the Home Secretary.

"If I'd had two of my men inside that apartment, he wouldn't have done," Cramer reminded him.

"Yes, well, that's water over the dam. Find the man, but quietly, discreetly."

The Home Secretary's private views were that if this Quinn fellow could recover Simon Cormack alone, well and good. Britain could ship them both home to America as quickly as possible. But if the Americans were going to make a mess of it, let it be their mess, not his.

At the same hour, Irving Moss received a telephone call from Houston. He jotted down the list of produce prices on offer from the vegetable gardens of Texas, put down the phone, and decoded the message. Then he whistled in amazement. The more he thought about it, the more he realized that only a slight change would need to be made to his own plans.

· · ·

After the fiasco on the road outside Mill Hill, Kevin Brown had descended on the Kensington apartment in high temper. Patrick Seymour and Lou Collins came with him. Together the three senior men debriefed their two junior colleagues for several hours.

Sam Somerville and Duncan McCrea explained at length what had happened that morning, how it had happened, and why they had not foreseen it. McCrea, as ever, was disarmingly apologetic.

"If he has reestablished phone contact with Zack, he's totally out of control," said Brown. "If they're using a phone-booth-to-phone-booth system, there's no way the British can get a tap on it. We don't know what they're up to."

"Maybe they're arranging to exchange Simon Cormack for the diamonds," said Seymour.

Brown growled.

"When this thing's over, I'm going to have that smartass."

"If he returns with Simon Cormack," Collins pointed out, "we're all going to be happy to carry his bags to the airport."

It was agreed that Somerville and McCrea would stay on at the apartment in case Quinn called in. The three phone lines would remain open to take his call, and tapped. The senior men returned to the embassy, Seymour to liaise with Scotland Yard on progress on what had now become two searches instead of one, the others to wait and listen.

Quinn woke at six, washed and shaved with the new toiletries he had bought in the High Street the previous day, had a light supper, and chanced the two-hundred-yard walk back to the phone booth in Chiltern Street at ten to eight. There was an old lady in it, but she left at five to eight. Quinn stood in the booth facing away from the street pretending to consult the telephone directories until the machine rang at two minutes after eight.

"Quinn?"

"Yeah."

"You may be on the level about having quit them, or maybe not. If it's a trick, you'll pay for it."

"No trick. Tell me where and when to show up."

"Ten tomorrow morning. I'll call you on this number at nine and tell you where. You'll have just enough time to get there by ten. My men will have had the place staked out since dawn. If the fuzz shows up, or the SAS; if there's any movement around the place at all, we'll spot it and pull out. Simon Cormack will die a phone call later. You'll never see us; we'll see you, or anyone else that shows up. If you're trying to trick me, tell your pals that. They might get one of us, or two, but it'll be too late for the boy."

"You got it, Zack. I come alone. No tricks."

"No electronic devices, no direction finders, no microphones. We'll check you out. If you're wired up, the boy gets it."

"Just what I said, no tricks. Just me and the diamonds."

"Be there in that phone box at nine."

There was a click and the line buzzed. Quinn left the booth and walked back to his hotel. He watched television for a while, then emptied his grip and worked for two hours on his purchases of that afternoon. It was two in the morning when he was satisfied.

He showered again to get rid of the telltale smell, set the clock, then lay on his bed and stared at the ceiling, quite immobile, thinking. He never slept much before combat; that was why he had caught three hours' rest during the afternoon. He catnapped just before dawn and rose when the alarm went off at seven.

The charming receptionist was on duty when he approached the desk at half past eight. He was dressed in his heavy-rimmed eyeglasses and tweed hat, and the Burberry was buttoned to the throat. He explained he had to go to Heathrow to collect his luggage, and he would like to settle up and check out.

At quarter to nine he sauntered up the street to the phone booth. There could be no old ladies this time. He stood in it for fifteen minutes, until it rang on the dot of nine. Zack's voice was husky with his own tension.

"Jamaica Road, Rotherhithe," he said.

Quinn did not know the area, but he knew of it. The old docks, partly converted to smart new houses and flats for the Yuppies who worked in the City, but with areas still near-derelict, abandoned wharves and warehouses.

"Go on."

Zack gave the directions. Off Jamaica Road down a street leading to the Thames.

"It's a single-story steel warehouse, open at both ends. The name Babbidge still written over the doors. Pay off the cab at the top of the street. Walk down alone. Go in the south entrance. Walk to the center of the floor and wait. Anyone follows, we don't show."

The phone went dead. Quinn left the booth and dropped his empty calfskin grip into a trash can. He looked around for a cab. Nothing, the morning rush hour. He caught one ten minutes later in Marylebone

High Street and was dropped at Marble Arch underground station. At that hour a cab would be ages getting through the twisting streets of the old City and across the Thames to Rotherhithe.

He took the underground due east to the Bank, then the Northern Line under the Thames to London Bridge. It was a main-line railway station; there were cabs waiting in front. He was in Jamaica Road fifty-five minutes after Zack had hung up.

The street he had been told to walk down was narrow, dirty, and empty. To one side, derelict tea warehouses, ripe for development, fronted the river. To the other, abandoned factories and steel sheds. He knew he was being watched from somewhere. He walked along the center of the street. The steel hangar with the faded painted name of Babbidge above one door was at the end. He turned inside.

Two hundred feet long, eighty wide. Rusted chains hung from roof girders; the floor was concrete, fouled by the windswept detritus of years of abandonment. The door he had entered by would take a pedestrian but not a vehicle; the one at the far end was wide enough and high enough to take a truck. He walked to the middle of the floor and stopped. He took off the phony eyeglasses and tweed hat and stuffed them in his pocket. He would not need them again. Either he walked out of here with a deal for Simon Cormack, or he would need a police escort anyway.

He waited an hour, quite immobile. At eleven o'clock the big Volvo appeared at the far end of the hangar and drove slowly toward him, coming to a stop with its engine running forty feet away. There were two men in the front, both masked so that only their eyes showed through the slits.

He sensed more than heard the scuffle of running shoes on concrete behind him and threw a casual glance over his shoulder. A third man stood there; black track suit without insignia, ski mask covering the head. He was alert, poised on the balls of his feet, with the submachine carbine held easily, at the port but ready for use if need be.

The passenger door of the Volvo opened and a man got out. Medium height, medium build.

He called: "Quinn?"

Zack's voice. Unmistakable.

"You got the diamonds?"

"Right here."

"Hand them over."

"You got the kid, Zack?"

"Don't be a fool. Trade him for a sack of glass pebbles? We examine the stones first. Takes time. One piece of glass, one piece of paste— you've blown it. If they're okay, then you get the boy."

"That's what I figured. Won't work."

"Don't play games with me, Quinn."

"No games, Zack. I have to see the kid. You could get pieces of glass—you won't, but you want to be sure. I could get a corpse."

"You won't."

"I need to be sure. That's why I have to go with you."

Behind the mask Zack stared at Quinn in disbelief. He gave a grating laugh.

"See that man behind you? One word and he blows you away. Then we take the stones anyway."

"You could try," admitted Quinn. "Ever seen one of these?"

He opened his raincoat all the way down, took something that hung free from near his waist and held it up.

Zack studied Quinn and the assembly strapped to his chest over his shirt, and swore softly but violently.

From below his sternum to his waist, Quinn's front was occupied by the flat wooden box of what had once contained liqueur chocolates. The bonbons were gone, along with the box's lid. The tray of the box formed a flat container strapped with surgical tape across his chest.

In the center was the velour package of diamonds, framed on each side by a half-pound block of tacky beige substance. Jammed into one of the blocks was a bright-green electrical wire, the other end of which ran to one of the spring-controlled jaws of the wooden clothespin Quinn held aloft in his left hand. It went through a tiny hole bored in the wood, to emerge inside the jaws of the peg.

Also in the chocolate box was a PP3 nine-volt battery, wired to another bright green cord. In one direction the green cord linked both blocks of beige substance to the battery; in the other direction the wire ran to the opposite jaw of the clothespin. The jaws of the pin were held apart by a stub of pencil. Quinn flexed the fingers of his hand; the stub of pencil fell to the floor.

"Phony," said Zack without conviction. "That's not real."

With his right hand Quinn twisted off a blob of the light-brown substance, rolled it into a ball, and tossed it across the floor to Zack. The criminal stooped, picked it up, and sniffed. The odor of marzipan filled his nostrils.

"Semtex," he said.

"That's Czech," said Quinn. "I prefer RDX."

Zack knew enough to know all explosive gelatins both look and smell like the harmless confection marzipan. There the difference ends. If his man opened fire now they would all die. There was enough plastic explosive in that box to clear the floor of the warehouse clean, lift off the roof, and scatter the diamonds on the other side of the Thames.

"Knew you were a bastard," said Zack. "What do you want?"

"I pick up the pencil, put it back, climb into the trunk of the car, and you drive me to see the boy. No one followed me. No one will. I can't recognize you, now or ever. You're safe enough. When I see the kid alive, I dismantle this and give you the stones. You check them through; when you're satisfied, you leave. The kid and I stay imprisoned. Twenty-four hours later you make an anonymous phone call. The fuzz comes to release us. It's clean, it's simple, and you get away."

Zack seemed undecided. It was not his plan, but he'd been outmaneuvered and he knew it. He reached into the side pocket of his track suit and pulled out a flat black box.

"Keep your hand up and those jaws open. I'm going to check you out for wiretaps."

He approached and ran the circuit detector over Quinn's body from head to foot. Any live electrical circuit, of the kind contained in an emitting direction finder or wiretap, would have caused the detector to give out a shrill whoop. The battery in the bomb Quinn wore was dormant. The original briefcase would have triggered the detector.

"All right," said Zack. He stood back, a yard away. Quinn could smell the man's sweat. "You're clean. Put that pencil back, and climb in the trunk."

Quinn did as he was bid. The last light he saw was before the large rectangular lid of the trunk came down on him. Air holes had already been punched in the floor to accommodate Simon Cormack three weeks earlier. It was stuffy but bearable and, despite his length, large enough, provided he remained crouched in fetal position—which meant he nearly gagged from the smell of almonds.

Though he could not see it, the car swung in a U-turn, and the gunman ran forward and climbed into the back seat. All three men removed their masks and track-suit tops, revealing shirts, ties, and jackets. The track-suit tops went into the back, on top of the Skorpion machine pistol. When they were ready, the car glided out of the warehouse, Zack himself now back behind the wheel, and headed toward their hideaway.

It took an hour and a half to reach the attached garage of the house forty miles out of London. Zack drove always at the proper speed, his companions upright and silent in their seats. For both these men it had been their first time out of the house in three weeks.

When the garage door was closed, all three men pulled on their track suits and masks, and one went into the house to warn the fourth. Only when they were ready did Zack open the trunk of the Volvo. Quinn was stiff, and blinked in the electric light of the garage. He had removed the pencil from the jaws of the clothespin and held it in his teeth.

"All right, all right," said Zack. "No need for that. We're going to show you the kid. But when you go through the house you wear this."

He held up a cowled hood. Quinn nodded. Zack pulled it over Quinn's head. There was a chance they would try to rush him, but it would take only a fraction of a second to release his grip on the open clothespin. They led him, left hand aloft, through into the house, down a short passage and then some cellar steps. He heard three loud knocks on a door of some kind, then a pause. He heard a door creak open and he was pushed into a room. He stood there alone, hearing the rasp of bolts.

"You can take the hood off," said Zack's voice. He was speaking through the peephole in the cellar door. Quinn used his right hand to remove his hood. He was in a bare cellar: concrete floor, concrete walls, perhaps a wine cellar converted to a new purpose. On a steel-frame bed against the far wall sat a lanky figure, his head and shoulders covered by another black hood. There were two knocks on the door. As if on command the figure on the bed tugged off his hood.

Simon Cormack stared in amazement at the tall man near the door, his raincoat half open, holding up a clothespin in his left hand. Quinn looked back at the President's son.

"Hi there, Simon. You okay, kid?" A voice from home.

"Who are you?" he whispered.

"Well, the negotiator. We've been worried about you. You okay?"

"Yeah, I'm . . . fine."

There were three knocks on the door. The young man pulled on his hood. The door opened. Zack stood there. Masked. Armed.

"Well, there he is. Now, the diamonds."

"Sure," said Quinn. "You kept your deal. I keep mine."

He replaced the pencil in the jaws of the clothespin, and let it hang from its wires to his waist. He slipped off the raincoat and ripped the wooden box from his chest. From the center he took the flat velour package of gems and held them out. Zack took them and passed them to a man in the passage behind him. His gun was still on Quinn.

"I'll take the bomb, too," he said. "You're not blowing your way out of here with it."

Quinn folded the wires and clothespin into the space left in the open box, pulled the wires out of the beige substance. The wires had no detonators attached to the ends of them. Quinn twisted a piece of the substance off one of the blocks and tasted it.

"Never could develop a taste for marzipan," he said. "Too sweet for me."

Zack stared at the assembly of household items lying in the box in his free hand.

"Marzipan?"

"The best that Marylebone High Street can offer."

"I should bloody kill you, Quinn."

"You could, but I hope you won't. No need, Zack. You got what you want. Like I said, pros kill when they have to. Examine the diamonds in peace, make your escape, let the kid and me stay here till you phone the police."

Zack closed the door and bolted it behind him. He spoke through the peephole.

"I'll say this for you, Yank. You got balls."

Then the peephole closed. Quinn turned to the figure on the bed and pulled off his hood for him. He sat down beside the boy.

"Now, I'd better bring you up to date a bit. A few more hours, if all goes well, and we should be out of here and heading for home. By the way, your mom and dad send their love."

He ruffled the young man's tangled hair. Simon Cormack's eyes filled with tears and he began to cry uncontrollably. He tried to wipe them away on the sleeve of his plaid shirt, but it was no good. Quinn wrapped one arm around the thin shoulders and remembered a day long ago in the jungles along the Mekong; the first time he was ever in combat, and how he survived while others died, and how afterward the sheer relief caused the tears to come and he could not stop them.

When Simon stopped and began to bombard him with questions about home, Quinn had a chance to have a look at the youth. Bearded, moustached, dirty, but otherwise in good shape. They'd fed him and had the decency to give him fresh clothes: the plaid shirt, blue jeans, and a broad leather belt with an embossed brass buckle to hold them up—camping-shop gear but adequate against the chill of November.

There seemed to be some kind of a row going on upstairs. Quinn could vaguely hear raised voices, principal among them Zack's. The sounds were too indistinct for him to hear the words, but the tone was clear enough. The man was angry. Quinn's brow furrowed; he had not checked the stones himself—he had not the skill to tell real diamonds from good forgeries—but now prayed no one had been foolish enough to insert a proportion of paste among the gems.

In fact that was not the reason for the dispute. After several minutes it calmed down. In an upstairs bedroom—the kidnappers tended to avoid the downstairs rooms during daylight hours, despite the thick net curtains that screened them—the South African was seated at a table brought up there for the purpose. The table was covered by a bed sheet, the slit velvet packet lay empty on the bed, and all four men gazed in awe at a small mountain of uncut diamonds.

Using a spatula, the South African began to divide the pile into smaller ones, then smaller again, until he had separated the mountain into twenty-five small hillocks. He gestured to Zack to choose one mound. Zack shrugged, picked one in the middle—approximately a thousand stones out of the twenty-five thousand on the table.

Without a word the South African began to scoop up the other twenty-four piles and tip them one by one into a stout canvas bag with a drawstring at the top. When the selected pile alone remained, he switched on a powerful reading lamp above the table, took a jeweler's loupe from his pocket, a pair of tweezers in his right hand, and held up the first stone to the light.

After several seconds he grunted and nodded, dropping the diamond into the open-topped canvas bag. It would take six hours to examine all thousand stones.

The kidnappers had chosen well. Top quality diamonds, even small ones, are normally "sourced" with a certificate when released to the trade by the Central Selling Organization, which dominates the world diamond trade, handling over 85 percent of stones passing from the mines to the trade. Even the U.S.S.R. with its Siberian extractions is smart enough not to break this lucrative cartel. Large stones of lesser quality are also usually sold with a certificate of provenance.

But in picking melees of medium quality gems between a fifth- and a half-carat, the kidnappers had gone for an area of the trade that is almost uncontrollable. These stones are the bread and butter of the manufacturing and retailing jewelers around the world, changing hands in packages of several hundred at a time without certification. Any manufacturing jeweler would honestly be able to take over a consignment of several hundred stones, especially if he was offered a 10 or

15 percent discount off the market price. Transferred into the settings around larger stones, they would simply disappear into the trade.

If they were genuine. Uncut diamonds do not glitter and gleam like the cut and polished article that appears at the end of the process. They look like dull pieces of glass, with a milky, opaque surface. But they cannot be confused with glass by an examiner of moderate skill and experience.

Real diamonds have a quite distinctive, soapy texture to the surface and are immune from water. If a piece of glass is dipped in water, the drops of liquid stay on the surface for several seconds; with a diamond they run off instantly, leaving the gem dry as a bone.

Moreover, under a magnifying loupe, diamonds have a perceivable triangular crystallography on the surface. The South African was looking for this patterning, to ensure they had not been foisted off with sand-blasted bottle glass or the other principal substitute, cubic zirconia.

As this scrutiny was going on, Senator Bennett R. Hapgood rose to his feet on the podium erected for the purpose in the sweeping grounds of the open-air Hancock Center in the heart of Austin and surveyed the crowd with satisfaction.

Straight ahead of him he could see the dome of the Texas State Capitol, second largest in the nation after the Capitol in Washington, gleaming in the late morning sun. The crowd might have been larger, considering the massive paid-for publicity that had presaged this important launch, but the media—local, state, and national—were well in attendance and this pleased him.

He raised his hands in a boxer's victory salute to acknowledge the roar of applause from the cheerleaders that began as soon as the encomium that announced him had ended. As the chants of the high-kicking girls continued and the crowd felt obliged to join in, he shook his head in well-simulated disbelief at such honor and held his hands high, palms outward, in a gesture to indicate there was no need to afford an insignificant junior senator from Oklahoma such an ovation.

When the cheering died down he took the microphone and began his speech. He used no notes; he had rehearsed his words many times since receiving the invitation to inaugurate and become president of the new movement that would soon sweep America.

"My friends, my fellow Americans, everywhere."

Though his present audience was overwhelmingly composed of

Texans, he was aiming through the lens of the television camera at a much larger audience.

"We may come from different parts of this great nation of ours. We may have different backgrounds, inhabit different walks of life, possess different hopes, fears, and aspirations. But one thing we share, wherever we may be, whatever we may do—we are all, men, women, and children, patriots of this great land. . . ."

The statement was undeniable and the cheering testified to that.

"This above all we share: We want our nation to be strong . . ." More cheering. ". . . and proud . . ." Ecstasy.

He talked for an hour. The evening newscasts across the United States would use between thirty seconds and one minute, according to taste. When he had finished and sat down, the breeze scarcely ruffling his snow-white, blow-dried, and spray-fixed hair above the cattleman's suntan, the Citizens for a Strong America movement was well and truly launched.

Dedicated, in broad terms, to the regeneration of national pride and honor through strength—the notion that it had never perceivably degenerated was overlooked—the CSA would specifically oppose the Nantucket Treaty root and branch, and demand its repudiation in Congress.

The enemy to pride and honor through strength had been clearly and incontrovertibly identified; it was Communism, meaning socialism, which ran from Medicaid through welfare checks to tax increases. Those fellow travelers of Communism who sought to dupe the American people into arms control at lower levels were not identified, but implied. The campaign would be conducted at every level—regional offices, media-oriented information kits, lobbying at the national and constituency levels, and public appearances by true patriots who would speak against the treaty and its progenitor—an oblique reference to the stricken man in the White House.

By the time the crowd was invited to sample the barbecues scattered around the periphery of the park, and made available by the generosity of a local philanthropist and patriot, Plan Crockett, the second campaign to destabilize John Cormack to the point of resignation, was on the road.

Quinn and the President's son spent a fitful night in the cellar. The boy took the bed, at Quinn's insistence, but could not sleep. Quinn sat on the floor, his back against the hard wall, and would have dozed but for the questions from Simon.

"Mr. Quinn?"

"It's Quinn. Just Quinn."

"Did you see my dad? Personally?"

"Sure. He told me about Aunt Emily . . . and Mr. Spot."

"How was he?"

"Fine. Worried of course. It was just after the kidnap."

"Did you see Mom?"

"No, she was with the White House doctor. Worried but okay."

"Do they know I'm okay?"

"As of two days ago, I told them you were still alive. Try and get some sleep."

"Okay . . . When do you figure we'll get out of here?"

"Depends. In the morning, I hope, they'll quit and run. If they make a phone call twelve hours later, the British police should be here minutes afterward. It depends on Zack."

"Zack? He's the leader?"

"Yep."

At two in the morning the overstrung youth finally ran out of questions and dozed. Quinn stayed awake, straining to identify the muffled sounds from upstairs. It was almost 4:00 A.M. when the three loud knocks came at the door.

Simon swung his legs off the bed and whispered, "The hoods." Both men pulled on the cowled hoods to prevent their seeing the abductors. When they were blindfolded, Zack entered the cellar with two men behind him. Each carried a pair of handcuffs. He nodded toward the two captives. They were turned around and their wrists cuffed behind their backs.

What they did not know was that the examination of the diamonds had finished before midnight, to the complete satisfaction of Zack and his accomplices. The four men had spent the night scouring their living quarters from top to bottom. Every surface that might have had a fingerprint was wiped; every trace they could think of, expunged. They did not bother to dismantle the cellar of its bolted-down bed or the length of chain that had tethered Simon to it for over three weeks. Their concern was not that others might come here one day and identify the place as having been the kidnappers' hideout; rather, that those examiners would never discover who the kidnappers had been.

Simon Cormack was detached from his ankle chain and both men were led upstairs, through the house, and into the garage. The Volvo awaited. Its trunk was stuffed with the carryalls of the kidnappers and had no room left. Quinn was forced into the back seat and down to the floor, then covered with a blanket. He was uncomfortable but optimistic.

If the kidnappers had intended to kill them both, the cellar would have been the place. He had proposed they be left in the cellar, to be liberated later by the police following a phone call from abroad. That was evidently not to be. He guessed, rightly, that the kidnappers did not want their hideout discovered, at least not yet. So he lay hunched on the floor of the car and breathed as best he could through the thick hood.

He felt the depression of the seat cushions above him as Simon Cormack was made to lie along the back seat. He, too, was covered by a blanket. The two smallest men climbed in the back, sitting on the edge of the seat with the slim body of Simon behind their backs, their feet on Quinn. The giant climbed into the passenger seat; Zack took the wheel.

At his command all four took off their masks and track-suit tops and threw them through the windows onto the garage floor. Zack started the engine and operated the door-opener. He backed out into the driveway, closed the garage door, reversed into the street, and drove off. No one saw the car. It was still dark, with another two and a half hours to dawn.

The car ran steadily for about two hours. Quinn had no idea where he was or where he was going. Eventually (it would later be established it must have been within a few minutes of six-thirty), the car slowed to a halt. No one had spoken during the drive. They all sat bolt upright in their seats, in business suits and ties, and remained silent. When they stopped, Quinn heard the rear near-side door open and the two sets of feet on his body were removed. Someone dragged him out of the car by the feet. He felt wet grass under his cuffed hands, knew he was on the grassy edge of a road somewhere. He scrambled to his knees, then his feet, and stood up. He heard two men reentering the rear of the car and the slamming of the door.

"Zack," he called. "What about the boy?"

Zack was standing on the road by the driver's open door, looking at him across the roof of the car.

"Ten miles up the road," he said, "by the roadside, same as you."

There was the purr of a powerful engine and the crunch of gravel under wheels. Then the car was gone. Quinn felt the chill of a November morning on his shirt-sleeved torso. The moment the car was gone, he got to work.

Hard labor in the vineyards had kept him in shape. His hips were narrow, like those of a man fifteen years his junior, and his arms were long. When the handcuffs went on he had braced the sinews of his wrists to secure the maximum space when he relaxed. Tugging the cuffs down over his hands as far as they would go, he worked his cuffed wrists down his back and around his behind. Then he sat in the grass, brought his wrists up under his knees, kicked off his shoes, and worked his legs through his locked arms, one after the other. With his wrists now in front of him he tore off the hood.

The road was long, narrow, straight, and utterly deserted in the predawn half-light. He sucked in lungsful of the cool fresh air and looked around for human habitation. There was none. He pulled on his shoes, rose, and began to jog along the road in the direction the car had taken.

After two miles he came to a garage on the left, a small affair with old-style hand-operated pumps and a little office. Three kicks brought the door down and he found the telephone on a shelf behind the pump attendant's chair. He lifted the receiver two-handed, leaned his ear against it to make sure he had a dial tone, laid it down, dialed 01 for London, and then the flash line in the Kensington apartment.

In London the chaos took three seconds to get into full gear. A British engineer in the Kensington exchange came jolting out of his chair and began to search for a lock on the transmitting number. He got it in nine seconds.

In the basement of the U.S. embassy the duty ELINT man gave a yell as his warning light blazed red in his face and the sound of a phone ringing came into his headset. Kevin Brown, Patrick Seymour, and Lou Collins ran into the listening post from the cots where they had been dozing.

"Throw sound onto the wall speaker," snapped Seymour.

In the apartment Sam Somerville had been dozing on the couch, once so favored by Quinn because it was right next to the flash phone. McCrea was asleep in one of the armchairs. It was their second night like this.

When the phone rang, Sam jolted awake but for two seconds did not register which phone was ringing. The pulsing red bulb on the flash line told her. She picked it up at the third ring.

"Yes?"

"Sam?"

There was no mistaking the deep voice at the other end.

"Oh, Quinn!" she said. "Are you all right?"

"Screw Quinn. What about the boy?" fumed Brown, unheard beneath the embassy.

"Fine. I've been released. Simon's due for release about now, maybe already. But farther up the road."

"Quinn, where are you?"

"I don't know. In a beat-up garage on a long stretch of road—the number on this phone is unreadable."

"Bletchley number," said the engineer in the Kensington exchange. "Here we are . . . got it. Seven-four-five-oh-one."

His colleague was already talking to Nigel Cramer, who had spent the night at Scotland Yard.

"Where the hell is it?" he hissed.

"Hang about . . . here, Tubbs Cross Garage, on the A.421 between Fenny Stratford and Buckingham."

At the same time Quinn saw an invoice pad belonging to the garage. It bore the address of the garage also, and he relayed it to Sam. Seconds later the line was dead. Sam and Duncan McCrea raced down to the street, where Lou Collins had left a CIA car should the listeners in the apartment need transport. Then they were off, McCrea driving and Sam map-reading.

From Scotland Yard, Nigel Cramer and six officers set off in two patrol cars, their sirens howling up Whitehall and down the Mall to pick up Park Lane and the road north out of London. Two big limousines sped out of Grosvenor Square at the same time, bearing Kevin Brown, Lou Collins, Patrick Seymour, and six of Brown's Washington-based FBI men.

The A.421 between Fenny Stratford and the county town of Buckingham twelve miles farther west is a long, almost straight road devoid of towns or villages, running through largely flat agricultural country studded by the occasional clump of trees. Quinn jogged steadily west, the direction taken by the car. The first light of day began to filter through gray clouds above, giving visibility that rose steadily to three hundred yards. That was when he saw the thin figure jogging toward him in the gloom, and heard the roar of engines coming up fast behind him. He turned his head: a British police car, one of two, two black American limousines just ahead of them, and an unmarked Company car behind them. The leading car saw him and started to slow; due to the narrowness of the road the ones behind slowed as well.

No one in the cars had seen the tottering figure farther down the road. Simon Cormack had also worked his wrists around to the front of his body, and had covered five miles to Quinn's four and a half. But he had made no phone call. Weakened by his captivity, dazed by his release, he was running slowly, rolling from side to side. The lead car from the embassy was beside Quinn.

"Where's the boy?" roared Brown from the front seat.

Nigel Cramer leaped from the red-and-white squad car and shouted the same question. Quinn stopped, sucked air into his lungs, and nodded forward along the road.

"There," he gasped.

That was when they saw him. Already out from their cars and on the road, the group of Americans and the British police officers began to run toward the figure two hundred yards away. Behind Quinn the car of McCrea and Sam Somerville swerved to a stop.

Quinn had stopped; there was nothing more he could do. He felt Sam run up behind him and grab his arm. She said something but he could never later recall what it was.

Simon Cormack, seeing his rescuers approaching him, slowed until he was hardly jogging at all. Just under a hundred yards separated him from the police officers of two nations when he died.

The witnesses would say later that the searingly brilliant white flash seemed to last for several seconds. The scientists would tell them it actually lasted for three milliseconds, but the human retina retains such a flash for some seconds afterward. The fireball that came with the flash lasted for half a second and enveloped the whole stumbling figure.

Four of the watchers, experienced men, not easy to shock, later had to undergo therapy. They described how the figure of the youth was picked up and hurled twenty yards toward them, like a rag doll, first flying, then bouncing and rolling in a twisted assembly of disjointed limbs. They all felt the blast wave.

Most would agree, with hindsight, that everything seemed to happen in slow motion, during and after the murder. Recollections came in bits and pieces, and the patient interrogators would listen, and note down the bits and pieces until they had a sequence, usually overlapping in parts.

There was Nigel Cramer, rock-still, pale as a sheet, repeating "Oh, God, oh, my God" over and over again. A Mormon FBI man dropped to his knees at the roadside and began to pray. Sam Somerville screamed once, buried her face in Quinn's back, and began to cry. There was Duncan McCrea, behind both of them, on his knees, head down over a ditch, hands deep in the water supporting his weight, retching up his guts.

Quinn, they would say, was standing still, having been overtaken by the main group but able to see what had happened up the road, shaking his head in disbelief and murmuring, "No . . . no . . . no."

It was a gray-haired British sergeant who was the first to break the spell of immobility and shock, moving forward toward the tangled body sixty yards away. He was followed by several FBI men, among them Kevin Brown, pale and shaking, then Nigel Cramer and three more men from the Yard. They looked at the body in silence. Then background and training took over.

"Clear the area, please," said Nigel Cramer. It was in a tone no one was prepared to argue. "Tread very carefully."

They all walked back toward the cars.

"Sergeant, get on to the Yard. I want the CEO up here, by chopper, within the hour. Photographs, forensics, the best team Fulham have got. You"—to the men in the second car—"get up and down the road. Block it off. Raise the local boys—I want barriers beyond the garage that way and up to Buckingham that way. No one enters this stretch of road until further notice except those I authorize."

The officers designated to take the stretch of road beyond the body had to walk, crossing into the fields for a while to avoid treading on fragments, then running up the road to head off approaching cars. The second squad car went east toward Tubbs Cross Garage to block the road in the other direction. The first squad car was used for its radio.

Within sixty minutes police out of Buckingham to the west and Bletchley to the east would seal the road completely with steel barriers. A screen of local officers would fan out across the fields to fend off the curious seeking to approach cross-country. At least this time there would be no press for a while. They could put the road closing down to a burst water main—enough to deter the local small-town reporters.

Within fifty minutes the first Metropolitan Police helicopter swung in across the fields, guided by the radio of the squad car, to deposit on the road behind the cars a small, birdlike man called Dr. Barnard, the Chief Explosives Officer of the Met., a man who, thanks to the bomb outrages of the I.R.A. in mainland Britain, had examined more explosion scenes than he would have wished. He brought with him, apart from his "bag of tricks," as he liked to call it, an awesome reputation.

They said of Dr. Barnard that from fragments so minuscule as almost to deceive a magnifying glass, he could reconstitute a bomb to the point of identifying the factory that had made its components and the man who had assembled it. He listened to Nigel Cramer for several minutes, nodded, and gave his own orders to the dozen men who had clambered out of the second and third helicopters—the team from the Fulham forensic laboratories.

Impassively they set about their work, and the machinery of post-crime science rolled into action.

Long before any of this, Kevin Brown had returned from looking at the corpse of Simon Cormack to the point where Quinn still stood. He was gray with shock and rage.

"You bastard," he grated. Both tall men, they were eyeball to eyeball. "This is your fault. One way or another you caused this, and I'm going to make you pay for it."

The punch, when it came, surprised the two younger FBI men by Brown's side, who took his arms and tried to calm him down. Quinn may have seen the punch coming. Whatever, he made no attempt to dodge it. Still with his hands cuffed in front of him, he took it full on the jaw. It was enough to knock him backwards; then his head caught the edge of the roof of the car behind him, and he went down unconscious.

"Put him in the car," growled Brown when he had recovered his self-control.

There was no way Cramer could hold the American group. Seymour and Collins had diplomatic immunity; he let them all depart back to London in their two cars fifteen minutes later, warning them that he would want Quinn, for whom there was no diplomatic status, available for the taking of lengthy statements in London. Seymour gave his word Quinn would be available. When they had gone, Cramer used the phone in the garage to put through a call to Sir Harry Marriott at his home and give him the news; the phone was more secure than a police radio band.

The politician was shocked to his core. But he was still a politician.

"Mr. Cramer, were we, in the form of the British authorities, in any way involved in all this?"

"No, Home Secretary. From the time Quinn ran out of that apartment, this was wholly his affair. He handled it the way he wanted to, without involving us or his own people. He chose to play a lone hand, and it has failed."

"I see," said the Home Secretary. "I shall have to inform the Prime Minister at once. Of all aspects." He meant that the British authorities had had no hand in the affair at all. "Keep the media out of it at all costs for the moment. At worst we will have to say that Simon Cormack has been found murdered. But not yet. And, of course, keep me in touch on every development, no matter how small."

•   •   •

This time the news reached Washington from its own sources in London. Patrick Seymour telephoned Vice President Odell personally, on a secure line. Thinking he was taking a call from the FBI liaison man in London to announce Simon Cormack's release, Michael Odell did not mind the hour—5:00 A.M. in Washington. When he heard what Seymour had to tell him, he went white.

"But how? Why? In God's name, why?"

"We don't know, sir," said the voice from London. "The boy had been released safe and sound. He was running toward us, ninety yards away, when it happened. We don't even know what 'it' was. But he's dead, Mr. Vice President."

The committee was convened within the hour. Every member felt ill with shock when told the news. The question was, who should tell the President. As chairman of the committee, the man saddled with the task of "Get my son back for me" twenty-four days earlier, it fell to Michael Odell. With a heavy heart he walked from the West Wing to the White House living quarters.

President Cormack did not need to be awakened. He had slept little these past three and a half weeks, often waking of his own accord in the predawn darkness, and walking through to his personal study to attempt to concentrate on papers of state. Hearing the Vice President was downstairs and wished to see him, President Cormack went into the Yellow Oval Room and said he would greet Odell there.

The Yellow Oval Room, on the second floor, is a spacious reception room between the study and the Treaty Room. Beyond its windows, looking over the South Lawn, is the Truman Balcony. Both are at the geometric center of the White House, beneath the cupola and right above the South Portico.

Odell entered. President Cormack was in the center of the room, facing him. Odell was silent. He could not bring himself to say it. The air of expectancy on the President's face drained away.

"Well, Michael?" he said dully.

"He . . . Simon . . . has been found. I'm afraid he is dead."

President Cormack did not move, not a muscle. His voice when it came was flat; clear but emotionless.

"Leave me, please."

Odell turned and left, moving into the Center Hall. He closed the door and turned toward the stairs. From behind him he heard a single cry, like that of a wounded animal in mortal pain. He shuddered and walked on.

Secret Service agent Lepinsky was at the end of the hall, by a desk against the wall, a raised phone in his hand.

"It's the British Prime Minister, Mr. Vice President," he said.

"I'll take it. Hello, this is Michael Odell. Yes, Prime Minister, I've just told him. No, ma'am, he's not taking any calls right now. *Any* calls."

There was a pause on the line.

"I understand," she said quietly. Then: "Do you have a pencil and paper?"

Odell gestured to Lepinsky, who produced his duty notebook. Odell scribbled what he was asked.

President Cormack got the slip of paper at the hour most Washingtonians, unaware of what had happened, were drinking their first cup of coffee. He was still in a silk robe, in his office, staring dully at the gray morning beyond the windows. His wife slept on; she would wake and hear it later. He nodded as the servant left and flicked open the folded sheet from Lepinsky's notebook.

It said just: *Second Samuel XVIII 33.*

After several minutes he rose and walked to the shelf where he kept some personal books, among them the family Bible, bearing the signatures of his father and his grandfather and his great-grandfather. He found the verse toward the end of the Second Book of Samuel.

"And the king was much moved, and went up to the chamber over the gate, and wept: and as he went, thus he said, O my son Absalom! my son, my son Absalom! would God I had died for thee, O Absalom, my son, my son!"

CHAPTER ELEVEN

D r. Barnard declined to use the services of the hundred young police constables offered by the Thames Valley Police in the search for clues on the road and the verges. He took the view that mass searches were fine for discovering the hidden body of a murdered child, or even a murder weapon like a knife, gun, or bludgeon.

But for this work, skill, patience, and extreme delicacy were needed. He used only his trained specialists from Fulham.

They taped off an area one hundred yards in diameter 'round the scene of the explosion; it turned out to be overkill. All the evidence was eventually found inside a circle of thirty yards' diameter. Literally on hands and knees, his men crawled over every inch of the designated area with plastic bags and tweezers.

Every tiny fragment of fiber, denim, and leather was picked up and dropped in the bags. Some had hair, tissue, or other matter attached to them. Smeared grass stems were included. Ultrafine-tuned metal detectors covered every square centimeter of the road, the ditches, and the surrounding fields, yielding inevitably a collection of nails, tin cans, rusty screws, nuts, bolts, and a corroded plowshare.

The sorting and separation would come later. Eight big plastic garbage cans were filled with clear plastic bags and flown to London. The oval area from where Simon Cormack had been standing when he died to the point where he stopped rolling, at the heart of the larger circle, was treated with special care. It was four hours before the body could be removed.

First it was photographed from every conceivable angle, in long-shot, mid-shot, and extreme close-up. Only when every part of the grass verge around the body had been scoured, and only the piece of turf actually under the body remained to be examined, would Dr. Barnard allow human feet to walk on the ground to approach the body.

Then a body bag was laid beside the corpse, and what remained of Simon Cormack was gently lifted from where it lay and placed on the spread-out plastic. The bag was folded over him and zipped up, then placed on a stretcher, into a pannier beneath a helicopter, and flown to the post-mortem laboratory.

The death had taken place in the countryside of Buckinghamshire, one of the three counties comprising the Thames Valley Police area. So it was that in death Simon Cormack returned to Oxford, to the Radcliffe Infirmary, whose facilities are a match even for Guy's Hospital, London.

From Guy's came a friend and colleague of Dr. Barnard, a man who had worked with the Chief Explosives Officer of the Metropolitan on many cases and had formed a close professional relationship with him. Indeed, they were often regarded as a team, though they followed different disciplines. Dr. Ian Macdonald was a senior consultant patholo-gist at the great London hospital and also a retained Home Office pathologist, and was usually asked for by Scotland Yard if he was avail-able. It was he who received the body of Simon Cormack at the Rad-cliffe.

Throughout the day, as the men crawled over the grass by the side of the A.421, continuous consultation took place between London and Washington regarding the release of the news to the media and the world. It was agreed that the statement should come from the White House, with immediate confirmation in London. The statement would simply say that an exchange had been arranged in conditions of total secrecy, as demanded by the kidnappers, an unspecified ransom had been paid, and that they had broken their word. The British authorities, responding to an anonymous phone call, had gone to a roadside in Buck-inghamshire and there found Simon Cormack dead.

Needless to say, the condolences of the British monarch, govern-ment, and people to the President and to the American people were without limit of sincerity or depth, and a search of unparalleled vigor was now in progress to identify, find, and arrest the culprits.

Sir Harry Marriott was adamant that the phrase referring to the arrangement of the exchange should include an extra seven words: "between the American authorities and the kidnappers." The White House, albeit reluctantly, agreed to this.

"The media are going to have our hides," growled Odell.

"Well, you wanted Quinn," said Philip Kelly.

"Actually, *you* wanted Quinn," snapped Odell at Lee Alexander and David Weintraub, who sat with them in the Situation Room. "By the way, where is he now?"

"Being detained," said Weintraub. "The British refused to allow him to be lodged on sovereign U.S. territory inside the embassy. Their MI-5 people have lent us a country house in Surrey. He's there."

"Well, he has a hell of a lot of explaining to do," said Hubert Reed. "The diamonds are gone, the kidnappers are gone, and that poor boy is dead. How exactly did he die?"

"The Brits are trying to find that out," said Brad Johnson. "Kevin Brown says it was almost as if he was hit by a bazooka, right in front of them, but they saw nothing like a bazooka. Or he stepped on a land mine of some sort."

"On a roadside in the middle of nowhere?" asked Stannard.

"As I told you, the post-mortem will indicate what happened."

"When the British have finished interviewing him, we have to have him back over here," said Kelly. "We need to talk to him."

"The Deputy Assistant Director of your Division is doing that already," said Weintraub.

"If he refuses to come, can we force him to return?" asked Bill Walters.

"Yes, Mr. Attorney General, we can," said Kelly. "Kevin Brown believes he may have been involved in some way. We don't know how . . . yet. But if we issued a material-witness warrant, I believe the British would put him on the plane."

"We'll give it another twenty-four hours, see what the British come up with," said Odell finally.

The Washington statement was issued at 5:00 P.M. local time and rocked the United States as little had done since the assassinations of Bobby Kennedy and Martin Luther King. The media went into a furor, not helped by Press Secretary Craig Lipton's refusal to answer the two hundred supplementary questions they had to ask. Who had arranged the ransom, how much was it, in what form, how had it been handed over, by whom, why had no attempt been made to arrest the kidnappers at the handover, was the package or packet of ransom money bugged, had the kidnappers been tracked too clumsily and killed the boy as they fled, what level of negligence had been shown by the authorities, did the White House blame Scotland Yard, if not why not, why did the U.S. not leave it to Scotland Yard in the first place, had any descriptions of the kidnappers been obtained, were the British police closing in on them . . . ? The questions went on and on. Craig Lipton definitely decided to resign before he was lynched.

The time in London was five hours later than Washington's but the reaction was similar: Late TV shows were interrupted by news flashes that left the nation stunned. The switchboards at Scotland Yard, the Home Office, Downing Street, and the American embassy were jammed. Teams of journalists just about to go home around 10:00 P.M. were told to work through the night as fresh editions were prepared for issue as late as 5:00 A.M. By dawn they were staking out the Radcliffe Infirmary, Grosvenor Square, Downing Street, and Scotland Yard. In chartered helicopters they hovered over the empty stretch of road between Fenny Stratford and Buckingham to photograph, at first light, the bare tarmac and the last few barriers and police cars parked there.

Few slept. Impelled by a personal plea for haste from Sir Harry Marriott himself, Dr. Barnard and his team worked through the night. The forensic scientist had finally quit the road as night fell, certain it had nothing more to yield. Ten hours of scouring had left the thirty-yard circle cleaner than any piece of ground in England. What that ground had yielded now reposed in a series of gray plastic drums along the wall of his laboratory. For him and his team it was the night of the microscopes.

Nigel Cramer spent the night in a plain, bare room in a Tudor grange, screened from the nearest road by a belt of trees, in the heart of Surrey. Despite its elegant exterior aspect, the old house was well equipped for interrogation. The British Security Service used its ancient cellars as a training school for such delicate matters.

Brown, Collins, and Seymour were present, at their own insistence. Cramer did not object—his brief from Sir Harry Marriott was to cooperate with the Americans wherever and whenever possible. Any information Quinn had would go to both governments anyway. A relay of tapes filled themselves in the machines on the table beside them.

Quinn had a long and livid bruise on the side of his jaw, a lump and a Band-Aid on the back of his head. He was still in his shirt, now filthy, and slacks. Shoes had been removed, along with belt and tie. He was unshaven and looked exhausted. But he answered the questions calmly and clearly.

Cramer started at the beginning: Why had he quit the flat in Kensington? Quinn explained. Brown glowered at him.

"Did you have any reason, Mr. Quinn, to believe that a person or persons unknown might have attempted to interfere in the ransom exchange, to the effect of endangering the safety of Simon Cormack?" Nigel Cramer was phrasing it by the book.

"Instinct," said Quinn.

"Just instinct, Mr. Quinn?"

"May I ask you a question, Mr. Cramer?"

"I don't promise to answer it."

"The attaché case with the diamonds in it. It was bugged, wasn't it?"

He got his answer from the four faces in the room.

"If I had shown up at any exchange with that case," said Quinn, "they'd have spotted it and killed the boy."

"They did that anyway, smartass," Brown grunted.

"Yes, they did," said Quinn grimly. "I admit I did not think they would do that."

Cramer took him back to the moment he left the flat. He told them about Marylebone, the night at the hotel, the terms Zack had laid down for the rendezvous, and how he had just made the deadline. For Cramer the meat was in the head-to-head in the abandoned factory. Quinn gave him the car, a Volvo sedan, and its registration number; both men surmised, rightly, that the plates would have been changed for that meeting, then changed back again. Ditto the road-tax disc stuck in the windshield. These men had shown they were careful.

He could describe the men only as he had seen them, masked, in shapeless track suits. One he had not seen at all, the fourth, who had stayed at the hideout ready to kill Simon Cormack at a phone call or a no-show by his colleagues by a certain time. He described the physiques of the two men he had seen upright, Zack and the gunman. Medium height, medium build. Sorry.

He identified the Skorpion submachine gun, and of course the Babbidge warehouse. Cramer left the room to make a phone call. A second team of forensic men from Fulham visited the warehouse before dawn and spent the morning there. It yielded nothing but a small ball of marzipan and a set of perfect tire tracks in the dust. These would eventually identify the abandoned Volvo, but not for two weeks.

The house used by the kidnappers was of particular interest. A gravel drive—Quinn had heard the crunching of the gravel—about ten yards from front gate to garage doors; automatic door-opening system, attached garage; a house with a concrete cellar beneath it—the real estate agents could help there. But direction from London—nothing. Quinn had been in the trunk the first time, and masked on the floor of the back seat the second. Driving time, one and a half hours the first time, two hours the second. If they drove by an indirect route, that could be anywhere; right in the heart of London or up to fifty miles in any direction.

"There's nothing we can charge him with, Home Secretary," Cramer reported to the Minister early next morning. "We can't even detain him any longer. And frankly, I don't think we should. I don't believe he was criminally involved in the death."

"Well, he seems to have made a complete balls of it," said Sir Harry. The pressure from Downing Street for some new lead was becoming intense.

"So it would seem," said the police officer. "But if those criminals were determined to kill the boy, and it seems with hindsight that they were, they could have done it any time, before or after receiving the diamonds, in the cellar, on the road, or on some lonely Yorkshire moorland. And Quinn with him. The mystery is why they let Quinn live, and why they first released the boy and then killed him. It's almost as if they were looking to make themselves the most hated and hunted men on earth."

"Very well," sighed the Home Secretary. "We have no further interest in Mr. Quinn. Are the Americans still holding him?"

"Technically, he's their voluntary guest," said Cramer carefully.

"Well, they can let him go back to Spain when they wish."

While they were talking, Sam Somerville was pleading with Kevin Brown. Collins and Seymour were present, in the manor's elegant drawing room.

"What the hell do you want to see him for?" asked Brown. "He failed. He's a busted flush."

"Look," she said, "in those three weeks I got closer to him than anybody. If he's holding out at all, on anything, maybe I could get it out of him, sir."

Brown seemed undecided.

"Couldn't do any harm," said Seymour.

Brown nodded. "He's downstairs. Thirty minutes."

That afternoon Sam Somerville took the regular flight from Heathrow to Washington, landing just after dark.

· · ·

When Sam Somerville took off from Heathrow, Dr. Barnard was sitting in his laboratory at Fulham staring at a small collection of pieces of debris spread on a crisp white sheet of paper across a tabletop. He was very tired. Since the urgent call to his small London house just after dawn the previous day, he had not stopped working. Much of that work was a strain on the eyes, peering through magnifying glasses and into microscopes. But if he rubbed his eyes that late afternoon, it was more from surprise than exhaustion.

He now knew what had happened, how it had happened, and what had been the effect. Stains on fabric and leather had yielded to chemical analysis to reveal the exact chemical components of the explosive; the extent of burn- and impact-deterioration had shown him how much was used, where it had been placed, and how it had been triggered. There were some pieces missing, of course. Some would never appear, vaporized, lost forever, having ceased to exist. Others would emerge from the ruin of the body itself, and he had been in constant contact with Ian Macdonald, who was still at work in Oxford. The yield from Oxford would arrive shortly. But he knew what he was looking at, though to the untrained eye it was just a pile of minuscule fragments.

Some of them made up the remnants of a tiny battery, source identified. Others were tiny pieces of polyvinyl-chloride insulated plastic covering, source identified. Strands of copper wire, source identified. And a mess of twisted brass bonded with what had once been a small but efficient pulse-receiver. No detonator. He was 100 percent sure, but he wanted to be 200 percent. He might have to go back to the road and start again. One of his assistants poked his head around the door.

"Dr. Macdonald on the line from the Radcliffe."

The pathologist had also been working since the previous afternoon, at a task many would find horribly gruesome but which to him was more full of detective fascination than any other he could imagine. He lived for his profession, so much so that instead of limiting himself to examining the remains of bomb-blast victims, he attended the courses and lectures available only to a very few on bomb-making and disarming offered at Fort Halstead. He wished to know not simply that he was looking for something, but what it was and what it looked like.

He had begun by studying the photographs for two hours before he even touched the cadaver itself. Then he carefully removed the clothes, not relying on an assistant but doing it himself. The running shoes came first, then the ankle socks. The rest was snipped off, using fine scissors. Each item was bagged and sent direct to Barnard in London. The yield from the clothes had reached Fulham by sunrise.

When the body was naked, it was X-rayed from top to toe. Macdonald studied the prints for an hour and identified forty nonhuman particles. Then he swabbed the body down with a sticky powder, which removed a dozen infinitely small particles stuck to the skin. Some were crumbs of grass and mud; some were not. A second police car took this grim harvest to Dr. Barnard in Fulham.

He did an external autopsy, dictating into a recorder in his measured Scottish lilt. He only began to cut just before dawn. The first task was to excise from the cadaver all the "relevant tissue." This happened to be all of the middle section of the body, which had lost almost everything from and including the bottom two ribs down to the top of the pelvis. Within the excised matter were the small particles that remained of eight inches of lower spine, which had come straight through the body and the ventral wall to lodge in the front of the jeans.

The autopsy—establishment of cause of death—was no problem. It was massive explosive injury to spine and abdomen. The full postmortem needed more. Dr. Macdonald had the excised matter X-rayed again, in much finer grain. There were things in there, all right, some so small they would defy tweezers. The excised flesh and bone was finally "digested" in a brew of enzymes to create a thick soup of dissolved human tissue, bone included. It was the centrifuge that yielded the last cull, a final ounce of bits of metal.

When this ounce was available for examination Dr. Macdonald selected the largest piece, the one he had spotted in the second X-ray, deeply impacted into a piece of bone and buried inside the young man's spleen. He studied it for a while, whistled, and rang Fulham.

Barnard came on the line. "Ian, glad you called. Anything else for me?"

"Aye. There's something here you have got to see. If I'm right, it's something I've never seen before. I think I know what it is, but I can hardly believe it."

"Use a squad car. Send it now," said Barnard grimly.

Two hours later the men were speaking again. It was Barnard who called this time.

"If you were thinking what I believe you were thinking, you were right," he said. Barnard had his 200 percent.

"It couldn't come from anywhere else?" asked Macdonald.

"Nope. There's no way one of these gets into anybody's hands but the manufacturer's."

"Bloody hell," said the pathologist quietly.

"Mum's the word, matey," said Barnard. "Ours but to do or die, right? I'm having my report with the Home Secretary in the morning. Can you do the same?"

Macdonald glanced at his watch. Thirty-six hours since he had been roused. Another twelve to go.

"Sleep no more. Barnard does murder sleep," he parodied *Macbeth*. "All right, on his desk by breakfast."

That evening he released the body, or both parts of it, to the coroner's officer. In the morning the Oxford coroner would open and adjourn the inquest, enabling him to release the body to the next of kin, in this case Ambassador Fairweather in person, representing President John Cormack.

As the two British scientists wrote their reports through the night, Sam Somerville was received, at her own request, by the committee in the Situation Room beneath the West Wing. She had appealed right up to the Director of the Bureau, and after she had telephoned Vice President Odell, he had agreed to bring her along.

When she entered the room they were all already seated. Only David Weintraub was missing, away in Tokyo talking to his opposite number there. She felt intimidated; these men were the most powerful in the land, men you only saw on television or in the press. She took a deep breath, held her head up, and walked forward to the end of the table. Vice President Odell gestured to a chair.

"Sit down, young lady."

"We understand you wanted to ask us to let Mr. Quinn go free," said Attorney General Bill Walters. "May we ask why?"

Sam took a deep breath. "Gentlemen, I know some may suspect Mr. Quinn was in some way involved in the death of Simon Cormack. I ask you to believe me. I have been in close contact with him in that apartment for three weeks and I'm convinced he genuinely tried to secure that young man's release safe and unharmed."

"Then why did he run?" asked Philip Kelly. He did not appreciate having his junior agents brought to the committee to speak for themselves.

"Because there were two freak news leaks in the forty-eight hours before he went. Because he had spent three weeks trying to gain that animal's trust and he had done it. Because he was convinced Zack was about to scuttle and run, if he couldn't get to him alone and unarmed, without a shadow from either the British or American authorities."

No one failed to grasp that by "American authorities" she meant Kevin Brown. Kelly scowled.

"There remains a suspicion he could have been involved in some way," he said. "We don't know how, but it needs to be checked out."

"He couldn't, sir," said Sam. "If he had proposed himself as the negotiator, maybe. But the choice to ask him was made right here. He told me he didn't even want to come. And from the moment Mr. Weintraub saw him in Spain he has been in someone's company twenty-four hours a day. Every word he spoke to the kidnappers, you listened to."

"Except those missing forty-eight hours before he showed up on a roadside," said Morton Stannard.

"But why should he make a deal with the kidnappers during that time?" she asked. "Except for the return of Simon Cormack."

"Because two million dollars is a lot of money to a poor man," suggested Hubert Reed.

"But if he had wanted to disappear with the diamonds," she persisted, "we'd still be looking for him now."

"Well," said Odell unexpectedly, "he did go to the kidnappers alone and unarmed—except for some goddam marzipan. If he didn't know them already, that takes grit."

"And yet Mr. Brown's suspicions may not be entirely unfounded," said Jim Donaldson. "He could have made his contact, struck a deal. They kill the boy, leave Quinn alive, take the stones. Later they meet up and split the booty."

"Why should they?" asked Sam, bolder now, with the Vice President apparently on her side. "They had the diamonds. They could have killed him too. Even if they didn't, why should they split with him? Would *you* trust them?"

None of them would trust such men an inch. There was silence as they thought it over.

"If he's allowed to go, what has he in mind? Back to his vineyard in Spain?" asked Reed.

"No, sir. He wants to go after them. He wants to hunt them down."

"Hey, hold on, Agent Somerville," said Kelly indignantly. "That's Bureau work. Gentlemen, we have no need of discretion to protect the life of Simon Cormack anymore. He's been murdered, and that murder is indictable under our laws, just like that murder on the cruise ship, the *Achille Lauro*. We're putting teams into Britain and Europe with the cooperation of all the national police authorities. We want them and we're going to get them. Mr. Brown controls the operations out of London."

Sam Somerville played her last card.

"But, gentlemen, if Quinn was not involved, he got closer than anyone to them, saw them, spoke to them. If he *was* involved, then he will know where to go. That could be our best lead."

"You mean, let him run and tail him?" asked Walters.

"No, sir. I mean let me go with him."

"Young lady"—Michael Odell leaned forward to see her better—"do you know what you're saying? This man has killed before—okay, in combat. If he's involved, you could end up very dead."

"I know that, Mr. Vice President. That's the point. I believe he's innocent and I'm prepared to take the risk."

"Mmmmm. All right. Stay in town, Miss Somerville. We'll let you know. We need to discuss this—in private," said Odell.

Home Secretary Marriott spent a disturbed morning reading the reports of Drs. Barnard and Macdonald. Then he took them both to Downing Street. He was back in the Home Office by lunchtime. Nigel Cramer was waiting for him.

"You've seen these?" asked Sir Harry.

"I've read copies, Home Secretary."

"This is appalling, utterly dismaying. If this ever gets out . . . Do you know where Ambassador Fairweather is?"

"Yes. He's at Oxford. The coroner released the body to him an hour ago. I believe Air Force One is standing by at Upper Heyford to fly the casket back to the States. The Ambassador will see it depart, then return to London."

"Mmm. I'll have to ask the Foreign Office to set up an interview. I want no copies of this to anybody. Ghastly business. Any news on the manhunt?"

"Not a lot, sir. Quinn made plain that none of the other two kidnappers he saw uttered a word. It could be they were foreigners. We're concentrating the hunt for the Volvo at major ports and airports connecting to Europe. I fear they may have slipped away. Of course, the hunt for the house goes on. No further need for discretion—I'm having a public appeal issued this evening, if you agree. A detached house with an attached garage, a cellar, and a Volvo of that color—someone must have seen something."

"Yes, by all means. Keep me posted," said the Home Secretary.

That evening in Washington, a very tense Sam Somerville was summoned from her apartment in Alexandria to the Hoover Building. She was shown to the office of Philip Kelly, her ultimate departmental boss, to hear the White House decision.

"All right, Agent Somerville, you've got it. The powers-that-be say you get to return to England and release Mr. Quinn. But this time, you stay with him, right with him, all the time. And you let Mr. Brown know what he's doing and where he's going."

"Yes, sir. Thank you, sir."

She was just in time to catch the overnight red-eye for Heathrow. There was a slight delay in the departure of her scheduled plane out of Dulles International. A few miles away, at Andrews, Air Force One was landing with the casket of Simon Cormack. At that hour, right across America, all airports ceased traffic for two minutes' silence.

She landed at Heathrow at dawn. It was the dawn of the fourth day since the murder.

Irving Moss was awakened early that morning by the sound of the ringing phone. It could only be one source—the only one that had his number here. He checked his watch: 4:00 A.M., 10:00 the previous evening in Houston. He took down the lengthy list of produce prices, all in U.S. dollars and cents, eradicated the zeros or "nulls"—which indicated a space in the message—and according to the day of the month set the lines of figures against prepared lines of letters.

When he had finished decoding, he sucked in his cheeks. Something extra, something not foreseen, something else he would have to take care of. Without delay.

Aloysius Fairweather, Jr., United States Ambassador to the Court of St. James's, had received the message conveyed by the British Foreign Office the previous evening on his return from the Upper Heyford U.S. Air Force Base. It had been a bad, sad day: receiving permission from Oxford's coroner to take charge of the body of his President's son, collecting the casket from the local morticians, who had done their best with little chance of success, and dispatching the tragic cargo back to Washington on Air Force One.

He had been in this post almost three years, the appointee of the new administration, and he knew he had done well, even though he had to succeed the incomparable Charles Price of the Reagan years. But these past four weeks had been a nightmare no ambassador should have to live through.

The Foreign Office request puzzled him, for it was not to see the Foreign Secretary, with whom he normally dealt, but the Home Secretary, Sir Harry Marriott. He knew Sir Harry, as he knew most of the British Ministers, well enough to drop titles in private and revert to first names. But to be called to the Home Office itself, and at the breakfast hour, was unusual, and the Foreign Office message had lacked explanation. His long black Cadillac swept into Victoria Street at five to nine.

"My dear Al." Marriott was all charm, albeit backed by the gravity the circumstances demanded. "I hope I don't need to tell you the level of shock that the last few days have brought to this entire country."

Fairweather nodded. He had no doubt the reaction of the British government and people was totally genuine. For days the queue to sign the condolence book in the embassy lobby had stretched twice around Grosvenor Square. Near the top of the first page was the simple inscription "Elizabeth R," followed by the entire Cabinet, the two archbishops, the leaders of all the other churches, and thousands of names of the high and the obscure. Sir Harry pushed two manila-bound reports across the desk at him.

"I wanted you to see these first, in private, and I suggest now. There may be matters we should discuss before you leave."

Dr. Macdonald's report was the shorter; Fairweather took it first. Simon Cormack had died of massive explosive damage to spine and abdomen, caused by a detonation of small but concentrated effect near the base of his back. At the time he died he was carrying the bomb on his person. There was more, but it was technical jargon about his physique, state of health, last known meal, and so on.

Dr. Barnard had more to say. The bomb Simon Cormack had been carrying on his person was concealed in the broad leather belt he wore around his waist and which had been given him by his abductors to hold up the denim jeans they had also provided him.

The belt had been three inches wide and made of two strips of cowhide sewn together along their edges. At the front it was secured by a heavy and ornate brass buckle, four inches long and slightly wider than the belt itself, decorated at its front by the embossed image of a longhorn steer's head. It was the sort of belt sold widely in shops specializing in Western or camping equipment. Although appearing solid, the buckle had in fact been hollow.

The explosive had been a two-ounce wafer of Semtex, composed of 45 percent penta tetro ether nitrate (or PETN), 45 percent RDX, and 10 percent plasticizer. The wafer had been three inches long and one-and-a-half inches wide, and had been inserted between the two strands of leather precisely against the young man's backbone.

Buried within the plastic explosive had been a miniature detonator, or mini-det, later extracted from within a fragment of vertebra that had itself been buried in the spleen. It was distorted but still recognizable—and identifiable.

From the explosive and detonator, a wire ran around the belt to the side, where it connected with a lithium battery similar to and no larger than the sort used to power digital watches. This had been inside a hollow, sculpted within the thickness of the double leather. The same wire then ran on to the pulse-receiver hidden inside the buckle. From the receiver a further wire, the aerial, ran right around the belt, between the layers of leather.

The pulse receiver would have been no larger than a small matchbox, probably receiving, on something like 72.15 megahertz, a signal sent from a small transmitter. This was not, of course, found at the scene, but it was probably a flat plastic box pack, smaller than a crushproof cigarette pack, with a single flush button depressed by the ball of the thumb to effect detonation. Range: something over three hundred yards.

Al Fairweather was visibly shaken. "God, Harry, this is . . . satanic."

"And complex technology," agreed the Home Secretary. "The sting is in the tail. Read the summary."

"But why?" asked the ambassador when he looked up at last. "In God's name, why, Harry? And how did they do it?"

"As to how, there's only one explanation. Those animals pretended to let Simon Cormack go free. They must have driven on awhile, circled back, and approached the stretch of road from the direction of the fields on foot. Probably hidden in one of those clumps of trees standing two hundred yards away from the road across the fields. That would be within range. We have men scouring the woods now for possible footprints.

"As to why, I don't know, Al. We none of us know. But the scientists are adamant. They have not got it wrong. For the moment I would suggest that report remain extremely confidential. Until we know more. We are trying to find out. I'm sure your own people will want to try also, before anything goes public."

Fairweather rose, taking his copies of the reports.

"I'm not sending these by courier," he said. "I'm flying home with them this afternoon."

The Home Secretary escorted him down to the ground level.

"You do realize what this could do if it gets out?" he asked.

"No need to underline it," said Fairweather. "There'd be riots. I have to take this to Jim Donaldson and maybe Michael Odell. *They'll* have to tell the President. God, what a thing."

Sam Somerville's rental car had been where she left it in the short-stay parking lot at Heathrow. She drove straight to the manor house in Surrey. Kevin Brown read the letter she brought and glowered.

"You're making a mistake, Agent Somerville," he said. "Director Edmonds is making a mistake. That man down there knows more than he lets on—always has, always will. Letting him run sticks in my craw. He should be on a flight Stateside—in handcuffs."

But the signature on the letter was clear. Brown sent Moxon down to the cellars to bring Quinn up. He was still in cuffs; they had to remove those. And unwashed, unshaven, and hungry. The FBI team began to clear out and hand the building back to their hosts. At the door Brown turned to Quinn.

"I don't want to see you again, Quinn. Except behind a row of steel bars. And I think one day I will."

On the drive back to London, Quinn was silent as Sam told him the outcome of her trip to Washington and the decision of the White House to let him have his head so long as she went with him.

"Quinn, just be careful. Those men have to be animals. What they did to that boy was savage."

"It was worse," said Quinn. "It was illogical. That's what I can't get over. It doesn't make sense. They had it all. They were away clean and clear. Why come back to kill him?"

"Because they were sadists," said Sam. "You know these people—you've dealt with their type for years. They have no mercy, no pity. They relish inflicting pain. They intended to kill him from the start."

"Then why not in the cellar? Why not me too? Why not with a gun, knife, or rope? Why at all?"

"We'll never know. Unless they can be found. And they've got the whole world to disappear into. Where do you want to go?"

"The apartment," said Quinn. "I have my things there."

"Me too," said Sam. "I went to Washington with only the clothes on my back."

She was driving north up Warwick Road.

"You've gone too far," said Quinn, who knew London like a cabdriver. "Take a right at Cromwell Road, the next intersection."

The lights were red. Across in front of them cruised a long black Cadillac bearing the fluttering pennant of the Stars and Stripes. Ambassador Fairweather was in the back, studying a report, heading for the airport. He looked up, glanced at the pair of them without recognition, and went on his way.

Duncan McCrea was still in residence, as if overlooked in the mayhem of the past few days. He greeted Quinn like a Labrador puppy reunited with his master.

Earlier that day, he reported, Lou Collins had sent in the cleaners. These were not men who wielded feather dusters. They had cleaned out the bugs and wiretaps. The apartment was "burned" as far as the Company was concerned and they had no further use for it. McCrea had been told to stay on, pack, tidy up, and return the keys to the landlord when he left the next morning. He was about to pack Sam's and Quinn's clothes when they arrived.

"Well, Duncan, it's here or a hotel. Mind if we stay one last night?"

"Oh, of course, no problem. Be the Agency's guest. I'm awfully sorry, but in the morning we have to vacate."

"The morning will do fine," said Quinn. He was tempted to ruffle the younger man's hair in a paternal gesture. McCrea's smile was infectious. "I need a bath, shave, food, and about ten hours' sleep."

McCrea went out to Mr. Patel's across the road and came back with two large grocery bags. He made steak, fries, and salad, with two bottles of red wine. Quinn was touched to note he had picked a Spanish Rioja—not from Andalusia, but the nearest he could get.

Sam saw no need for further secrecy over her affair with Quinn. She came to his room as soon as he turned in, and if young McCrea heard them making love, so what? After the second time she fell asleep, on her front, her face against his chest. He placed one hand on the nape of her neck and she murmured at the touch.

But despite his tiredness he could not sleep. He lay on his back, as on so many previous nights, and stared at the ceiling and thought. There was something about those men in the warehouse, something he had missed. It came to him in the small hours. The man behind him, holding the Skorpion with practiced casualness, not the careful tension of one unused to handguns; balanced, relaxed, self-confident, knowing he could bring the machine pistol to aim, and fire in a fraction of a second. His stance, his poise—Quinn had seen it before.

"He was a soldier," he said quietly into the darkness. Sam murmured "Mmmmm" but went on sleeping. Something else, something as he passed the door of the Volvo to climb into the trunk. It eluded him and he fell asleep at last.

In the morning Sam rose first and went back to her own room to dress. Duncan McCrea may have seen her leave Quinn's room but he made no mention. He was more concerned that his guests should have a good breakfast.

"Last night . . . I forgot eggs," he called, and scampered off down the stairs to get some from an early dairy around the corner.

Sam brought Quinn his breakfast in bed. He was lost in thought. She had become accustomed to his reveries, and left him. Lou Collins's cleaners had certainly not done any proper cleaning, she thought. The rooms were dusty after four weeks without attention.

Quinn was not concerned with the dust. He was watching a spider in the top far corner of his room. Laboriously the little creature laced up the last two strands of an otherwise perfect web, checked to see that every strand was in place, then scuttled to the center and sat there waiting. It was that last movement by the spider that recalled to Quinn the tiny detail that had eluded him last night.

The White House committee had the full reports of Drs. Barnard and Macdonald in front of them. It was the former they were studying. One by one they finished the summary and sat back.

"Goddam bastards," said Michael Odell with feeling. He spoke for all of them. Ambassador Fairweather sat at the end of the table.

"Is there any possibility," Secretary of State Donaldson asked, "that the British scientists could have gotten it wrong? About the origins?"

"They say no," answered the ambassador. "They've invited us to send anyone we like over to double-check, but they're good. I'm afraid they've got it right."

As Sir Harry Marriott had said, the sting was in the tail, the summary. Every single component, Dr. Barnard had said with the full concurrence of his military colleagues at Fort Halstead—the copper wires, their plastic covering, the Semtex, the pulse-receiver, the battery, the brass, and the leather stitching—was of Soviet manufacture.

He conceded it was possible for such items, though manufactured in the Soviet Union, to fall into the hands of others outside the U.S.S.R. But the clincher was the mini-det. No larger than a paper clip, these miniature detonators are used, and *only* used, within the Soviet space program at Baikonur. They are employed to give infinitesimal steering changes to the Salyut and Soyuz vehicles as they maneuver to dock in space.

"But it doesn't make sense," protested Donaldson. "Why should they?"

"A whole lot in this mess doesn't make sense," said Odell. "If this is true, I don't see how Quinn could have known about it. It looks like they duped him all along, duped all of us."

"The question is, what do we do about it?" asked Reed of Treasury.

"The funeral's tomorrow," said Odell. "We'll get that over with first. Then we'll decide how we handle our Russian friends."

Over four weeks Michael Odell had found that the authority of acting-President was sitting more and more lightly on him. The men around this table had come to accept his leadership also, more and more, he realized, as if he were the President.

"How is the President," asked Walters, "since . . . the news?"

"According to the doctor, bad," said Odell. "Very bad. If the kidnapping was bad enough, the death of his son, and done that way, has been like a bullet in his gut."

At the word *bullet* each man around the table thought the same thought. No one dared say it.

Julian Hayman was the same age as Quinn and they had known each other when Quinn lived in London and worked for the underwriting firm affiliated with Lloyd's, specializing in protection and hostage release. Their worlds had overlapped, for Hayman, a former major in the SAS, ran a company dedicated to the provision of anticrime alarm systems and personal protection, including bodyguards. His clientele was exclusive, wealthy, and careful. They were people who had reason to be suspicious, or they would not have paid so highly for Hayman's services.

The office in Victoria, to which Quinn guided Sam in the middle of the morning after leaving the flat and saying a final goodbye to Duncan McCrea, was as well-protected as it was discreet.

Quinn told Sam to sit in the window of a café down the street and wait for him.

"Why can't I come with you?" she asked.

"Because he wouldn't receive you. He may not even see me. But I hope he will—we go back a long way. Strangers he doesn't like, unless they are paying heavily, and we aren't. When it comes to women from the FBI, he'd be like shy game."

Quinn announced himself through the door phone, aware he was being scanned by the overhead video camera. When the door clicked he walked right through to the back, past two secretaries who did not even look up. Julian Hayman was in his office at the far end of the ground floor. The room was as elegant as its occupant. It had no windows; neither did Hayman.

"Well, well, well," he drawled. "Long time, soldier." He held out a languid hand. "What brings you to my humble shop?"

"Information," said Quinn. He told Hayman what he wanted.

"In earlier times, dear boy, no problem. But things change, don't you see? Fact is, the word's out on you, Quinn. Persona non grata, they're saying at the club. Not the flavor of the month exactly, especially with your own people. Sorry, old boy, you're bad news. Can't help."

Quinn lifted the phone off the desk and hit several buttons. It began to ring at the other end.

"What are you doing?" asked Hayman. The drawl had gone.

"No one saw me come in here, but half Fleet Street's going to see me leave," said Quinn.

"*Daily Mail*," said a voice on the phone. Hayman reached forward and killed the call. Many of his best-paying clients were American corporations in Europe, the sort to whom he would prefer to avoid making laborious explanations.

"You're a bastard, Quinn," he said thinly. "Always were. All right, a couple of hours in the files, but I lock you in. Nothing is to be missing."

"Would I do that to you?" asked Quinn amiably. Hayman led him downstairs to the basement archive.

Partly in the course of his business, partly out of a personal interest, Julian Hayman had amassed over the years a remarkably comprehensive archive of criminals of every kind. Murderers, bank robbers, gangsters, swindlers, dope peddlers, arms traffickers, terrorists, kidnappers, shifty bankers, accountants, lawyers, politicians, and policemen; dead, alive, in jail, or simply missing—if they had appeared in print, and often if they had not, he had them filed. The archive ran right under the building.

"Any particular section?" asked Hayman as he switched on the lights. The file cabinets ran in all directions, and these were only the cards and the photographs. The main data was on computer.

"Mercenaries," said Quinn.

"As in Congo?" asked Hayman.

"As in Congo, Yemen, South Sudan, Biafra, Rhodesia."

"From here to here," said Hayman, gesturing to ten yards of chin-high steel filing cabinets. "The table's at the end."

It took Quinn four hours, but no one disturbed him. The photograph showed four men, all white. They were grouped around the front end of a Jeep, on a thin and dusty road edged by the bush vegetation of what looked like Africa. Several black soldiers could be discerned behind them. They were all in camouflage combat uniform and calf boots. Three had bush hats. All carried Belgian FLN automatic rifles. Their camouflage was of the leopard-spot type favored by Europeans rather than the streaked variety used by the British and Americans.

Quinn took the photo to the table, put it under the spot lamp, and found a powerful magnifying glass in the drawer. Under its gaze, the design on the hand of one of the men showed up more clearly, despite the sepia tint of the old photo. A spider's web motif, on the back of the left hand, the spider crouching at the center of the web.

He went on through the files but found nothing else of interest. Nothing that rang a bell. He pressed the buzzer to be let out.

In his office Julian Hayman held out his hand for the photograph.

"Who?" said Quinn. Hayman studied the rear of the picture. Like every other card entry and photo in his collection, it bore a seven-figure number on the back. He tapped the number into the console of his desktop computer. The full file flashed up on the screen.

"Hmm, you *have* picked some charmers, old boy." He read off the screen. "Picture almost certainly taken in Maniema Province, eastern Congo, now Zaire, some time in the winter of 1964. The man on the left is Jacques Schramme, Black Jack Schramme, the Belgian mercenary."

He warmed to his narration. It was his speciality.

"Schramme was one of the first. He fought against the United Nations troops in the attempted Katangan secession of 1960 to '62. When they lost he had to quit and took refuge in neighboring Angola, which was then Portuguese and ultra-right wing. Returned on invitation in the autumn of 1964 to help put down the Simba revolt. Reconstituted his old Leopard Group and set about pacifying Maniema Province. That's him all right. Any more?"

"The others," said Quinn.

"Mmmm. The one on the extreme right is another Belgian, Commandant Wauthier. At the time he commanded a contingent of Katangan levies and about twenty white mercenaries at Watsa. Must have been on a visit. You interested in Belgians?"

"Maybe." Quinn thought back to the Volvo in the warehouse. He was passing the open door, caught the odor of cigarette smoke. Not Marlboro, not Dunhill. More like French Gauloises. Or Bastos, the Belgian brand. Zack did not smoke; he had smelt his breath.

"The one without the hat in the middle is Roger Lagaillarde, also Belgian. Killed in a Simba ambush on the Punia road. No doubt about that."

"And the big one?" said Quinn. "The giant?"

"Yes, he is big," agreed Hayman. "Must be six feet six at least. Built like a barn door. Early twenties, by the look of him. Pity he's turned his head away. With the shadow of his bush hat you can't see much of his face. Probably why there's no name for him. Just a nickname. Big Paul. That's all it says."

He flicked off the screen. Quinn had been doodling on a pad. He pushed his drawing across to Hayman.

"Ever seen that before?"

Hayman looked at the design of the spider's web, the spider at its center. He shrugged.

"A tattoo? Worn by young hooligans, punks, football thugs. Quite common."

"Think back," said Quinn. "Belgium, say thirty years ago."

"Ah, wait a minute. What the hell did they call it? *Araignée*—that was it. Can't recall the Flemish word for spider, just the French."

He tapped at his keys for several seconds.

"Black web, red spider at the center, worn on the back of the left hand?"

Quinn tried to recall. He was passing the open passenger door of the Volvo, on his way to climb into the trunk. Zack behind him. The man in the driver's seat had leaned across to watch him through the hood slits. A big man, almost touched the roof in the sitting position. Leaning sideways, left hand supporting his weight. And in order to smoke he had removed his left glove.

"Yeah," said Quinn. "That's it."

"Insignificant bunch," said Hayman dismissively, reading from his screen. "Extreme right-wing organization formed in Belgium in the late fifties, early sixties. Opposed to decolonization of Belgium's only colony, the Congo. Anti-black, of course, anti-Semitic—what else is new? Recruited young tearaways and hooligans, street thugs and riffraff. Specialized in throwing rocks through Jewish shop windows, heckling leftist speakers, beat up a couple of Liberal members of Parliament. Died out eventually. Of course, the dissolution of the colonial empires threw up all sorts of these groups."

"Flemish movement or Walloon?" asked Quinn. He was referring to the two cultural groups within Belgium: the Flemings, mainly in the northern half near Holland, who speak Flemish, and the Walloons from the South, nearer France, who speak French. Belgium is a two-language country.

"Both, really," said Hayman after consulting his screen. "But it says here it started and was always strongest in the city of Antwerp. So, Flemish, I suppose."

Quinn left him and returned to the café. Any other woman would have been spitting angry at being kept waiting for four and a half hours. Fortunately for Quinn, Sam was a trained agent, and had been through her apprenticeship in stakeout duties, than which nothing is more boring. She was nursing her fifth cup of awful coffee.

"When do you check your car in?" he asked.

"Due tonight. I could extend it."

"Can you hand it back at the airport?"

"Sure. Why?"

"We're flying to Brussels."

She looked unhappy.

"Please, Quinn, do we have to fly? I do it if I really have to, but if I can avoid it I chicken out, and I've had too much flying lately."

"Okay," he said. "Check the car in London. We'll take the train and the hovercraft. We'll have to rent a Belgian car anyway. Might as well be Ostende. And we'll need money. I have no credit cards."

"You *what*?" She had never heard anyone say that.

"I don't need them in Alcántara del Rio."

"Okay, we'll go to the bank. I'll use a check and hope I have enough in the account back home."

On the way to the bank she turned on the radio. The music was somber. It was four on a London afternoon and getting dark. Far away across the Atlantic, the Cormack family was burying their son.

CHAPTER TWELVE

They laid him down on Prospect Hill, the cemetery on the island of Nantucket, and the chill November wind keened out of the north across the Sound.

The service was in the small Episcopalian church on Fair Street, far too small to hold all who wanted to attend. The First Family was in the front two rows of pews, with the Cabinet behind them and a variety of other dignitaries in the rear. At the family's request it was a small and private service—foreign ambassadors and delegates were asked to attend a memorial service in Washington to be held later.

The President had asked for privacy from the media, but a number had turned up anyway. The islanders—there were no vacationers on the island in that season—took his wish very literally. Even the Secret Service men, not known for their exquisite manners, were surprised to be upstaged by the grim and silent Nantucketers, who quietly lifted several cameramen physically out of the way and left two of them protesting the ruin of their exposed film rolls.

The casket was brought to the church from the island's only funeral parlor on Union Street, where it had rested during the time between its arrival by military C-130—the small airfield could not take the Boeing 747—and the start of the service.

Halfway through the ceremony the first rains came, glittering on the gray slate roof of the church, washing down the stained-glass windows and the pink and gray stone blocks of the building.

When it was over, the casket was placed in a hearse, which proceeded at walking pace the half mile to the Hill; out of Fair Street, over the bumpy cobblestones of Main Street, and up New Mill Street to Cato Lane. The mourners walked in the rain, headed by the President, whose eyes were fixed on the flag-draped coffin a few feet in front of him. His younger brother supported a weeping Myra Cormack.

The way was flanked by the people of Nantucket, bareheaded and silent. There were the tradesmen who had sold the family fish, meat, eggs, and vegetables; restaurateurs who had served them in the scores of good eating houses around the island. There were the walnut faces of the old fishermen who had once taught the tow-haired youngster from New Haven to swim and dive and fish, or taken him scalloping off the Sankaty Light.

The caretaker and the gardener stood weeping on the corner of Fair Street and Main, to take a last look at the boy who had learned to run on those hard, tide-washed beaches from Coatue up to Great Point and back to Siasconset Beach. But bomb victims are not for the eyes of the living and the casket was sealed.

At Prospect Hill they turned into the Protestant half of the cemetery, past hundred-year-old graves of men who had hunted whales in small open boats and carved scrimshaw by oil lamps through the long winter nights. They came to the new section where the grave had been prepared.

The people filed in behind and filled the ground, row on row, and in that high open place the wind tore across the Sound and through the town to tug at hair and scarves. No shop was open that day, no garage, no bar. No planes landed, no ferries docked. The islanders had locked out the world to mourn one of their own, even by adoption. The minister began to intone the old words, his voice carried away on the wind.

High above, a single gyrfalcon, drifting down from the Arctic like a snowflake on the blast, looked down, saw every detail with his incredible eyes, and his single lost-soul scream was pulled away down the wind.

The rain, which had held off since the church service, resumed again, coming in flurries and squalls. The locked sails of the Old Mill creaked down the road. The men from Washington shivered and huddled into their heavy coats. The President stood immobile and stared down at what was left of his son, immune to the cold and the rain.

A yard from him stood the First Lady, her face streaked with rain and tears. When the preacher reached "the Resurrection and the Life," she seemed to sway as if she might fall.

By her side a Secret Service man, open-coated to reach the handgun beneath his left armpit, crew-cut and built like a linebacker, overlooked protocol and training to wrap his right arm around her shoulders. She leaned against him and wept into his soaked jacket.

John Cormack stood alone, isolated in his pain, unable to reach out, an island.

A photographer, smarter than the rest, took a ladder from a backyard a quarter of a mile away and climbed the old wooden windmill on the corner of South Prospect Street and South Mill Street. Before anyone saw him using a telephoto lens, and by the light of a single wintry shaft that penetrated the clouds, he took one picture over the heads of the crowd of the group by the side of the grave.

It was a picture that would flash around America and the world. It showed the face of John Cormack as none had ever seen it: the face of an old man, a man aged beyond his years, sick, tired, drained. A man who could take no more; a man ready to go.

At the entrance to the cemetery the Cormacks stood later as the mourners passed by. None could find words to say. The President nodded as if he understood, and shook hands formally.

After the few from the immediate family came his closest friends and colleagues, headed by the Vice President and the six members of the Cabinet who formed the core of the committee seeking to handle the crisis for him. With four of them—Odell, Reed, Donaldson, and Walters—he went back a long time.

Michael Odell paused for a moment in an attempt to find something to say, shook his head, and turned away. The rain pattered on his bowed head, plastering the thick gray hair to his scalp.

Jim Donaldson's precise diplomacy was equally disarmed by his emotions; he, too, could only stare in mute sympathy at his friend, shake his limp, dry hand, and pass on.

Bill Walters, the Attorney General, hid what he felt behind formality. He murmured, "Mr. President, my condolences. I'm sorry, sir."

Morton Stannard, the banker from New York translated to the Pentagon, was the oldest man there. He had attended many funerals, of friends and colleagues, but nothing like this. He was going to say something conventional, but could only blurt out: "God, I'm so sorry, John."

Brad Johnson, the black academic and National Security adviser, just shook his head as if in bewilderment.

Hubert Reed of the Treasury surprised those standing close to the Cormacks. He was not a demonstrative man, too shy for overt demonstrations of affection, a bachelor who had never felt the need for wife or children. But he stared up at John Cormack through streaked glasses, held out his hand, and then reached up spontaneously to embrace his old friend with both arms. As if surprised at his own impulsiveness, he then turned and hurried away to join the others climbing into their waiting cars for the airfield.

The rain eased again and two strong men began to shovel wet earth into the hole. It was over.

Quinn checked the ferry times out of Dover for Ostende and found they had missed the last of the day. They spent the night at a quiet hotel and took the train from Charing Cross in the morning.

The crossing was uneventful and by the late morning Quinn had rented a blue medium-sized Ford from a local rental agency and they were heading for the ancient Flemish port that had been trading on the Schelde since before Columbus sailed.

Belgium is interlaced by a very modern system of high-class motorways; distances are short and times even shorter. Quinn chose the E.5 east out of Ostende, cut south of Bruges and Ghent, then northeast down the E.3 and straight into the heart of Antwerp in time for a late lunch.

Europe was unknown territory for Sam; Quinn seemed to know his way around. She had heard him speak rapid and fluent French several times during the few hours they had been in the country. What she had not realized was that each time Quinn had asked if the Fleming would mind if he spoke French before he launched into it. The Flemish usually speak some French, but like to be asked first. Just to establish that they are not Walloons.

They parked the car, took lodgings in a small hotel on the Italie Lei, and walked around the corner to one of the many restaurants flanking both sides of the De Keyser Lei for lunch.

"What exactly are you looking for?" asked Sam as they ate.

"A man," said Quinn.

"What kind of a man?"

"I'll know when I see him."

After lunch Quinn consulted a taxi driver in French and they took off. He paused at an art shop, made two purchases, bought a street map from a curbside kiosk, and had another conference with the driver. Sam heard the words *Falcon Rui* and then *Schipperstraat*. The driver gave her a bit of a leer as Quinn paid off the taxi.

The Falcon Rui turned out to be a run-down street fronted by several low-budget clothing shops, among others. In one, Quinn bought a seaman's sweater, canvas jeans, and rough boots. He stuffed these into a canvas bag and they set off toward Schipperstraat. Above the roofs she could see the beaks of great cranes, indicating they were close to the docks.

Quinn turned off the Falcon Rui into a maze of narrow, mean streets that seemed to make up a zone of old and seedy houses between the Falcon Rui and the River Schelde. They passed several rough-looking men who appeared to be merchant seamen. There was an illuminated plate-glass window to Sam's left. She glanced in. A hefty young woman, bursting out of a skimpy pair of briefs and a bra, lounged in an armchair.

"Jesus, Quinn, this is the red light district," she protested.

"I know," he said. "That's what I asked the cabdriver for."

He was still walking, glancing left and right at the signs above the shops. Apart from the bars and the illuminated windows where the whores sat and beckoned, there were few shops. But he found three of the sort he wanted, all within the space of two hundred yards.

"Tattooists?" she queried.

"Docks," he said simply. "Docks mean sailors; sailors mean tattoos. They also mean bars and girls and the thugs who live off girls. We'll come back tonight."

Senator Bennett Hapgood rose at his appointed time on the floor of the Senate and strode to the podium. The day after the funeral of Simon Cormack both houses of Congress had once again put on the record their shock and revulsion at what had happened on a lonely roadside far away in England the previous week.

Speaker after speaker had called for action to trace the culprits and bring them to justice, American justice, no matter what the cost. The President pro tem of the Senate hammered with his gavel.

"The junior senator from Oklahoma has the floor," he intoned.

Bennett Hapgood was not known as a heavyweight within the Senate. The session might have been thinly attended but for the matter under discussion. It was not thought the junior senator from Oklahoma would have much more to add. But he did. He uttered the habitual words of condolence to the President, revulsion at what had happened, and eagerness to see the guilty brought to justice. Then he paused and considered what he was about to say.

He knew it was a gamble, one hell of a gamble. He had been told what he had been told, but he had no proof of it. If he was wrong, his fellow senators would put him down as just another hayseed who used serious words with no serious intent. But he knew he had to go on or lose the support of his new and very impressive financial backer.

"But maybe we do not have to look too far to find out who were the culprits of this fiendish act."

The low buzz in the chamber died away. Those in the aisles, about to depart, stopped and turned.

"I would like to ask one thing: Is it not true that the bomb which killed that young man, the only son of our President, was designed, made, and assembled wholly within the Soviet Union, and provably so? Did that device not come from Russia?"

His natural demagoguery might have carried him further. But the scene disintegrated in confusion and uproar. The media carried his question to the nation within ten minutes. For two hours the administration fenced and hedged. Then it had to concede the contents of the summary of Dr. Barnard's report.

By nightfall the bleak and black rage against someone unknown, which had run like a growling current through the people of Nantucket the previous day, had found a target. Spontaneous crowds stormed and wrecked the offices of the Soviet airline Aeroflot at 630 Fifth Avenue in New York, before the police could throw a cordon 'round the building. Its panic-stricken staff ran upstairs seeking shelter from the mob, only to be rebuffed by the office workers on the floors above them. They escaped, along with the others in the building, through the help of the Fire Department when the Aeroflot floors were set afire and the whole building evacuated.

The NYPD got reinforcements to the Soviet Mission to the United Nations at 136 East 67th Street just in time. A surging mob of New Yorkers tried to force their way into the cordoned-off street; fortunately for the Russians the blue-uniformed lines held. The New York police found themselves wrestling with a crowd intent on doing something with which many of the policemen privately sympathized.

It was the same in Washington. The capital's police were forewarned and sealed off both the Soviet embassy and the consulate on Phelps Place just in time. Frenzied telephone appeals from the Soviet ambassador to the State Department were met with an assurance that the British report was still under examination and might prove to be false.

"We wish to see that report," insisted Ambassador Yermakov. "It is a lie. I will be categorical. It is a lie."

The agencies Tass and Novosti, along with every Soviet embassy in the world, issued a late-night flat denial of the findings of the Barnard report, accusing London and Washington of a vicious and deliberate calumny.

"How the hell did it get out?" demanded Michael Odell. "How the hell did that man Hapgood get to hear of it?"

There was no answer. Any major organization, let alone a government, cannot function without a host of secretaries, stenographers, clerks, messengers, any one of whom can leak a confidential document.

"One thing is certain," mused Stannard of Defense. "After this, the Nantucket Treaty is dead as a dodo. We have to review our defense appropriations now on the basis that there will be no reductions, no limits at all."

Quinn had begun trawling the bars in the maze of narrow streets running off Schipperstraat. He was there by ten that evening and stayed till the bars closed just before dawn, a rangy seaman who seemed half drunk, spoke slurred French, and nursed a small beer in bar after bar. It was cold outside and the thinly clad prostitutes shivered over their electric heaters behind their windows. Sometimes they came off shift, pulled on a coat, and scuttled down the pavement to one of the bars for a drink and the usual exchange of crude pleasantries with the barman and regulars.

Most of the bars had names like Las Vegas, Hollywood, California, their optimistic owners hoping that names redolent of foreign glamour would entice the wandering sailor to think that opulence lay beyond the chipped doors. By and large they were sleazy places, but warm and serving good beer.

Quinn had told Sam she would have to wait, either at the hotel or in the car parked two corners away on Falcon Rui. She chose the car, which did not prevent her receiving a fair share of propositions through the windows.

Quinn sat and drank slowly, watching the surging tide of locals and foreigners that ebbed in and out of these streets and their bars. On his left hand, picked out in India ink from the art shop, slightly smudged to give the impression of age, was the motif of the black spider's web, the bright red spider at its center. All night he scanned other left hands but saw nothing like it.

He wandered up the Guit Straat and the Pauli Plein, took a small beer in each of the bars, then cut back into Schipperstraat and started again. The girls thought he wanted a woman but was having trouble making up his mind. The male customers ignored him, since they were always on the move themselves. A couple of barmen, on his third visit, nodded and grinned: "Back again, no luck?"

They were right, but in a different sense. He had no luck and before dawn rejoined Sam in the car. She was half asleep, the engine running to keep the heater on.

"What now?" she asked as she drove him back to the hotel.

"Eat, sleep, eat, start again tomorrow night," he said.

She was particularly erotic through the morning they spent in bed, suspecting Quinn might have been tempted by some of the girls and their outfits on display in Schipperstraat. He was not, but saw no reason to disabuse her.

Peter Cobb saw Cyrus Miller at his own request atop the Pan-Global Building in Houston the same day.

"I want out," he said flatly. "This has gone too far. What happened to that young boy was awful. My associates feel the same. Cyrus, you said it would never come to that. You said the kidnap alone would suffice to . . . to change things. We never thought the boy would die. But what those animals did to him . . . that was horrible . . . immoral . . ."

Miller rose from behind his desk and his eyes blazed at the younger man.

"Don't you lecture me about morality, boy. Don't you ever do that. I didn't want that to happen either, but we all knew it might have to. You, too, Peter Cobb, as God will be your judge—you, too. And it had to be. Unlike you I have prayed for His guidance; unlike you I have spent nights on my knees praying for that young man.

"And the Lord answered me, my friend; and the Lord said: Better that one young lamb go to the slaughter than that the whole flock perish. We are not talking about one man here, Cobb. We are talking of the safety, of the survival, of the very lives of the entire American people. And the Lord has told me: what must be, must be. That Communist in Washington must be brought down before he destroys the temple of the Lord, the temple that is this entire land of ours. Go back to your factory, Peter Cobb. Go back and turn the plowshares into the swords we must have to defend our nation and destroy the Antichrists of Moscow. And be silent, sir. Talk to me no more of morality, for this is the Lord's work and He has spoken to me."

Peter Cobb went back to his factory a very shaken man.

• • •

Mikhail Sergeevich Gorbachev also had a serious confrontation that day. Once again Western newspapers were spread over the long conference table running almost the length of the room, their pictures telling part of the story, their screaming headlines the rest. Only for the latter did he need a Russian translation. The Foreign Ministry translations were pinned to each newspaper.

On his desk were more reports that needed no translation. They were in Russian, coming from ambassadors across the world, from consuls general and the U.S.S.R.'s own foreign correspondents. Even the East European satellites had had their anti-Soviet demonstrations. Moscow's denials had been constant and sincere, and yet . . .

As a Russian, and a Party apparatchik of years of practice, Mikhail Gorbachev was no milksop in the business of realpolitik. He knew about disinformation; had not the Kremlin founded an entire department devoted to it? Was there not in the KGB a whole directorate dedicated to the sowing of anti-Western sentiment by the well-placed lie or the even more damaging half-truth? But this act of disinformation was unbelievable.

He awaited the man he had summoned with impatience. It was close to midnight and he had had to cancel a weekend of duck-shooting on the northern lakes, along with spicy Georgian food, one of his two great passions.

The man came just after midnight.

A General Secretary of the U.S.S.R., of all people, should not expect a Chairman of the KGB to be a warm, lovable fellow, but there was a cold cruelty about the face of Colonel-General Vladimir Kryuchkov that Gorbachev found personally unlikable.

True, he had promoted the man from the post of First Deputy Chairman when he had secured the ouster of his old antagonist Chebrikov three years earlier. He had had little choice. One of the four Deputy Chairmen had to take the slot, and he had been sufficiently taken with Kryuchkov's lawyer background to offer him the job. Since then he had begun to nurture reservations.

He recognized that he might have been swayed by his desire to turn the U.S.S.R. into a "socialist law-based state," in which the law would be supreme, a concept formerly regarded by the Kremlin as bourgeois. It had been a pretty frantic time, those first few days of October 1988, when he had summoned a sudden extraordinary meeting of the Central Committee and inaugurated his own Night of the Long

Knives against his opponents. Maybe in his hurry he had overlooked a few things. Like Kryuchkov's background.

Kryuchkov had worked in Stalin's Public Prosecutor office, not a job for the squeamish, and had been involved in the savage repression of the 1956 Hungarian uprising, joining the KGB in 1967. It was in Hungary he had met Andropov, who went on to head the KGB for fifteen years. It was Andropov who had nominated Chebrikov as his successor, and Chebrikov who had picked Kryuchkov to head up the foreign espionage arm, the First Chief Directorate. Maybe he, the General Secretary, had underestimated the old loyalties.

He looked up at the high-domed forehead, the freezing eyes, thick gray sideburns, and grim, down-turned mouth. And he realized this man might, after all, be his opponent.

Gorbachev came around the desk and shook hands; a dry, firm grip. As always when he talked, he maintained vigorous eye contact, as if seeking shiftiness or timidity. Unlike most of his predecessors, he was pleased if he found neither. He gestured at the overseas reports. The general nodded. He had seen them all, and more. He avoided Gorbachev's eye.

"Let's keep it short," said Gorbachev. "We know what they are saying. It's a lie. Our denials continue to go out. This lie must not be allowed to stick. But where does it come from? On what is it based?"

Kryuchkov tapped the massed Western reports with contempt. Though a former KGB *rezident* in New York, he hated America.

"Comrade General Secretary, it appears to be based on a British report by the scientists who carried out the forensic examination of the way that American died. Either the man lied, or others took his report and altered it. I suspect it is an American trick."

Gorbachev walked back behind his desk and resumed his seat. He chose his words carefully.

"Could there . . . under any circumstances . . . be any part of truth in this accusation?"

Vladimir Kryuchkov was startled. Within his own organization there was a department that specifically designed, invented, and made in its laboratories the most devilish devices for the ending of life, or simply for incapacitation. But that was not the point; they had not assembled any bomb to be concealed in Simon Cormack's belt.

"No, Comrade, no, surely not."

Gorbachev leaned forward and tapped his blotter.

"Find out," he ordered. "Once and for all, yes or no, find out."

The general nodded and left. The General Secretary stared down the long room. He needed—perhaps he should say "had needed"—the Nantucket Treaty more than the Oval Office knew. Without it his country faced the specter of the invisible B-2 Stealth bomber, and he the nightmare of trying to find 300 billion rubles to rebuild the air-defense network. Until the oil ran out.

Quinn saw him on the third night. He was short and stocky, with the puffed ears and broadened nose of a pug, a knuckle-fighter. He sat alone at the end of the bar in the Montana, a grubby dive in Oude Mann Straat, the aptly named Old Man Street. There were another dozen people in the bar, but no one talked to him and he looked as if he did not wish them to.

He held his beer in his right hand, his left clutching a hand-rolled cigarette, and on the back was the black web and the spider. Quinn strolled down the length of the bar and sat down two barstools away from the man.

They both sat in silence for a while. The pug glanced at Quinn but took no other notice. Ten minutes went by. The man rolled another cigarette. Quinn gave him a light. The pug nodded but gave no verbal thanks. A surly, suspicious man, not easy to draw into conversation.

Quinn caught the barman's eye and gestured to his glass. The barman brought another bottle. Quinn gestured to the empty glass of the man beside him and raised an eyebrow. The man shook his head, dug in his pocket, and paid for his own.

Quinn sighed inwardly. This was hard going. The man looked like a bar-brawler and a petty crook without even the brains to be a pimp, which does not need much. The chances that he spoke French were slim, and he was certainly surly enough. But his age was about right, late forties, and he had the tattoo. He would have to do.

Quinn left the bar and found Sam slumped in the car two corners away. He told her quietly what he wanted her to do.

"Are you out of your mind?" she said. "I can't do that. I'd have you know, Mr. Quinn, I am a Rockcastle preacher's daughter." She was grinning as she said it.

Ten minutes later Quinn was back on his barstool when she came in. She had hiked her skirt so high the waistband must have been under her armpits, but covered by her polo-neck sweater. She had used the entire Kleenex box from the glove compartment to fill out her already full bosom to startling proportions. She swayed over to Quinn and took the barstool between him and the pug. The pug stared at her. So did everyone else. Quinn ignored her.

She reached up and kissed his cheek, then stuck her tongue in his ear. He still ignored her. The pug returned to staring at his glass, but darted an occasional glance at the bosom that jutted over the bar. The barman came up, smiled, and looked inquiring.

"Whisky," she said. It is an international word, and uttering it does not betray country of origin. He asked her in Flemish if she wanted ice; she did not understand, but nodded brightly. She got the ice. She toasted Quinn, who ignored her. With a shrug she turned to the pug and toasted him instead. Surprised, the bar-brawler responded.

Quite deliberately Sam opened her mouth and ran her tongue along her lower lip, bright with gloss. She was vamping the pug unashamedly. He gave her a broken-toothed grin. Without waiting for more she leaned over and kissed the pug on the mouth.

With a backward sweep Quinn swept her off the barstool onto the floor, got up, and leaned toward the pug.

"What the shit do you think you're up to, messing with my broad?" he snarled in drunken French. Without waiting for an answer he hauled off a left hook that took the pug squarely on the jaw and knocked him backwards into the sawdust.

The man fell well, blinked, rolled back on his feet, and came for Quinn. Sam, as instructed, left hastily by the door. The barman reached quickly for the phone beneath the counter, dialed 101 for the police, and, when they came on the line, muttered "Bar fight" and the address of his bar.

There are always prowl cars cruising that district, especially at night, and the first white Sierra with the word POLITIE along the side in blue was there in four minutes. It disgorged two uniformed officers, closely followed by two more from a second car twenty seconds afterward.

Still, it is surprising how much damage two good fighters can do to a bar in four minutes. Quinn knew he could outpace the pug, who was slowed by drink and cigarettes, and outpunch him. But he let the man land a couple of blows in the ribs, just for encouragement, then put a hard left hook under his heart to slow him a mite. When it looked as if the pug might call it a day, Quinn closed with him to help him a bit.

In a double bear hug the two men flattened most of the bar furniture, rolling through the sawdust in a melee of chair legs, tabletops, glasses, and bottles.

When the police arrived, the two brawlers were arrested on the spot. The police HQ for that area is Zone West P/1 and the nearest precinct house is in the Blindenstraat. The two squad cars deposited them there separately two minutes later and delivered them into the care of Duty Sergeant Van Maes. The barman totted up his damage and made a statement from behind his bar. No need to detain the man—he had a business to run. The officers divided his damage estimate by two and made him sign it.

Fighting prisoners are always separated at Blindenstraat. Sergeant Van Maes slung the pug, whom he knew well from previous encounters, into the bare and stained *wachtkamer* behind his desk; Quinn was made to sit on a hard bench in the reception area while his passport was examined.

"American, eh?" said Van Maes. "You should not get involved in fights, Mr. Quinn. This Kuyper we know; he is always in trouble. This time he does down. He hit you first, no?"

Quinn shook his head.

"Actually, I slugged him."

Van Maes studied the barman's statement.

"Hmm. *Ja*, the barman says you were both to blame. Pity. I must hold you both now. In the morning you go to the Magistraat. Because of the damage to the bar."

The Magistraat would mean paperwork. When at 5:00 A.M. a very smart American lady in a severe business suit came into the precinct house with a roll of money to pay for the damage to the Montana, Sergeant Van Maes was relieved.

"You pay for the half this American caused, *ja*?" he asked.

"Pay the lot," said Quinn from his bench.

"You pay Kuyper's share, too, Mr. Quinn? He is a thug, in and out of here since he was a boy. A long record, always small things."

"Pay for him too," said Quinn to Sam. She did so. "Since there's now nothing owing, do you want to press charges, Sergeant?"

"Not really. You can leave."

"Can he come too?" Quinn gestured to the *wachtkamer* and the snoring form of Kuyper, which could be seen through the door.

"You want *him*?"

"Sure, we're buddies."

The sergeant raised an eyebrow, shook Kuyper awake, told him the stranger had paid his damages for him, and just as well or Kuyper would see a week inside jail, again. As it was, he could go. When Sergeant Van Maes looked up, the lady had gone. The American draped an arm around Kuyper and together they staggered down the steps of the precinct house. Much to the sergeant's relief.

In London the two quiet men met during the lunch hour in a discreet restaurant whose waiters left them alone once their food had arrived. The men knew each other by sight, or more properly by photograph. Each knew what the other did for a living. A curious inquirer, had he had the impudence to ask, might have learned that the Englishman was a civil servant in the Foreign Office and the other the Assistant Cultural Attaché at the Soviet embassy.

He would never have learned, no matter how many records he checked, that the Foreign Office official was Deputy Head of Soviet Section at Century House, headquarters of Britain's Secret Intelligence Service; nor that the man who purported to arrange visits of the Georgian State Choir was the Deputy *Rezident* of the KGB within the mission. Both men knew they were there with the approval of their respective governments, that the meeting had been at the request of the Russians, and that the Chief of the SIS had reflected deeply before permitting it. The British had a fair idea what the Russian request would be.

As the remains of the lamb cutlets were cleared away and the waiter headed off for their coffee, the Russian asked his question.

"I'm afraid it is, Vitali Ivanovich," replied the Englishman gravely. He spoke for several minutes, summarizing the findings of the Barnard forensic report. The Russian looked shaken.

"This is impossible," said the Russian at last. "My government's denials are wholly truthful."

The British intelligence man was silent. He might have said that if you tell enough lies, when you finally tell the truth it is hard to keep an audience. But he did not. From his breast pocket he withdrew a photograph. The Russian studied it.

It was blown up many times from its original paper-clip size. In the photograph it was four inches long. A mini-det from Baikonur.

"This was found in the body?"

The Englishman nodded.

"Embedded in a fragment of bone, driven into the spleen."

"I am not technically qualified," said the Russian. "May I keep this?"

"That's why I brought it," said the SIS man.

For answer the Russian sighed and produced a sheet of paper of his own. The Englishman glanced at it and raised an eyebrow. It was an address in London. The Russian shrugged.

"A small gesture," he said. "Something that came to our notice."

The men settled up and parted company. Four hours later the Special Branch and the Anti-Terrorist squad jointly raided a semidetached house in Mill Hill, arresting all four members of an I.R.A. Active Service Unit and taking possession of enough bomb-making equipment to have created a dozen major attacks in the capital.

Quinn proposed to Kuyper that they find a bar still open and have a drink to celebrate their release. This time there was no objection. Kuyper bore no grudge for the fight in the bar; in fact he had been bored and the scrap had lifted his spirits. Having his fine paid for him was an added bonus. Moreover, his hangover needed the solace of a further beer or two, and if the tall man was paying . . .

Kuyper's French was slow but passable. He seemed to understand more of the language than he could speak. Quinn introduced himself as Jacques Degueldre, a French national of Belgian parentage, departed these many years to work on ships in the French Merchant Navy.

By the second beer Kuyper noticed the tattoo on the back of Quinn's hand, and proudly offered his own for comparison.

"Those were the days, eh?" Quinn grinned. Kuyper cackled at the memory.

"Broke a few heads in those days," he recalled with satisfaction. "Where did you join?"

"Congo, 1962," said Quinn.

Kuyper's brow furrowed as he tried to work out how one could join the Spider organization in the Congo. Quinn leaned forward conspiratorially.

"Fought there from '62 to '67," he said. "With Schramme and Wauthier. They were all Belgians in those days down there. Mostly Flemings. Best fighters in the world."

That pleased Kuyper. He nodded somberly at the truth of it all.

"Taught those black bastards a lesson, I can tell you."

Kuyper liked that even more.

"I nearly went," he said regretfully. He had evidently missed a major opportunity to kill a lot of Africans. "Only I was in jail."

Quinn poured another beer, their seventh.

"My best mate down there came from here," said Quinn. "There were four with the Spider tattoo. But he was the best. One night we all went into town, found a tattooist, and they initiated me, seeing as I'd already passed the tests, like. You might remember him from here. Big Paul."

Kuyper let the name sink in slowly, thought for a while, furrowed his brow, and shook his head. "Paul who?"

"Damned if I can remember. We were both twenty then. Long time ago. We just called him Big Paul. Huge chap, over six feet six. Wide as a truck. Must have weighed two hundred fifty pounds. Damn . . . what *was* his last name . . . ?"

Kuyper's brow lightened.

"I remember him," he said. "Yeah, useful puncher. He had to get out, you know. One step ahead of the fuzz. That's why he went to Africa. The bastards wanted him on a rape charge. Hold on . . . Marchais. That was it, Paul Marchais."

"Of course," said Quinn. "Good old Paul."

Steve Pyle, General Manager of the SAIB in Riyadh, got the letter from Andy Laing ten days after it was posted. He read it in the privacy of his office and when he put it down his hand was shaking. This whole thing was becoming a nightmare.

He knew the new records in the bank computer would stand up to electronic check—the colonel's work at erasing one set and substituting another had been at near-genius level—but . . . Supposing anything happened to the Minister, Prince Abdul? Suppose the Ministry did their April audit and the Prince declined to admit he had sanctioned the fundraising? And he, Steve Pyle, had only the colonel's word . . .

He tried to reach Colonel Easterhouse by phone, but the man was away, unknown to Pyle, up in the mountainous North near Ha'il making plans with a Shi'ah Imam who believed that the hand of Allah was upon him and the shoes of the Prophet on his feet. It would be three days before Pyle could reach the colonel.

Quinn plied Kuyper with beer until mid-afternoon. He had to be careful. Too little and the man's tongue would not be loosed enough to overcome his natural wariness and surliness; too much and he would simply pass out. He was that sort of drinker.

"I lost sight of him in '67," said Quinn, of their missing and mutual buddy Paul Marchais. "I got out when it all turned nasty for us mercs. I bet he never got out. Probably ended up dead in some rain ditch."

Kuyper chortled, looked around, and tapped the side of his nose in the gesture of the foolish who think they know something special.

"He came back," he said with glee. "He got out. Came back here."

"To Belgium?"

"Yup—1968, must have been. I'd just got out of the nick. Saw him myself."

Twenty-three years, thought Quinn. He could be anywhere. "Wouldn't mind having a beer with Big Paul, for old times' sake," he mused.

Kuyper shook his head. "No chance," he said drunkenly. "He's disappeared. Had to, didn't he, with the police thing and all that. Last I heard, he was working on a fun fair somewhere in the South."

Five minutes later he was asleep. Quinn returned to the hotel, somewhat unsteadily. He, too, felt the need to sleep.

"Time to earn your keep," he told Sam. "Go to the tourist information office and ask about fun fairs, theme parks, whatever. In the South of the country."

It was 6:00 P.M. He slept for twelve hours.

"There are two," Sam told him as they had breakfast in their room. "There's Bellewaerde. That's outside the town of Ieper in the extreme West, up near the coast and the French border. Or there's Walibi outside Wavre. That's south of Brussels. I've got the brochures."

"I don't suppose the brochures announce they might have an ex-Congo mercenary working there," said Quinn. "That cretin said 'South.' We'll try Walibi first. Plot a route and let's check out."

Just before ten he hoisted their luggage into the car. Once they picked up the motorway system it was another fast run, due south past Mechelen, around Brussels on the orbital ring road, and south again on the E.40 to Wavre. After that the theme park was signposted.

It was closed, of course. All fun fairs look sad in the grim chill of winter, with the dodgem cars huddled in canvas shrouds, the pavilions cold and empty, the gray rain tumbling off the girders of the roller coaster, and the wind running wet brown leaves into Ali Baba's cave. Because of the rain, even maintenance work was suspended. There was no one in the administration office either. They repaired to a café farther down the road.

"What now?" asked Sam.

"Mr. Van Eyck, at his home," said Quinn and asked for the local telephone directory.

The jovial face of the theme park's director, Bertie Van Eyck, beamed out of the title page of the brochure, above his written welcome to all visitors. Being a Flemish name, and Wavre being deep in French-speaking country, there were only three Van Eycks listed. One was listed as Albert. Bertie. An address out of town. They lunched and drove out there, Quinn asking for directions several times.

It was a pleasant detached house on a long country road called the Chemin des Charrons. Mrs. Van Eyck answered the door and called for her husband, who soon appeared in cardigan and carpet slippers. From behind him came the sound of a sports program on the television.

Though Flemish-born, Bertie Van Eyck was in the tourist business and so was bilingual in French and Flemish. His English was also perfect. He summed up his visitors as Americans at a glance and said, "Yes, I am Van Eyck. Can I help you?"

"I sure hope you can, sir. Yes, I surely do," said Quinn. He had dropped into his pose of folksy American innocence, which had fooled the receptionist at Blackwood's Hotel. "Me and my lady wife here, we're over in Belgium trying to look up relatives from the old country. See, my grandpa on my mother's side, he came from Belgium, so I have cousins in these parts and I thought maybe if I could find one or two, that would be real nice to tell the family back Stateside. . . ."

There was a roar from the television. Van Eyck looked visibly worried. The Belgian league leaders Tournai were playing French champions Sainte Étienne, a real needle match not to be missed by a football buff.

"I fear I am not related to any Americans," he began.

"No, sir, you do not understand. I've been told up in Antwerp my mother's nephew could be working in these parts, in a fun fair. Paul Marchais?"

Van Eyck's brow furrowed and he shook his head.

"I know all my staff. We have no one of that name."

"Great big guy. Big Paul, they call him. Six feet six, wide as this, tattoo on his left hand . . ."

"*Ja, ja,* but he is not Marchais. Paul Lefort, you mean."

"Well now, maybe I do mean that," said Quinn. "I seem to recall his ma, my mom's sister, *did* marry twice, so probably his name was changed. Would you by any chance know where he lives?"

"Wait, please."

Bertie Van Eyck was back in two minutes with a slip of paper. Then he fled back to his football match. Tournai had scored and he had missed it.

"I have never," said Sam as they drove back into Wavre town, "heard such an appalling caricature of an American meathead on a visit to Europe."

Quinn grinned.

"Worked, didn't it?"

They found the boardinghouse of Madame Garnier behind the railway station. It was already getting dark. She was a desiccated little widow who began by telling Quinn that she had no rooms vacant, but relented when he told her he sought none, but simply a chance to talk to his old friend Paul Lefort. His French was so fluent she took him for a Frenchman.

"But he is out, monsieur. He has gone to work."

"At the Walibi?" asked Quinn.

"But of course. The Big Wheel. He overhauls the engine for the winter months."

Quinn made a Gallic gesture of frustration.

"Always I miss my friend," he complained. "Early last month I came by the fair, and he was on vacation."

"Ah, not vacation, monsieur. His poor mother died. A long illness. He nursed her to the end. In Antwerp."

So that was what he had told them. For the second half of September and all of October he had been away from his dwelling and his workplace. I bet he was, thought Quinn, but he beamed and thanked Madame Garnier, and they drove back the four kilometers to the fun fair.

It was as abandoned as it had been six hours earlier, but now in the darkness it seemed like a ghost town. Quinn scaled the outer fence and helped Sam over after him. Against the deep velvet of the night sky he could see the inky girders of the Ferris wheel, the highest structure in the park.

They walked past the dismantled carrousel, whose antique wooden horses would now be in storage, the shuttered hot-dog stand. The Ferris wheel towered above them in the night.

"Stay here," murmured Quinn. Leaving Sam in the shadows, he walked forward to the base of the machine.

"Lefort," he called softly. There was no reply.

The double seats, hanging on their steel bars, were canvas-shrouded to protect the interiors. There was no one in or under the bottommost seats. Perhaps the man was crouching in the shadows waiting for them. Quinn glanced behind him.

To one side of the structure was the machine house, a big green steel shed housing the electric motor, and on top of it the control cabin in yellow. The doors of both opened to the touch. There was not a sound from the generator. Quinn touched it lightly. The machine contained a residual warmth.

He climbed to the control booth, flicked on a pilot light above the console, studied the levers, and depressed a switch. Beneath him the engine purred into life. He engaged the gears and moved the forward lever to "slow." Ahead of him the giant wheel began to turn through the darkness. He found a floodlight control, touched it, and the area around the base of the wheel was bathed in white light.

Quinn descended and stood by the boarding ramp as the bucket seats swung silently by him. Sam joined him.

"What are you doing?" she whispered.

"There was a spare canvas seat-cover in the engine house," he said. To their right, the booth that had once been at the zenith of the wheel began to appear. The man in it was not enjoying the ride.

He lay on his back across the double seat, his huge frame filling most of the space destined for two passengers. The hand with the tattoo lay limply across his belly, his head lolled back against the seat, sightless eyes staring up at the girders and the sky. He passed slowly in front of them, a few feet away. His mouth was half open, the nicotine-stained teeth glinting wetly in the floodlight. In the center of his forehead was a drilled round hole, its edges darkened by scorch marks. He passed and began his climb back into the night sky.

Quinn returned to the control booth and stopped the Ferris wheel where it had been, the single occupied booth at the very top out of sight in the darkness. He closed down the motor, switched off the lights, and locked both doors; took the ignition key and both door keys and hurled them far into the ornamental lake. The spare canvas seat-cover was locked inside the engine room. He was very thoughtful; Sam, when he glanced at her, looked pale and shaken.

On the road out of Wavre and back to the motorway they passed down the Chemin des Charrons again, past the house of the fun-fair director who had just lost a worker. It began to rain again.

Half a mile farther on they spotted the Domaine des Champs hotel, its lights beaming a welcome through the wet darkness.

When they had checked in, Quinn suggested Sam take her bath first. She made no objection. While she was in the tub he went through her luggage. The garment bag was no problem; the suitcase was soft-sided and took him thirty seconds to check out.

The square, hard-framed vanity case was heavy. He tipped out the collection of hair spray, shampoo, perfume, makeup kit, mirrors, brushes, and combs. It was still heavy. He measured its depth from rim to base on the outside and again on the inside. There are reasons why people hate to fly, and X-ray machines can be one of them. There was a two-inch difference in height. Quinn took his penknife and found the crack in the interior floor of the case.

Sam came out of the bathroom ten minutes later, brushing her wet hair. She was about to say something when she saw what lay on the bed, and stopped. Her face crumpled.

It was not what tradition calls a lady's weapon. It was a Smith & Wesson long-barreled .38 revolver, and the shells laid on the coverlet beside it were hollow-point. A man-stopper.

CHAPTER THIRTEEN

"Quinn," said Sam, "I swear to God, Brown sicked that piece onto me before he'd agree to let me come with you. In case things got rough, he said."

Quinn nodded and toyed with his food, which was excellent. But he had lost his appetite.

"Look, you know it hasn't been fired. And I haven't been out of your sight since Antwerp."

She was right, of course. Though he had slept for twelve hours the previous night, long enough for someone to motor from Antwerp to Wavre and back with time to spare, Madame Garnier had said her lodger left for work on the Ferris wheel that morning after breakfast. Sam had been in bed with Quinn when he woke at six.

But there *are* telephones in Belgium.

Sam had not got to Marchais before him; but someone had. Brown and his FBI hunters? Quinn knew they, too, were out in Europe, with the full backing of the national police forces behind them. But Brown would want his man alive, able to talk, able to identify the accomplices. Maybe. He pushed his plate away.

"Been a long day," he said. "Let's go sleep."

But he lay in the darkness and stared at the ceiling. At midnight he slept; he had decided to believe her.

They left in the morning after breakfast. Sam took the wheel.

"Where to, O Master?"

"Hamburg," said Quinn.

"Hamburg? What's with Hamburg?"

"I know a man in Hamburg" was all he would say.

They took the motorways again, south to cut into the E.41 north of Namur, then the long die-straight highway due east, to pass Liège and cross the German frontier at Aachen. She turned north through the dense industrial sprawl of the Ruhr past Düsseldorf, Duisburg, and Essen, to emerge finally into the agricultural plains of Lower Saxony.

Quinn spelled her at the wheel after three hours, and after two more they paused for fuel and a lunch of meaty Westphalian sausages and potato salad at a *Gasthaus*, one of the myriad that appear every two or three miles along the major German routes. It was already getting dark when they joined the columns of traffic moving through the southern suburbs of Hamburg.

The old Hanseatic port city on the Elbe was much as Quinn recalled it. They found a small, anonymous, but comfortable hotel behind the Steindammtor and checked in.

"I didn't know you spoke German too," said Sam when they reached their room.

"You never asked," said Quinn. In fact he had taught himself the language years before, because in the days when the Baader-Meinhof gang was on the rampage, and then its successor, the Red Army Faction, was in business, kidnaps had been frequent in Germany, and often very bloody. Three times in the late seventies he had worked on cases in the Federal Republic.

He made two phone calls, but learned the man he wanted to speak to would not be in his office until the following morning.

General Vadim Vassilievich Kirpichenko stood in the outer office and waited. Despite his impassive exterior he felt a twinge of nervousness. Not that the man he wished to see was unapproachable; his reputation was the opposite and they had met several times, though always formally and in public. His qualms stemmed from another factor: To go over the heads of his superiors in the KGB, to ask for a personal and private meeting with the General Secretary without telling them, was risky. If it went wrong, badly wrong, his career would be on the line.

A secretary came to the door of the private office and stood there.

"The General Secretary will see you now, Comrade General," he said.

The Deputy Head of the First Chief Directorate, senior professional intelligence officer of the espionage arm, walked straight down the long room toward the man who sat behind his desk at the end. If Mikhail Gorbachev was puzzled by the request for the meeting, he did not show it. He greeted the KGB general in comradely fashion, calling him by his first name and patronymic, and waited for him to proceed.

"You have received the report from our London station regarding the so-called evidence extracted by the British from the corpse of Simon Cormack."

It was a statement, not a question. Kirpichenko knew the General Secretary must have seen it. He had demanded the results of the London meeting as soon as they came in. Gorbachev nodded shortly.

"And you will know, Comrade General Secretary, that our colleagues in the military deny the photograph was of a piece of their equipment."

The rocket programs of Baikonur come under the military. Another nod. Kirpichenko bit the bullet.

"Four months ago I submitted a report received from my *rezident* in Belgrade which I believed to be of such importance that I marked it for passing on by the Comrade Chairman to this office."

Gorbachev stiffened. The matter was out. The officer in front of him, though a very senior man, was going behind Kryuchkov's back. It had better be serious, Comrade General, he thought. His face remained impassive.

"I expected to receive instructions to investigate the matter further. None came. It occurred to me to wonder if you ever saw the August report—it is, after all, the vacation month. . . ."

Gorbachev recalled his broken vacation. Those Jewish refuseniks being hammered right in front of the whole Western media on a Moscow street.

"You have a copy of that report with you, Comrade General?" he asked quietly. Kirpichenko took two folded sheets from his inner jacket pocket. He always wore civilian clothes, hated uniforms.

"There may be no linkage at all, General Secretary. I hope not. But I do not like coincidences. I am trained not to like them."

Mikhail Gorbachev studied the report from Major Kerkorian in Belgrade, and his brow furrowed in puzzlement.

"Who are these men?" he asked.

"Five American industrialists. The man Miller we have tagged as an extreme right-winger, a man who loathes our country. The man

Scanlon is an entrepreneur, what the Americans call a hustler. The other three manufacture extremely sophisticated weaponry for the Pentagon. With the technical details that they carry in their heads alone, they should never have exposed themselves to the danger of possible interrogation by visiting our soil."

"But they came?" asked Gorbachev. "Covertly, by military transport? To land at Odessa?"

"That's the coincidence," said the spy chief. "I checked with the Air Force traffic control people. As the Antonov left Romanian air space to enter Odessa control area, it varied its own flight plan, overflew Odessa, and touched down at Baku."

"Azerbaijan? What the hell were they doing in Azerbaijan?"

"Baku, Comrade General Secretary, is the headquarters of High Command South."

"But that's a top-secret military base. What did they do there?"

"I don't know. They disappeared when they landed, spent sixteen hours inside the base, and flew back to the same Yugoslav air base in the same plane. Then they went back to America. No boar-hunting, no vacation."

"Anything else?"

"One last coincidence. On that day, Marshal Kozlov was on an inspection visit of the Baku headquarters. Just routine. So it says."

When he had gone, Mikhail Gorbachev stopped all calls and reflected on what he had learned. It was bad, all bad, almost all. There was one recompense. His adversary, the diehard general who ran the KGB, had made a very serious mistake.

The bad news was not confined to New Square, Moscow. It pervaded the lush top-floor office of Steve Pyle in Riyadh. Colonel Easterhouse put down the letter from Andy Laing.

"I see," he said.

"Christ, that little shit could still land us all in deep trouble," protested Pyle. "Maybe the records in the computer do show something different from what he says. But if he goes on saying it, maybe the Ministry accountants will want to have a look, a real look. Before April. I mean, I know this is all sanctioned by Prince Abdul himself, and for a good cause, but hell, you know these people. Supposing he withdraws his protection, says he knows nothing of it . . . They can do that, you know. Look, maybe you should just replace that money, find the funds someplace else. . . ."

Easterhouse continued to stare out over the desert with his pale-blue eyes. It's worse than that, my friend, he thought. There *is* no connivance by Prince Abdul, no sanction by the Royal House. And half the money has gone, disbursed to bankroll the preparations for a coup that would one day bring order and discipline, *his* order and discipline, to the crazed economics and unbalanced political structures of the entire Middle East. He doubted the House of Sa'ud would see it that way; or the State Department.

"Calm yourself, Steve," he said reassuringly. "You know whom I represent here. The matter will be taken care of. I assure you."

Pyle saw him out but was not calmed. Even the CIA fouled up sometimes, he reminded himself too late. Had he known more, and read less fiction, he would have known that a senior officer of the Company could not have the rank of colonel. Langley does not take ex-Army officers. But he did not know. He just worried.

On his way down, Easterhouse realized he was going to have to return to the States for consultations. It was time, anyway. All was in place, ticking like a patient time bomb. He was even ahead of schedule. He ought to give his patrons a situation report. While there he would mention Andy Laing. Surely the man could be bought off, persuaded to hold his fire, at least until April?

He was unaware how wrong he was.

"Dieter, you owe me, and I'm calling in the marker."

Quinn sat with his contact in a bar two blocks away from the office where the man worked. Sam listened and the contact looked worried.

"But, Quinn, please try to understand. It is not a question of house rules. Federal law itself forbids non-employees to have access to the morgue."

Dieter Lutz was a decade younger than Quinn, but far more prosperous. He had the gloss of a flourishing career. He was in fact a senior staff reporter with *Der Spiegel*, Germany's biggest and most prestigious current affairs magazine.

It had not always been so. Once he had been a free-lancer, scratching a living, trying to be one step ahead of the opposition when the big stories broke. In those days there had been a kidnapping that had made every German headline day after day. At the most delicate point of the negotiations with the kidnappers Lutz had inadvertently leaked something that almost destroyed the deal.

The angry police had wanted to know where the leak had come

from. The kidnap victim was a big industrialist, a party benefactor, and Bonn had been leaning on the police heavily. Quinn had known who the guilty party was, but had kept silent. The damage was done, had to be repaired, and the breaking of a young reporter with too much enthusiasm and too little wisdom was not going to help matters.

"I don't need to break in," said Quinn patiently. "You're on the staff. You have the right to go and get the material, if it's there."

The head offices of *Der Spiegel* are at 19 Brandstwiete, a short street running between the Dovenfleet canal and the Ost-West-Strasse. Beneath the modern eleven-story building slumbers the biggest newspaper morgue in Europe. More than 18 million documents are filed in it. Computerizing the files had been going on for a decade before Quinn and Lutz took their beer that November afternoon in the Dom-Strasse bar. Lutz sighed.

"All right," he said. "What is his name?"

"Paul Marchais," said Quinn. "Belgian mercenary. Fought in the Congo 1964 to 1968. And any general background on the events of that period."

Julian Hayman's files in London might have had something on Marchais, but Quinn had not then been able to give him a name. Lutz was back an hour later with a file.

"These must not pass out of my possession," he said. "And they must be back by nightfall."

"Crap," said Quinn amiably. "Go back to work. Return in four hours. I'll be here. You can have it then."

Lutz left. Sam had not understood the talk in German, but now she leaned over to see what Quinn had got.

"What are you looking for?" she asked.

"I want to see if the bastard had any pals, any really close friends," said Quinn. He began to read.

The first piece was from an Antwerp newspaper of 1965, a general review of local men who had signed on to fight in the Congo. For Belgium it was a highly emotional issue in those days—the stories of the Simba rebels raping, torturing, and slaughtering priests, nuns, planters, missionaries, women, and children, many of them Belgian, had endowed the mercenaries who put down the Simba revolt with a kind of glamour. The article was in Flemish, with a German translation attached.

Marchais, Paul: born in Liège 1943, son of a Walloon father and Flemish mother—that would account for the French-sounding name of a boy who grew up in Antwerp. Father killed in the liberation of Belgium in 1944/45. Mother returned to her native Antwerp.

Slum boyhood, spent around the docks. In trouble with the police from early teens. A string of minor convictions to spring 1964. Turned up in the Congo with Jacques Schramme's Leopard Group. There was no mention of the rape charge; perhaps the Antwerp police were keeping quiet in the hope he would show up again and be arrested.

The second piece was a passing mention. In 1966 he had apparently quit Schramme and joined the Fifth Commando, by then headed by John Peters, who had succeeded Mike Hoare. Principally manned by South Africans—Peters had quickly ousted most of Hoare's British. So Marchais's Flemish could have enabled him to survive among Afrikaners, since Afrikaans and Flemish are fairly similar.

The other two pieces mentioned Marchais, or simply a giant Belgian called Big Paul, staying on after the disbanding of the Fifth Commando and the departure of Peters, and rejoining Schramme in time for the 1967 Stanleyville mutiny and the long march to Bukavu.

Finally Lutz had included five photocopies of sheets extracted from Anthony Mockler's classic, *Histoire des Mercenaires*, from which Quinn could fill in the events of Marchais's last months in the Congo.

In late July 1967, unable to hold Stanleyville, Schramme's group set off for the border and cut a swath clean through all opposition until they reached Bukavu, once a delightful watering hole for Belgians, a cool resort on the edge of a lake. Here they holed up.

They held out for three months until they finally ran out of ammunition. Then they marched over the bridge across the lake into the neighboring republic of Ruanda.

Quinn had heard the rest. Though out of ammunition they terrified the Ruandan government, which thought they might, if not appeased, simply terrorize the entire country. The Belgian consul was overwhelmed. Many of the Belgian mercenaries had lost their identity papers, accidentally or on purpose. The harassed consul issued temporary Belgian ID cards according to the name he was given. That would be where Marchais became Paul Lefort. It would not be beyond the wit of man to convert those papers into permanent ones at a later date, especially if a Paul Lefort had once existed and died down there.

On April 23, 1968, two Red Cross airplanes finally repatriated the mercenaries. One plane flew direct to Brussels with all the Belgians on board. All except one. The Belgian public was prepared to hail their mercenaries as heroes; not so the police. They checked everyone descending from the plane against their own wanted lists. Marchais must have taken the other DC-6, the one that dropped off human cargoes at Pisa, Zurich, and Paris. Between them the two planes carried 123 mixed European and South African mercenaries back to Europe.

Quinn was convinced Marchais had been on the second plane, that he had disappeared into twenty-three years of dead-end jobs on fairgrounds until being recruited for his last foreign assignment. What Quinn wanted was the name of one other who had been with him on that last assignment. There was nothing in the papers to give a clue. Lutz returned.

"One last thing," said Quinn.

"I can't," protested Lutz. "There's already talk that I'm writing a background piece on mercenaries. I'm not—I'm on the Common Market meeting of agriculture Ministers."

"Broaden your horizons," suggested Quinn. "How many German mercenaries were in the Stanleyville mutiny, the march to Bukavu, the siege of Bukavu, and the internment camp in Ruanda."

Lutz took notes.

"I have a wife and kids to go home to, you know."

"Then you're a lucky man," said Quinn.

The area of information he had asked for was narrower, and Lutz was back from the morgue in twenty minutes. This time he stayed while Quinn read.

What Lutz had brought him was the entire file on German mercenaries from 1960 onward. A dozen at least. Wilhelm had been in the Congo, at Watsa. Dead of wounds on the Paulis road ambush. Rolf Steiner had been in Biafra; still living in Munich, but was never in the Congo. Quinn turned the page. Siegfried "Congo" Muller had been through the Congo from start to finish; died in South Africa in 1983.

There were two other Germans, both living in Nuremberg, addresses given, but both had left Africa in the spring of 1967. That left one.

Werner Bernhardt had been with the Fifth Commando but skipped to join Schramme when it was disbanded. He had been in the mutiny, on the march to Bukavu, and in the siege of the lakeside resort. There was no address for him.

"Where would he be now?" asked Quinn.

"If it's not listed, he disappeared," said Lutz. "That was 1968, you know. This is 1991. He could be dead. Or anywhere. People like that . . . you know . . . Central or South America, South Africa . . ."

"Or here in Germany," suggested Quinn.

For answer, Lutz borrowed the bar's telephone directory. There were four columns of Bernhardts. And that was just for Hamburg. There are ten states in the Federal Republic, and they all have several such directories. "If he's listed at all," said Lutz.

"Criminal records?" asked Quinn.

"Unless it's federal, there are ten separate police authorities to go through," said Lutz. "You know that, since the war, when the Allies were kind enough to write our constitution for us, everything is decentralized. So we can never have another Hitler. Makes tracking someone down enormous fun. I know—it's part of my job. But a man like this . . . very little chance. If he wants to disappear, he disappears. This one does, or he'd have given *some* interview in twenty-three years, appeared in the papers. But, nothing. If he had, he'd be in our files."

Quinn had one last question. Where had he originally come from, this Bernhardt? Lutz scanned the sheets.

"Dortmund," he said. "He was born and raised in Dortmund. Maybe the police there know something. But they won't tell you. Civil rights, you see—we're very keen on civil rights in Germany."

Quinn thanked him and let him go. He and Sam wandered down the street looking for a promising restaurant.

"Where do we go next?" she asked.

"Dortmund," he said. "I know a man in Dortmund."

"Darling," she said, "you know a man everywhere."

In the middle of November, Michael Odell faced President Cormack alone in the Oval Office. The Vice President was shocked by the change in his old friend. Far from having recovered since the funeral, John Cormack seemed to have shrunk.

It was not simply the physical appearance that worried Odell; the former power of concentration was gone, the old incisiveness dissipated. He tried to draw the President's attention to the appointments diary.

"Ah, yes," said Cormack, with an attempt at revival. "Let's have a look."

He studied the page for Monday.

"John, it's Tuesday," said Odell gently.

As the pages turned Odell saw broad red lines through canceled appointments. There was a NATO Head of State in town. The President should greet him on the White House lawn; not negotiate with him—the European would understand that—but just greet him.

Besides, the issue was not whether the European leader would understand; the problem was whether the American media would understand if the President failed to show. Odell feared they might understand only too well.

"Stand in for me, Michael," pleaded Cormack.

The Vice President nodded. "Sure," he said gloomily. It was the tenth canceled appointment in a week. The paperwork could be handled in-house; there was a good team at the White House nowadays. Cormack had chosen well. But the American people invest a lot of power in that one man who is President, Head of State, Chief Executive, Commander in Chief of the armed forces, the man with his finger on the nuclear button. Under certain conditions. One is that they have the right to see him in action—often. It was the Attorney General who articulated Odell's worries an hour later in the Situation Room.

"He can't just sit there forever," said Walters.

Odell had reported to them all on the state in which he had found the President. There were just the inner six of them present—Odell, Stannard, Walters, Donaldson, Reed, and Johnson—plus Dr. Armitage, who had been asked to join them as an adviser.

"The man's a husk, a shadow of what he once was. Dammit, only five weeks ago," said Odell. His listeners were gloomy and depressed.

Dr. Armitage explained that President Cormack was suffering from deep postshock trauma, from which he seemed unable to recover.

"What does that mean, minus the jargon?" snapped Odell.

What it meant, said Armitage patiently, was that the Chief Executive was stricken by a personal grief so profound that it was depriving him of the will to continue.

In the aftermath of the kidnapping, the psychiatrist reported, there had been a similar trauma, but not so profound. Then the problem had been the stress and anxiety stemming from ignorance and worry—not knowing what was happening to his son, whether the boy was alive or dead, in good shape or maltreated, or when or if he would be freed.

During the kidnap the load had lightened slightly. He had learned indirectly from Quinn that at least his son was alive. As the exchange neared, he had recovered somewhat.

But the death of his only son, and the savagely brutal manner of it, had been like a body blow. Too introverted a man to share easily, too inhibited to express his grief, he had settled into an abiding melancholy that was sapping his mental and moral strength, those qualities humans call the will.

The committee listened morosely. They relied on the psychiatrist to tell them what was in their President's mind. On the few occasions when they saw him, they needed no doctor to tell them what they were seeing. A man lackluster and distraught; tired to the point of deep exhaustion, old before his time, devoid of energy or interest. There had been Presidents before who had been ill in office; the machinery of state could cope. But nothing like this. Even without the growing media questioning, several present were also beginning to ask themselves whether John Cormack could, or should, continue much longer in office.

Bill Walters listened to the psychiatrist with an expressionless face. At forty-four he was the youngest man in the Cabinet, a tough and brilliant corporate lawyer from California. John Cormack had brought him to Washington as Attorney General to use his talents against organized crime, much of it now hiding behind corporate façades. Those who admired him admitted he could be ruthless, albeit in pursuit of the supremacy of the law; those who were his enemies, and he had made a few, feared his relentlessness.

He was personable to look at, sometimes almost boyish, with his youthful clothes and blow-dried, carefully barbered hair. But behind the charm there could be a coldness, an impassivity that hid the inner man. Those who had negotiated with him noticed that the only sign he was homing in was that he ceased to blink. Then his stare could be unnerving. When Dr. Armitage had left the room Walters broke the grim silence.

"It may be, gentlemen, we will have to look seriously at the Twenty-fifth."

They all knew about it, but he had been the first to invoke its availability. Under the Twenty-fifth Amendment, the Vice President and a majority of the Cabinet may together, in writing, communicate to the President pro tempore of the Senate and the Speaker of the House of Representatives their view that the President is no longer able to discharge the powers and duties of his office. Section 4 of the Twenty-fifth Amendment, to be precise.

"No doubt you've memorized it, Bill," snapped Odell.

"Easy, Michael," said Jim Donaldson. "Bill just mentioned it."

"He would resign before that," said Odell.

"Yes," said Walters soothingly. "On health grounds, with absolute justification, and with the sympathy and gratitude of the nation. We just might have to put it to him. That's all."

"Not yet, surely," protested Stannard.

"Hear, hear. There is time," said Reed. "The grief will pass, surely. He will recover. Become his old self."

"And if not?" asked Walters. His unblinking stare went across the face of every man in the room. Michael Odell rose abruptly. He had been in some political fights in his time, but there was a coldness about Walters he had never liked. The man did not drink, and by the look of his wife he probably made love by the book.

"Okay, we'll keep an eye on it," he said. "Now, however, we'll defer decision on that. Right, gentlemen?"

Everyone else nodded and rose. They would defer consideration of the Twenty-fifth. For now.

It was a combination of the rich wheat and barley lands of Lower Saxony and Westphalia to the north and east, plus the crystal-clear water trickling out of the nearby hills, that first made Dortmund a beer town. That was in 1293, when King Adolf of Nassau gave the citizens of the small town in the southern tip of Westphalia the right to brew.

Steel, insurance, banking, and trade came later, much later. Beer was the foundation, and for centuries the Dortmunders drank most of it themselves. The industrial revolution of the middle and late nineteenth century provided the third ingredient for the grain and the water—the thirsty workers of the factories that mushroomed along the valley of the Ruhr. At the head of the valley, with views southwest as far as the towering chimneys of Essen, Duisburg, and Düsseldorf, the city stood between the grain prairies and the customers. The city fathers took advantage; Dortmund became the beer capital of Europe.

Seven giant breweries ruled the trade: Brinkhoff, Kronen, DAB, Stifts, Ritter, Thier, and Moritz. Hans Moritz was head of the second-smallest brewery and head of the dynasty that went back eight generations. But he was the last individual to own and control his empire personally, and that made him very seriously rich. It was partly his wealth and partly the fame of his name that had caused the savages of the Baader-Meinhof gang to snatch his daughter Renata ten years before.

Quinn and Sam checked into the Roemischer Kaiser Hotel in the center of the city and Quinn tried the telephone directory with little hope. The home number, of course, was not listed. He wrote a personal letter on the hotel stationery, called a cab, and had it delivered to the brewery's head office.

"Do you think your friend will still be here?" asked Sam.

"He'll be here, all right," said Quinn. "Unless he's away abroad, or at any of his six homes."

"He likes to move around a lot," observed Sam.

"Yeah. He feels safer that way. The French Riviera, the Caribbean, the ski chalet, the yacht . . ."

He was right in supposing that the villa on Lake Constanz had long been sold; that was where the snatch had taken place.

He was also in luck. They were eating dinner when Quinn was called to the phone.

"Herr Quinn?"

He recognized the voice, deep and cultured. The man spoke four languages, could have been a concert pianist. Maybe should have been.

"Herr Moritz. Are you in town?"

"You remember my house? You should. You spent two weeks in it, once."

"Yes, sir. I remember it. I didn't know whether you still retained it."

"Still the same. Renata loves it, wouldn't let me change it. What can I do for you?"

"I'd like to see you."

"Tomorrow morning. Coffee at ten-thirty."

"I'll be there."

They drove out of Dortmund due south along the Ruhrwald Strasse until the industrial and commercial sprawl dropped away behind and they entered the outer suburb of Syburg. The hills began, rolling and forested, and the estates situated within the forests contained the homes of the wealthy.

The Moritz mansion was set in four acres of parkland down a lane off the Hohensyburg Strasse. Across the valley the Syburger monument stared down the Ruhr toward the spires of Sauerland.

The place was a fortress. Chain-link fencing surrounded the entire plot and the gates were high-tensile steel, remote-controlled and with a TV camera discreetly attached to a pine tree nearby. Someone watched Quinn climb out of the car and announce himself through the steel grille beside the gates. Two seconds later the gates swung open on electric motors. When the car passed through they closed again.

"Herr Moritz enjoys his privacy," said Sam.

"He has reason to," said Quinn.

He parked on the tan gravel in front of the white stucco house and a uniformed steward let them in. Hans Moritz received them in the elegant sitting room, where coffee waited in a sterling-silver pot. His hair was whiter than Quinn recalled, his face more lined, but the handshake was as firm and the smile as grave.

They had hardly sat down when the door opened and a young woman stood there hesitantly. Moritz's face lit up. Quinn turned to look.

She was pretty in a vacuous sort of way, shy to the point of self-effacement. Both her little fingers ended in stumps. She must be twenty-five now, Quinn thought.

"Renata, kitten, this is Mr. Quinn. You remember Mr. Quinn? No, of course not."

Moritz rose, crossed to his daughter, murmured a few words in her ear, kissed the top of her head. She turned and left. Moritz resumed his seat. His face was impassive, but the twisting of his fingers revealed his inner turmoil.

"She . . . um . . . never really recovered, you know. The therapy goes on. She prefers to stay inside, seldom goes out. She will not marry . . . after what those animals did . . ."

There was a photograph on the Steinbeck grand; of a laughing, mischievous fourteen-year-old on skis. That was a year before the kidnapping. A year afterward Moritz had found his wife in the garage, the exhaust gases pumping down the rubber tube into the closed car. Quinn had been told in London.

Moritz made an effort. "I'm sorry. What can I do for you?"

"I'm trying to find a man. One who came from Dortmund long ago. He may still be here, or in Germany, or dead, or abroad. I don't know."

"Well, there are agencies, specialists. Of course, I can engage . . ."

Quinn realized that Moritz thought he needed money to engage private investigators.

"Or you could ask through the Einwohnermeldeant."

Quinn shook his head.

"I doubt if they would know. He almost certainly does not willingly cooperate with the authorities. But I believe the police might keep surveillance on him."

Technically speaking, German citizens who move to a new home within the country are required by law to notify the Inhabitants Registration Office of changes of address, both where from and where to the move took place. Like most bureaucratic systems, this works better in theory than in practice. The ones the police and/or the income tax authorities would like to contact are often those who decline to oblige.

Quinn sketched in the background of the man Werner Bernhardt.

"If he is still in Germany, he would be of an age to be in employment," said Quinn. "Unless he has changed his name, that will mean he has a social security card, pays income tax—or someone pays it for him. Because of his background he might have been in trouble with the law."

Moritz thought it over.

"If he is a law-abiding citizen—and even a former mercenary might never have committed an offense inside Germany—he would not have a police record," he said. "As for the income tax and social security people, they would regard this as privileged information, not to be divulged to an inquiry from you, or even me."

"They *would* respond to a police inquiry," said Quinn. "I thought you might perhaps have a friend or two in the city or state police."

"Ah," said Moritz. Only he would ever know just how much he had donated to the police charities of the city of Dortmund and the state of Westphalia. As in any country in the world, money is power and both buy information. "Give me twenty-four hours. I'll phone you."

He was true to his word, but his tone when he called the Roemischer Kaiser the following morning after breakfast was distant, as if someone had given him a warning along with the information.

"Werner Richard Bernhardt," he said as if reading from notes, "aged forty-eight, former Congo mercenary. Yes, he's alive, here in Germany. He works on the personal staff of Horst Lenzlinger, the arms dealer."

"Thank you. Where would I find Herr Lenzlinger?"

"Not easily. He has an office in Bremen but lives outside Oldenburg, in Ammerland County. Like me, a very private man. There the resemblance ends. Be careful of Lenzlinger, Herr Quinn. My sources tell me that despite the respectable veneer he is still a gangster."

He gave Quinn both addresses.

"Thank you," said Quinn as he noted them. There was an embarrassed pause on the line.

"One last thing. I am sorry. A message from the Dortmund police. Please leave Dortmund. Do not come back. That is all."

The word of Quinn's role in what had happened on the side of a Buckinghamshire road was spreading. Soon doors would start to close in many places.

"Feel like driving?" he asked Sam when they were packed and checked out.

"Sure. Where to?"

"Bremen." She studied the map.

"Good God, it's halfway back to Hamburg."

"Two thirds, actually. Take the E.37 for Osnabruck and follow the signs. You'll love it."

That evening Colonel Robert Easterhouse flew out of Jiddah for London, changed planes, and flew on directly to Houston. On the flight across the Atlantic he had access to the whole range of American newspapers and magazines.

Three of them carried articles on the same theme, and the reasoning of all the writers was remarkably similar. The presidential election of November 1992 was now just twelve months away. In the normal course of events the Republican party choice would be no choice at all. President Cormack would secure the nomination unopposed for a second term of office.

But the course of events these past six weeks had not been normal, the scribes told their readers—as if they needed to be told. They went on to describe the effect on President Cormack of the loss of his son as traumatic and disabling.

All three writers listed a chronicle of lapses of concentration, canceled speaking engagements, and abandoned public appearances in the previous fortnight since the funeral on Nantucket island. "The Invisible Man," one of them called the Chief Executive.

The summary of each was also similar. Would it not be better, they wrote, if the President stepped down in favor of Vice President Odell, giving Odell a clear twelve months in office to prepare for reelection in November '92?

After all, reasoned *Time*, the main plank of Cormack's foreign, defense, and economic policy, the shaving of $100 billion off the defense budget with a matching reduction by the U.S.S.R., was already dead in the water.

"Belly up" was how *Newsweek* described the chances of the treaty's ratification by the Senate after the Christmas recess.

Easterhouse landed at Houston close to midnight, after twelve hours in the air and two in London. The headlines on the newsstands in the Houston airport were more overt: Michael Odell was a Texan and would be the first Texan President since Lyndon Johnson if he stepped into Cormack's shoes.

The conference with the Alamo Group was scheduled in two days' time in the Pan-Global Building. A company limousine took Easterhouse to the Remington, where a suite had been reserved for him. Before turning in, he caught a late news summary. Again, the question was being asked.

The colonel had not been informed of Plan Travis. He did not need to know. But he did know that a change of Chief Executive would remove the last stumbling block to the fruition of all his endeavors—the securing of Riyadh and the Hasa oil fields by an American Rapid Deployment Force sent in by a President prepared to do it.

Fortuitous, he thought as he drifted into sleep. Very fortuitous.

The small brass plaque on the wall of the converted warehouse beside the paneled teak door said simply: THOR SPEDITION AG. Lenzlinger apparently hid the true nature of his business behind the façade of a trucking company, though there were no rigs to be seen and the smell of diesel had never penetrated the carpeted privacy of the fourth-floor suite of offices to which Quinn mounted.

There was an intercom to seek admittance from street level, and another with closed-circuit TV camera at the end of the corridor on the fourth floor. The conversion of the warehouse in a side street off the old docks—where the river Weser pauses on its way to the North Sea to provide the reason for old Bremen's existence—had not been cheap.

The secretary, when he met her in the outer office, seemed typecast. Had Lenzlinger had any trucks, she could easily have kick-started them.

"*Ja, bitte?*" she asked, though her gaze made plain it was he, not she, who was the supplicant.

"I would like the opportunity of speaking with Herr Lenzlinger," said Quinn.

She took his name and vanished into the private sanctum, closing the door behind her. Quinn had the impression that the mirror set into the partition wall was one-way. She returned after thirty seconds.

"And your business, please, Herr Quinn."

"I would like the chance to meet an employee of Herr Lenzlinger, a certain Werner Bernhardt," he said.

She went backstage again. This time she was gone more than a minute. When she returned she closed the door firmly on whoever sat within.

"I regret, Herr Lenzlinger is not available to speak with you," she said. It sounded final.

"I'll wait," said Quinn.

She gave him a look that regretted she had been too young to run a labor camp with him in it, and disappeared a third time. When she returned to her desk she ignored him and began to type with concentrated venom.

Another door into the reception area opened and a man came out. The sort who might well have been a truck driver; a walking refrigerator-freezer. The pale-gray suit was well enough cut almost to conceal the masses of beefy muscle beneath; the short, blow-dried hairstyle, aftershave, and veneer of civility were not cheap. Under all that he was pure knuckle-fighter.

"Herr Quinn," he said quietly, "Herr Lenzlinger is not available to see you or answer your questions."

"Now, no," agreed Quinn.

"Not now, not ever, Mr. Quinn. Please go."

Quinn had the impression the interview was over. He descended to the street and crossed the cobbles to where Sam waited in the car.

"He's not available in working hours," said Quinn. "I'll have to see him at his home. Let's get to Oldenburg."

Another very old city, its inland port trading for centuries on the Hunte River, it was once the seat of the Counts of Oldenburg. The inner core, the Old Town, is still girdled by sections of the former city wall and a moat made up of a series of linked canals.

Quinn found the sort of hotel he preferred, a quiet inn with a walled courtyard called the Graf von Oldenburg, in Holy Ghost Street.

Before the shops closed he had time to visit a hardware store and a camping shop; from a kiosk he bought the largest-scale map of the surrounding area he could find. After dinner he puzzled Sam by spending an hour in their room, tying knots every twenty inches down the length of the fifty feet of rope he had bought from the hardware shop, finally tying a three-prong grapnel to the end.

"Where are you going?" she asked.

"I suspect, up a tree" was all he would say. He left her still asleep in the predawn darkness.

He found the Lenzlinger domain an hour later, due west of the city, south of the great Bad Zwischenahn Lake, between the villages of Portsloge and Janstrat. It was all flat country, running without a mountain due west across the Ems to become northern Holland sixty miles farther on.

Intersected by myriad rivers and canals, draining the wet plain toward the sea, the country between Oldenburg and the border is studded with forests of beech, oak, and conifers. Lenzlinger's estate lay between two forests, a former fortified manor now set in its own five-acre park, the whole bounded by an eight-foot wall.

Quinn, dressed from head to toe in camouflage green, his face masked with scrim netting, spent the morning lying along the branch of a mighty oak in the woods across the road from the estate. His high-definition binoculars showed him all he needed to know.

The gray stone manor and its outbuildings formed an *L* shape. The shorter arm was the main house, with two stories plus attics. The longer arm had once been the stables, now converted to self-contained apartments for the staff. Quinn counted four domestic staff: a butler/steward, a male cook, and two cleaning women. It was the security arrangements that held his attention. They were numerous and expensive.

Lenzlinger had started as a young hustler in the late fifties, selling penny packets of war surplus weaponry to all comers. Without a license, his end-user certificates were forged and his questions nil. It was the age of the anticolonial wars and Third World revolutions. But operating on the fringe, he had made a living, not much more.

His big break came with the Nigerian civil war. He swindled the Biafrans of more than half a million dollars; they paid for bazookas but received cast-iron rain pipes. He was right in supposing they were too busy fighting for their lives to come north to settle accounts.

In the early seventies he got a license to trade—how much that cost him Quinn could only guess—which enabled him to supply half a dozen African, Central American, and Middle Eastern war groups, and still have time to conclude the occasional illegal deal (much more lucrative) with the E.T.A., the I.R.A., and a few others. He bought from Czechoslovakia, Yugoslavia, and North Korea, all needing hard currency, and sold to the desperate. By 1985 he was parlaying new North Korean hardware to both sides in the Iran–Iraq war. Even some governmental intelligence agencies had used his stocks when they wanted no-source weaponry for arm's-length revolutions.

This career had made him very wealthy. It had also made him a lot of enemies. He intended to enjoy the former and frustrate the latter.

All the windows, up and down, were electronically protected. Though he could not see the devices, Quinn knew that the doors would be, as well. That was the inner ring. The outer ring was the wall. It ran right around the estate without a break, topped with two strands of razor-wire, the trees inside the park lopped back to prevent any overhanging branches. Something else, glinting in the occasional ray of wintry sunshine. A tight wire, like piano wire, running along the top of the wall, supported by ceramic studs; electrified, linked to the alarm system, sensitive to the touch.

Between the wall and the house was open ground—fifty yards of it at the closest point, swept by cameras, patrolled by dogs. He watched the two Dobermans, muzzled and leashed, being given their morning constitutional. The dog handler was too young to be Bernhardt.

Quinn observed the black-windowed Mercedes 600 leave for Bremen at five to nine. The walking refrigerator-freezer ushered a muffled, fur-hatted figure into the rear seat, took the front passenger seat for himself, and the chauffeur swept them out through the steel gates and onto the road. They passed just below the branch where Quinn lay.

Quinn reckoned on four bodyguards, maybe five. The chauffeur looked like one; the refrigerator-freezer, definitely. That left the dog handler and probably another inside the house. Bernhardt?

The security nerve center seemed to be a ground-floor room where the staff wing joined the main house. The dog handler came and went to it several times, using a small door that gave directly onto the lawns. Quinn surmised that the night guard could probably control the floodlights, the TV monitors, and the dogs from within. By noon Quinn had his plan. He descended from his tree, and returned to Oldenburg.

He and Sam spent the afternoon shopping, he for a rental van and a variety of tools, she to complete a list he had given her.

"Can I come with you?" she asked. "I could wait outside."

"No. One vehicle on that country lane in the middle of the night is bad enough. Two is a traffic jam."

He told her what he wanted her to do.

"Just be there when I arrive," he said. "I suspect I may be in a hurry."

He was outside the stone wall, parked in the lane, at 2:00 A.M. His high-roofed panel van was driven close enough to the wall for him to be able to see over it clearly when he stood on the van's roof. The side of the van, in case of inquiry, bore the logo, created in masking tape, of a TV aerial installer. That would also account for the telescoping aluminum ladder fixed to the roof rack.

When his head came over the wall he could see by the light of the moon the leaf-bare trees of the park, the lawns running up to the house, and the dim light from the window of the guard's control room.

The spot he had chosen for the diversion was where a single tree inside the park grew only eight feet from the wall. He stood on the roof of the van and swung the small plastic box on the end of the fishing line gently 'round and 'round. When it had enough momentum he let go the line. The plastic case curved out in a gentle parabola, went into the branches of the tree, and fell toward the ground. The fishing line jerked it up short. Quinn paid out enough line to leave the box swinging from the tree just eight feet above the turf of the park, then tied off the line.

He started the engine and ran the van quietly down the wall a hundred yards, to a point opposite the guard's control house. The van now had steel brackets bolted to its sides, something that would perplex the rental company in the morning. Quinn slotted the ladder into them so that the aluminum structure jutted high above the wall. From its topmost rung he could jump forward and down into the park, avoiding the razor-wire and sensor cord. He climbed the ladder, attached his escape rope to the topmost rung, and waited. He saw the loping shape of a Doberman cross a patch of moonlight inside the park.

The sounds, when they came, were too low for him to hear, but the dogs heard them. He saw one stop, pause, listen, and then race off toward the spot where the black box swung from its nylon line among the trees. The other followed seconds later. Two cameras on the house wall swiveled to follow them. They did not return.

After five minutes the narrow door opened and a man stood there. Not the morning's dog handler, the night guard.

"Lothar, Wotan, *was ist denn los?*" he called softly. Now he and Quinn could hear the Dobermans growling, snarling with rage, somewhere in the tree line. The man went back, studied his monitors, but could see nothing. He emerged with a flashlight, drew a handgun, and went after the dogs. Leaving the door unlocked.

Quinn came off the top of the ladder like a shadow, forward and out, then twelve feet down. He took the landing in a paratroop roll, came up and ran through the trees, across the lawn, and into the control house, turning and locking the door from the inside.

A glance at the TV monitors told him the guard was still trying to retrieve his Dobermans a hundred yards up along the wall. Eventually the man would see the tape recorder hanging from its twine eight feet above the ground, the dogs leaping in rage to try to attack it as the recorder uttered its endless stream of growls and snarls at them. It had taken Quinn an hour in the hotel room to prepare that tape, to the consternation of the other guests. By the time the guard realized he had been tricked, it would be too late.

There was a door inside the control room, communicating with the main house. Quinn took the stairs to the bedroom floor. Six carved-oak doors, all probably to bedrooms. But the lights Quinn had seen at dawn that morning indicated the master bedroom must be at the end. It was.

Horst Lenzlinger awoke to the sensation of something hard and painful being jabbed into his left ear. Then the bedside light went on. He squealed once in outrage, then stared silently at the face above him. His lower lip wobbled. It was the man who had come to his office; he had not liked the look of him then. He liked him now even less, but most of all he disliked the barrel of the pistol stuck half an inch into his earhole.

"Bernhardt," said the man in the camouflage combat suit. "I want to speak to Werner Bernhardt. Use the phone. Bring him here. Now."

Lenzlinger scrabbled for the house phone on his night table, dialed an extension, and got a bleary response.

"Werner," he squeaked, "get your arse up here. Now. Yes, my bedroom. Hurry."

While they waited, Lenzlinger looked at Quinn with a mixture of fear and malevolence. On the black silk sheets beside him the bought-in-Vietnam child whimpered in her sleep, stick-thin, a tarnished doll. Bernhardt arrived, polo-neck sweater over his pajamas. He took in the scene and stared in amazement.

He was the right age, late forties. A mean, sallow face, sandy hair going gray at the sides, gray-pebble eyes.

"*Was ist denn hier*, Herr Lenzlinger?"

"I'll ask the questions," said Quinn in German. "Tell him to answer them, truthfully and fast. Or you'll need a spoon to get your brains off the lampshade. No problem, sleazebag. Just tell him."

Lenzlinger told him. Bernhardt nodded.

"You were in the Fifth Commando under John Peters?"

"*Ja.*"

"Stayed on for the Stanleyville mutiny, the march to Bukavu, and the siege?"

"*Ja.*"

"Did you ever know a big Belgian called Paul Marchais? Big Paul, they called him."

"Yes, I remember him. Came to us from the Twelfth Commando, Schramme's crowd. So what?"

"Tell me about Marchais."

"What about him?"

"Everything. What was he like?"

"Big, huge, six feet six or more, good fighter, a former motor mechanic."

Yeah, thought Quinn, someone had to put that Ford Transit van back in shape, someone who knew motors and welding. So the Belgian was the mechanic.

"Who was his closest buddy, from start to finish?"

Quinn knew that combat soldiers, like policemen on the beat, usually form partnerships; trust and rely on one man more than any other when the going gets really rough. Bernhardt furrowed his brow in concentration.

"Yes, there was one. They were always together. They palled up during Marchais's time in the Fifth. A South African. They could speak the same language, see? Flemish or Afrikaans."

"Name?"

"Pretorius—Janni Pretorius."

Quinn's heart sank. South Africa was a long way off, and Pretorius a very common name.

"What happened to him? Back in South Africa? Dead?"

"No, the last I heard he had settled in Holland. It's been a bloody long time. Look, I don't know where he is now. That's the truth, Herr Lenzlinger. It's just something I heard ten years back."

"He doesn't know," protested Lenzlinger. "Now get that thing out of my ear."

Quinn knew he would get no more from Bernhardt. He grabbed the front of Lenzlinger's silk nightshirt and swung him off the bed.

"We walk to the front door," said Quinn. "Slow and easy. Bernhardt, hands on top of the head. You go first. One move and your boss gets a second navel."

In single file they went down the darkened stairs. At the front door they heard a hammering from outside—the dog handler trying to get back in.

"The back way," said Quinn. They were halfway through the passage to the control house when Quinn hit an unseen oak chair and stumbled. He lost his grip on Lenzlinger. In a flash the tubby little man was off toward the main hall, screaming his head off for his bodyguards. Quinn flattened Bernhardt with a swipe from the gun and ran on to the control room and its door to the park.

He was halfway across the grass when the screaming Lenzlinger appeared in the door behind him, yelling for the dogs to come around from the front. Quinn turned, drew a bead, squeezed once, turned and ran on. There was a shriek of pain from the arms dealer and he vanished back inside the house.

Quinn jammed his gun in his waistband and made his escape rope just ten yards ahead of the two Dobermans. He swung up the wall as they leaped after him, trod on the sensor wire—triggering a shrill peal of alarm bells from the house—and dropped to the roof of the van. He had discarded the ladder, got the van in gear, and raced off down the lane before a pursuit group could be organized.

Sam was waiting as promised in their car, all packed and checked out, opposite the Graf von Oldenburg. He abandoned the van and climbed in beside her.

"Head west," he said. "The E.22 for Lier and Holland."

Lenzlinger's men were in two cars and radio-linked, with each other and to the manor house. Someone in the house phoned the city's best hotel, the City Club, but were told Quinn was not registered there. It took the caller another ten minutes, running down the hotel list, to ascertain from the Graf von Oldenburg that Herr and Frau Quinn had checked out. But the caller got an approximate description of their car.

Sam had cleared the Ofener Strasse and reached the 293 ring road when a gray Mercedes appeared behind them. Quinn slid down and curled up until his head was below the sill. Sam turned off the ring road onto the E.22 autobahn; the Mercedes followed.

"It's coming alongside," she said.

"Drive normally," mumbled Quinn from his hiding place. "Give 'em a nice bright smile and a wave."

The Mercedes pulled up alongside. It was still dark, the interior of the Ford invisible from outside. Sam turned her head. She knew neither of them, the refrigerator-freezer or the dog handler of the previous morning.

Sam flashed a beaming smile and a little wave. The men stared, expressionless. Frightened people on the run do not smile and wave. After several seconds, the Mercedes accelerated ahead, did a U-turn at the next intersection, and went back toward town. After ten minutes Quinn emerged and sat up again.

"Herr Lenzlinger doesn't seem to like you," said Sam.

"Apparently not," said Quinn sadly. "I've just shot his pecker off."

CHAPTER FOURTEEN

"I t is now confirmed that the Saudi jamboree to celebrate the Diamond Jubilee of the declaration of the Kingdom will be on April 17th next," Colonel Easterhouse told the Alamo Group later that morning.

They were seated in the spacious office of Cyrus Miller atop the Pan-Global Tower in downtown Houston.

"The half-billion-dollar stadium, entirely covered with a two-hundred-meter-wide acrylic dome, is complete, ahead of schedule. The other half of this billion-dollar exercise in self-glorification will be spent on food, jewelry, gifts, hospitality, extra hotels and guest mansions for the statesmen of the world, and on the pageant.

"Seven days before the actual pageant, before the expected fifty thousand international guests arrive, there will be a full dress rehearsal. The climax of the entire four-hour pageant will be the storming of a life-size replica model of the old Musmak Fortress, as it stood in 1902. The structure will be completed by Hollywood's most skilled set designers and builders. The 'defenders' will be drawn from the Royal Guard and dressed in the Turkish clothes of those days. The attacking group will be composed of fifty younger princes of the House, all on horseback, and led by a young relative of the King who bears a resemblance to the Sheikh Abdal Aziz of 1902."

"Fine," drawled Scanlon. "Love the local color. What about the coup?"

"That's when the coup takes place," said the colonel. "In that vast stadium, on rehearsal night, the only audience will be the topmost six hundred of the Royal House, headed by the King himself. All will be fathers, uncles, mothers, and aunts of the participants. All will be packed into the royal enclosure. As the last participants of the previous presentation leave, I will computer-lock the exit doors. The entrance doors will open to admit the fifty riders. What is not foreseen, except by me, is that they will be followed by ten fast-driving trucks disguised as Army vehicles and parked near the entrance gates. Those gates will stay open until the last truck has passed inside, then be computer-locked. After that, no one leaves.

"The assassins will leap out of the trucks, run toward the royal enclosure, and begin firing. One group alone will stay on the floor of the arena to dispatch the fifty princes and the Royal Guard 'defenders' of the dummy Musmak Fortress, all armed only with blanks.

"The five hundred Royal Guards surrounding the royal enclosure will attempt to defend their charges. Their ammunition will be defective. In most cases it will detonate in the magazines, killing the man holding the gun. In other cases it will jam. The complete destruction of the Royal House will take about forty minutes. Every stage will be filmed by the video cameras and patched through to Saudi TV; from there the spectacle will be available to most of the Gulf States."

"How you going to get the Royal Guard to agree to a reissue of ammunition?" asked Moir.

"Security in Saudi Arabia is an obsession," replied the colonel, "and for that very reason arbitrary changes in procedure are constant. So long as the authority on the order looks genuine, they will obey orders. These will be given in a document prepared by me, over the real signature of the Minister of the Interior, which I have obtained on a blank sheet. Never mind how. Major General Al-Shakry, of Egypt, is in charge of the ordnance depot. He will provide the defective issue of bullets. Later, Egypt will have to have access to Saudi oil at a price she can afford."

"And the regular Army?" asked Salkind. "There are fifty thousand of them."

"Yes, but they are not all in Riyadh. The locally-based Army units will have been on maneuvers a hundred miles away, due back in Riyadh the day before the dress rehearsal. The Army's vehicles are maintained by Palestinians, part of the huge foreign presence in the country of foreign technicians who do the jobs the Saudis cannot. They will immobilize the vehicles, marooning the nine thousand Army troops from Riyadh in the desert."

"What's the Palestinians' kickback?" asked Cobb.

"A chance of naturalization," said Easterhouse. "Although the technical infrastructure of Saudi depends on the quarter-million Palestinians employed at every level, they are always denied nationality. However loyally they serve, they can never have it. But under the post-Imam regime they could acquire it on the basis of six months' residence. That measure alone will eventually suck a million Palestinians south from the West Bank and Gaza, Jordan, and Lebanon, to reside in their new homeland south of the Nefud, bringing peace to the northern Middle East."

"And after the massacre?" Cyrus Miller asked the question. He had no time for euphemisms.

"In the last stages of the firefight inside the stadium, it will catch fire," said Colonel Easterhouse smoothly. "This has been arranged. The flames will engulf the structure fast, disposing of the remains of the Royal House and their assassins. The cameras will continue to run until meltdown, followed on screen by the Imam himself."

"What is he going to say?" queried Moir.

"Enough to terrify the entire Middle East and the West. Unlike Khomeini, who always spoke very quietly, this man is a firebrand. When he speaks he becomes carried away, for he speaks the message of Allah and Mohammed, and wishes to be heard."

Miller nodded understandingly. He, too, knew the conviction of being a divine mouthpiece.

"By the time he has finished threatening all the secular and Sunni orthodox regimes around Saudi's borders with their imminent destruction; promising to use the entire four-hundred-and-fifty-million-dollars-a-day income in the service of Holy Terror, and to destroy the Hasa oil fields if thwarted, every Arab kingdom, emirate, sheikhdom, and republic, from Oman in the south up north to the Turkish border, will be appealing to the West for help. That means America."

"What about this pro-Western Saudi Prince who is going to replace him?" asked Cobb. "If he fails . . ."

"He won't," said the colonel with certainty. "Just as the Army's trucks and the Air Force fighter-bombers were immobilized when they might have prevented the massacre, they will reenter service in time to rally to the Prince's call. The Palestinians will see to that.

"Prince Khalidi bin Sudairi will stop by my house on his way to the dress rehearsal. He will have a drink—no doubt about that; he's an alcoholic. The drink will be drugged. For three days he will be detained by two of my Yemenite house servants in the cellar. There he will prepare video and radio tapes announcing he is alive, the legitimate successor to his uncle, and appealing for American help to restore legitimacy. Note the phrase, gentlemen: the United States will intervene, not to conduct a countercoup, but to restore legitimacy with the full backing of the Arab world.

"I will then transfer the Prince to the safekeeping of the U.S. embassy, forcing America to become involved whether it likes it or not, since the embassy will have to defend itself against Shi'ah mobs demanding the Prince be handed over to them. The Religious Police, the Army, and the people will still need a trigger to turn on the Shi'ah usurpers and eliminate them, to a man. That trigger will be the arrival of the first U.S. airborne units."

"What about the aftermath, Colonel?" asked Miller slowly. "Will we get what we want—the oil for America?"

"We will all get what we want, gentlemen. The Palestinians get a homeland; the Egyptians, an oil quota to feed their masses. Uncle Sam gets to control the Saudi and Kuwaiti reserves, and thus the global oil price for the benefit of all mankind. The Prince becomes the new King, a drunken sot with me at his elbow every minute of the day. Only the Saudis will be disinherited, and return to their goats.

"The Sunni Arab states will learn their lesson from such a close call. Faced with the rage of the Shi'ah at having been so near and then defeated, the secular states will have no option but to hunt down and extirpate Fundamentalism before they all fall victim. Within five years there will be a huge crescent of peace and prosperity from the Caspian Sea to the Bay of Bengal."

The Alamo Five sat in silence. Two of them had thought to divert Saudi's oil flow America's way, nothing more. The other three had agreed to go along. They had just heard a plan to redraw a third of the world. It occurred to an appalled Moir and Cobb, though not to the other three, and certainly not to the colonel, that Easterhouse was a completely unbalanced egomaniac. Each realized too late that they were on a roller coaster, unable to slow down or get off.

Cyrus Miller invited Easterhouse to a private lunch in his adjacent dining room.

"No problems, Colonel?" he queried over the fresh peaches from his greenhouse. "Really, no problems?"

"There could be one, sir," said the colonel carefully. "I have one hundred and forty days to H-hour. Long enough for a single bad leak to blow it all away. There is a young man, a former bank official . . . he lives in London now. Name of Laing. I would like someone to have a word with him."

"Tell me," said Miller. "Tell me about Mr. Laing."

Quinn and Sam drove into the northern Dutch town of Groningen two and a half hours after fleeing Oldenburg. The capital of the province of the same name, Groningen, like the German city across the border, dates from medieval times, with an inner heart, the Old Town, protected by a ring canal. In olden days the inhabitants could flee into the center and lift their fourteen bridges to seal themselves behind their watery ramparts.

The wisdom of the city council decreed that the Old Town should not be despoiled by the industrial sprawl and poured-concrete obsession of the late twentieth century. Instead, it has been renovated and restored, a circular half-mile of alleys, markets, streets, squares, churches, restaurants, hotels, and pedestrian malls, almost all of them cobbled. At Quinn's direction Sam drove to the De Doelen Hotel on Grote Markt and they registered.

Modern buildings are few in the Old Town, but one is the five-story red-brick block on Rade Markt, which houses the police station.

"You know somebody here?" asked Sam as they approached the building.

"I used to," admitted Quinn. "He may be retired. Hope not."

He was not. The young blond officer at the reception desk confirmed that, yes, Inspector De Groot was now Chief Inspector and commanded the Gemeente Politie. Whom should he announce?

Quinn could hear the shout over the telephone when the policeman phoned upstairs. The young man grinned.

"He seems to know you, *mijnheer.*"

They were shown up to the office of Chief Inspector De Groot without delay. He was waiting for them, advancing across the floor to greet them, a big florid bear of a man with thinning hair, in uniform but wearing carpet slippers to favor a pair of feet that had pounded many miles of cobbled streets in thirty years.

The Dutch police has three branches: the Gemeente, or Community, Police, the criminal branch, known as the Recherche, and the highway patrol, the Rijkspolitie. De Groot looked the part, a Community Police chief whose avuncular frame and manner had long earned him among his own officers and the populace the nickname Papa De Groot.

"Quinn, good heavens alive, Quinn. It's been a long time since Assen."

"Fourteen years," admitted Quinn as they shook hands, and he introduced Sam. He made no mention of her FBI status. She had no jurisdiction in the kingdom of the Netherlands, and they were there unofficially. Papa De Groot ordered coffee—it was still shortly after breakfast—and asked what brought them to his town.

"I'm looking for a man," said Quinn. "I believe he may be living in Holland."

"An old friend, perhaps? Someone from the old days?"

"No, I've never met him."

The beam in De Groot's twinkling eyes did not falter, but he stirred his coffee a little more slowly.

"I heard you had retired from Lloyd's," he said.

"True," said Quinn. "My friend and I are just trying to do a favor for some friends."

"Tracing missing people?" queried De Groot. "A new departure for you. Well, what's his name and where does he live?"

De Groot owed him a favor. In May 1977, a group of South Moluccan fanatics, seeking to reestablish their old homeland in the former Dutch colony of Indonesia, had sought to publicize their cause by hijacking a train and a school at nearby Assen. There were fifty-four passengers on the train and a hundred children in the school. This sort of thing was new to Holland; they had no trained hostage-recovery teams in those days.

Quinn had been in his first year with the Lloyd's firm that specialized in such things. He was sent to advise, along with two soft-spoken sergeants from the British SAS, London's official contribution. Assen being in next-door Drente Province, De Groot had commanded the local police; the SAS men liaised with the Dutch Army.

De Groot had listened to the lean American who seemed to understand the men of violence inside the train and the school. He suggested what would probably happen when the troops went in and the terrorists opened fire. De Groot ordered his men to do as the American suggested, and two stayed alive because of that. Both the train and the school were eventually stormed; six terrorists died, and two train passengers in the crossfire. No soldiers or policemen were killed.

"His name is Pretorius, Janni Pretorius," said Quinn. De Groot pursed his lips.

"A common enough name, Pretorius," he said. "You know which town or village he lives in?"

"No. But he is not Dutch. He's South African by birth and I suspect may never have naturalized."

"Then you have a problem," said De Groot. "We do not have a central list of all foreign nationals living in Holland. Civil rights, you see."

"He's a former Congo mercenary. I'd have thought a background like that, plus being from a country Holland hardly approves of, would give him a card in some index somewhere."

De Groot shook his head.

"Not necessarily. If he is here illegally, then he will not be on file, or we'd have expelled him for illegal entry. If he's here legally, there'd be a card for him when he came in, but after that, if he committed no offenses against Dutch law, he could move freely around without checks. Part of our civil rights."

Quinn nodded. He knew about Holland's obsession with civil rights. Though benign to the law-abiding citizen, it also made life a rose garden for the vicious and squalid. Which was why lovely old Amsterdam had become Europe's capital for drug dealers, terrorists, and child-porn filmmakers.

"How would a man like that get entry and residence permits in Holland?" he asked.

"Well, if he married a Dutch girl he'd get it. That would even give him the right to naturalization. Then he could just disappear."

"Social security, income tax, Immigration?"

"They wouldn't tell you," said De Groot. "The man would have the right to privacy. Even to tell me, I'd have to present a criminal case against the man to justify my inquiry. Believe me, I just can't do that."

"No way at all you could help me?" asked Quinn.

De Groot stared out of the window.

"I have a nephew with the BVD," he said. "It would have to be unofficial. . . . Your man might be listed with them."

"Please ask him," said Quinn. "I'd be very grateful."

While Quinn and Sam strolled up the Oosterstraat looking for a place to lunch, De Groot called his nephew in The Hague. Young Koos De Groot was a junior officer with the Binnenlandse Veiligheids Dienst, Holland's small Internal Security Service. Though he had great affection for the bearlike uncle who used to slip him ten-guilder notes when he was a boy, he needed a deal of persuading. Tapping into the BVD computer was not the sort of thing a Community cop from Groningen called for every day of the week.

Papa De Groot called Quinn the next morning and they met an hour later at the police station.

"He's some fellow, your Pretorius," said De Groot, studying his notes. "It seems our BVD were interested enough when he arrived in Holland ten years ago to file his details, just in case. Some of them come from him—the flattering bits. Others come from newspaper cuttings. Jan Pieter Pretorius, born Bloemfontein 1942—that makes him forty-nine now. Gives his profession as sign painter."

Quinn nodded. Someone had repainted the Ford Transit, put the BARLOW'S ORCHARD PRODUCE sign on the side, and painted apple crates on the inside of the rear windows. He surmised Pretorius was also the bomb man whose device had torched the Transit in the barn. He knew it could not be Zack. In the Babbidge warehouse Zack had sniffed marzipan and thought it might be Semtex. Semtex is odorless.

"He returned to South Africa in 1968 after leaving Ruanda, then worked for a while as a security guard on a De Beers diamond mine in Sierra Leone."

Yes, the man who could tell diamonds from paste, and knew about cubic zirconia.

"He had wandered as far as Paris twelve years ago; met a Dutch girl working for a French family, married her. That gave him access to Holland. His father-in-law installed him as barman—apparently the father-in-law owns two bars. The couple divorced five years ago, but Pretorius had saved enough to buy his own bar. He runs it and lives above it."

"Where?" asked Quinn.

"A town called Den Bosch. You know it?"

Quinn shook his head. "And the bar?"

"De Gouden Leeuw—the Golden Lion," said De Groot.

Quinn and Sam thanked him profusely and left. When they had gone, De Groot looked down from the window and watched them cross the Rade Markt and head back to their hotel. He liked Quinn, but he was worried by the inquiry. Perhaps it was all legitimate, no need to worry. But he would not want Quinn on a manhunt coming into *his* town to face a South African mercenary. . . . He sighed and reached for the phone.

"Find it?" asked Quinn as he drove south out of Groningen. Sam was studying the road map.

"Yep. Way down south, near the Belgian border. Join Quinn and see the Low Countries," she said.

"We're lucky," said Quinn. "If Pretorius *was* the second kidnapper in Zack's gang, we could have been heading for Bloemfontein."

The E.35 motorway ran straight as an arrow south-southeast to Zwolle, where Quinn turned onto the A.50 highroad due south for Apeldoorn, Arnhem, Nijmegen, and Den Bosch. At Apeldoorn, Sam took the wheel. Quinn put the backrest of the passenger seat almost horizontal and fell asleep. He was still asleep, and it was his seatbelt that saved his life, in the crash.

Just north of Arnhem and west of the highway is the gliding club of Terlet. Despite the time of year it was a bright sunny day, rare enough in Holland in November to have brought out the enthusiasts. The driver of the truck thundering along in the opposite lane was so busy gazing at the glider, which wing-tilted right over the highway in front of him as it lined up to land, that he failed to notice he was drifting over to the oncoming lane.

Sam was sandwiched between the timber stakes running along the edge of the sandy moorland to her right and the bulk of the swerving juggernaut to her left. She tried to brake and almost made it. The last three feet of the swaying trailer clipped the front left fender of the Sierra and flicked it off the road, as a finger and thumb will flick a fly off a blotter. The truck driver never even noticed and drove on.

The Sierra mounted the curb as Sam tried to bring it back onto the road, and she would have made it but for the vertical stakes in a line beyond the curb. One of them mashed her right front wheel and she went out of control. The Sierra careered down the bank, almost rolled, recovered, and ended up axle-deep in the soft wet sand of the moor.

Quinn straightened his seat and looked across at her. Both were shaken but unhurt. They climbed out. Above them, cars and trucks roared on south to Arnhem. The ground all around was flat; they were in easy view of the road.

"The piece," said Quinn.

"The what?"

"The Smith & Wesson. Give it to me."

He wrapped the pistol and its ammunition in one of her silk scarves from the vanity case and buried it under a bush ten yards from the car, mentally marking the place in the sand where it lay. Two minutes later a red-and-white Range Rover of the Rijkspolitie, the Highway Patrol, stood above them on the hard shoulder.

The officers were concerned, relieved to see they were unhurt, and asked for their papers. Thirty minutes later, with their luggage, they were deposited in the rear courtyard of the gray concrete-slab police headquarters in Arnhem's Beek Straat. A sergeant showed them up to an interview room, where he took copious particulars. It was past lunch when he had finished.

The car-rental agency representative had not had a busy day—tourists tend to become thin on the ground in mid-November—and was quite pleased to take a call in his Heuvelink Boulevard office from an American lady inquiring about an agency car. His joy faded somewhat when he learned she had just totaled one of his company's Sierras on the A.50 at Terlet, but he recalled his firm's admonition to try harder, and he did.

He came around to the police station and conversed with the sergeant. Neither Quinn nor Sam could understand a word. Fortunately, both Dutchmen spoke good English.

"The police recovery team will bring the Sierra in from where it is . . . parked," he said. "I will have it collected from here and taken to our company workshops. You are fully insured, according to your papers. It is a Dutch-hired car?"

"No, Ostende, Belgium," said Sam. "We were touring."

"Ah," said the man. He thought: paperwork, a lot of paperwork. "You wish to rent another car?"

"Yes, we would," said Sam.

"I can let you have a nice Opel Ascona, but in the morning. It is being serviced right now. You have a hotel?"

They did not, but the helpful police sergeant made a call and they had a double room at the Rijn Hotel. The skies had clouded over again; the rain began to come down. The agency man drove them a mile up the Rijnkade embankment to the hotel, dropped them off, and promised to have the Opel at the front door at eight next day.

The hotel was two-thirds empty and they had a large double room on the front, overlooking the river. The short afternoon was closing in; the rain lashed the windows. The great gray mass of the Rhine flowed past toward the sea. Quinn took an upright armchair by the window bay and gazed out.

"I should call Kevin Brown," said Sam. "Tell him what we've found."

"I wouldn't," said Quinn.

"He'll be mad."

"Well, you can tell him we found one of the kidnappers and left him on top of a Ferris wheel with someone else's bullet in his skull. You can tell him you've been carrying an illegal gun through Belgium, Germany, and Holland. You want to say all that on an open line?"

"Yeah, okay. So I should write up some notes."

"You do that," said Quinn.

She raided the mini-bar, found a half-bottle of red wine, and brought him a glass. Then she sat at the desk and began to write on hotel notepaper.

Three miles upstream of the hotel, dim in the deepening dusk, Quinn could make out the great black girders of the old Arnhem Bridge, the "bridge too far," where in September 1944, Colonel John Frost and a small handful of British paratroopers had fought and died for four days, trying to hold off SS Panzers with bolt-action rifles and Sten guns while Thirty Corps vainly fought up from the south to relieve them on the northern end of the bridge. Quinn raised his glass toward the steel joists that reared into the rainy sky.

Sam caught the gesture and walked over to the window. She looked down to the embankment.

"See someone you know?" she asked.

"No," said Quinn. "They have passed by."

She craned to look up the street.

"Don't see anyone."

"A long time ago."

She frowned, puzzled. "You're a very enigmatic man, Mr. Quinn. What is it you can see that I can't?"

"Not a lot," said Quinn, rising. "And none of it very hopeful. Let's go see what the dining room has to offer."

The Ascona was there promptly at eight, along with the friendly sergeant and two motorcycle police outriders.

"Where are you heading, Mr. Quinn?" asked the sergeant.

"Vlissingen, Flushing," said Quinn, to Sam's surprise. "To catch the ferry."

"Fine," said the sergeant. "Have a good trip. My colleagues will guide you to the motorway southwest."

At the junction to the motorway the outriders pulled over and watched the Opel out of sight. Quinn had that Dortmund feeling again.

General Zvi ben Shaul sat behind his desk and looked up from the report at the two men in front of him. One was the head of the Mossad department covering Saudi Arabia and the entire peninsula from the Iraqi border in the north to the shores of South Yemen. It was a territorial fiefdom. The other man's speciality knew no borders and was in its way even more important, especially for the security of Israel. He covered all Palestinians, wherever they might be. It was he who had written the report on the Director's desk.

Some of those Palestinians would dearly have loved to know the building where the meeting was taking place. Like many of the curious, including a number of foreign governments, the Palestinians still imagined that the Mossad's headquarters remained in the northern suburbs of Tel Aviv. But since 1988 their new home had been a large modern building right in the center of Tel Aviv, around a corner from Rehov Shlomo Ha'melekh (King Solomon Street) and close to the building occupied by AMAN, the military intelligence service.

"Can you get any more?" the general asked David Gur Arieh, the Palestinian expert. The man grinned and shrugged.

"Always you want more, Zvi. My source is a low-level operative, a technician in the motor vehicle workshops for the Saudi Army. That's what he's been told. The Army's to be marooned in the desert for three days during next April."

"It smells of a coup," said the man who ran the Saudi department. "We should pull their chestnuts out of the fire for them?"

"If someone toppled King Fahd and took over, who would it likely be?" asked the Director. The Saudi expert shrugged.

"Another Prince," he said. "Not one of the brothers. More likely the younger generation. They're greedy. However many billions they skim through the Oil Quota Commission, they want more. No, it may be they want it all. And of course the younger men tend to be more . . . modern, more Westernized. It could be for the better. It is time the old men went."

It was not the thought of a younger man ruling in Riyadh that intrigued Ben Shaul. It was what the Palestinian technician who had given the orders to Gur Arieh's source had let slip. Next year, he had gloated, we Palestinians will have the right to become naturalized citizens here.

If that was true, if that was what the unnamed conspirators had in mind, the perspectives were astounding. Such an offer by a new Saudi government would suck a million homeless and landless Palestinians out of Israel, Gaza, the West Bank, and Lebanon to a new life far in the South. With the Palestinian sore cauterized, Israel, with her energy and technology, could enter into a relationship with her neighbors that could be beneficial and profitable. It had been the dream of the founders, back to Weizmann and Ben-Gurion. Ben Shaul had been taught the dream as a boy, never thought to see it happen. But . . .

"You going to tell the politicians?" asked Gur Arieh.

The Director thought of them squabbling away up in the Knesset, splitting semantic and theological hairs while his service tried to tell them on which side of the sky the sun rose. April was a long way off still. There would be a leak if he did. He closed the report.

"Not yet," he said. "We have too little. When we have more I will tell them."

Privately, he had decided to sit on it.

Lest they fall asleep, visitors to Den Bosch are met with a quiz game devised by the town's planners. It is called Find a Way to Drive into the Town Center. Win, and the visitor finds Market Square and a parking space. Lose, and a labyrinthine system of one-way streets dumps him back on the ring road.

The city center is a triangle: Along the northwest runs the Dommel river; along the northeast, the Zuid-Willemsvaart canal; and along the southern third side, the city wall. Sam and Quinn beat the system at the third attempt, reached the market, and claimed their prize: a room at the Central Hotel on Market Square.

In their room Quinn consulted the telephone directory. It listed only one Golden Lion bar, on a street called Jans Straat. They set off on foot. The hotel reception desk had provided a line-drawing map of the town center, but Jans Straat was not listed. A number of citizens around the square shook their heads in ignorance. Even the street-corner policeman had to consult his much-thumbed town plan. They found it eventually.

It was a narrow alley, running between the St. Jans Singel, the old towpath along the Dommel, and the parallel Molenstraat. The whole area was old, most of it dating back three hundred years. Much of it had been tastefully restored and renovated, the fine old brick structures retained, along with their antique doors and windows, but fitted out with smart new apartments inside. Not so the Jans Straat.

It was barely a car's width wide and the buildings leaned against each other for support. There were two bars in it, for at one time the bargemen plying their trade up the Dommel and along the canals had moored here to quench their thirst.

The Gouden Leeuw was on the south side of the street, twenty yards from the towpath, a narrow-fronted two-story building with a faded sign that announced its name. The ground floor had a single bow window whose small panes were of opaque and colored glass. Beside it was the single door giving access to the bar. It was locked. Quinn rang the bell and waited. No sound, no movement. The other bar in the street was open. Every bar in Den Bosch was open.

"Now what?" asked Sam. Down the street a man in the window of the other bar lowered his paper, noted them, and raised the paper again. Beside the Golden Lion was a six-foot-high wooden door apparently giving access to a passage to the rear.

"Wait here," said Quinn. He went up and over the gate in a second and dropped into the passage. A few minutes later Sam heard the tinkling of glass, the pad of footsteps, and the bar's front door opened from inside. Quinn stood there.

"Get off the street," he said. She entered and he closed the door behind her. There were no lights. The bar was gloomy, lit only by the filtered daylight through the colored bay window.

It was a small place. The bar was L-shaped around the bay window. From the door a gangway ran along the bar, then around the corner of the L to become a larger drinking area near the back. Behind the bar was the usual array of bottles; upturned beer glasses were in rows on a towel on the bar top, along with three Delft-china beer-pump handles. At the very back was a door, through which Quinn had entered.

The door led to a small washroom, whose window Quinn had broken to get in. Also to a set of stairs leading to an apartment upstairs.

"Maybe he's up there," said Sam. He was not. It was a studio apartment, very small, just a bed-sitting room with a kitchenette in an alcove and a small bathroom/lavatory. There was a picture of a scene that could have been the Transvaal on one wall; a number of African memorabilia, a television set, an unmade bed. No books. Quinn checked every cupboard and the tiny loft above the ceiling. No Pretorius. They went downstairs.

"Since we've broken into his bar, we might as well have a beer," suggested Sam. She went behind the counter, took two glasses, and pulled one of the china pump handles. The foaming ale ran into the glasses.

"Where's that beer come from?" asked Quinn.

Sam checked under the counter.

"The tubes run straight through the floor," she said.

Quinn found the trapdoor under a rug at the end of the room. Wooden steps led downward, and beside them was a light switch. Unlike the bar, the cellars were spacious.

The whole house and its neighbors were supported by the vaulted brick arches that created the cellars. The tubes that led upward to the beer pumps above them came from modern steel beer barrels, evidently lowered through the trapdoor before being connected. It had not always been so.

At one end of the cellars was a tall and wide steel grille. Beyond it flowed the Dieze Canal, which ran out under Molenstraat. Years before, men had poled the great beer vats in shallow boats along the canal, to roll them through the grille and into position beneath the bar. That was in the days when potboys had to scurry up and down the stairs bringing pitchers of ale to the customers above.

There were still three of these antique barrels standing on their brick plinths in the largest hall created by the arches, each with a spigot tap at its base. Quinn idly flicked one of the spigots; a gush of sour old beer ran into the lamplight. The second was the same. He kicked the third with his toe. The liquid ran a dull yellow, then changed to pink.

It took three heaves from Quinn to turn the beer vat on its side. When it fell, it came with a crash and the contents tumbled onto the brick floor. Some of those contents were the last two gallons of ancient beer that had never reached the bar upstairs. In a puddle of the beer lay a man, on his back, open eyes dull in the light from the single bulb, a hole through one temple and a pulped exit wound at the other. From his height and build, Quinn estimated, he could be the man behind him in the warehouse, the man with the Skorpion. If he was, he had chopped down a British sergeant and two American Secret Service men on Shotover Plain.

The other man in the cellar pointed his gun straight at Quinn's back and spoke in Dutch. Quinn turned. The man had come down the cellar steps, his treads masked by the crash of the falling barrel. What he actually said was: "Well done, *mijnheer*. You found your friend. We missed him."

Two others were descending the steps, both in the uniform of the Dutch Community Police. The man with the gun was in civilian clothes, a sergeant in the Recherche.

"I wonder," said Sam as they were marched into the police station on Tolbrug Straat, "whether there is a market for the definitive anthology of Dutch precinct houses?"

By chance the Den Bosch police station is right across the street from the Groot Zieken Gasthaus—literally the Big Sick Guesthouse—to whose hospital morgue the body of Jan Pretorius was taken to await autopsy.

Chief Inspector Dykstra had thought little of Papa De Groot's warning call of the previous morning. An American trying to look up a South African did not necessarily spell trouble. He had dispatched one of his sergeants in the lunch hour. The man had found the Golden Lion bar closed and had reported back.

A local locksmith had secured them entry, but everything had seemed in order. No disturbance, no fight. If Pretorius wished to lock up and go away, he had the right to do so. The proprietor of the bar across and down the street said he thought the Golden Lion had been open until about midday. The weather being the way it was, the door would normally be closed. He had seen no customers enter or leave the Golden Lion, but that was not odd. Business was slack.

It was the sergeant who asked to stake out the bar a little longer, and Dykstra had agreed. It had paid dividends; the American arrived twenty-four hours later.

Dykstra sent a message to the Gerechtelijk Laboratorium in Voorburg, the country's central pathology laboratory. Hearing it was a bullet wound, and a foreigner, they sent Dr. Veerman himself, and he was Holland's leading forensic pathologist.

In the afternoon Chief Inspector Dykstra listened patiently to Quinn explaining that he had known Pretorius fourteen years ago in Paris and had hoped to look him up for old time's sake while touring Holland. If Dykstra disbelieved the story, he kept a straight face. But he checked. His own country's BVD confirmed that the South African had been in Paris at that time; Quinn's former Hartford employers confirmed that, yes, Quinn had been heading their Paris office in that year.

The rented car was brought around from the Central Hotel and thoroughly searched. No gun. Their luggage was retrieved and searched. No gun. The sergeant admitted neither Quinn nor Sam had had a gun when he found them in the cellar. Dykstra believed Quinn had killed the South African the previous day, just before his sergeant mounted the stakeout, and had come back because he had forgotten something that might be in the man's pockets. But if that were the case, why had the sergeant seen him trying to gain access via the front door? If he had locked the door after him following the killing of the South African, he could have let himself back in. It was puzzling. Of one thing Dykstra was certain: He did not think much of the Paris connection as a reason for the visit.

Professor Veerman arrived at six and was finished by midnight. He crossed the road and took a coffee with a very tired Chief Inspector Dykstra.

"Well, Professor?"

"You'll have my full report in due course," said the doctor.

"Just the outline, please."

"All right. Death from massive laceration of the brain caused by a bullet, probably nine millimeter, fired at close range through the left temple, exiting through the right. I should look for a hole in the woodwork somewhere in that bar."

Dykstra nodded. "Time of death?" he asked. "I am holding two Americans who discovered the body, supposedly on a friendly visit. Though they broke into the bar to find it."

"Midday yesterday," said the professor. "Give or take a couple of hours. I'll know more later, when the tests have been analyzed."

"But the Americans were in Arnhem police station at midday yesterday," said Dykstra. "That's unarguable. They crashed their car at ten and were released to spend the night at the Rijn Hotel at four. They could have left the hotel in the night, driven here, done it, and got back by dawn."

"No chance," said the professor, rising. "That man was dead no later than two P.M. yesterday. If they were in Arnhem, they're innocent parties. Sorry. Facts."

Dykstra swore. His sergeant must have mounted his stakeout within thirty minutes of the killer's leaving the bar.

"My Arnhem colleagues tell me you were heading for the ferry at Vlissingen when you left yesterday," he told Sam and Quinn as he released them in the small hours.

"That's right," said Quinn, collecting his much-examined luggage.

"I would be grateful if you would continue there," said the Chief Inspector. "Mr. Quinn, my country likes to welcome foreign visitors, but wherever you go it seems the Dutch police are put to a lot of extra work."

"I'm truly sorry," said Quinn with feeling. "Seeing as how we've missed the last ferry, and are hungry and tired, could we finish the night at our hotel and go in the morning?"

"Very well," said Dykstra. "I'll have a couple of my men escort you out of town."

"I'm beginning to feel like royalty," said Sam as she went into the bathroom back at the Central Hotel. When she emerged, Quinn was gone. He returned at 5:00 A.M., stashed the Smith & Wesson back in the base of Sam's vanity case, and caught two hours' sleep before the morning coffee arrived.

The drive to Flushing was uneventful. Quinn was deep in thought. Someone was wasting the mercenaries one after the other, and now he really had run out of places to go. Except maybe . . . back to the archives. There might be something more to drag from them, but it was unlikely, very unlikely. With Pretorius dead, the trail was cold as a week-dead cod, and stank as badly.

A Flushing police car was parked near the ramp of the ferry for England. The two officers in it noted the Opel Ascona driving slowly into the hull of the roll-on roll-off car-carrier, but waited till the doors closed shut and the ferry headed out into the estuary of the Westerschelde before informing their headquarters.

The trip passed quietly. Sam wrote up her notes, now becoming a travelogue of European police stations; Quinn read the first London newspapers he had seen in ten days. He missed the paragraph that began: "Major KGB Shake-up?" It was a Reuters report out of Moscow, alleging that the usual informed sources were hinting at forthcoming changes at the top of the Soviet secret police.

Quinn waited in the darkness of the small front garden in Carlyle Square, as he had for the previous two hours, immobile as a statue and unseen by anyone. A laburnum tree cast a shadow that shielded him from the light of the streetlamp; his black zip-up leather windbreaker and his immobility did the rest. People came past within a few feet but none saw the man in the shadows.

It was half past ten; the inhabitants of this elegant Chelsea square were returning from their dinners in the restaurants of Knightsbridge and Mayfair. David and Carina Frost went by in the back of their elderly Bentley toward their house farther up. At eleven the man Quinn waited for arrived.

He parked his car in a residents' bay across the road, mounted the three steps to his front door, and inserted his key in the lock. Quinn was at his elbow before it turned.

"Julian."

Julian Hayman spun in alarm.

"Good God, Quinn, don't do that. I could have flattened you."

Hayman was still, years after leaving the regiment, a very fit man. But years of city living had blurred the old cutting edge, just a fraction. Quinn had spent those years toiling in vineyards beneath a blazing sun. He declined to suggest it might have been the other way around, if it ever came to it.

"I need to go back into your files, Julian."

Hayman had quite recovered. He shook his head firmly.

"Sorry, old boy. Not again. No chance. Word is, you're taboo. People have been muttering—on the circuit, you know—about the Cormack affair. Can't risk it. That's final."

Quinn realized it was final. The trail had ended. He turned to go.

"By the way," Hayman called from the top of the steps. "I had lunch yesterday with Barney Simkins. Remember old Barney?"

Quinn nodded. Barney Simkins, a director of Broderick-Jones, the Lloyd's underwriters who had employed Quinn for ten years all over Europe.

"He says someone's been ringing in, asking for you."

"Who?"

"Dunno. Barney said the caller played it very close. Just said if you wanted to contact him, put a small ad in the *International Herald Tribune*, Paris edition, any day for the next ten, and sign it Q."

"Didn't he give any name at all?" asked Quinn.

"Only one, old boy. Odd name. Zack."

CHAPTER FIFTEEN

Quinn climbed into the car beside Sam, who had been waiting around the corner in Mulberry Walk. He looked pensive.

"Won't he play?"

"Mmmm?"

"Hayman. Won't he let you go back into his files?"

"No. That's out. And it's final. But it appears someone else does want to play. Zack has been phoning."

She was stunned.

"Zack? What does he want?"

"A meeting."

"How the hell did he find you?"

Quinn let in the clutch and pulled away from the curb.

"A long shot. Years ago there was an occasional mention of me when I worked for Broderick-Jones. All he had was my name and my job. Seems I'm not the only one who checks back through old newspaper clippings. By a fluke, Hayman was lunching with someone from my old company when the subject came up."

He turned into Old Church Street and right again on the King's Road.

"Quinn, he's going to try to kill you. He's wiped out two of his own men already. With them gone he gets to keep all the ransom for himself; with you out of the way the hunt dies. He obviously reckons you're more likely to trace him than the FBI."

Quinn laughed shortly.

"If only he knew. I haven't the faintest idea who he is or where he is."

He decided not to tell her he no longer believed Zack was the killer of Marchais and Pretorius. Not that a man like Zack would balk at eliminating his own kind if the price was right. Back in the Congo several mercenaries had been wasted by their own kind. It was the coincidence of the timing that worried him.

He and Sam had got to Marchais a few hours after his death; fortunately for them, there were no police about. But for a fluke crash outside Arnhem they would have been in Pretorius's bar with a loaded gun an hour after *he* died. They would have remained in detention for weeks while the Den Bosch police investigated the case.

He turned left off King's Road into Beaufort Street, heading for Battersea Bridge, and ran straight into a traffic jam. London traffic is no stranger to snarls, but at that hour on a winter's night the run south through London should have been clear enough.

The line of cars he was in edged forward and he saw a uniformed London policeman directing them around a series of cones that blocked off the nearside lane. Turn and turn about the cars heading north and those heading south had to use the single remaining lane in the street.

When they came abreast of the obstruction Quinn and Sam saw two police cars, the blue lights on their roofs flashing as they turned. The police cars hemmed in an ambulance, parked with its doors open. Two attendants were climbing out of the rear with a stretcher, and approached a shapeless mass on the pavement, hidden under a blanket.

The traffic control policeman impatiently waved them on. Sam squinted up at the face of the building outside which the form on the pavement lay. The windows on the top floor were open and she saw a policeman's head poking out as he gazed down.

"Someone seems to have fallen eight floors," she remarked. "The police are looking out the open window up there."

Quinn grunted and concentrated on not hitting the taillights of the car in front of him, whose driver was also gawping at the accident. Seconds later the road cleared and Quinn gunned the Opel over the bridge across the Thames, leaving behind him the dead body of a man he had never heard of and never would: the body of Andy Laing.

"Where are we going?" asked Sam.

"Paris," said Quinn.

Coming back to Paris for Quinn was like coming home. Though he had spent a longer time based in London, Paris held a special place in his life.

He had wooed and won Jeannette there, had married her there. For two blissful years they had lived in a small flat just off the rue de Grenelle; their daughter had been born at the American Hospital in Neuilly.

He knew bars in Paris, dozens of bars, where after the death of Jeannette and their baby Sophie on the Orléans highway he had tried to obliterate the pain with drink. He had been happy in Paris, been in heaven in Paris, known hell in Paris, waked up in gutters in Paris. He knew the place.

They spent the night at a motel just outside Ashford and caught the 9:00 A.M. Hovercraft from Folkestone to Calais, arriving in Paris in time for lunch.

Quinn checked them into a small hotel just off the Champs-Élysées and disappeared with the car to find a place to park it. The Eighth Arrondissement of Paris has many charms, but ample parking is not one of them. To have parked outside the Hôtel du Colisée in the street of the same name would have been to invite a wheel-clamp. Instead he used the twenty-four-hour underground parking lot in rue Chauveau-Lagarde, just behind the Madeleine, and took a cab back to the hotel. He intended to use cabs anyway. While in the area of the Madeleine he noted two other items he might need.

After lunch Quinn and Sam took a cab to the offices of the *International Herald Tribune* at 181 Avenue Charles-de-Gaulle in Neuilly.

"I'm afraid we can't get it in tomorrow's edition," said the girl at the front desk. "It will have to be the day after. Insertions are only for the following day if entered by eleven-thirty A.M."

"That'll be fine," said Quinn and paid cash. He took a complimentary copy of the paper and read it in the taxi back to the Champs-Élysées.

This time he did not miss the story, datelined out of Moscow, whose headline read: GEN. KRYUCHKOV OUSTER. There was a sub-headline: KGB CHIEF FIRED IN BIG SECURITY SHAKE-UP. He read the story out of interest but it signified nothing to him.

The agency correspondent reported that the Soviet Politburo had received "with regret" the resignation and retirement of KGB Chairman General Vladimir Kryuchkov. A deputy chairman would head the Committee pro tem, until the Politburo appointed a successor.

The report surmised that the changes appeared to have been in response to Politburo dissatisfaction, particularly with the performance of the First Chief Directorate, of which Kryuchkov himself had been a former head. The reporter finished his piece with the suggestion that the Politburo—a thinly veiled reference to Gorbachev himself—wished to see newer and younger blood moving into the top slot of the U.S.S.R.'s overseas espionage service.

That evening and through the following day, Quinn gave Sam, who had never seen Paris before, the tourist's menu. They took in the Louvre, the Tuileries Gardens in the rain, the Arc de Triomphe, and the Eiffel Tower, rounding off their free day at the Lido cabaret.

The ad appeared the following morning. Quinn rose early and bought a copy from a vendor on the Champs-Élysées at seven to make sure it was in. It said simply: "Z. I'm here. Call me on . . . Q." He had given the hotel number, and warned the operator in the small lobby that he expected a call. He waited for it in his room. It came at nine-thirty.

"Quinn?" The voice was unmistakable.

"Zack, before we go any further, this is a hotel. I don't like hotel phones. Call me at this public booth in thirty minutes."

He dictated the number of a phone booth just off the Place de la Madeleine. He left Sam behind, still in her nightgown, calling, "I'll be back in an hour."

The phone in the booth rang at exactly ten.

"Quinn, I want to talk to you."

"We are talking, Zack."

"I mean face-to-face."

"Sure, no problem. You say when and where."

"No tricks, Quinn. Unarmed, no backup."

"You got it."

Zack dictated the time and the place. Quinn made no notes—there was no need. He returned to the hotel. He found Sam in the lounge-cum-bar, with croissants and milky coffee before her. She looked up eagerly.

"What did he want?"

"A meeting, face-to-face."

"Quinn, darling, be careful. He's a killer. When and where?"

"Not here," he said. There were other tourists having a late breakfast. "In our room."

"It's a hotel room," he told her when they were upstairs. "Tomorrow at eight in the morning. His room at the Hôtel Roblin. Reserved in the name of—would you believe it?—Smith."

"I have to be there, Quinn. I don't like the sound of it. Don't forget I'm weapon-trained too. And you are definitely carrying the Smith & Wesson."

"Sure," said Quinn.

Several minutes later Sam made an excuse and went down to the bar. She was back after ten minutes. Quinn recalled that there was a phone on the end of the bar.

She was asleep when he left at midnight, the bedside alarm clock set for six in the morning. He moved through the bedroom like a shadow, picking up his shoes, socks, trousers, shorts, sweater, jacket, and gun as he went. There was no one in the corridor. He dressed there, stuck the pistol in his belt, adjusted the windbreaker to cover it, and went silently downstairs.

He found a cab on the Champs-Élysées and was at the Hôtel Roblin ten minutes later.

"*La chambre de Monsieur Smith, si'l vous plaît,*" he told the night porter. The man checked a list and gave him the key. Number 10. Second floor. He mounted the stairs and let himself in.

The bathroom was the best place for the ambush. The door was in the corner of the bedroom and from it he could cover every angle, especially the door to the corridor. He removed the bulb from the main light in the bedroom, took an upright chair and placed it inside the bathroom. With the bathroom door open just enough to give him a two-inch crack, he began his vigil. When his night-sight came he could clearly make out the empty bedroom, dimly lit by the light from the street coming through the windows, whose curtains he had left open.

By six no one had come; he had heard no footsteps in the corridor. At half past six the night porter brought coffee to an early riser down the corridor; he heard the footsteps passing the door, then returning to the stairs to the lobby. No one came in; no one tried to come in.

At eight he felt the sense of relief washing over him. At twenty past the hour he left, paid his bill, and took a cab back to the Hôtel du Colisée. She was in the bedroom and nearly frantic.

"Quinn, where the hell have you been? I've been desperate with worry. I woke at five . . . you weren't there. . . . For God's sake, we've missed the rendezvous."

He could have lied, but he was genuinely remorseful. He told her what he had done. She looked as if he had hit her in the face.

"You thought it was me?" she whispered.

"Yes," he admitted. After Marchais and Pretorius he had become obsessed with the idea that someone was tipping off the killer or killers; how else could they twice get to the vanished mercenaries before he and Sam did? She swallowed hard, composed herself, hid the hurt inside her.

"Okay, so when is the real rendezvous, may I ask? That is, if you trust me enough now."

"It's in an hour, at ten o'clock," he said. "A bar off the rue de Chalon, right behind the Gare de Lyon. It's a long haul—let's go now."

It was another cab ride. Sam sat silently reproachful as they rode down the quays along the north bank of the Seine from the northwest to the southeast of the city. Quinn dismissed the taxi on the corner of the rue de Chalon and the Passage de Gatbois. He decided to walk the rest.

The rue de Chalon ran parallel to the railway tracks heading out of the station toward the south of France. From beyond the wall they could hear the clang of trains moving over the numerous points outside the terminus. It was a dingy street.

Off the rue de Chalon a number of narrow streets, each called *Passage*, connected up to the bustling Avenue Daumesnil. One block down from where he had paid off the cab Quinn found the street he sought, the Passage de Vautrin. He turned into it.

"It's a hell of a dingy place," remarked Sam.

"Yeah, well, he picked it. The meeting is in a bar."

There were two bars in the street and neither was any threat to the Ritz.

Chez Hugo was the second one, across the street and fifty yards up from the first. Quinn pushed open the door. The bar counter was to his left; to his right, two tables near the street window, which was masked by thick lace curtains. Both tables were empty. The whole bar was empty except for the unshaven proprietor, who tended his espresso machine behind the counter. With the open door behind him and Sam standing there, Quinn was visible, and he knew it. Anyone in the dark recesses at the rear would be hard to see. Then he saw the bar's only customer. Right at the back, alone at a table, a coffee in front of him, staring at Quinn.

Quinn walked the length of the room, followed by Sam. The man made no move. His eyes never left Quinn, except to flicker once over Sam. Eventually Quinn stood above him. He wore a corduroy jacket and open-necked shirt. Thinning sandy hair, late forties, a thin, mean face, badly pockmarked.

"Zack?" said Quinn.

"Yeah. Siddown. Who's she?"

"My partner. I stay, she stays. You wanted this. Let's talk."

He sat down opposite Zack, hands on the table. No tricks. The man stared at him malevolently. Quinn knew he had seen the face before, thought back to Hayman's files, and those of Hamburg. Then he got it. Sidney Fielding, one of John Peters's section commanders in the Fifth Commando at Paulis, ex-Belgian Congo. The man trembled with a barely controlled emotion. After several seconds Quinn realized it was rage, but mixed with something else. Quinn had seen the look in the eyes many times, in Vietnam and elsewhere. The man was afraid, bitter and angry but also very badly frightened. Zack could contain himself no longer.

"Quinn, you're a bastard. You and your people are lying bastards. You promised no manhunt, said we'd just have to disappear and after a couple of weeks the heat would be off. Some shit. Now I hear Big Paul's gone missing and Janni's in a morgue in Holland. No manhunt, hell. We're being wasted."

"Hey, ease up, Zack. I'm not one of the ones who told you that. I'm on the other side. Why don't we start at the beginning? Why did you kidnap Simon Cormack?"

Zack looked at Quinn as if he had just asked if the sun was hot or cold.

"Because we was paid to," he said.

"You were paid up front? Not for the ransom?"

"No, that was extra. Half a million dollars was the fee. I took two hundred for me, one hundred each for the other three. We was told the ransom was extra—we could get as much as we could, and keep it."

"All right. Who paid you to do it? I swear I wasn't one of them. I was called in the day after the snatch, to try and get the kid back. Who set it up?"

"I dunno his name. Never did. He was American, that's all I know. Short, fat man. Contacted me here. God knows how he found me—must have had contacts. We always met in hotel rooms. I'd come there and he would always be masked. But the money was up front and in cash."

"What about expenses? Kidnappings come expensive."

"On top of the fee. In cash. Another hundred thousand dollars I had to spend."

"Did that include the house you hid in?"

"No, that was provided. We met in London a month before the job.

He gave me the keys, told me where it was, told me to get it ready as a bunk-hole."

"Give me the address."

Zack gave it to him. Quinn noted it. Nigel Cramer and the forensic scientists from the labs of the Metropolitan Police would later visit the place and take it apart in their search for clues. Records would show it was not rented at all. It had been bought quite legitimately for £200,000 through a firm of British lawyers acting for a Luxembourg-registered company.

The company would prove to be a bearer-share shell corporation represented quite legally by a Luxembourg bank acting as nominee, and who had never met the owner of the shell company. The money used to buy the house had come to Luxembourg in the form of a draft issued by a Swiss bank. The Swiss would declare that the draft had been bought for cash in U.S. dollars at their Geneva branch, but no one could recall the buyer.

The house, moreover, was not north of London at all; it was in Sussex to the south, near East Grinstead. Zack had simply been motoring around the orbital M.25 to make his phone calls from the northern side of the capital.

Cramer's men would scour the place from top to bottom; despite the cleaning-up efforts by the four mercenaries, there were some overlooked fingerprints, but they belonged to Marchais and Pretorius.

"What about the Volvo?" asked Quinn. "You paid for that?"

"Yeah, and the van, and most of the other gear. Only the Skorpion was given us by the fat man. In London."

Unknown to Quinn, the Volvo had already been found outside London. It had overstayed its time in a multistory parking lot at London's Heathrow Airport. The mercenaries, after driving through Buckingham on the morning of the murder, had turned south again and back to London. From Heathrow they had taken the airport shuttle bus to London's other air terminus at Gatwick, ignored the airport, and boarded the train for Hastings and the coast. Separate taxis had brought them to Newhaven to catch the noon ferry to Dieppe. Once in France they had split up and gone to earth.

The Volvo, examined by the Heathrow Airport police, was seen to have breathing holes punctured in the floor of the trunk, and a lingering smell of almonds. Scotland Yard was called in, the original owner traced. But it had been bought for cash, the change-of-owner documentation had never been completed, and the description of the buyer matched that of the ginger-haired man who had bought the Ford Transit.

"It was the fat man who was giving you all the inside information?" asked Quinn.

"What inside information?" said Sam suddenly.

"How did you know about that?" asked Zack suspiciously. He evidently still suspected that Quinn might be one of his employers-turned-persecutors.

"You were too good," said Quinn. "You knew to wait until I was in place, then ask for the negotiator in person. I've never known that before. You knew when to throw a rage and when to back off. You changed from dollars to diamonds, knowing it would cause a delay when we were ready to exchange."

Zack nodded. "Yeah, I was briefed before the kidnap on what to do, when and how to do it. While we were hiding, I had to make another series of phone calls. Always while out of the house, always from one phone booth to another, according to an arranged list. It was the fat man; I knew his voice by then. He occasionally made changes—fine-tuning, he called it. I just did what I was told."

"All right," said Quinn. "And the fat man told you there'd be no problem getting away afterward. Just a manhunt for a month or so, but with no clues to go on, it would all die down and you could live happily ever after. You really believed that? You really thought you could kidnap and kill the son of an American President and get away? Then why did you kill the kid? You didn't have to."

Zack's facial muscles worked in something like a frenzy. His eyes bulged with anger.

"That's the point, you shit. We didn't kill him. We dumped him on the road like we was told. He was alive and well—we hadn't hurt him at all. And we drove on. First we knew he was dead was when it was made public the next day. I couldn't believe it. It was a lie. We didn't do it."

Outside in the street a car cruised around the corner from the rue de Chalon. One man drove; the other was in back, cradling the rifle. The car came up the street as if looking for someone, paused outside the first bar, advanced almost to the door of Chez Hugo, then backed up to come to rest halfway between the two. The engine was kept idling.

"The kid was killed by a bomb planted in the leather belt he wore around his waist," said Quinn. "He wasn't wearing that when he was snatched on Shotover Plain. You gave it to him to wear."

"I didn't," shouted Zack. "I bloody didn't. It was Orsini."

"Okay, tell me about Orsini."

"Corsican, a hit man. Younger than us. When the three of us left to meet you in the warehouse, the kid was wearing what he had always worn. When we got back he was in new clothes. I tore Orsini off a hell of a strip over that. The silly bastard had left the house, against orders, and gone and bought them."

Quinn recalled the shouting row he had heard above his head when the mercenaries had retired to examine their diamonds. He had thought it was about the gems.

"Why did he do it?" asked Quinn.

"He said the kid had complained he was cold. Said he thought it would do no harm, so he walked into East Grinstead, went to a camping shop, and bought the gear. I was angry because he speaks no English and would stand out like a sore thumb, the way he looks."

"The clothes were almost certainly delivered in your absence," said Quinn. "All right, what does he look like, this Orsini?"

"About thirty-three, a pro, but never been in combat. Very dark chin, black eyes, knife scar down one cheek."

"Why did you hire him?"

"I didn't. I contacted Big Paul and Janni 'cos I knew them from the old days and we'd stayed in touch. The Corsican was sicked on me by the fat man. Now I hear Janni's dead and Big Paul has vanished."

"And what do you want with this meeting?" asked Quinn. "What am I supposed to do for you?"

Zack leaned forward and gripped Quinn's forearm.

"I want out," he said. "If you're with the people who set me up, tell 'em there's no way they need to come after me. I'd never, never talk. Not to the fuzz anyway. So they're safe."

"But I'm not with them," said Quinn.

"Then tell your people I never killed the kid," said Zack. "That was never part of the deal. I swear on my life I never intended that boy to die."

Quinn mused that if Nigel Cramer or Kevin Brown ever got their hands on Zack, "life" was exactly what he would be serving, as a guest either of Her Majesty or of Uncle Sam.

"A few last points, Zack. The diamonds. If you want to make a play for clemency, they'd better have the ransom back for starters. Have you spent them?"

"No," said Zack abruptly. "No chance. They're here. Every single bloody one."

He dived a hand under the table and dumped a canvas bag on the table. Sam's eyes popped.

"Orsini," said Quinn impassively. "Where is he now?"

"God knows. Probably back in Corsica. He came from there ten years ago to work in the gangs of Marseilles, Nice, and later Paris. That was all I could get out of him. Oh, and he comes from a village called Castelblanc."

Quinn rose, took the canvas bag, and looked down at Zack.

"You're in it, mate. Right up to your ears. I'll talk to the authorities. They might accept your turning state's evidence. Even that's a long shot. But I'll tell them there *were* people behind you, and probably people behind them. If they believe that, and you tell all, they might leave you alive. The others, the ones you worked for . . . no chance."

He turned to go. Sam got up to follow. As if preferring the shelter the American gave him, Zack rose also and they headed for the door. Quinn paused.

"One last thing. Why the name Zack?"

He knew that during the kidnapping, the psychiatrists and code breakers had puzzled long over the name, seeking a possible clue to the real identity of the man who had chosen it. They had worked on variations of Zachary, Zachariah, looked for relatives of known criminals who had such names or initials.

"It was really Z-A-K," said Zack. "The letters on the number plate of the first car I ever owned."

Quinn raised a single eyebrow. So much for psychiatry. He stepped outside. Zack came next. Sam was still in the doorway when the crash of the rifle tore apart the quiet of the side street.

Quinn did not see the car or the gunman. But he heard the distinctive "whap" of a bullet going past his face and felt the breath of cool wind it made on his cheek. The bullet missed his ear by half an inch, but not Zack. The mercenary took it in the base of the throat.

It was Quinn's quick reflexes that saved his life. He was no stranger to that sound, which gave him an edge. Zack's body was thrown back into the doorpost, then forward on the rebound. Quinn was back in the door arch before Zack's knees began to buckle. For the second that the mercenary's body was still upright, it acted as a shield between Quinn and the car parked thirty yards away.

Quinn hurled himself backwards through the door, twisting, grabbing Sam, and pulling them both down to the floor in one movement. As they hit the grubby tiles a second bullet passed through the closing door above them and tore plaster off the side wall of the café. Then the spring-loaded door closed.

Quinn went across the bar's floor at a fast crawl, elbows and toes, dragging Sam behind him. The car moved up the alley to straighten the rifleman's angle, and a volley of shots shattered the plate-glass window and riddled the door. The barman, presumably Hugo, was slower. He stood open-mouthed behind his bar until a shower of splinters from his disintegrating stock of bottles sent him to the floor.

The shots stopped—change of magazine. Quinn was up and racing for the rear exit, his left hand pulling Sam by the wrist, his right still clutching the bag of diamonds. The door at the back of the bar gave onto a corridor, with the toilets on each side. Straight ahead was a grubby kitchen. Quinn raced through the kitchen, kicked open the door at the end, and they found themselves in a rear yard.

Crates of beer bottles were stacked, awaiting collection. Using them as steps, Quinn and Sam went over the back wall of the yard and dropped into another backyard, which itself belonged to a butcher shop on the parallel street, the Passage de Gatbois. Three seconds later they emerged from the establishment of the astounded butcher and into the street. By good luck there was a taxi, thirty yards up. From its rear an old lady was climbing unsteadily, reaching into her bag for small change as she did so. Quinn got there first, swung the lady physically onto the pavement, and told her: "*C'est payé, madame.*"

He dived into the rear seat of the cab, still clutching Sam by the wrist, dropped the canvas bag on the seat, reached for a bundle of French banknotes, and held them under the driver's nose.

"Let's get out of here, fast," he said. "My girl's husband has just showed up with some hired muscle."

Marcel Dupont was an old man with a walrus moustache who had driven a cab on the streets of Paris for forty-five years. Before that he had fought with the Free French. He had bailed out of a few places in his time, one step ahead of the hard squad. He was also a Frenchman and the blond girl being dragged into his cab was quite an eyeful. He was also a Parisian and knew a fat bundle of banknotes when he saw one. It had been a long time since Americans gave $10 tips. Nowadays most of them seemed to be in Paris on a $10-a-day budget. He left a stream of black rubber smoke as he went up the passage and into Avenue Daumesnil.

Quinn had reached across Sam to give the swinging door a hard tug. It hit some impediment, closed at the second slam. Sam leaned back in the seat, white as a sheet. Then she noticed her treas-ured crocodile-skin handbag from Harrods. The force of the closing door had shattered the frame near the base, splitting the stitching. She examined the damage and her brow furrowed in puzzlement.

"Quinn, what the hell's this?"

"This" was the jutting end of a black-and-orange wafer-thin bat-tery, of the type used to power Polaroid cameras. Quinn's penknife slit the rest of the stitching along the base of the bag's frame to reveal the battery was one of a linked set of three, two and a half inches wide, four inches long. The transmitter and bleeper were in a printed circuit board, also in the base, with a wire leading to a microphone in the stud that formed the bottom of the hinge. The aerial was in the shoulder strap. It was a miniature, professional, state-of-the-art device and voice-activated to save power.

Quinn looked at the components on the rear seat between them. Even if it still worked, it would now be impossible to pass disinforma-tion through it. Sam's exclamation would have alerted the listeners to its discovery. He emptied all her effects from the upturned handbag, asked the driver to pause by the curb, and threw the handbag and elec-tronic bug into a garbage bin.

"Well, that accounts for Marchais and Pretorius," said Quinn. "There must have been two of them; one staying close to us, listening to our progress, phoning forward to his friend who could get to the target before us. But why the hell didn't they show up at this morning's phony rendezvous?"

"I didn't have it," said Sam suddenly.

"Didn't have what?"

"Didn't have the purse with me. I was having breakfast in the bar—you wanted to talk upstairs. I forgot my purse, left it on the ban-quette. I had to go back for it, thought it might have been stolen. Wish to God it had been."

"Yeah. All they heard was me telling the cabdriver to drop us on the rue de Chalon, at the corner of the street. And the word *bar*. There were two in that street."

"But how the hell could they have done that to my bag?" she asked. "It's been with me ever since I bought it."

"That's not your bag—that was a duplicate," said Quinn. "Someone spotted it, made up the replica, and did the switch. How many people came to that apartment in Kensington?"

"After you ran out? The world and his mother. There was Cramer and the Brits, Brown, Collins, Seymour, another three or four FBI men. I was up at the embassy, down at that manor house in Surrey where they kept you for a while, over to the States, back again—hell, I've been everywhere with it."

And it would take five minutes to empty the old bag, put the contents in the duplicate, and effect the switch.

"Where do you want to go, mate?" asked the driver.

The Hôtel du Colisée was out; the killers would know of that. But not the garage where he had parked the Opel. He had been there alone, without Sam and her lethal handbag.

"Place de la Madeleine," he said, "corner of Chauveau-Lagarde."

"Quinn, maybe I should head back to the States with what we just heard. I could go to our embassy here and insist on two U.S. marshals as escort. Washington's got to hear what Zack told us."

Quinn stared out at the passing streets. The cab was moving up the rue Royale. It skirted the Madeleine and dropped them at the entrance to the garage. Quinn tipped the friendly cabdriver heavily.

"Where are we going?" asked Sam when they were in the Opel and heading south across the Seine toward the Latin Quarter.

"You're going to the airport," said Quinn.

"For Washington?"

"Absolutely not for Washington. Listen, Sam, now more than ever you should not go back there unprotected. Whoever's behind this, they're much higher than a bunch of former mercenaries. They were just the hired hands. Everything that was happening on our side was being fed to Zack. He was forewarned of police progress, the dispositions in Scotland Yard, London, and Washington. Everything was choreographed, even the killing of Simon Cormack.

"When that kid ran along that roadside, someone had to be up in those trees with the detonator. How did he know to be there? Because Zack was told exactly what to do at every stage, including the release of both of us. The reason he didn't kill me was because he wasn't told to. He didn't think he was going to kill anybody."

"But he told us who," protested Sam. "It was this American, the one who set it up and paid him, the one he called the fat man."

"And who told the fat man?"

"Oh. There's someone behind the fat man."

"There has to be," said Quinn. "And high—real high. 'Way up there. We know what happened and how, but not who or why. You go back to Washington now and you tell them what we heard from Zack. What have we got? The claims of a kidnapper, criminal, and mercenary, now conveniently dead. A man running scared at the aftermath of what he's done, trying to buy his freedom by wasting his own colleagues and handing back the diamonds, with a cock-and-bull story that he was put up to it all."

"So where do we go from here?"

"You go into hiding. I go after the Corsican. He's the key. He's the fat man's employee, the one who provided the deadly belt and put it on Simon. Five will get you ten Zack was ordered to spin out the negotiations by an extra six days, switching his demand from cash to diamonds, because the new clothes were not ready. The schedule was being thrown out of kilter, moving too fast, had to be slowed down. If I can get to Orsini, take him alive, get him to talk, he probably knows the name of his employer. When we have the name of the fat man, *then* we can go to Washington."

"Let me come with you, Quinn. That was the deal we made."

"It was the deal Washington made. The deal's off. Everything Zack told us was recorded by that bug in your purse. They know that we know. For them now the hunt is on for you and me. Unless we can deliver the fat man's name. Then the hunters become the hunted. The FBI will see to that. And the CIA."

"So where do I go to ground, and for how long?"

"Until I call you and tell you we're in the clear, one way or the other. As to where—Málaga. I have friends in the South of Spain who'll look after you."

Paris, like London, is a two-airport city. Ninety percent of overseas flights leave from Charles de Gaulle to the north of the capital. But Spain and Portugal are still served from the older airport at Orly in the south. To add to the confusion, Paris also has two separate terminuses, each serving different airports. Buses for Orly depart from Maine-Montparnasse in the Latin Quarter. Quinn drew up there thirty minutes after leaving the Madeleine, parked, and led Sam inside the main hall.

"What about my clothes, my things at the hotel?" she complained.

"Forget them. If the hoods are not staking out the hotel by now, they're stupid. And they're not. You have your passport?"

"Yep. Always carry it on me."

"Same here. And your credit cards?"

"Sure. Same thing."

"Go over to that bank and get as much money as your credit card account can stand."

While Sam was at the bank, Quinn used the last of his cash to buy her a single ticket from Paris to Málaga. She had missed the 12:45 flight but there was another at 5:35 P.M.

"Your friend has five hours to wait," said the ticket-counter agent. "Coaches leave from Gate J every twelve minutes for Orly South terminal."

Quinn thanked her, crossed the floor to the bank, and gave Sam her ticket. She had drawn $5,000, and Quinn took $4,000.

"I'm taking you to the bus right now," said Quinn. "It'll be safer at Orly than right here, just in case they're checking flight departures. When you get there, go straight through passport control into the duty-free area. Harder to get at. Get yourself a new handbag, a suitcase, some clothes—you know what you'll need. Then wait for the flight and don't miss it. I'll have people at Málaga to meet you."

"Quinn, I don't even speak Spanish."

"Don't worry. These people all speak English."

At the steps of the bus Sam reached up and wrapped her arms around his neck.

"Quinn, I'm sorry. You'd have done better alone."

"Not your fault, baby." Quinn turned her face up and kissed her. A common enough scene at terminals—no one took any notice. "Besides, without you I wouldn't have the Smith & Wesson. I think I may need that."

"Take care of yourself," she whispered. A chill wind blew down the Boulevard de Vaugirard. The last heavy luggage was stacked underneath the bus and the last passengers boarded. Sam shivered in his arms. He smoothed the shining blond hair.

"I'll be okay. Trust me. I'll be in touch by phone in a couple of days. By then, either way, we'll be able to go home in safety."

He watched the bus head down the boulevard, waved at the small hand in the rear window. Then it turned the corner and was gone.

Two hundred yards from the terminus and across Vaugirard is a large post office. Quinn bought sheet cardboard and wrapping paper in a stationery shop and entered the post office. With penknife and gummed tape, paper and string, he made up a stout parcel of the diamonds and mailed it by registered post, express rate, to Ambassador Fairweather in London.

From the bank of international telephone booths he called Scotland Yard and left a message for Nigel Cramer. It consisted of an address near East Grinstead, Sussex. Finally he called a bar in Estepona. The man he spoke to was not Spanish, but a London Cockney.

"Yeah, all right, mate," said the voice on the phone. "We'll take care of the little lady for you."

With his last loose ends tied up, Quinn retrieved his car, filled the tank to the brim at the nearest gasoline station, and headed through the lunchtime traffic for the orbital ring road. Sixty minutes after making his phone call to Spain he was on the A.6 autoroute heading south for Marseilles.

He broke for dinner at Beaune, then put his head back in the rear seat of the car and caught up on some missing sleep. It was three in the morning when he resumed his journey south.

While he slept a man sat quietly in the San Marco restaurant across the road from the Hôtel du Colisée and kept watch on the hotel's front door. He had been there since midday, to the surprise and eventual annoyance of the staff. He had ordered lunch, sat through the afternoon, and then ordered dinner. To the waiters he appeared to be reading quietly in the window seat.

At eleven the restaurant wished to close. The man left and went next door to the Royal Hôtel. Explaining that he was waiting for a friend, he took a seat at the window of the lobby and continued his vigil. At two in the morning he finally gave up.

He drove to the twenty-four-hour-a-day post office in the rue du Louvre, went up to the first-floor bank of telephones, and placed a person-to-person call. He stayed in the booth until the operator rang back.

"*Allô, monsieur,*" she said. "I have your call. On the line. Go ahead, Castelblanc."

CHAPTER SIXTEEN

The Costa del Sol has long been the favored place of retirement of sought-after members of the British underworld. Several dozen such villains, having contrived to separate banks or armored cars from their contents or investors from their savings, having skipped the land of their fathers one inch ahead of the grasping fingers of Scotland Yard and sought refuge in the sun of the South of Spain, there to enjoy their newfound affluence. A wit once said that on a clear day in Estepona you can see more Category A men than in Her Majesty's Prison, Parkhurst, during roll call.

That evening four of their number were waiting at Málaga airport as a result of a phone call from Paris. There were Ronnie and Bernie and Arthur, pronounced Arfur, who were all mature men, and the youngster Terry, known as Tel. Apart from Tel they all wore pale suits and panama hats, and despite the fact that it was long after dark, sunglasses. They checked the arrivals board, noted that the Paris plane had just landed, and stood discreetly to one side of the exit door from the customs area.

Sam emerged among the first three passengers. She had no luggage but her new, Orly-bought handbag and a small leather suitcase, also new, with a collection of toiletries and overnight clothes. Otherwise she had only the two-piece outfit in which she had attended the morning's meeting at Chez Hugo.

Ronnie had a description of her but it had failed to do her justice. Like Bernie and Arfur he was married, and like the others his old lady was a peroxide blonde, bleached even whiter by constant sun-worshipping, with the lizardlike skin that is the heritage of too much ultraviolet radiation. Ronnie appraised the pale northern skin and hour-glass figure of the newcomer with approval.

"Gorblimey," muttered Bernie.

"Tasty," said Tel. It was his favorite, if not only, adjective. Anything that surprised or pleased him he designated "tasty."

Ronnie moved forward.

"Miss Somerville?"

"Yes."

"Evening. I'm Ronnie. This is Bernie and Arfur and Tel. Quinn asked us to look after you. The car's right over here."

Quinn drove into Marseilles in a cold and rainy dawn, the last day of November. He had the choice of flying to Ajaccio, the capital of Corsica, from Marignane Airport, and arriving the same day, or of taking the evening ferry and his car with him.

He elected the ferry. For one thing he would not have to rent a car in Ajaccio; for another, he could safely take the Smith & Wesson, still stuck in his waistband; and for a third, he felt he ought as a precaution to make some small purchases for the stay in Corsica.

The signs to the ferry port on the Quai de la Joliette were clear enough. The port was almost empty. The morning's ferry from Ajaccio was docked, its passengers gone an hour before. The SNCM ticket office on the Boulevard des Dames was still closed. He parked and enjoyed breakfast while he waited.

At nine he bought himself a crossing on the ferry *Napoléon* for the coming night, due to leave at 8:00 P.M. and arrive at 7:00 the morning after. With his ticket he could lodge the Ascona in the passengers' parking lot close to the J4 *quai*, from which the ferry would leave. This done, he walked back into the city to make his purchases.

The canvas holdall was easy enough to find, and a pharmacy yielded the washing things and shaving tackle to replace what he had abandoned at the Hôtel du Colisée in Paris. The search for a specialist men's outfitters caused a number of shaken heads, but he eventually found it in the pedestrians-only rue St.-Ferréol just north of the Old Port.

The young salesman was helpful and the purchase of boots, jeans, belt, shirt, and hat posed no problem. When Quinn mentioned his last request, the young man's eyebrows went up.

"You want *what*, m'sieur?"

Quinn repeated his need.

"I'm sorry, I don't think such a thing could be for sale."

He eyed the two large-denomination notes moving seductively through Quinn's fingers.

"Perhaps in the storeroom? An old one of no further use?" suggested Quinn.

The young man glanced around.

"I will see, sir. May I take the holdall?"

He was in the storeroom at the rear for ten minutes. When he returned he opened the holdall for Quinn to peer inside.

"Marvelous," said Quinn. "Just what I needed."

He settled up, tipped the young man as promised, and left. The skies cleared and he lunched at an open café in the Old Port, spending an hour over coffee studying a large-scale map of Corsica. The only thing the attached gazeteer would say of Castelblanc was that it was in the Ospédale Range in the deep south of the island.

At eight the *Napoléon* eased herself out of the Gare Maritime and headed backwards into the roads. Quinn was enjoying a glass of wine in the Bar des Aigles, almost empty at that season of the year. As the ferry swung to bring her nose to the sea, the lights of Marseilles passed in review before the window, to be replaced by the old prison fortress of Château d'If, drifting past half a cable's length away.

Fifteen minutes later she cleared Cap Croisette and was enveloped by the darkness and the open sea. Quinn went to dine in the Malmaison, returned to his cabin on D Deck, and turned in before eleven, his bedside clock set for six.

At about that hour Sam sat with her hosts in a small and isolated former farmhouse high in the hills behind Estepona. None of them lived in the house; it was used for storage and the occasional moment when one of their friends needed a little "privacy" from marauding detectives waving extradition warrants.

The five of them sat in a closed and shuttered room, now blue with cigarette smoke, playing poker. It had been Ronnie's suggestion. They had been at it for three hours; only Ronnie and Sam remained in the game. Tel did not play; he served beer—drunk straight from the bottle and with an ample supply available in the crates along one wall. The other walls were also stacked, but with bales of an exotic leaf fresh in from Morocco and destined for export to countries farther north.

Arfur and Bernie had been cleaned out and sat glumly watching the last two players at the table. The "pot" of 1,000-peseta notes in the center of the table contained all they had brought with them, plus half of what Ronnie had and half the dollars in Sam's possession, exchanged at the going dollar/peseta rate.

Sam eyed Ronnie's remaining stash, pushed most of her own banknotes to the center, and raised him. He grinned, matched her raise, and asked to see her cards. She turned four of her cards face-up. Two kings, two tens. Ronnie grinned and up-faced his own hand: full house, three queens and two jacks. He reached for the pile of notes containing all he had, plus all Bernie and Arfur had brought, plus nine tenths of Sam's thousand dollars. Sam flicked over her fifth card. The third king.

"Bloody 'ell," he said and leaned back. Sam scooped the notes into a pile.

"S'truth," said Bernie.

"'Ere, what you do for a living, Sam?" asked Arfur.

"Didn't Quinn tell you?" she asked. "I'm a special agent with the FBI."

"Gorblimey," said Ronnie.

"Tasty," said Tel.

The *Napoléon* docked on the dot of seven at the Gare Maritime of Ajaccio, halfway between the jetties Capucins and Citadelle. Ten minutes later Quinn joined the few other vehicles emerging from her hold and drove down the ramp into the ancient capital of this wildly beautiful and secretive island.

His map had made clear enough the route he should take, due south out of town, down the Boulevard Sampiero to the airport, there to take a left into the mountains on the N.196. Ten minutes after he took the turnoff, the land began to climb, as it always will in Corsica, which is almost entirely covered by mountains. The road swerved and switchbacked up past Cauro to the Col St. Georges, from which for a second he could look back and down to the narrow coastal plain far behind and below. Then the mountains enfolded him again, dizzying slopes and cliffs, clothed in these low-lying hills with forests of oak, olive, and beech. After Bicchisano the road wound down again, back toward the coast at Propriano. There was no way of avoiding the dogleg route to the Ospédale—a straight line would lead clear across the valley of the Baraci, a region so wild no roadmakers could penetrate it.

After Propriano he followed the coastal plain again for a few miles before the D.268 allowed him to turn toward the mountains of Ospédale. He was now off the N (national) roads and onto D (departmental) roads, little more than narrow lanes, yet broad highways compared to the tracks high in the mountains to come.

He passed tiny perched villages of local gray stone houses, sitting on hills and escarpments from which the views were vertiginous, and he wondered how these farmers could make a living from their tiny meadows and orchards.

Always the road climbed, twisting and turning, dipping to cross a fold in the ground but always climbing again after the respite. Beyond Ste. Lucie de Tallano the tree line ended and the hills were covered with that thick, thigh-high cover of heather and myrtle that they call the *maquis*. During the Second World War, fleeing from one's home into the mountains to avoid arrest by the Gestapo was called "taking to the *maquis*"; thus the French underground resistance became known as the *maquisards*, or just "the Maquis."

Corsica is as old as her mountains, and men have lived in these hills since prehistoric times. Like Sardinia and Sicily, Corsica has been fought over more times than she can remember, and always the strangers came as conquerors, invaders, and tax-gatherers, to rule and to take, never to give. With so little to live on for themselves, the Corsicans reacted by turning to their hills, the natural ramparts and sanctuaries. Generations of rebels and bandits, guerrillas and partisans have taken to the hills to avoid the authorities marching up from the coast to levy taxes and imposts from people ill able to pay.

Out of these centuries of experience the mountain folk developed their philosophy: clannish and secretive. Authority represented injustice and Paris gathered taxes just as harshly as any other conqueror. Though Corsica is part of France, and gave France Napoléon Bonaparte and a thousand other notables, for the mountain people the foreigner is still the foreigner, harbinger of injustice and the tax levy, whether from France or anywhere else. Corsica might send her sons by the tens of thousands to mainland France to work, but if ever such a son were in trouble, the old mountains would still offer sanctuary.

It was the mountains and the poverty and the perceived persecution that gave rise to the rocklike solidarity, and to the Corsican Union, deemed by some to be more secretive and dangerous than the Mafia. It was into this world, which no twentieth century had managed to change with its Common Markets and European Parliaments, that Quinn drove in the last month of 1991.

Just before the town of Levie there was a sign pointing to Carbini, along a small road called the D.59. The road ran due south and, after four miles, crossed the Fiumicicoli, by now a small stream tumbling out of the Ospédale Range. At Carbini, a one-street village where old men in blue smocks sat outside their stone cottages and a few chickens scratched the dust, Quinn's gazetteer ran out of steam. Two lanes left the village; the D.148 ran back west, the way he had come, but along the south flank of the valley.

Straight ahead ran the D.59 toward Orone and, much farther south, to Sotta. He could see the jutting peak of Mount Cagna to the southwest, the silent mass of the Ospédale Range to his left, topped by one of Corsica's highest peaks, the Punta di la Vacca Morta, so called because from a certain angle it seems to resemble a dead cow. He chose to drive straight on.

Just after Orone the mountains were closer to his left, and the turning for Castelblanc was two miles beyond Orone. It was no more than a track, and since no road led through the Ospédale, it had to be a cul-de-sac. He could see from the road the great pale-gray rock set in the flank of the range that had once caused someone to think he was looking at a white castle, a mistake that had given the hamlet its name long ago. Quinn drove slowly up the track. Three miles farther on, high above the D.59, he entered Castelblanc.

The road ended at the village square, which lay at the end of the village, back to the mountain. The narrow street that led to the square was flanked by low stone houses, all closed and shuttered. No chickens scratched the dirt. No old men sat on their stoops. The place was silent. He drove into the square, stopped, climbed out, and stretched. Down the main street a tractor engine started. The tractor emerged from between two houses, rolled to the center of the road, and stopped. The driver removed the ignition keys, dropped to the ground, and disappeared between the houses. There was enough space between the rear of the tractor and the wall for a motorcycle, but no car could drive back down that street until the tractor was removed.

Quinn looked around. The square had three sides, apart from the road. To the right were four cottages; ahead, a small gray stone church. To his left was what must be the center of life in Castelblanc, a low tavern of two floors under a tiled roof and an alley leading to what else there was of Castelblanc that was not on the road—a cluster of cottages, barns, and yards that terminated in the flank of the mountain.

From the church door a small and very old priest emerged, failed to see Quinn, and turned to lock the door behind him.

"*Bonjour, mon père,*" Quinn called cheerfully. The man of God jumped like a shot rabbit, glanced at Quinn in near panic, and scuttled across the square to disappear down the alley beside the tavern. As he did so he crossed himself.

Quinn's appearance would have surprised any Corsican priest, for the specialist menswear shop in Marseilles had done him proud. He had tooled Western boots, pale-blue jeans, a bright-red plaid shirt, fringed buckskin jacket, and a tall Stetson hat. If he wished to look like a caricature off a dude ranch, he had succeeded. He took his ignition keys and his canvas bag and strolled into the bar.

It was dark inside. The proprietor was behind the bar, earnestly polishing glasses—something of a novelty, Quinn surmised. Otherwise there were four plain oak tables, each surrounded by four chairs. Only one was occupied; four men sat studying hands of cards.

Quinn went to the bar and set down his bag, but kept his tall hat on. The barman looked up.

"Monsieur?"

No curiosity, no surprise. Quinn pretended not to notice, flashed a beaming smile.

"A glass of red wine, if you please," he said formally. The wine was local, rough but good. Quinn sipped appreciatively. From behind the bar the landlord's plump wife appeared, deposited several dishes of olives, cheese, and bread, cast not a glance at Quinn and, at a short word in the local dialect from her husband, disappeared back into the kitchen. The men playing cards refused to look at him either. Quinn addressed the barman.

"I am looking," he said, "for a gentleman I believe lives here. Name of Orsini. Do you know him?"

The barman glanced at the card players as if for a prompt. None came.

"Would that be Monsieur Dominique Orsini?" asked the barman. Quinn looked thoughtful. They had blocked the road, admitted Orsini existed. For both reasons they wished him to stay. Until when? He glanced behind him. The sky outside the windows was pale-blue in the wintry sun. Until dark perhaps. Quinn turned back to the bar and drew a fingertip down his cheek.

"Man with a knife scar? Dominique Orsini?"

The barman nodded.

"Can you tell me where I can find his house?"

Again the barman looked urgently at the card players for a prompt. This time it came. One of the men, the only one in a formal suit, looked up from his cards and spoke.

"Monsieur Orsini is away today, monsieur. He will return tomorrow. If you wait, you will meet him."

"Well, thank you, friend. That's real neighborly of you." To the barman he said, "Could I take a room here for the night?"

The man just nodded. Ten minutes later Quinn had his room, shown him by the proprietor's wife, who still refused to meet his gaze. When she left, Quinn examined the room. It was at the back, overlooking a yard surrounded by lean-to open-fronted barns. The mattress on the bed was thin, stuffed with lumpy horsehair, but adequate for his purpose. With his penknife he eased up two floorboards under the bed and secreted one of the items contained in his bag. The rest he left for inspection. He closed the bag, left it on the bed, took a hair from his head, and stuck it with saliva across the zip.

Back in the bar he made a good lunch of goat cheese, fresh crusty bread, local pork pâté, and juicy olives, washed down with wine. Then he took a walk around the village. He knew he was safe until sundown; his hosts had received and understood their orders.

There was not a lot to see. No people came to the street to greet him. He saw one small child hastily pulled back into a doorway by a pair of hard-worked female hands. The tractor on the main street had its big rear wheels just clear of the alley from which it had emerged, leaving a two-foot gap. Its front was up against a timber barn.

A chill came into the air about five o'clock. Quinn retired to the bar, where a cheerful fire of olive logs crackled in the hearth. He went to his room for a book, satisfied himself that his bag had been searched, nothing taken, and the floorboards beneath the bed had not been discovered.

He spent two hours in the bar reading, still refusing to remove his hat, then ate again, a tasty ragout of pork, beans, and mountain herbs, with lentils, bread, apple tart, and coffee. He took water instead of wine. At nine he retired to his room. An hour later the last light in the village was extinguished. No one watched television in the bar that night, though it boasted one of only three sets in the village. No one played cards. By ten the village was in darkness, save only for the single bulb in Quinn's room.

It was a low-power bulb, unshaded and hanging from a dusty cord in the middle of the room. The best light it gave was directly beneath, and that was where the figure in the tall Stetson hat sat reading in the upright armchair.

The moon rose at half past one, climbed from behind the Ospédale Range, and bathed Castelblanc in an eerie white light thirty minutes later. The lean, silent figure moved through the street by its dim illumination as one who knows exactly where he is going. The figure slid down two narrow alleys and into the complex of barns and yards behind the tavern.

Without a sound the shape leaped onto a hay wain parked in one of the yards and from there to the top of a wall. It ran effortlessly along the top of the wall and jumped another alley to land nimbly on the lean-to roof of the barn directly opposite Quinn's window.

The curtains were half-drawn—they reached only halfway across the window at full stretch. In the twelve-inch gap Quinn could be plainly seen, book on lap, head tilted slightly forward to read the print in the dim light, the shoulders in the red plaid shirt visible above the window sill, the tan Stetson on his head.

The young man on the roof grinned; such foolishness would prevent his having to come through the bedroom window to do what had to be done. He unslung the Lupara shotgun on the leather strap across his shoulders, flicked the catch off safety, and took aim. Forty feet away the hatted head filled the space above the twin barrels; the triggers were wired together to detonate both barrels simultaneously.

When he fired, the roar would have waked the entire village, but no lights went on. The heavy buckshot from both barrels vaporized the panes in the window and shredded the thin cotton curtains. Beyond the window, the head of the sitting man seemed to explode. The gunman saw the pale Stetson whipped away by the blast. The skull fragmented and a great spray of brilliant-red blood flew in all directions. Without a head, the red-plaid torso toppled sideways to the floor and out of vision.

Satisfied, the young cousin of the Orsini clan, who had just made his bones for the family, ran back off the roof, along the wall, down to the hay cart, to the ground, and into the alley from which he had come. Unhurried, and safe in his triumph, the youth walked through the village to the cottage on the fringes of the hamlet where the man he idolized awaited him. He did not see or hear the quieter and taller man who eased himself out of a darkened doorway and followed him.

The devastation in the room above the bar would later be cleared up by the owner's wife. Her mattress was beyond salvation, slit from end to end, its springy stuffing used to fill the plaid shirt, the torso, and the arms, until it was stiff enough to sit unaided in the upright chair. She would find long strips of clear gummed tape that had held the dummy torso in the upright position, and the remains of the Stetson hat and the book.

She would pick up, piece by piece, the remnants of the polystyrene head of the store dummy that Quinn had persuaded the Marseilles attendant to filch from the stockroom and sell him. Of the two condoms, bloated with ketchup from the ferry's dining room, which had once hung inside the dummy head, she would find little trace— just the red splotches all over her room, but these would come off with a damp cloth.

The landlord would wonder why he had not seen the head of the store dummy when he searched the American's luggage, and would eventually find the loose planks beneath the bed where it had been hidden by Quinn as soon as he arrived.

Finally the angry man in the dark suit who had been playing cards in the bar the previous afternoon would be shown the abandoned tooled cowboy boots, the jeans, the fringed buckskin jacket, and the landlord would inform the local *capu* that the American must now be dressed in his other set of clothes: dark trousers, black zip-up windbreaker, crepe-soled desert boots, and polo-neck sweater. They would all examine the canvas holdall and find nothing else left in it. This would happen in the hour before dawn.

When the youth reached the cottage he sought, he tapped gently on the door. Quinn slipped into a shadowed doorway fifty yards behind him. There must have been a command to enter, for the youth flipped the door latch and went inside. As the door closed, Quinn moved closer, circled the house, and found a shuttered window with a crack in the timbers large enough to peer through.

Dominique Orsini sat at a rough wooden table, and cut slices off a fat salami sausage with a razor-sharp knife. The teenager with the Lupara stood in front of him. They were talking in the Corsican language, nothing like French, incomprehensible to a foreigner. The boy was describing the events of the last thirty minutes; Orsini nodded several times.

When the boy had finished, Orsini rose, came around the table, and embraced him. The younger man glowed with pride. As Orsini turned, the lamplight caught the livid scar running down one cheek from the point of the bone to the jaw. He took a wad of notes from his pocket; the boy shook his head and protested. Orsini stuffed the wad in the youth's top pocket, patted him on the back, and dismissed him. The boy disappeared from view.

To have killed the Corsican hit man would have been easy. Quinn wanted him alive, in the back of his car, and in a cell in Ajaccio police headquarters by sunup. He had noticed the powerful motorcycle parked in the lean-to log store.

Thirty minutes later, in the deep shadow cast by the wooden barn and the parked tractor, Quinn heard the rumble of the motorcycle's engine starting. Orsini turned the motorcycle slowly out of a side passage and into the main square, then headed down the track out of town. There was enough room for him to pass between the rear of the tractor and the nearest house wall. He passed through a bright patch of moonlight and Quinn stepped out of the shadows, drew a bead, and fired once. The motorcycle's front tire shredded; the machine slewed violently and went out of control. It fell to its side, threw the rider, and rolled to a stop.

Orsini was hurled by his own momentum into the side of the tractor, but he came back up with remarkable speed. Quinn stood ten yards away, the Smith & Wesson pointing at the Corsican's chest. Orsini was breathing deeply, in pain, favoring one leg as he leaned against the tractor's high rear wheel. Quinn could see the glittering black eyes, the dark stubble around the chin. Slowly Orsini raised his hands.

"Orsini," said Quinn quietly. *"Je m'appelle Quinn. Je veux te parler."*

Orsini's reaction was to put pressure on his damaged leg, gasp in pain, and lower his left hand to his knee. He was good. The left hand moved slowly to massage the knee, taking Quinn's attention with it for a second. The right hand moved much faster, sweeping down and letting go of the sleeve-knife in the same second. Quinn caught the flicker of steel in the moonlight and jerked sideways. The blade missed his throat, twitched the shoulder of his leather jacket, and dug deep into the planks of the barn behind him.

It took Quinn only a second to grab the bone haft and jerk it out of the wood to release his jacket. But it was enough for Orsini. He was behind the tractor and running down the alley behind the vehicle like a cat. But a wounded cat.

Had he been unhurt Quinn would have lost him. Fit though the American was, when a Corsican hits the *maquis* there are very few who can keep up with him. The tough strands of heather, up to waist height, cling and drag at the clothes like a thousand fingers. The sensation is of wading through water. Within two hundred meters the energy is sapped away; the legs feel like lead. A man can drop to the ground anywhere in that sea of *maquis* and vanish, invisible at ten feet.

But Orsini was slowed. His other enemy was the moonlight. Quinn saw his shadow reach the end of the alley, which marked the last houses of the hamlet, and then move out into the heather of the hillside. Quinn went after him, down the alley, which became a track, and then into the *maquis*. He could hear the swish of branches ahead and guided himself by the noise.

Then he saw Orsini's head again, twenty yards ahead, moving across the flank of the mountain but steadily uphill. A hundred yards farther on, the sounds ceased. Orsini had gone to earth. Quinn stopped and did the same. To go forward with the moon behind him would be madness.

He had hunted before, and been hunted, by night. In the dense bush by the Mekong, through the thick jungle north of Khe Sanh, in the high country with his Montagnard guides. All natives are good in their own terrain, the Viet Cong in their jungle, the Kalahari bushmen in their own desert. Orsini was on his own ground, where he had been born and brought up, slowed by a damaged knee, without his knife but almost certainly with his handgun. And Quinn needed him alive. So both men crouched in the heather and listened to the sounds of the night, to discern that one sound that was not a cicada or coney or fluttering bird, but could only be made by a man. Quinn glanced at the moon; an hour to set. After that he would see nothing until dawn, when help would come for the Corsican from his own village a quarter-mile down the mountain.

For forty-five minutes of that hour neither man moved. Each listened for the other to move first. When Quinn heard the scrape he knew it was the sound of metal against rock. Trying to ease the pain in his knee, Orsini had let his gun touch rock. There was only one rock; fifteen yards to Quinn's right, and Orsini behind it. Quinn began to crawl slowly through the heather at ground level. Not toward the rock—that would have been to take a bullet in the face. But to a larger clump of heather ten yards in front of the rock.

In his back pocket he still had the residue of the fishing line he had used at Oldenburg to dangle the tape recorder over the branch of the tree. He tied one end around the tall clump of heather two feet off the ground, then retreated to where he had started, paying out the line as he went. When he was certain he was far enough away, he began to tug gently at the line.

The bush moved and rustled. He let it stop, let the sound sink in to the listening ears. Did it again, and again. Then he heard Orsini begin to crawl.

The Corsican finally came to his knees ten feet from the bush. Quinn saw the back of his head, gave the twine one last sharp tug. The

bush jerked, Orsini raised his gun, double-handed, and put seven bullets one after the other into the ground around the base of the bush.
When he stopped, Quinn was behind him, upright, the Smith & Wesson
pointing at Orsini's back.

As the echoes of the last shots died away down the mountain the
Corsican sensed he had been wrong. He turned slowly, saw Quinn.

"Orsini . . ."

He was going to say: I just want to talk to you. Any man in Orsini's
position would have been crazy to try it. Or desperate. Or convinced he
was dead if he did not. He pulled his torso about and fired his last round.
It was hopeless. The shot went into the sky because half a second before
he fired, Quinn did the same. He had no choice. His bullet took the
Corsican full in the chest and tossed him backwards, faceup in the
maquis.

It was not a heart-shot, but bad enough. There had been no time to
take him in the shoulder, and the range was too close for half-measures.
He lay on his back, staring up at the American above him. His chest
cavity was filling with blood, gurgling out of the punctured lungs, filling
the throat.

"They told you I had come to kill you, didn't they?" said Quinn. The
Corsican nodded slowly.

"They lied to you. He lied to you. And about the clothes for the boy.
I came to find out his name. The fat man. The one who set it up. You owe
him nothing now. No code applies. Who is he?"

Whether, in his last moments, Dominique Orsini still stuck by the
code of silence, or whether it was the blood pumping up his throat,
Quinn would never know. The man on his back opened his mouth in
what might have been an effort to speak or might have been a mocking
grin. He gave a low cough instead, and a stream of bright-pink frothing
blood filled his mouth and ran onto his chest. Quinn heard the sound he
had heard before and knew too well; the low clatter of the lungs empty-
ing for the last time. Orsini rolled his head sideways and Quinn saw the
hard bright glitter fade from the black eyes.

The village was still silent and dark when he padded down the alley
to the main square. They must have heard the boom of the shotgun, the
single roar of a handgun on the main street, the fusillade from up the
mountain. But if their orders were to stay inside, they were obeying
them. Yet someone, probably the youth, had become curious. Perhaps
he had seen the motorcycle lying by the tractor and feared the worst.
Whatever, he was lying in wait.

Quinn got into his Opel in the main square. No one had touched it.

He strapped himself in tightly, turned to face the street, and gunned the engine. When he hit the side of the timber barn, just in front of the tractor's wheels, the old planks shattered. There was a thump as he collided with several bales of hay inside the barn and another crash of splintering woodwork as the Ascona demolished the farther wall.

The buckshot hit the rear of the Ascona as it came out of the barn, a full charge that blew holes in the trunk but failed to hit the tank. Quinn tore down the track in a hail of pieces of wood and tufts of flying straw, corrected the steering, and headed down toward the road for Orone and Carbini. It was just short of four in the morning and he had a three-hour drive to Ajaccio airport.

Six time zones to the west it was nudging 10:00 P.M. in Washington the previous evening and the Cabinet officers whom Odell had summoned to grill the professional experts were not in an easily appeasable mood.

"What do you mean, no progress so far?" demanded the Vice President. "It's been a month. You've had unlimited resources, all the manpower you asked for, and the cooperation of the Europeans. What goes on?"

The target of his inquiry was Don Edmonds, Director of the FBI, who sat next to Assistant Director (CID) Philip Kelly. Lee Alexander of the CIA had David Weintraub with him. Edmonds coughed, glanced at Kelly, and nodded.

"Gentlemen, we are a lot further forward than we were thirty days ago," said Kelly defensively. "The Scotland Yard people are even now examining the house where, we now know, Simon Cormack was held captive. That has already yielded a mass of forensic evidence, including two sets of fingerprints which are in the process of being identified."

"How did they find the house?" asked the Secretary of State.

Philip Kelly studied his notes.

Weintraub answered Jim Donaldson's question: "Quinn called them up from Paris and told them."

"Great," said Odell sarcastically. "And what other news of Quinn?"

"He seems to have been active in several parts of Europe," said Kelly diplomatically. "We are expecting a full report on him momentarily."

"What do you mean, active?" asked Bill Walters, the Attorney General.

"We may have a problem with Mr. Quinn," said Kelly.

"We've always had a problem with Mr. Quinn," observed Morton Stannard of Defense. "What's the new one?"

"You may know that my colleague Kevin Brown has long harbored suspicions that Mr. Quinn knew more about this thing from the start than he was letting on; could even have been involved at some stage. Now it appears adduced evidence may support that theory."

"What adduced evidence?" asked Odell.

"Well, since he was released, on this committee's instructions, to pursue his own investigations into the identities of the kidnappers, he has been located in a number of European situations and then vanished again. He was detained in Holland at the scene of a murder, then released by the Dutch police for lack of evidence. . . ."

"He was released," said Weintraub quietly, "because he could prove he was miles away when the crime was committed."

"Yeah, but the dead man was a former Congo mercenary whose fingerprints have now been found in the house where Simon Cormack was detained," said Kelly. "We regard that as suspicious."

"Any other evidence on Quinn?" asked Hubert Reed.

"Yes, sir. The Belgian police have just reported finding a body with a bullet hole in the head, stuck on top of a Ferris wheel. Time of death, three weeks ago. A couple answering the description of Quinn and Agent Somerville were asking the dead man's whereabouts from his employer around the same time the man disappeared.

"Then in Paris another mercenary was shot dead on a sidewalk. A cabdriver reported two Americans answering the same description fleeing from the scene in his cab at the time."

"Marvelous," said Stannard. "Wonderful. We let him go to pursue inquiries and he leaves a trail of bodies all over northern Europe. We have, or used to have, allies over there."

"Three bodies in three countries," observed Donaldson acidly. "Anything else we should know about?"

"There's a German businessman recovering from remedial surgery in Bremen General Hospital; claims it was because of Quinn," said Kelly.

"What did he do to him?" asked Walters.

Kelly told him.

"Good God, the man's a maniac," exclaimed Stannard.

"Okay, we know what Quinn's been doing," said Odell. "He's wiping out the gang before they can talk. Or maybe he makes them talk to him first. What has the FBI been doing?"

"Gentlemen," said Kelly, "Mr. Brown has been pursuing the best lead we have—the diamonds. Every diamond dealer and manufacturing jeweler in Europe and Israel, not to mention right here in the States, is now on the lookout for those stones. Small though they are, we are confident we will be on top of the seller the instant they show up."

"Damn it, Kelly, they *have* shown up," shouted Odell. With a dramatic gesture he pulled a canvas bag from the floor near his feet and turned it upside down over the conference table. A river of stones clattered out and flowed across the mahogany. There was a stunned silence.

"Mailed to Ambassador Fairweather in London two days ago. From Paris. Handwriting identified as Quinn's. Now what the hell is going on over there? We want you to get Quinn back over here to Washington to tell us what happened to Simon Cormack, who did it, and why. We figure he seems about the only one who knows anything. Right, gentlemen?"

There was a concerted series of nods from the Cabinet members.

"You got it, Mr. Vice President," said Kelly. "We ... er ... may have a bit of a problem there."

"And what is that?" asked Reed sardonically.

"He's vanished again," said Kelly. "We know he was in Paris. We know he rented an Opel in Holland. We'll ask the French police to trace the Opel, put a port watch all over Europe in the morning. His car or his passport will show up in twenty-four hours. Then we'll extradite him back here."

"Why can't you telephone Agent Somerville?" asked Odell suspiciously. "She's with him. She's our bird dog."

Kelly coughed defensively.

"We have a slight problem there, too, sir. . . ."

"You haven't lost her as well?" asked Stannard in disbelief.

"Europe's a big place, sir. She seems to be temporarily out of contact. The French confirmed earlier today she had left Paris for the south of Spain. Quinn has a place there; the Spanish police checked it out. She didn't show. Probably in a hotel. They're checking them too."

"Now look," said Odell. "You find Quinn and you get his ass back over here. Fast. And Miss Somerville. We want to talk to Miss Somerville."

The meeting broke up.

"They're not the only ones," growled Kelly as he escorted a less-than-pleased Director out to their limousines.

Quinn was in a despondent mood as he drove the last fifteen miles from Cauro down to the coastal plain. He knew that with Orsini dead the trail was at last well and truly cold. There had been only four men in the gang, now all dead. The fat man, whoever he was, and the men behind him if there *were* any other paymasters, could bury themselves forever, their identities secure. What really happened to the President's only son, why, how, and who did it, would remain in history like the Kennedy killing and the *Marie Celeste*. There would be the official record to close the file, and there would be the theories to try to explain the ambiguities . . . forever.

Southeast of the Ajaccio airport, where the road from the mountains joins the coast highway, Quinn crossed the Prunelli River, then in spate as the winter rains tumbled out of the hills to the sea. The Smith & Wesson had served him well at Oldenburg and Castelblanc, but he could not wait for the ferry and would have to fly—without luggage. He bade the FBI-issue weapon farewell and tossed it far into the river, creating another bureaucratic headache for the Hoover Building. Then he drove the last four miles to the airport.

It is a low, wide modern building, light and airy, divided into two tunnel-linked parts, dedicated to arrivals and departures. He parked the Opel Ascona in the lot and walked into the departures terminal. The place was just opening up. Half-right, just after the magazine shop, he found the Flight Information desk and inquired about the first flight out. Nothing to France for the next two hours, but he could do better. Mondays, Tuesdays, and Sundays there is a 9:00 A.M. Air France flight direct to London.

He was going there anyway, to make a full report to Kevin Brown and Nigel Cramer; he thought Scotland Yard had as much right as the FBI to know what had happened through October and November, half of it in Britain and half in Europe. He bought himself a single ticket to Heathrow and asked for the phone booths. They were in a row beyond the information desk. He needed coins and went to change a bank note at the magazine shop. It was just after seven; he had two hours to wait.

Changing his money and heading back to the telephones, he failed to notice the British businessman who entered the terminal from the direction of the forecourt. The man appeared not to notice him either. He brushed several drops of rain off the shoulders of his beautifully cut three-piece dark suit, folded his charcoal-gray Crombie overcoat across one arm, hung his still-furled umbrella in the crook of the same elbow, and went to study the magazines. After several minutes he bought one, looked around, and selected one of the eight circular banquettes that surround the eight pillars supporting the roof.

The one he selected gave him a view of the main entrance doors, the passenger check-in desk, the row of phone booths, and the embarka-

tion doors leading to the departure lounge. The man crossed his ele-
gantly suited legs and began to read his magazine.

Quinn checked the directory and made his first call to the rental
company. The agent was in early. He, too, tried harder.

"Certainly, monsieur. At the airport? The keys under the driver's
foot mat? We can collect it from there. Now about payment . . . By the
way, what car is it?"

"An Opel Ascona," said Quinn. There was a doubtful pause.

"Monsieur, we do not have any Opel Asconas. Are you sure you
rented it from us?"

"Certainly, but not here in Ajaccio."

"Ah, perhaps you went to our branch in Bastia? Or Calvi?"

"No, Arnhem."

By now the man was trying very hard indeed.

"Where is Arnhem, monsieur?"

"In Holland," said Quinn.

At this point the man just stopped trying.

"How the hell am I going to get a Dutch-registered Opel back
there from Ajaccio airport?"

"You could drive it," said Quinn reasonably. "It will be fine after it's
been fixed up."

There was a long pause.

"Fixed up? What's wrong with it?"

"Well, the front end's been through a barn and the rear end's got a
dozen bullet holes."

"What about payment for all this?" whispered the agent.

"Just send the bill to the American ambassador in Paris," said
Quinn. After that he hung up. It seemed the kindest thing to do.

He called the bar in Estepona and spoke to Ronnie, who gave him
the number of the mountain villa where Bernie and Arfur were keeping
an eye on Sam but making a point of not playing poker with her. He
rang the new number and Arfur called her to the phone.

"Quinn, darling, are you all right?" Her voice was faint but clear.

"I'm fine. Listen, honey, it's over. You can take a plane from Málaga to Madrid and on to Washington. They'll want to talk to you; probably that fancy committee will want to hear the story. You'll be safe.
Tell 'em this: Orsini died without talking. Never said a word. Whoever
the fat man Zack mentioned may be, or his backers, no one can ever get
to them now. I have to run. Bye now."

He hung up, cutting off her stream of questions.

Drifting silently in space, a National Security Agency satellite heard the phone call, along with a million others that morning, and beamed the words down to the computers at Fort Meade. It took time to process them, work out what to keep and what to throw away, but Sam's use of the name Quinn ensured that this message was filed. It was studied in the early afternoon, Washington time, and passed to Langley.

Passengers for the London flight were being called when the truck drew up in the forecourt of the departures building. The four men who descended and marched through the front doors did not look like passengers for London, but no one took any notice. Except the elegant businessman. He looked up, folded his magazine, stood with his coat over his arm and his umbrella in his other hand, and watched them.

The leader of the four, in the black suit with open-necked shirt, had been playing cards the previous afternoon in a bar in Castelblanc. The other three were in the blue shirts and trousers of men who worked the vineyards and olive groves. The shirts were worn outside the trousers, a detail that was not lost on the businessman. They looked around the concourse, ignored the businessman, studied the other passengers filing through the embarkation doors. Quinn was out of sight in the men's washroom. The public address system repeated the final call for boarding. Quinn emerged.

He turned sharp right, toward the doors, pulling his ticket from his breast pocket, failing to see the four from Castelblanc. They began to move toward Quinn's back. A porter pushing a long line of interlinked baggage carts began to traverse the floor of the hall.

The businessman crossed to the porter and eased him to one side. He paused until the moment was right and gave the column of carts an almighty shove. On the smooth marble floor the column gathered speed and momentum and bore down on the four walking men. One saw them in time, threw himself to one side, tripped, and sprawled. The column hit the second man in the hip, knocked him over, split into several sections, and rattled in three directions. The black-suited *capu* collected a section of eight trolleys in the midriff and doubled over. The fourth man went to his help. They recovered and regrouped, in time to see Quinn's back disappearing into the departure lounge.

The four men from the village ran to the glass door. The waiting hostess gave her professional smile and suggested there could be no more fond farewells—departure had been called long since. Through the glass they could see the tall American go through passport control and onto the tarmac. A polite hand eased them aside.

"I say, excuse me, old boy," said the businessman, and he passed through as well.

On the flight he sat in the smoking section, ten rows behind Quinn, took orange juice and coffee for breakfast, and smoked two filter kings through a silver holder. Like Quinn, he had no luggage. At Heathrow he was four passengers behind Quinn at passport control and ten paces behind as they crossed the customs hall where others waited for their suitcases. He watched Quinn take a cab as his turn came, then nodded to a long black car across the road. He climbed in it on the move, and as they entered the tunnel from the airport to the M.4 motorway and London, the limousine was three vehicles behind Quinn's cab.

When Philip Kelly said he would ask the British for a port watch on Quinn's passport in the morning, he meant a Washington morning. Because of the time difference, the British received the request at 11:00 A.M. London time. Half an hour later the port-watch notice was brought by a colleague to the passport officer at Heathrow who had seen Quinn pass in front of him—half an hour earlier. He handed over his post to the colleague and told his superior.

Two Special Branch officers, on duty behind the immigration desk, queried the men in the customs hall. One customs man in the "Green" channel recalled a tall American whom he had briefly stopped because he had no luggage at all. Shown a photograph, he identified it.

Out on the taxi rank the traffic wardens who allocate taxis to prevent line-crashing did the same. But they had not noted the number of the cab he took.

Cabdrivers are sometimes sources of vital information to the police, and as the cabbies are a law-abiding breed, save for an occasional lapse in the declaring of income tax, which does not concern the Met., relations are good and kept that way. Moreover, the cabbies plying the lucrative Heathrow run do so according to a strict and jealously guarded rotation system. It took another hour to trace and contact the one who had carried Quinn, but he too recognized his passenger.

"Yerse," he said. "I took him to Blackwood's Hotel in Marylebone."

In fact he dropped Quinn at the base of the hotel steps at twenty to one. Neither noticed the black limousine that drew up behind. Quinn paid off the cab and mounted the steps. By this time a dark-suited London businessman was beside him. They reached the revolving doors at the same time. It was a question of who should pass first. Quinn's eyes narrowed when he saw the man beside him. The businessman preempted him.

"I say, weren't you the chap on the plane from Corsica this morning? By Jove, so was I. Small world, what? After you, m'dear fellow."

He gestured to Quinn to pass ahead of him. The needle tip jutting from the ferrule of the umbrella was already bared. Quinn hardly felt the sting of the jab as it entered the calf of his left leg. It remained for half a second and was withdrawn. Then Quinn was inside the revolving doors. They jammed when he was halfway through; trapped in the segment between the portico and the lobby. He was stuck there for only five seconds. As he emerged he had the impression of feeling slightly dizzy. The heat, no doubt.

The Englishman was beside him, still chattering.

"Damn door, never did like them. I say, old boy, are you feeling all right?"

Quinn's vision blurred again and he swayed. A uniformed porter approached, concern on his face.

"You all right, sir?"

The businessman took over with smooth efficiency. He leaned toward the porter, holding Quinn under one armpit with a grip of surprising strength, and slipped a £10 note into the porter's hand.

"Touch of the pre-lunch martinis, I'm afraid. That and jet lag. Look, my car's outside. . . . If you'd be so kind . . . Come on, Clive. Let's get you home, old son."

Quinn tried to resist but his limbs seemed to be made of Jell-O. The porter knew his duty to his hotel, and a real gentleman when he saw one. The real gentleman took Quinn at one side, the porter at the other. They eased him through the baggage door, which did not revolve, and down the three steps to the curb. There, two of the real gentleman's colleagues climbed out of the car and helped Quinn into the rear seat. The businessman nodded his thanks to the porter, who turned to attend to other arriving guests, and the limousine drew away.

As it did so, two police cars came around the corner of Blandford Street and headed for the hotel. Quinn leaned back against the upholstery of the car, his mind still aware but his body helpless and his tongue a soggy lump. Then the blackness swam up and over him in waves and he passed out.

CHAPTER SEVENTEEN

When Quinn awoke he was in a bare white room, flat on his back on a cot. Without moving he looked around. A solid door, also white; a recessed bulb protected by a steel grille. Whoever had set the place up did not wish the inhabitant to smash the bulb and slice his wrists. He recalled the too-smooth English businessman, the sting in the rear of the calf, the slide into unconsciousness. Damn the Brits.

There was a peephole in the door. He heard it click. An eye stared at him. There was no more point in pretending to be unconscious or asleep. He pulled back the blanket that covered him and swung his legs to the floor. Only then did he realize he was naked but for his shorts.

There was a rasp as two bolts were pulled back and the door opened. The man who came in was short, chunky, with close-cropped hair and a white jacket, like a steward. He said nothing. Just marched in bearing a plain deal table, which he set down against the far wall. He went back out and reappeared with a large tin bowl and a pitcher from whose top a wisp of steam emerged. These he put on the table. Then he went out again, but only to the corridor. Quinn wondered if he should flatten the man and seek to escape. He decided against it. The lack of windows indicated he was below ground somewhere; he wore only shorts, the servant looked as though he could handle himself in a fight, and there would have to be other "heavies" out there somewhere.

When the man came back the second time he bore a fluffy towel, washcloth, soap, toothpaste, a new toothbrush still in its wrapper, safety razor and foam, and a self-standing shaving mirror. Like a perfect valet, he arranged these on the table, paused at the door, gestured to the table, and left. The bolts went home.

Well, thought Quinn, if the British undercover people who had snatched him wished him to look presentable for Her Majesty, he was prepared to oblige. Besides, he needed to freshen up.

He took his time. The hot water felt good and he sponged himself right down. He had showered on the ferry *Napoléon*, but that had been forty-eight hours ago. Or was it? His watch was gone. He knew he had been kidnapped about lunchtime, but was that four hours ago, twelve, or twenty-four? Whatever, the sharp mint of the toothpaste felt good in the mouth. It was when he took up the razor, lathered his chin, and gazed in the small round mirror that he got a shock. The bastards had given him a haircut.

Not a bad one, either. His brown hair was trimmed and barbered, but styled in a different way. There was no comb among the wash things; he could not push it the way he liked it except with his fingertips. Then it stood up in tufts, so he pushed it back the way the unknown barber had left it. He had hardly finished when the steward came back again.

"Well, thanks for that, pal," said Quinn. The man gave no sign of having heard; just removed the wash things, left the table, and reappeared with a tray. On it was fresh orange juice, cereal, milk, sugar, a platter containing eggs and bacon, toast, butter, and orange marmalade, and coffee. The coffee was fresh and smelled great. The steward set a plain wooden chair by the table, gave a stiff bow, and left.

Quinn was reminded of an old British tradition: When they take you to the Tower to chop your head off, they always give you a hearty breakfast. He ate anyway. Everything.

Hardly had he finished than Rumpelstiltskin was back, this time with a pile of clothes, fresh-laundered and pressed. But not his. A crisp white shirt, tie, socks, shoes, and a two-piece suit. Everything fitted as if tailor-made for him. The servant gestured to the clothes and tapped his watch as if to say there was little time to lose.

When Quinn was dressed, the door opened again. This time it was the elegant businessman, and he at least could speak.

"My dear chap, you're looking a hundred percent better, and feeling it, I hope. My sincere apologies for the unconventional invitation here. We felt that without it you might not care to join us."

He still looked like a fashion plate and talked like an officer from one of the Guards regiments.

"I'll give you assholes credit where it's due," said Quinn. "You have style."

"How very kind," murmured the businessman. "And now, if you would come with me, my superior officer would like a word with you."

He led Quinn down a plain corridor to an elevator. As it hummed upward, Quinn asked what time it was.

"Ah, yes," said the businessman. "The American obsession with the hour of the day. Actually it is close to midnight. I fear that breakfast was all our night-duty chef was very good at."

They got out of the lift into another corridor, plushly carpeted this time, with several paneled wooden doors leading off it. But his guide led Quinn to the far end, opened the door, ushered Quinn inside, withdrew, and closed the door.

Quinn found himself in a room that might have been office or drawing room. Sofas and armchairs were grouped around a gas-log fire, but there was an imposing desk in the window bay. The man who rose from behind it and came to greet him was older than he, mid-fifties he guessed, in a Savile Row suit. He also wore an air of authority in his bearing and in his hard, no-nonsense face. But his tone was amiable enough.

"My dear Mr. Quinn, how good of you to join me."

Quinn began to get annoyed. There was a limit to this game-playing.

"Okay, can we quit playing charades? You had me jabbed in a hotel lobby, drugged unconscious, brought here. Fine. Totally unnecessary. If you British spooks had wanted to talk to me, you could have had a couple of bobbies pick me up without need of hypodermic needles and all that crap."

The man in front of him paused, seeming genuinely surprised.

"Oh, I see. You think you are in the hands of MI-Five or MI-Six? I fear not. The other side, so to speak. Allow me. I am General Vadim Kirpichenko, newly appointed head of the First Chief Directorate, KGB. Geographically you are still in London; technically you are on sovereign Soviet territory—our embassy in Kensington Park Gardens. Won't you sit down?"

For the second time in her life Sam Somerville was shown into the Situation Room in the basement below the West Wing of the White House.

She had barely been off the Madrid plane five hours. Whatever the men of power wanted to ask her, they did not wish to be kept waiting.

The Vice President was flanked by the four senior Cabinet members and Brad Johnson, the National Security Adviser. Also in attendance were the Director of the FBI and Philip Kelly. Lee Alexander of the CIA sat alone. The one other man was Kevin Brown, repatriated from London to report personally, something he had just finished doing when Sam was shown in. The atmosphere toward her was clearly hostile.

"Sit down, young lady," said Vice President Odell. She took the chair at the end of the table, where they could all see her. Kevin Brown glowered at her; he would have preferred to conduct her debriefing personally, then reported to this committee. It was not pleasing to have his subordinate agents interrogated directly.

"Agent Somerville," said the Vice President, "this committee let you return to London and released the man Quinn to your charge for one reason: your assertion that he might make some progress in identifying Simon Cormack's abductors because he had actually seen them. You were also told to stay in touch, report back. Since then . . . nothing. Yet we've been getting a stream of reports about bodies being left all over Europe, and always you and Quinn a few yards away at the time. Now will you please tell us what the hell you've been doing?"

Sam told them. She started at the beginning, Quinn's vague recall of a spider tattoo on the back of the hand of one of the men in the Babbidge warehouse; the trail via the Antwerp thug Kuyper to Marchais, already dead under a pseudonym in a Ferris wheel in Wavre. She told them of Quinn's hunch that Marchais might have brought a long-time buddy into the operation, and the unearthing of Pretorius in his bar in Den Bosch. She told them of Zack, the mercenary commander Sidney Fielding. What he had had to say, minutes before he died, kept them in riveted silence. She finished with the bugged handbag and Quinn's departure alone to Corsica to find and interrogate the fourth man, the mysterious Orsini, who, according to Zack, had actually provided the booby-trapped belt.

"Then he called me, twenty hours ago, and told me it was over, the trail cold, Orsini dead and never said a word about the fat man. . . ."

There was silence when she finished.

"Jesus," said Reed, "that is incredible. Do we have any evidence that might tend to support all this?"

Lee Alexander looked up.

"The Belgians report that the slug that killed Lefort, alias Marchais, was a forty-five, not a thirty-eight. Unless Quinn had another gun . . ."

"He didn't," said Sam quickly. "The only one we had between us was my thirty-eight, the one Mr. Brown gave me. And Quinn was never out of my sight for long enough to get from Antwerp to Wavre and back, or from Arnhem to Den Bosch and back. As for the Paris café, Zack was killed by a rifle fired from a car in the street."

"That checks," said Alexander. "The French have recovered the slugs fired at that café. Armalite rounds."

"Quinn could have had a partner," suggested Walters.

"Then there was no need to bug my handbag," said Sam. "He could just have slipped away while I was in the bath, or the john, and made a phone call. I ask you to believe, gentlemen, Quinn is clean. He damn near got to the bottom of this thing. There was someone ahead of us all the way."

"The fat man, referred to by Zack?" queried Stannard. "The one Zack swore set it all up, paid for it all? Maybe. But . . . an *American*?"

"May I make a suggestion?" asked Kevin Brown. "I may have been wrong in thinking that Quinn was involved here from the outset. And I admit that. But there is another scenario that makes even more sense."

He had their undivided attention.

"Zack claimed the fat man was American. How? By his accent. What would a Britisher know about American accents? They mistake Canadians for Americans. Say the fat man was Russian. Then it all fits. The KGB has dozens of agents perfect in English and with impeccable American accents."

There was a series of slow nods around the table.

"My colleague is right," said Kelly. "We have motive. The destabilization and demoralization of the United States has long been Moscow's top priority—no argument about that. Opportunity? No problem. There was publicity about Simon Cormack studying at Oxford, so the KGB mounts a major 'wet' operation to hurt us all. Financing? They have no problem there. Using the mercenaries—the employment of surrogates to do the dirty work is standard practice. Even the CIA does it. As for wasting the four mercenaries when the job is over—that's standard for the Mob, and the KGB has similarities to the Mob over here."

"If one accepts that the fat man was a Russian," added Brown, "it all checks out. I'll accept, on the basis of Agent Somerville's report, that there *was* a man who paid, briefed, and 'ran' Zack and his thugs. But for me, that man is now back where he came from—in Moscow."

"But why," queried Jim Donaldson, "should Gorbachev first set up the Nantucket Treaty, then blow it away in this appalling manner?"

Lee Alexander coughed gently.

"Mr. Secretary, there are known to be powerful forces inside the Soviet Union opposed to *glasnost, perestroika*, the reforms, Gorbachev himself, and most particularly the Nantucket Treaty. Let us recall that the former chairman of the KGB, General Kryuchkov, has just been fired. Maybe what we have been discussing is the reason why."

"I think you've got it," said Odell. "Those covert KGB bastards mount the operation to shaft America and the treaty in one. Gorbachev personally doesn't need to have been responsible."

"Doesn't change a damn thing," said Walters. "The American public is never going to believe that. And that includes Congress. If this was Moscow's doing, Mr. Gorbachev stands indicted, aware or not. Remember Irangate?"

Yes, they all remembered Irangate. Sam looked up.

"What about my handbag?" she asked. "If the KGB set it all up, why would they need us to lead them to the mercenaries?"

"No problem," suggested Brown. "The mercenaries didn't know the boy was going to die. When he did, they panicked, hid out. Maybe they never showed up someplace where the KGB was waiting for them. Besides, attempts were made to implicate you and Quinn, the American negotiator and an agent of the FBI, in two of the killings. Again, standard practice: Throw dust in the eyes of world opinion; make it look like the American establishment silencing the killers before they can talk."

"But my handbag was switched for a replica with the bug inside," protested Sam. "Somewhere in London."

"How do you know that, Agent Somerville?" asked Brown. "Could have been at the airport, or on the ferry to Ostende. Hell, it could have been one of the Brits—they came to the apartment after Quinn quit. And the manor house in Surrey. Quite a number have worked for Moscow in the past. Remember Burgess, Maclean, Philby, Vassall, Blunt, Blake—they were all traitors who worked for Moscow. Maybe they have a new one."

Lee Alexander studied his fingertips. He deemed it undiplomatic to mention Mitchell, Marshall, Lee, Boyce, Harper, Walker, Lonetree, Conrad, Howard, or any of the other twenty Americans who had betrayed Uncle Sam for money.

"Okay, gentlemen," said Odell an hour later, "we commission the report. A through Z. The findings have to be clear. The belt was Soviet-made. The suspicion will remain unproved but indelible for all that—this was a KGB operation and it ends with the vanished agent known only as the fat man, now presumably back behind the Iron Curtain. We know the 'what' of it, and the 'how.' We think we know the 'who,' and the 'why' is pretty clear. The Nantucket Treaty is belly-up for all time, and we have a President sick with grief. Jesus, I never thought I'd say it, even though I'm not known as a liberal, but right now I almost wish we could nuke those Commie bastards back to the Stone Age."

Ten minutes later the meeting was in closed session. It was only in her car on her way back to her apartment in Alexandria that Sam spotted the flaw in their beautiful solution. How did the KGB know to copy a Harrods-bought crocodile-skin handbag?

Philip Kelly and Kevin Brown shared a car back to the Hoover Building.

"That young lady got closer to Quinn, a lot closer, than I had intended," said Kelly.

"I smelled that in London, all through the negotiations," Brown agreed. "She fought in his corner all the way, and in my book we still want to talk to Quinn himself—I mean, really talk. Have the French or the British traced him yet?"

"No. I was going to tell you. The French tagged him out of Ajaccio airport on a London-bound plane. He abandoned his car, full of bulletholes, in the parking lot. The Brits traced him in London to a hotel, but when they got there he had vanished—never even checked in."

"Damn, that man's like an eel," Brown swore.

"Exactly," said Kelly. "But if you're right, there could be one person he'll contact. Somerville; the only one. I don't like doing this to one of our own people, but I want her apartment bugged, her phone tapped, and mail intercepted. As of tonight."

"Right away," said Brown.

When they were alone, the Vice President and the inner five members of the Cabinet again raised the issue of the Twenty-fifth Amendment.

It was the Attorney General who brought it up. Quietly and regretfully. Odell was on the defensive. He saw more of their reclusive President than the others. He had to admit John Cormack appeared as lackluster as ever.

"Not yet," he said. "Give him time."

"How much?" asked Morton Stannard. "It's been three weeks since the funeral."

"Next year is election year," Bill Walters pointed out. "If it's to be you, Michael, you will need a clear run from January."

"Jesus," exploded Odell. "That man in the White House is stricken and you talk of elections."

"Just being practical, Michael," said Donaldson.

"We all know that after Irangate, Ronald Reagan was so badly confused for a while that the Twenty-fifth was almost invoked then," Walters pointed out. "The Cannon Report at the time makes plain it was touch-and-go. But this crisis is worse."

"President Reagan recovered," pointed out Hubert Reed. "He resumed his functions."

"Yes, just in time," said Stannard.

"That's the issue," suggested Donaldson. "How much time do we have?"

"Not a lot," admitted Odell. "The media have been patient so far. He's a damn popular man. But it's cracking, fast."

"Deadline?" asked Walters quietly.

They held a vote. Odell abstained. Walters raised his silver pencil. Stannard nodded. Brad Johnson shook his head. Walters agreed. Jim Donaldson reflected and joined Johnson in refusing. It was locked, two and two. Hubert Reed looked around at the other five men with a worried frown. Then he shrugged.

"I'm sorry, but if it must be, it must."

He joined the ayes. Odell exhaled noisily.

"All right," he said. "We agree by a majority. By Christmas Eve, without a major turnaround, I'll have to go and tell him we're invoking the Twenty-fifth on New Year's Day."

He had only risen halfway when the others reached their feet in deference. He found he enjoyed it.

"I don't believe you," said Quinn.

"Please," said the man in the Savile Row suit. He gestured toward the curtained windows. Quinn glanced around the room. Above the mantel shelf, Lenin addressed the masses. Quinn walked to the window and peered out.

Across the gardens of bare trees and over the wall, the top section of a red London double-decker bus ran along Bayswater Road. Quinn resumed his seat.

"Well, if you're lying, it's a hell of a film set," he said.

"No film set," replied the KGB general. "I prefer to leave that to your people in Hollywood."

"So what brings me here?"

"You interest us, Mr. Quinn. Please don't be so defensive. Strange though it may sound, I believe we are for the moment on the same side."

"It does sound strange," said Quinn. "Too damn strange."

"All right, so let me talk it through. For some time we have known that you were the man chosen to negotiate the release of Simon Cormack from his abductors. We also know that after his death you have spent a month in Europe trying to track them down—with some success, it would appear."

"That puts us on the same side?"

"Maybe, Mr. Quinn, maybe. My job isn't to protect young Americans who insist on going for country runs with inadequate protection. But it *is* to try to protect my country from hostile conspiracies that do her huge damage. And this . . . this Cormack business . . . is a conspiracy by persons unknown to damage and discredit my country in the eyes of the entire world. We don't like it, Mr. Quinn. We don't like it at all. So let me, as you Americans say, level with you.

"The abduction and murder of Simon Cormack was not a Soviet conspiracy. But we are getting the blame for it. Ever since that belt was analyzed, we have been in the dock of world opinion. Relations with your country, which our leader was genuinely trying to improve, have been poisoned; a treaty to reduce weapons levels, on which we placed great store, is in ruins."

"It looks as though you don't appreciate disinformation when it works against the U.S.S.R., even though you're pretty good at it yourselves," said Quinn.

The general had the grace to shrug in acceptance of the barb.

"All right, we indulge in *disinformatsya* from time to time. So does the CIA. It goes with the territory. And I admit it's bad enough to get the blame for something we *have* done. But it is intolerable for us to be blamed for this affair, which we did not instigate."

"If I were a more generous man I might feel sorry for you," said Quinn. "But the fact is, there is absolutely nothing I can do about it. Not anymore."

"Possibly." The general nodded. "Let us see. I happen to believe you are smart enough to have worked out already that this conspiracy is not ours. If I had put this together, why the hell would I have Cormack killed by a device so provably Soviet?"

Quinn nodded. "All right. I happen to think you were not behind it."

"Thank you. Now, have you any ideas as to who might have been?"

"I think it came out of America. Maybe the ultra-right. If the aim was to kill off the Nantucket Treaty's chance of Senate ratification, it certainly succeeded."

"Precisely."

General Kirpichenko went behind the desk and returned with five enlarged photographs. He put them in front of Quinn.

"Have you ever seen these men before, Mr. Quinn?"

Quinn studied the passport photographs of Cyrus Miller, Melville Scanlon, Lionel Moir, Peter Cobb, and Ben Salkind. He shook his head.

"No, never seen them."

"Pity. Their names are on the reverse side. They visited my country several months ago. The man they conferred with—the man I *believe* they conferred with—would have been in a position to supply that belt. He happens to be a marshal."

"Have you arrested him? Interrogated him?"

General Kirpichenko smiled for the first time.

"Mr. Quinn, your Western novelists and journalists are happy to suggest that the organization I work for has limitless powers. Not quite. Even for us, to arrest a Soviet marshal without a shred of proof is way off base. Now, I've been frank with you. Would you return the compliment? Would you tell me what you managed to discover these past thirty days?"

Quinn considered the request. He could see no reason not to; the affair was over so far as any trail he would ever be able to follow was concerned. He told the general the story from the moment he ran out of the Kensington apartment to make his private rendezvous with Zack. Kirpichenko listened attentively, nodding several times, as if what he heard coincided with something he already knew. Quinn ended his tale with the death of Orsini.

"By the way," he added, "may I ask how you tracked me to Ajaccio airport?"

"Oh, I see. Well, my department has obviously been keenly interested in this whole affair from the start. After the boy's death and the deliberate leak of the details of the belt, we went into overdrive. You weren't exactly low-profile as you went through the Low Countries.

The shoot-out in Paris made all the evening papers. The description of the man the barman described as fleeing the scene matched yours.

"A check on airline departure and passenger lists—yes, we do have assets working for us in Paris—showed your FBI lady friend heading for Spain, but nothing on you. I assumed you might be armed, would wish to avoid airport security procedures, and checked ferry bookings. My man in Marseilles got lucky, tagged you on the ferry to Corsica. The man you saw at the airport flew in the same morning you arrived, but missed you. Now I knew you had gone up into the mountains. He took up station at the point where the airport road and the road to the docks meet each other, saw your car take the airport road just after sunup. By the way, did you know four men with guns came into the terminal while you were in the men's room?"

"No, I never saw them."

"Mmmm. They didn't seem to like you. From what you have just told me about Orsini, I can understand why. No matter. My colleague . . . took care of them."

"Your tame Englishman?"

"Andrei? He's not English. As a matter of fact, he's not even Russian. Ethnically, he's a Cossack. I don't underestimate your ability to handle yourself, Mr. Quinn, but please don't ever try to mix with Andrei. He really is one of my best men."

"Thank him for me," said Quinn. "Look, General, it's been a nice chat. But that's it. There's nowhere for me to go but back to my vineyard in Spain and try to start over."

"I disagree, Mr. Quinn. I think you should go back to America. The key lies there, somewhere in America. You should return."

"I'd be picked up within the hour," said Quinn. "The FBI doesn't like me—some of them think I was involved."

General Kirpichenko went back to his desk and beckoned Quinn across. He handed him a passport, a Canadian passport, not new, suitably thumbed, with a dozen exit and entry stamps. His own face, hardly recognizable with its different haircut, horn-rimmed glasses, and stubble of beard, stared at him.

"I'm afraid it was taken while you were drugged," said the general. "But then, aren't they all? The passport is quite genuine, one of our better efforts. You will need clothes with Canadian maker's labels, luggage—that sort of thing. Andrei has them all ready for you. And, of course, these."

He put three credit cards, a valid Canadian driver's license, and a wad of 20,000 Canadian dollars on the desk top. The passport, license, and credit cards were all in the name of Roger Lefevre. A French-Canadian; the accent for an American who spoke French would be no problem.

"I suggest Andrei drive you to Birmingham for the first morning flight to Dublin. From there you can connect to Toronto. In a rented car the border crossing into America should present no problem. Are you ready to go, Mr. Quinn?"

"General, I don't seem to be making myself clear. Orsini never said a word before he died. If he knew who the fat man was, and I think he did, he never let it out. I don't know where to start. The trail's cold. The fat man is safe, and the paymasters behind him, and the renegade I believe is somewhere high in the establishment—the information source. They're all safe because Orsini stayed silent. I have no aces, no kings, queens, or jacks. I have nothing in my hand."

"Ah, the analogy of cards. Always you Americans refer to aces of spades. Do you play chess, Mr. Quinn?"

"A bit, not well," said Quinn. The Soviet general walked to a shelf of books on one wall and ran his finger along the row, as if looking for a particular one.

"You should," he said. "Like my profession, it is a game of cunning and guile, not brute force. All the pieces are visible, and yet . . . there is more deception in chess than in poker. Ah, here we are."

He offered the book to Quinn. The author was Russian, the text in English. A translation, private edition. *The Great Grand Masters: A Study*.

"You are in check, Mr. Quinn, but perhaps not yet checkmate. Go back to America, Mr. Quinn. Read the book on the flight. May I recommend you pay particular attention to the chapter on Tigran Petrosian. An Armenian, long dead now, but perhaps the greatest chess tactician who ever lived. Good luck, Mr. Quinn."

General Kirpichenko summoned his operative Andrei and issued a stream of orders in Russian. Then Andrei took Quinn to another room and fitted him out with a suitcase of new clothes, all Canadian; plus luggage and airline tickets. They drove together to Birmingham and Quinn caught the first British Midland flight of the day to Dublin. Andrei saw him off, then drove back to London.

Quinn connected out of Dublin to Shannon, waited several hours, and caught the Air Canada flight to Toronto.

As promised, he read the book in the departure lounge in Shannon and again on the flight across the Atlantic. He read the chapter on Petrosian six times. Before he touched down at Toronto he realized why so many rueful opponents had dubbed the wily Armenian grandmaster the Great Deceiver.

At Toronto his passport was no more queried than it had been at Birmingham or Dublin or Shannon. He took his luggage off the carrousel in the customs hall and passed through with a cursory check. There was no reason why he should notice the quiet man who observed him emerge from the customs hall, followed him to the main railway station, and joined him on the train northeast to Montreal.

At a used-car lot in Quebec's first city, Quinn bought a used Jeep Renegade with heavy-duty winter tires and, from a camping store nearby, the boots, trousers, and down parka needed for the time of year in that climate. When the Jeep was tanked up he drove southeast, through St. Jean to Bedford, then due south for the American border.

At the border post on the shores of Lake Champlain, where State Highway 89 passes from Canada into Vermont, Quinn crossed into the United States.

There is a land in the northern fringes of the state of Vermont known to locals simply as the Northeast Kingdom. It takes in most of Essex County, with pieces of Orleans and Caledonia, a wild, mountainous place of lakes and rivers, hills and gorges, with here and there a bumpy track and a small village. In winter a cold descends on the Northeast Kingdom so terrible it is as if the land had been subjected to a state of freeze-frame—literally. The lakes become ice, the trees rigid with frost; the ground crackles beneath the feet. In winter nothing lives up there, save in hibernation, apart from the occasional lonely elk moving through the creaking forest. Wits from the South say there are only two seasons in the Kingdom—August and winter. Those who know the place say this is nonsense; it is August 15th and winter.

Quinn drove his Jeep south past Swanton and St. Albans to the town of Burlington, then turned away from Lake Champlain to follow Route 89 to the state capital, Montpelier. Here he quit the main highway to take Route 2 up through East Montpelier, following the valley of the Winooski past Plainfield and Marshfield to West Danville.

Winter had come early to the Northeast Kingdom and the hills closed in, huddled against the cold; the occasional vehicle coming the other way was another anonymous bubble of warmth, with heater full on, containing a human being surviving with technology a cold that would kill the unprotected body in minutes.

The road narrowed again after West Danville, banked high with snow on both sides. After passing through the shuttered community of Danville itself, Quinn put the Jeep in four-wheel drive for the final stage to St. Johnsbury.

The little town on the Passumpsic River was like an oasis in the freezing mountains, with shops and bars and lights and warmth. Quinn found a real estate agent on Main Street and put his request. It was not the man's busiest time of year. He considered the request with puzzlement.

"A cabin? Well, sure, we rent out cabins in the summer. Mostly the owners want to spend a month, maybe six weeks in their cabins, then rent out for the rest of the season. But now?"

"Now," said Quinn.

"Anywhere special?" asked the man.

"In the Kingdom."

"You really want to get lost, mister."

But the man checked his list and scratched his head.

"There might be a place," he said. "Belongs to a dentist from Barre, down in the warm country."

The warm country was at that time of year only fifteen below zero, as opposed to twenty. The realtor rang the dentist, who agreed to a one-month rental. He peered out at the Jeep.

"You got snow chains on that Renegade, mister?"

"Not yet."

"You'll need 'em."

Quinn bought and attached the chains, and they set off together. It was fifteen miles but the drive took more than an hour.

"It's on Lost Ridge," said the agent. "The owner only uses it in high summer for fishing and walking. You trying to avoid the wife's lawyers or something?"

"I need the peace and quiet to write a book," said Quinn.

"Oh, a writer," said the agent, satisfied. People make allowances for writers, as for all other lunatics.

They headed back toward Danville, then branched north up an even smaller road. At North Danville the agent guided Quinn west into the wilderness. Ahead the Kittredge Hills reared up to the sky, impenetrable. The track led to the right of the range, toward Bear Mountain. On the slopes of the mountain the agent gestured to a snow-choked track. Quinn needed all the power of the engine, the four-wheel drive, and the chains to get there.

The cabin was of logs, great tree trunks laid horizontally under a low roof with a yard of snow on it. But it was well built, with an inner skin and triple glazing. The agent pointed out the attached garage—a car left unheated in that climate would be a solid lump of metal and frozen gasoline by morning—and the log-burning stove that would heat the water and the radiators.

"I'll take it," said Quinn.

"You'll need oil for the lamps, butane bottles for cooking, an axe to split down the logs for the stove," said the agent. "And food. And spare gasoline. No use running out of anything up here. And the right clothing. What you're wearing's a bit thin. Be sure and cover your face or you'll get frostbite. No telephone. You *sure* you want it?"

"I'll take it," said Quinn again.

They drove back to St. Johnsbury. Quinn gave his name and nationality, and paid in advance.

The agent was either too courteous or too incurious to ask why a Quebecois should want to find sanctuary in Vermont when Quebec had so many tranquil places of her own.

Quinn located several public phone booths that he could use day or night, and spent the night in a local hotel. In the morning he stocked his Jeep with all he would need and set off back into the mountains.

Once, pausing on the road out of North Danville to check his bearings, he thought he heard the snarl of an engine down the mountain behind him, but deduced it must be a sound from the village or even his own echo.

He lit the stove and slowly the cabin thawed out. The stove was efficient, roaring behind its steel doors, and when he opened them it was like facing a blast furnace. The water tank defrosted and heated up, warming the radiators in the cabin's four rooms and the secondary tank for washing and bathing. By midday he was down to his shirt sleeves and feeling the heat. After lunch he took his axe and cut a week's supply of split timber from the cords of pine stacked in the back.

He had bought a transistor radio, but there was no television and no phone. When he was equipped with a week's supplies, he sat down with his new portable typewriter and began to type. The next day he drove to Montpelier and flew to Boston and on to Washington.

His destination was Union Station, on Massachusetts Avenue at Second Street, one of the most elegant railway stations in America, still gleaming from its recent refurbishment. Some of the layout had been changed from what he remembered from years ago. But the tracks were still there, running out of the basement departure concourse below the main hall.

He found what he wanted opposite the Amtrak boarding gates H and J. Between the door of the Amtrak Police office and the ladies' room was a row of eight public phone booths. All their numbers began with the 789 prefix; he noted all eight, mailed his letter, and left.

As his cab took him back across the Potomac to Washington National Airport it turned down 14th Street, and to his right he caught a glimpse of the White House. He wondered how fared the man who lived in the mansion, the man who had said, "Get him back for us," and whom he had failed.

In the month since the burial of their son a change had come over the Cormacks, and their relationship to each other, which only a psychiatrist would be able to rationalize or explain.

During the kidnapping the President, though he had deteriorated through stress, worry, anxiety, and insomnia, had still managed to retain control of himself. Toward the end of the abduction of his son, when reports from London seemed to indicate an exchange was near, he had even seemed to recover. It was his wife, less intellectual and without administrative responsibilities to distract her mind, who had abandoned herself to grief and sedation.

But since that awful day at Nantucket when they had consigned their only son to the cold ground, the roles of the parents had subtly reversed. Myra Cormack had wept against the chest of the Secret Service man by the graveside, and on the flight back to Washington. But as the days went by she seemed to recover. It might be she recognized that, having lost one dependent child, she had inherited another, the husband who had never been dependent on her before.

Her maternal and protective instincts seemed to have given her an inner strength denied to the man whose intelligence and willpower she had never before doubted. As Quinn's cab passed the White House that winter afternoon, John Cormack was sitting at his desk in his private study between the Yellow Oval Room and the bedroom. Myra Cormack stood at his side. She cradled the head of her devastated husband against her body and rocked him slowly and gently.

She knew her man was mortally stricken, unable to carry on for much longer. She knew that what had destroyed him as much as, if not more than, the actual death of his son was the bewilderment of not knowing who had done it, or why. Had the boy died in a car crash, she believed, John Cormack could have accepted the logic even of the illogic of death. It was the manner of his death that had destroyed the father as surely as if that demonic bomb had exploded against his own body.

She believed there would never be an answer now, and that her husband could not go on like this. She had come to hate the White House, and the job she had once been so proud to see her husband hold. All she wanted now was for him to lay down the burden of that office and retire with her, back to New Haven, so that she could nurse him.

The letter Quinn had mailed to Sam Somerville at her Alexandria condominium address was duly intercepted before she saw it and brought in triumph to the White House committee, which convened to hear it and discuss its implications. Philip Kelly and Kevin Brown bore it to their superiors' attention like a trophy.

"I have to admit, gentlemen," said Kelly, "that it was with the gravest reservations that I asked for one of my own trusted agents to be put under this kind of surveillance. But I think you will agree, it paid dividends."

He placed the letter on the table in front of him.

"This letter, gentlemen, was mailed yesterday, right here in Washington. That does not necessarily prove Quinn is here in the city, or even in the States; it would be possible for someone else to have mailed it on his behalf. But I take the view that Quinn is a loner, has no accomplices. How he disappeared from London and showed up here, we do not know. Yet my colleagues and I are of the opinion he mailed this letter himself."

"Read it," commanded Odell.

"It's . . . er . . . fairly dramatic," said Kelly. He adjusted his glasses and began to read.

" 'My darling Sam . . .' This form of address would seem to indicate that my colleague Kevin Brown was right—there was a relationship beyond the professional one required, between Miss Somerville and Quinn."

"So your hound dog fell in love with the wolf," said Odell. "Well done, very smart. What does he say?"

Kelly resumed.

" 'Here I am at last, back in the United States. I would very much love to see you again, but am afraid that for the moment it would not be safe.

" 'The point of my writing is to set the record straight over what really took place in Corsica. The fact is, when I called you out of Ajaccio airport, I lied to you. I decided that if I told you what really happened down there, you might not feel it would be safe for you to return. But the more I think about it, the more I feel you have the right to know. Make me only one promise: whatever you read in this letter you keep to yourself. No one else must know, at least not yet. Not until I have finished what I am doing.

"'The truth is, Orsini and I fought it out. I had no choice; someone had called him and said I was on my way to Corsica to kill him, when I only wanted to talk to him. He did take a bullet from my gun—yours, actually—but it did not kill him. When he learned he had been tricked, he realized his code of the vow of silence no longer bound him. He told me everything he knew, and it turned out to be a lot.

"'First, it was not the Russians who were behind this thing—at least, not the Soviet government. The conspiracy began right here in the United States. The real paymasters are still clothed in secrecy, but the man they employed to arrange the abduction and murder of Simon Cormack, the one Zack called the fat man, is known to me. Orsini had recognized him and gave me his name. When he is captured, as he will be, I have no doubt he will deliver the names of the men who paid him to do this thing.

"'For the moment, Sam, I am holed up writing everything down, chapter and verse: names, dates, places, events. The whole story from start to finish. When I am done I will mail copies of the manuscript to a dozen different authorities: the Vice President, the FBI, the CIA, et cetera. Then, if anything happens to me after that, it will be too late to stop the wheels of justice from rolling into motion.

"'I will not be in touch with you again until I have finished. Please understand—if I do not tell you where I am, it is only for your own protection.

"'All my love, Quinn.'"

There was a minute of stunned silence. One of those present was sweating profusely.

"Jesus," breathed Michael Odell. "Is this guy for real?"

"If what he says is true," suggested Morton Stannard, the former lawyer, "he should certainly not be at large. He should say what he has to say to us, right here."

"I agree," said the Attorney General. "Apart from anything else, he has just constituted himself a material witness. We have a witness protection program. He should be taken into protective custody."

The agreement was unanimous. By nightfall the Department of Justice had authorized a material-witness warrant for the arrest and detention of Quinn. The FBI operated all the resources of the National Crime Information System to alert every FBI bureau in the country to be on the lookout for him. To back this up, messages went out on the National Law Enforcement Teletype System to all other enforcement arms: city police departments, sheriffs' offices, U.S. marshals, and highway patrols. Quinn's picture accompanied them all. The "cover" used was that he was wanted in connection with a major jewel heist.

An all-points bulletin is one thing; America is a very big country with a lot of places to hide. Wanted felons have stayed at large for years despite a national alert for them. Moreover, the alert was out for Quinn, an American citizen, of known passport number and driving license. It was not an alert for a French Canadian called Lefevre with perfect IDs, a different hairstyle, horn-rimmed glasses, and a light beard. Quinn had let his beard grow since shaving in the Soviet embassy in London, and though not long, it now covered his lower face.

Back in his mountain cabin, he gave the White House committee three days to simmer over his deliberate letter to Sam Somerville, then set about contacting her covertly. The clue was in something she had told him in Antwerp. "A Rockcastle preacher's daughter," she had called herself.

A bookshop in St. Johnsbury yielded an atlas that showed three Rockcastles in the United States. But one was in the deep South, another the far West. Sam's accent was nearer to the East Coast. The third Rockcastle was in Goochland County, Virginia.

Telephone inquiries clinched it. They showed a Reverend Brian Somerville of Rockcastle, Virginia. There was just the one listing—the comparatively unusual spelling of the name kept it apart from the Summervilles and Sommervilles.

Quinn left his hideout again, flew from Montpelier to Boston and on to Richmond, landing at Byrd Field, now renamed with glorious optimism Richmond International Airport. The Richmond directory right in the airport had the usual yellow pages at the back, showing that the reverend was incumbent at the Smyrna Church of St. Mary's at Three Square Road, but resident at 290 Rockcastle Road. Quinn rented a compact and drove the thirty-five miles west on Route 6 to Rockcastle. It was Reverend Somerville who came to the door himself when Quinn rang the bell.

In the front parlor the quiet, silver-haired preacher served tea and confirmed that his daughter was indeed Samantha and worked for the FBI. Then he listened to what Quinn had to say. As he did so, he became grave.

"Why do you think my daughter is in danger, Mr. Quinn?" he asked.

Quinn told him.

"But under surveillance? By the Bureau itself? Has she done anything wrong?"

"No, sir, she has not. But there are those who suspect her, unjustly. And she does not know it. What I want to do is warn her."

The kindly old man surveyed the letter in his hands and sighed. Quinn had just lifted a corner of a curtain to reveal a world unknown to him. He wondered what his late wife would have done; she was always the dynamic one. He decided she would have taken the message to her child in trouble.

"Very well," he said. "I will go and see her."

He was as good as his word. He took his elderly car, drove sedately up to Washington, and visited his daughter at her apartment without announcement. As briefed, he kept the conversation to small talk and handed her the single sheet first. It said simply: "Keep talking naturally. Open the envelope and read it at your leisure. Then burn it and obey the instructions. Quinn."

She nearly choked when she saw the words and realized Quinn meant her apartment was bugged. It was something she had done in the course of duty to others, but never expected for herself. She gazed into the worried eyes of her father, kept talking naturally, and took the proffered envelope. When he left to drive back to Rockcastle she escorted him to his car and gave him a long kiss.

The paper in the envelope was just as brief. At midnight she should stand next to the phone booths opposite Amtrak boarding platforms H and J in Union Station and wait. One phone would ring; it would be Quinn.

She took his call from a booth in St. Johnsbury exactly at midnight. He told her about Corsica, and London, and the phony letter he had sent her, convinced it would be redirected to the White House committee.

"But, Quinn," she protested, "if Orsini really gave you nothing, it's over, just as you said. Why pretend he talked when he didn't?"

He told her about Petrosian, who even when he was down, with his opponents staring at the chessboard, could persuade them he had some master stroke in preparation and force them into error.

"I think they, whoever they are, will break cover because of that letter," he said. "Despite what I said about not contacting you anymore, you're still the only possible link if the police can't find me. As the days pass they ought to get more and more frantic. I want you to keep your eyes and ears open. I'll call you every second day, at midnight, on one of these numbers."

It took six days.

"Quinn, do you know a man called David Weintraub?"

"Yes, I do."

"He's the Company, right?"

"Yeah, he's the DDO. Why?"

"He asked to meet me. He said something's breaking. Fast. He doesn't understand it, thought you would."

"You met at Langley?"

"No, he said that would be too exposed. We met by appointment in the back of a Company car at a spot near the Tidal Basin. We talked as we drove around."

"Did he tell you what?"

"No. He said he didn't feel he could trust anybody, not anymore. Only you. He wants to meet you—your terms, any time or place. Can you trust him, Quinn?"

Quinn thought. If David Weintraub was crooked, there was no hope for the human race anyway.

"Yes," he said, "I do." He gave her the time and place of the rendezvous.

CHAPTER EIGHTEEN

Sam Somerville arrived at Montpelier airport the following evening.
She was accompanied by Duncan McCrea, the young CIA man who had
first approached her with the Deputy Director of Operations' request
for a meeting with her.

They arrived on the PBA Beechcraft 1900 shuttle from Boston,
rented an off-road Dodge Ram right at the airport, and checked into a
motel on the outskirts of the state capital. Both had brought the warm-
est clothing Washington had to offer, at Quinn's suggestion.

The DDO of the CIA, pleading a high-level planning meeting at
Langley that he could not afford to miss, was due the next morning, well
in time for the roadside rendezvous with Quinn.

He landed at 7:00 A.M. in a ten-seater executive jet whose logo Sam
did not recognize. McCrea explained it was a Company communications
plane, and that the charter company listed on its fuselage was a CIA
front.

He greeted them briefly but cordially as he came down the steps of
the jet onto the tarmac, dressed in heavy snow boots, thick trousers,
and quilted parka. He carried his suitcase in his hand. He climbed
straight into the back of the Ram and they set off. McCrea drove, Sam
directing him from her road map.

Out of Montpelier they took Route 2, up through the small township of East Montpelier and onto the road for Plainfield. Just after Plainmont Cemetery, but before the gates of Goddard College, there is a place where the Winooski River leaves the roadside to make a sweep to the south. In this half-moon of land between the road and the river is a stand of tall trees, at that time of year silent and caked with snow. Among the trees stand several picnic tables provided for summer vacationers, and a pull-off and parking area for camper vehicles. This was where Quinn had said he would be at 8:00 A.M.

Sam saw him first. He emerged from behind a tree twenty yards away as the Ram crunched to a halt. Without waiting for her companions she jumped down, ran to him, and threw her arms 'round his neck.

"You all right, kid?"

"I'm fine. Oh, Quinn, thank God you're safe."

Quinn was staring beyond her, over the top of her head. She felt him stiffen.

"Who did you bring?" he asked quietly.

"Oh, silly of me . . ." She turned. "You remember Duncan McCrea? He was the one who got me to Mr. Weintraub."

McCrea was standing ten yards away, having approached from the truck. He wore his shy smile.

"Hello, Mr. Quinn." The greeting was diffident, deferential as always. There was nothing diffident about the Colt .45 automatic in his right hand. It pointed unwaveringly at Sam and Quinn.

From the side door of the Ram the second man descended. He carried the folding-stock rifle he had taken from his suitcase, just after passing McCrea the Colt.

"Who's he?" asked Quinn.

Sam's voice was very small and very frightened.

"David Weintraub," she said. "Oh, God, Quinn, what have I done?"

"You've been tricked, darling."

It was his own fault, he realized. He could have kicked himself. Talking to her on the phone, it had not occurred to him to ask whether she had ever seen the Deputy Director of Operations of the CIA. She had twice been summoned to the White House committee to report. He assumed David Weintraub had been present on both, or at least one, of those occasions. In fact the secretive DDO, doing one of the most covert jobs in America, disliked coming into Washington very often and had been away on both occasions. In combat, as Quinn well knew, assuming things can present a serious hazard to health.

The short, chunky man with the rifle, made to look even plumper by his heavy clothes, walked up to take his place beside McCrea.

"So, Sergeant Quinn, we meet again. Remember me?"

Quinn shook his head. The man tapped the bridge of his flattened nose.

"You gave me this, you bastard. Now that's going to cost you, Quinn."

Quinn squinted in recollection, saw once again a clearing in Vietnam, a long time ago: a Vietnamese peasant, or what was left of him, still alive, pegged to the ground.

"I remember," he said.

"Good," said Moss. "Now, let's get moving. Where you been living?"

"Log cabin, up in the hills."

"Writing a little manuscript, I understand. That, I think, we have to have a look at. No tricks, Quinn. Duncan's handgun might miss you, but then the girl gets it. And as for you, you'll never outrun this."

He jerked the barrel of the rifle to indicate there was no chance of making ten yards toward the trees before being cut down.

"Go screw yourself," said Quinn. In answer Moss chuckled, his breath wheezing through the distorted nose.

"Cold must have frozen your brain, Quinn. Tell you what I have in mind. We take you and the girl down to the riverbank. No one to disturb us—no one within miles. You, we tie to a tree, and you watch, Quinn, you watch. I swear it will take two hours for that girl to die, and every second of it she'll be praying for death. Now, you want to drive?"

Quinn thought of the clearing in the jungle, the peasant with wrist, elbow, knee, and ankle joints shattered by the soft lead slugs, whimpering that he was just a peasant, knew nothing. It was when Quinn realized that the dumpy interrogator knew that already, had known it for hours, that he had turned and knocked him into the orthopedic ward.

Alone, he would have tried to fight it out, against all the odds, died cleanly with a bullet in the heart. But with Sam . . . He nodded.

McCrea separated them, handcuffed Quinn's wrists behind his back, Sam's also. McCrea drove the Renegade with Quinn beside him. Moss followed behind in the Ram, Sam lying in the back.

In West Danville, people were stirring but no one thought anything of two off-road vehicles heading toward St. Johnsbury. One man raised a hand in greeting, the salutation of fellow survivors of the bitter cold. McCrea responded, flashing his friendly grin, and turned north at

Danville toward Lost Ridge. At Pope Cemetery, Quinn signaled another left turn, in the direction of Bear Mountain. Behind them the Ram, without snow chains, was having trouble.

Where the paved road ran out, Moss abandoned the Ram and clambered into the back of the Renegade, pushing Sam ahead of him. She was white-faced and shaking with fear.

"You sure wanted to get lost," said Moss when they arrived at the log cabin.

Outside, it was thirty below zero, but the interior of the cabin was still snug and warm, as Quinn had left it. He and Sam were forced to sit several feet apart on a bunk bed at one end of the open-plan living area that formed the principal room of the cabin. McCrea still kept them covered while Moss made a quick check of the other rooms to ensure they were alone.

"Nice," he said at last and with satisfaction. "Nice and private. You couldn't have done it better for me, Quinn."

Quinn's manuscript was stacked in a drawer of the writing desk. Moss stripped off his parka, seated himself in an armchair, and began to read. McCrea, despite the fact that his prisoners were manacled, sat in an upright chair facing Sam and Quinn. He still wore his boy-next-door grin. Too late Quinn realized it was a mask, something the younger man had developed over the years to cover his inner self.

"You've won out," said Quinn after a while. "I'd still be interested to know how you did it."

"No problem," said Moss, still reading. "It's not going to change anything, either way."

Quinn started with a small and unimportant question. "How did McCrea get picked for the job in London?"

"That was a lucky break," said Moss. "Just a fluke. I never thought I'd have my boy in there to help me. A bonus, courtesy of the goddam Company."

"How did you two get together?"

Moss looked up.

"Central America," he said simply. "I spent years down there. Duncan was raised in those parts. Met him when he was just a kid. Realized we shared the same tastes. Dammit, I recruited him into the Company."

"Same tastes?" queried Quinn. He knew what Moss's tastes were. He wanted to keep them talking. Psychopaths love to talk about themselves when they feel they are safe.

"Well, almost," said Moss. "Except Duncan here prefers the ladies and I don't. Of course, he likes to mess 'em around a bit first—don't you, boy?"

He resumed reading. McCrea flashed a happy grin.

"Sure do, Mr. Moss. You know, these two were balling during those days in London? Thought I hadn't heard. Guess I've got some catching up to do."

"Whatever you say, boy," said Moss. "But Quinn is mine. You're going to go slow, Quinn. I'm going to have me some fun."

He went on reading. Sam suddenly leaned her head forward and retched. Nothing came up. Quinn had seen recruits in 'Nam do that. The fear generated a flood of acid in the stomach which irritated the sensitive membranes and produced dry retching.

"How did you stay in touch in London?" he asked.

"No problem," said Moss. "Duncan used to go out to buy things, food and so forth. Remember? We used to meet in the food stores. If you'd been smarter, Quinn, you'd have noticed he always went food-shopping at the same hour."

"And Simon's clothing, the booby-trapped belt?"

"Took it all to the house in Sussex while you were with the other three at the warehouse. Gave it to Orsini, by appointment. Good man, Orsini. I used him a couple of times in Europe, when I was with the Company. And afterwards."

Moss put the manuscript down; his tongue loosened.

"You spooked me, running out of the apartment like that. I'd have had you wasted then, but I couldn't get Orsini to do it. Said the other three would have stopped him. So I let it go, figured when the boy died you'd come under suspicion anyway. But I was really surprised those yo-yos in the Bureau let you go afterwards. Thought they'd put you in the pen, just on suspicion alone."

"That was when you needed to bug Sam's handbag?"

"Sure. Duncan told me about it. I bought a duplicate, fixed it up. Gave it to Duncan the morning you left Kensington for the last time. Remember he went out for breakfast eggs? Brought it back with him, did the switch while you were eating in the kitchen."

"Why not just waste the four mercenaries at a prearranged rendezvous?" asked Quinn. "Save you the trouble of trailing us all over."

"Because three of them panicked," said Moss with disgust. "They were supposed to show up in Europe for their bonuses. Orsini was going to take care of them, all three. I'd have silenced Orsini. But when they heard the boy was dead they split and disappeared. Happily, you were around to find them for me."

"You couldn't have handled it alone," said Quinn. "McCrea had to be helping you."

"Right. I was up ahead. Duncan was close to you all the time, even slept in the car. Didn't like that, did you, Duncan? When he heard you pin down Marchais and Pretorius he called me on the car phone, gave me a few hours' start."

Quinn still had a couple more questions. Moss had resumed reading, his face becoming angrier and angrier.

"The kid, Simon Cormack. Who blew him away? It was you, McCrea, wasn't it?"

"Sure. Carried the transmitter in my jacket pocket for two days."

Quinn recalled the scene by the Buckinghamshire roadside—the Scotland Yard men, the FBI group, Brown, Collins, Seymour near the car, Sam with her face pressed to his back after the explosion; recalled McCrea, on his knees over a ditch, pretending to gag, in actuality pushing the transmitter ten inches deep into the mud beneath the water.

"Okay," he said. "So you had Orsini keeping you abreast of what was going on inside the hideaway, baby Duncan here telling you about the Kensington end. What about the man in Washington?"

Sam looked up and stared at him in disbelief. Even McCrea looked startled. Moss glanced over and surveyed Quinn with curiosity.

On the drive up to the cabin Quinn had realized that Moss had taken a tremendous risk in approaching Sam and pretending to be David Weintraub. Or had he? There was only one way Moss could have known Sam had never actually seen the DDO.

Moss lifted the manuscript and dropped it in rage all over the floor.

"You're a bastard, Quinn," he said with quiet venom. "There's nothing new in here. The word in Washington is, this whole thing was a Communist operation mounted by the KGB. Despite what that shit Zack said. You were supposed to have something *new*, something to disprove that. Names, dates, places . . . *proof*, goddammit. And you know what you've got here? Nothing. Orsini never said a word, did he?"

He rose in his anger and paced up and down the cabin. He had wasted a lot of time and effort, a lot of worry. All for nothing.

"That Corsican should have wasted you, the way I asked him to. Even alive, you had nothing. That letter you sent the bitch here, it was a lie. Who put you up to this?"

"Petrosian," said Quinn.

"Who?"

"Tigran Petrosian. An Armenian. He's dead now."

"Good. And that's where you're going, Quinn."

"Another stage-managed scenario?"

"Yep. Seeing as it'll do you no good, I'll enjoy telling you. Sweat a little. That Dodge Ram we drove up in—it was rented by your lady friend here. The car-rental agent never saw Duncan at all. The police will find the cabin, after it's been burned down, and her inside it. The Ram will give them a name; dental records will prove who the corpse was. Your Renegade will be driven back and dumped at the airport. Within a week there'll be a murder rap on you, and the last ends will be tied up.

"Only the police will never find you. This terrain is great. There must be crevasses in these mountains where a man could disappear forever. Come the spring you'll be a skeleton; by summer, covered over and lost forever. Not that the police will be looking around here—they'll be checking for a man who flew out of Montpelier airport."

He picked up his rifle, jerked the barrel toward Quinn.

"Come on, asshole, walk. Duncan, have fun. I'll be back in an hour, maybe less. You have till then."

The bitter cold outside hit like a slap in the face. His hands cuffed behind him, Quinn was prodded through the snow behind the cabin, farther and farther up Bear Mountain. He could hear the wheezing of Moss, knew the man was out of shape. But with manacled hands there was no way he could outrun a rifle. And Moss was smart enough not to get too close, run the risk of taking a disabling kick from the former Green Beret.

It was only ten minutes until Moss found what he sought. At the edge of a clearing in the mountain's cloak of spruce and fir, the ground dropped away into a precipitous crevasse, barely ten feet across at the rim, vanishing to a narrow crack fifty feet down.

The depths were choked with soft snow into which a body would sink another three or four feet. Fresh snow through the last two weeks of December, plus January, February, March, and April, would fill the gully. In the spring thaw, all would melt, the crevasse become a freezing brook. The freshwater shrimp and crayfish would do the rest. When the crevasse choked up with summer growth, any remains far below would be covered for another season, and another and another.

Quinn had no illusions he would die with one clean shot through the head or heart. He had recognized Moss's face, recalled his name now.

Knew his warped pleasures. He wondered if he could take the pain and not give Moss the satisfaction of crying out. And he thought of Sam, and what she would go through before she died.

"Kneel down," said Moss. His breath was coming in short wheezes and snorts. Quinn knelt. He wondered where the first slug would take him. He heard the bolt of the rifle ten yards behind him clatter in the freezing dry air. He took a deep breath, closed his eyes, and waited.

The crash, when it came, seemed to fill the clearing and echo off the mountain. But the snow muffled it so quickly that no one on the road far below would have heard it, let alone the village ten miles away.

Quinn's first sensation was bewilderment. How could a man miss at that range? Then he realized it was all part of Moss's game. He turned his head. Moss was standing pointing the rifle at him.

"Get on with it, sleazeball," said Quinn. Moss gave a half-smile and began to lower the rifle. He dropped to his knees, reached forward, and placed both his hands in the snow in front of him.

It seemed longer in retrospect, but it was only two seconds that Moss stared at Quinn, on his knees with his hands in the snow, before he leaned his head forward, opened his mouth, and brought up a long bright stream of glittering blood. Then he gave a sigh and rolled quietly sideways into the snow.

It took several more seconds for Quinn to see the man, so good was his camouflage. He stood at the far side of the clearing between two trees, quite motionless. The country was wrong for skis, but the man wore snowshoes, like oversized tennis rackets, on each foot. His locally bought arctic clothing was caked with snow, but both the quilted trousers and parka were in the palest blue, the nearest the store had to the color white.

Stiff hoarfrost had clotted on the strands of fur that stuck out from his parka hood, and on his eyebrows and beard. Between the facial hair the skin was caked with grease and charcoal, the arctic soldier's protection against temperatures of thirty degrees below zero. He held his rifle easily across his chest, aware he would not need a second shot.

Quinn wondered how he could have survived up here, bivouacking in some ice hole in the hill behind the cabin. He supposed that if you could take a winter in Siberia you could take Vermont.

He braced his arms and pulled and tugged until his cuffed hands came under his backside, then squeezed one leg after another through his arms. When he had his hands in front of him he fumbled in Moss's parka until he found the key, then released his hands. He picked up

Moss's rifle and rose to his feet. The man across the clearing watched impassively.

Quinn called across to him: "As they say in your country—*spasibo.*"

The man's half-frozen face gave a flicker of a smile. When he spoke, Andrei the Cossack still used the tones of London's clubland.

"As they say in your country, old boy—Have a nice day."

There was a swish from the snowshoes, then another, and he was gone. Quinn realized that after dumping him at Birmingham, the Russian must have driven to London Heathrow, caught a direct flight to Toronto, and tailed him up into these mountains. He knew a bit about insurance. So, apparently, did the KGB. He turned and began to slog through the knee-deep snow back to the cabin.

He paused outside to peer through the small round hole in the mist that covered the living-room window. No one there. With the rifle pointed straight ahead, he eased open the latch and gave the front door a gentle kick. There was a whimper from the bedroom. He crossed the open floor of the living room and stood in the bedroom door.

Sam was naked, face-down on the bed, spread-eagled, her hands and feet knotted with ropes to the four corners. McCrea was in his shorts, his back to the door, two thin lengths of electric cord dangling from his right hand.

He was smiling still. Quinn caught a glimpse of his face in the mirror above the chest of drawers. McCrea heard the footfall and turned. The bullet took him in the stomach, an inch above the navel. It went on through and destroyed the spine. As he went down, he stopped smiling.

For two days Quinn nursed Sam like a child. The paralyzing fear she had experienced caused her to shiver and weep alternately, while Quinn held her in his arms and rocked her to and fro. Otherwise she slept, and that great healer had its benign effect.

When he felt he could leave her, Quinn drove to St. Johnsbury, phoning the FBI personnel officer to claim he was her father in Rockcastle. He told the unsuspecting officer she was visiting him and had caught a heavy cold. She would be back at her desk in three or four days.

At night, while she slept, he wrote the second and real manuscript of the events of the past seventy days. He could tell the tale from his own point of view, omitting nothing, not even the mistakes he had made. To this he could add the story from the Soviet side, as told him by the KGB general in London. The sheets Moss had read made no mention of this; he had not reached that point in the story when Sam had told him the DDO wanted a meeting.

He could add the story from the mercenaries' point of view, as told by Zack just before he died, and finally he could incorporate the answers given him by Moss himself. He had it all—almost.

At the center of the web was Moss; behind him, the five paymasters. Feeding into Moss had been the informants: Orsini from inside the kidnappers' hideout, McCrea from the Kensington apartment. But there was one more, he knew; someone who had to have known everything the authorities in Britain and America had known, someone who had monitored the progress of Nigel Cramer for Scotland Yard and Kevin Brown for the FBI, someone who knew the deliberations of the British COBRA committee and the White House group. It was the one question Moss had not answered.

He dragged the body of Moss back from the wilderness and laid him alongside McCrea in the unheated lean-to where the firewood was stored, where both bodies quickly became as rigid as the cords of pine among which they lay. He rifled the pockets of both men and surveyed the haul. Nothing was of value to him, save possibly the private phone book that came from Moss's inside breast pocket.

Moss had been a secretive man, created by years of training and of surviving on the run. The small book contained more than 120 telephone numbers, but each was referred to only by initials or a single first name.

On the third morning Sam came out of the bedroom after ten hours of unbroken sleep and no nightmares.

She curled up on his lap and leaned her head against his shoulder.

"How you feeling?" he asked her.

"I'm fine now. Quinn, it's okay. I'm all right. Where do we go now?"

"We have to go back to Washington," he said. "The last chapter will be written there. I need your help."

"Whatever," she said.

That afternoon he let the fire go out in the stove, shut everything down, cleaned and locked the cabin. He left Moss's rifle and the Colt .45 that McCrea had brandished. But he took the notebook.

On the way down the mountain he hitched the abandoned Dodge Ram behind the Jeep Renegade and towed it into St. Johnsbury. Here the local garage was happy to get it started again and he left them the Jeep with its Canadian plates to sell as best they could.

They drove the Ram to Montpelier airport, turned it in, and flew to

Boston and then to Washington National. Sam had her own car parked there.

"I can't stay with you," he told her. "Your place is still tapped."

They found a modest rooming house a mile from her apartment in Alexandria where the landlady was glad to rent her upper front room to the tourist from Canada. Late that night Sam took Moss's phone book with her, let herself back into her own place and, for the benefit of the phone tap, called the Bureau to say she would be at her desk in the morning.

They met again at a diner on the second evening. Sam had brought along the phone book and began to go through it with him. She had highlighted the numbers in fluorescent pen, colored according to the country, state, or city of the phone numbers listed in it.

"This guy really got around," she said. "The numbers highlighted in yellow are foreign."

"Forget them," said Quinn. "The man I want lives right here, or close. District of Columbia, Virginia, or Maryland. He has to be close to Washington itself."

"Right. The red highlights mean territorial United States, but outside this area. In the District and the two states there are forty-one numbers. I checked them all. By the ink analysis, most go back years, probably to when he was with the Company. They include banks, lobbyists, several CIA staffers at their private homes, a brokerage firm. I had to call in a big favor with a guy I know in the lab to get this stuff."

"What did your technician say about the dates of the entries?"

"All over seven years old."

"Before Moss was busted. No, this has to be a more recent entry."

"I said 'most,'" she reminded him. "There are four that were written in the past twelve months. A travel agency, two airline ticket offices, and a cab-call number."

"Damn."

"There's one other number, entered about three to six months ago. Problem is, it doesn't exist."

"Disconnected? Out of service?"

"No, I mean it never did exist. The area code is two-oh-two for Washington, but the remaining seven figures don't form a telephone number and never did."

Quinn took the number home with him and worked on it for two days and nights. If it was coded, there could be enough variations to give a computer headaches, let alone the human brain. It would depend how secretive Moss had wanted to be, how safe he thought his contacts book would stay. He began to run through the easier codes, writing the new numbers yielded by the process in a column for Sam to check out later.

He started with the obvious, the children's code; just reversing the order of the numbers from front to back. Then he transposed the first and last figures, the second-first and second-last, and third-from-first and third-from-last, leaving the middle number of the seven in place. He ran through ten variations of transposition. Then he moved into additions and subtractions.

He deducted one from every figure, then two, and so forth. Then one from the first figure, two from the second, three from the third, down the line to the seventh. Then repeated the process by adding numbers. After the first night he sat back and looked at his columns. Moss, he realized, could have added or subtracted his own birth date, or even his mother's birth date, his car registration number or his inseam measurement. When he had a list of 107 of the most obvious possibilities, he gave his list to Sam. She called him back in the late afternoon of the next day, sounding tired. The Bureau's phone bill must have gone up a smidgen.

"Okay, forty-one of the numbers still don't exist. The remaining sixty-six include laundromats, a senior citizens' center, a massage parlor, four restaurants, a hamburger joint, two hookers, and a military air base. Add to that fifty private citizens who seem to have nothing to do with anything. But there is one that might be paydirt. Number forty-four on your list."

He glanced at his own copy. Forty-four. He had reached it by reversing the order of the phone number, then subtracting 1,2,3,4,5,6,7, in that order.

"What is it?" he asked.

"It's a private unlisted number carrying a classified tag," she said. "I had to call in a few favors to get it identified. It belongs to a large town house in Georgetown. Guess who it belongs to?"

She told him. Quinn let out a deep breath. It could be a coincidence. Play around with a seven-figure number long enough and it is possible to come up with the private number of a very important person just by fluke.

"Thanks, Sam. It's all I have. I'll try it—let you know."

. . .

At half past eight that evening Senator Bennett Hapgood sat in the makeup room of a major television station in New York as a pretty girl dabbed a bit more ocher makeup onto his face. He lifted his chin to draw in a mite more of the sag beneath the jawbone.

"Just a little more hairspray here, honey," he told her, pointing out a strand of the blow-dried white locks that hung boyishly over one side of his forehead, but which might slip out of place if not attended to.

She had done a good job. The fine tracery of veins around the nose had vanished; the blue eyes glittered from the drops that had been applied; the cattleman's suntan, acquired in long hours toiling under a sunlamp, glowed with rugged health. An assistant stage manager popped her head around the door, clipboard like an insignia.

"We're ready for you, Senator," she said.

Bennett Hapgood rose, stood while the makeup girl removed the bib and dusted any last specks of powder off the pearl-gray suit, and followed the stage manager down the corridor to the studio. He was seated to the left of the host of the show, and a soundman expertly clipped a button-sized microphone to his lapel. The host, anchoring one of the country's most important prime-time current affairs programs, was busy going down his running order; the monitor showed a dog-food commercial. He looked up and flashed a pearly grin at Hapgood.

"Good to see you, Senator."

Hapgood responded with the obligatory yard-wide smile.

"Good to be here, Tom."

"We have just two more messages after this. Then we're on."

"Fine, fine. I'll just follow your lead."

Will you, hell, thought the anchorman, who came from the East Coast liberal tradition of journalism and thought the Oklahoma senator a menace to society. The dog food was replaced by a pickup truck and then a breakfast cereal. As the last image faded of a deliriously happy family tucking into a product that looked and tasted like straw, the stage manager pointed a finger directly at Tom. The red light above camera one lit up and the host gazed into the lens, his face etched with public concern.

"Despite repeated denials from White House Press Secretary Craig Lipton, reports continue to reach this program that the health of President Cormack still gives rise to deep concern. And this just two weeks before the project most closely identified with his name and his incumbency, the Nantucket Treaty, is due to go before the Senate for ratification.

"One of those who has most consistently opposed the treaty is the chairman of the Citizens for a Strong America movement, Senator Bennet Hapgood."

On the word *Senator*, the light of camera two went on, sending the image of the seated senator into 30 million homes. Camera three gave viewers a two-shot of both men as the host swung toward Hapgood.

"Senator, how do you rate the chances of ratification in January?"

"What can I say, Tom? They can't be good. Not after what has happened these past few weeks. But even those events apart, the treaty should not pass. Like millions of my fellow Americans, I can see no justification at this point in time for trusting the Russians—and that's what it comes down to."

"But surely, Senator, the issue of trust does not arise. There are verification procedures built into that treaty which give our military specialists unprecedented access to the Soviet weapons-destruction program. . . ."

"Maybe so, Tom, maybe so. Fact is, Russia is a huge place. We have to trust them not to build other, newer weapons deep in the interior. For me, it's simple: I want to see America strong, and that means keeping every piece of hardware we have—"

"And deploying more, Senator?"

"If we have to, if we have to."

"But these defense budgets are starting to cripple our economy. The deficits are becoming unmanageable."

"You say so, Tom. There are others who think the damage to our economy is caused by too many welfare checks, too many foreign imports, too many federal foreign aid programs. We seem to spend more looking after foreign critics than our military. Believe me, Tom, it's not a question of money for the defense industries, not at all."

Tom Granger switched topics.

"Senator, apart from opposing U.S. help to the hungry of the Third World and backing protectionist trade tariffs, you have also called for the resignation of John Cormack. Can you justify that?"

Hapgood could cheerfully have strangled the newsman. Granger's use of the words *hungry* and *protectionist* indicated where *he* stood on these issues. Instead, Hapgood kept his concerned expression in place and nodded soberly but regretfully.

"Tom, I just want to say this: I have opposed several issues espoused by President Cormack. That is my right in this free country. But . . ."

He turned away from the host, found the camera he wanted with its on-light dark, and stared at it for the half-second it took the director in the control booth to switch cameras and give him a personal close-up shot.

". . . I yield to no man in my respect for the integrity and courage in adversity of John Cormack. And it is precisely because of this that I say . . ."

His bronzed face would have oozed sincerity from every pore had they not been clogged with pancake makeup.

"'. . . John, you have taken more than any man should have to take. For the sake of the nation, but above all for the sake of yourself and Myra, lay down this intolerable burden of office, I beg you.'"

In his private study in the White House, President Cormack depressed a button on his remote control and switched off the TV screen across the room. He knew and disliked Hapgood, even though they were members of the same party; knew the man would never have dared call him "John" to his face.

And yet . . . He knew the man was right. He knew he could not go on much longer, was no longer capable of leadership. His misery was so great he had no further lust for the job he did, no further lust for life itself.

Though he did not know it, Dr. Armitage had noticed symptoms these past two weeks that had caused him profound concern. Once the psychiatrist, probably looking for what he found, had caught the President in the underground garage, descending from his car after one of his rare forays outside the White House grounds. He intercepted the Chief Executive staring at the exhaust pipe of the limousine, as if at an old friend to whom he might now turn to dull his pain.

John Cormack turned to the book he had been reading before the TV show. It was a book of poetry, something he had once taught his students at Yale. There was a verse he recalled. Something John Keats had written. The little English poet, dead at twenty-six, had known melancholy as few others had, and expressed it like no one else. He found the passage he sought: "Ode to a Nightingale."

> . . . and for many a time
> I have been half in love with easeful Death,
> Call'd him soft names in many a musèd rhyme,
> To take into the air my quiet breath;
> Now more than ever seems it rich to die,
> To cease upon the midnight with no pain . . .

He left the book open and leaned back, stared at the rich scrollwork around the cornices of the private study of the most powerful man in the world. *To cease upon the midnight with no pain.* How tempting, he thought. How very tempting . . .

Quinn chose half past ten that evening, an hour when most people were back home but not yet in bed asleep for the night. He was in a phone booth in a good hotel, the sort of place where the booths still have doors to give the caller privacy. He heard the number ring three times; then the phone was lifted.

"Yes?"

He had heard the man speak before, but that one word was not enough to identify the voice.

Quinn spoke in the quiet, almost whispering voice of Moss, the words punctuated by the occasional whistle of breath through the damaged nose.

"It's Moss," he said.

There was a pause.

"You should never call me here, except in an emergency. I told you that."

Pay dirt. Quinn let out a deep sigh.

"It is," he said softly. "Quinn has been taken care of. The girl too. And McCrea, he's been . . . terminated."

"I don't think I want to know these things," said the voice.

"You should," said Quinn before the man could cut the connection. "He left a manuscript behind. Quinn. I have it now, right here."

"Manuscript?"

"That's right. I don't know where he got the details, how he worked them out, but it's all here. The five names—you know, the men in back. Me, McCrea, Orsini, Zack, Marchais, Pretorius. Everything. Names, dates, places, times. What happened and why . . . and who."

There was a long pause.

"That include me?" asked the voice.

"I said, *everything.*"

Quinn could hear the breathing.

"How many copies?"

"Just the one. He was in a cabin up in northern Vermont. No Xerox machines up there. I have the only copy right here."

"I see. Where are you?"

"In Washington."

"I think you had better hand it over to me."

"Sure," said Quinn. "No problem. It names me too. I'd destroy it myself, except . . ."

"Except what, Mr. Moss?"

"Except they still owe me."

There was another long pause. The man at the other end of the line was swallowing saliva, several times.

"I understand you have been handsomely rewarded," he said. "If there is more due you, it will be provided."

"No good," said Quinn. "There was a whole mess of things I had to clear up that were not foreseen. Those three guys in Europe, Quinn, the girl . . . All that caused a deal of extra . . . work."

"What do you want, Mr. Moss?"

"I figure I ought to get what was offered to me originally, all over again. And doubled."

Quinn could hear the intake of breath. Doubtless the man was learning the hard way that if you mess with killers, you may end up being blackmailed.

"I will have to consult on this," said the man in Georgetown. "If . . . er . . . paperwork has to be prepared, it will take time. Don't do anything rash. I'm sure things can be worked out."

"Twenty-four hours," said Quinn. "I call you back this time tomorrow. Tell those five down there you had better be ready. I get my fee—you get the manuscript. Then I'll be gone, and you'll all be safe . . . forever."

He hung up the phone, leaving the other man to calculate the choice of paying up or facing ruin.

For transportation Quinn rented a motorcycle, and bought himself a chunky sheepskin bomber jacket to keep out the cold.

His call the next evening was picked up at the first ring.

"Well?" Quinn snuffled.

"Your . . . terms, excessive though they are, have been accepted," said the owner of the Georgetown house.

"You have the paperwork?" asked Quinn.

"I do. In my hand. You have the manuscript?"

"In mine. Let's swap and get it over with."

"I agree. Not here. The usual place, two in the morning."

"Alone. Unarmed. You get some hired muscle to try and jump me, you end up in a box."

"No tricks—you have my word on it. Since we are prepared to pay, there's no need. And none from your side either. A straight commercial deal, please."

"Suits me. I just want the money," said Quinn.

The other man cut off the call.

At five minutes to eleven John Cormack sat at his desk and surveyed the handwritten letter to the American people. It was gracious and regretful. Others would have to read it aloud, reproduce it in their newspapers and magazines, on their radio programs and TV shows. After he was gone. It was eight days to Christmas. But this year another man would celebrate the festive season in this mansion. A good man, a man he trusted. Michael Odell, forty-first President of the United States. The phone rang. He glanced at it with some irritation. It was his personal and private number, the one he gave only to close and trusted friends who might call him without introduction at any hour.

"Yes?"

"Mr. President?"

"Yes."

"My name is Quinn. The negotiator."

"Ah . . . yes, Mr. Quinn."

"I don't know what you think of me, Mr. President. It matters little now. I failed to get your son back to you. But I have discovered why. And who killed him. Please, sir, just listen. I have little time.

"At five tomorrow morning a motorcyclist will stop at the Secret Service post at the public entrance to the White House on Alexander Hamilton Place. He will hand over a package, a flat cardboard box. It will contain a manuscript. It is for your eyes and yours only. There are no copies. Please give orders for it to be brought to you personally when it arrives. When you have read it, you will make the dispositions you see fit. Trust me, Mr. President. This one last time. Good night, sir."

John Cormack stared at the buzzing phone. Still perplexed, he put it down, lifted another, and gave the order to the Secret Service duty officer.

Quinn had a small problem. He did not know "the usual place," and to have admitted that would have blown away his chances of the meeting. At midnight he found the Georgetown address Sam had given him, parked the big Honda down the street, and took up his station in the deep shadow of a gap between two other houses across the street and twenty yards up.

The house he watched was an elegant five-story red-brick mansion at the western end of N Street, a quiet avenue that terminates there with the campus of Georgetown University. Quinn calculated such a place would have to cost over $2 million.

Beside the house were the electronically operated doors of a double garage. Lights burned in the house on three floors. Just after midnight those in the topmost floor, the staff quarters, went out. At one o'clock only one floor remained illuminated. Someone was still awake.

At twenty past one the last lights above the ground floor went out; others downstairs came on. Ten minutes later a crack of yellow appeared behind the garage doors—someone was getting into a car. The light went out and the doors began to rise. A long black Cadillac limousine emerged, turned slowly into the street, and the doors closed. As the car headed away from the university Quinn saw there was just one man at the wheel, driving carefully. He walked unobtrusively to his Honda, started up, and cruised down the street in the wake of the limousine.

It turned south on Wisconsin Avenue. The usually bustling heart of Georgetown, with its bars, bistros, and late shops, was quiet at that hour of a deep mid-December night. Quinn stayed back as far as he dared, watching the taillights of the Cadillac swing east onto M Street and then right on Pennsylvania Avenue. He followed it around the Washington Circle and then due south on Twenty-third Street, until it turned left into Constitution Avenue and pulled to a halt by the curb under the trees just beyond Henry Bacon Drive.

Quinn slewed quickly off the avenue, over the curb, and into a clump of bushes, killing his engine and lights as he did so. He watched the taillights die on the Cadillac and the driver climb out. The man glanced around him, watched a taxi cruise past looking forlornly for a fare, noticed nothing else, and began to walk. Instead of coming down the pavement he stepped over the railing bordering the greensward of West Potomac Park and began to cross the grass in the direction of the Reflecting Pool.

Out of the range of the streetlamps the darkness enveloped the figure in the black overcoat and hat. To Quinn's right the bright illumination of the Lincoln Memorial lit the bottom end of Twenty-third Street, but the light hardly reached across the grass and into the trees of the park. Quinn was able to close up to fifty yards and keep the moving shadow in vision.

The man skirted the western end of the Vietnam Memorial, then cut half-left to slant away toward the high ground, heavily studded with trees, between the Constitution Gardens lake and the bank of the Reflecting Pool.

Far to Quinn's left he could make out the glimmer of light from the two bivouacs where veterans kept vigil for the Missing in Action of that sad and distant war. His quarry was using a diagonal route to avoid passing too close to this single sign of life in the park at that hour.

The Memorial is a long wall of black marble, ankle-high at each end but seven feet deep at the center, recessed into the ground of the Mall and shaped like a very shallow chevron. Quinn stepped over the wall in the path of his quarry at the point where it was only a foot high, then crouched low in the shadow of the stone as the man ahead of him turned, as if hearing some scrape of shoe on gravel. With his head above the level of the surrounding lawn, Quinn could see him scan the park and the Mall before moving on.

A pale sickle moon emerged from behind the clouds. By its light Quinn could see the length of the marble wall incised with the names of the fifty-eight thousand men who died in Vietnam. He stooped briefly to kiss the icy marble and moved on, crossing the further stretch of lawn to the grove of towering oaks where stand the life-size bronze statues of veterans of the war.

Ahead of Quinn, the man in the black coat stopped and turned again to survey the ground behind him. He saw nothing; the moonlight picked out the oaks, bare of leaf and stark against the glow from the now-distant Lincoln Memorial, and glinted on the figures of the four bronze soldiers.

Had he known or cared more, the man in the coat would have known there are only three soldiers on the plinth. As he turned to walk on, the fourth detached himself and followed.

Finally the man reached "the usual place." At the height of the knoll between the lake in the gardens and the Reflecting Pool itself, surrounded by discreet trees, stands a public toilet, illuminated by a single lamp, still burning at that hour. The man in the black coat took up his station near the lamp and waited. Two minutes later Quinn emerged from the trees. The man looked at him. He probably went pale—it was too dim to see. But his hands shook; Quinn could see that. They looked at each other. The man in front of Quinn was fighting back a rising tide of panic.

"Quinn," said the man. "You're dead."

"No," said Quinn reasonably. "Moss is dead. And McCrea. And Orsini, Zack, Marchais, and Pretorius. And Simon Cormack—oh, yes, he's dead. And you know why."

"Easy, Quinn. Let's behave like reasonable people. He had to go. He was going to ruin us all. Surely you can see that." He knew he was talking for his life now.

"*Simon?* A college student?"

The surprise of the man in the dark coat overcame his nervousness. He had sat in the White House, heard the details of what Quinn could do.

"Not the boy. The father. He has to go."

"The Nantucket Treaty?"

"Of course. Those terms will ruin thousands of men, hundreds of corporations."

"But why you? From what I know, you're an extremely wealthy man. Your private fortune is enormous."

The man Quinn faced laughed shortly.

"So far," he said. "When I inherited my family wealth I used my talents as a broker in New York to place the estate in a variety of stock portfolios. Good stocks, high-growth, high-yield portfolios. It's still in them. The trustees of my blind trust haven't moved them."

"In the armaments industry."

"Look, Quinn, I brought this for Moss. Now it could be for you. Have you ever seen one before?"

He brought a slip of paper out of his breast pocket and held it out. By the light of the single lantern and the moon Quinn looked at it. A bank draft, drawn on a Swiss bank of unimpeachable reputation, payable to the bearer. In the sum of 5 million U.S. dollars.

"Take it, Quinn. You've never seen money like that before. Never will again. Think what you can do with it, the life you can lead with it. Comfort, luxury even, for the rest of your life. Just the manuscript, and it's yours."

"It really was about money all along, wasn't it?" said Quinn thoughtfully. He toyed with the check, thinking things over.

"Of course. Money and power. Same thing."

"But you were his friend. He trusted you."

"Please, Quinn, don't be naïve. It always comes down to money. This entire nation is about money. No one can change that. Always has been, always will. We worship the almighty dollar. Everything and everyone in this land can be bought—bought and paid for."

Quinn nodded. He thought of the fifty-eight thousand names on the black marble four hundred yards behind him. Bought and paid for. He sighed and reached inside his sheepskin bomber jacket. The smaller man jumped back, startled.

"No need for that, Quinn. You said, no guns."

But when Quinn's hand emerged it clutched two hundred sheets of white typescript. He held out the manuscript. The other man relaxed, took the sheaf.

"You won't regret it, Quinn. The money is yours. Enjoy it."

Quinn nodded again. "There is just one thing . . ."

"Anything."

"I paid off my cab on Constitution Avenue. Could you give me a ride back to the Circle?"

For the first time the other man smiled. With relief.

"No problem," he said.

CHAPTER NINETEEN

The men in the long leather coats decided to discharge their duties during the weekend. There were fewer people about, and their instructions were to be very discreet. They had observers up the street from the Moscow office building who told them by radio when the quarry left the city that Friday evening.

The arrest party waited patiently on the long, narrow road by the curve of the Moskva River, just a mile short of the turning into Peredelkino village where the senior members of the Central Committee, the most prestigious academicians, and the military chiefs have their weekend *dacha*s.

When the car they were awaiting came in sight, the lead vehicle of the arresting party pulled across the road, blocking it completely. The speeding Chaika slowed, then came to a halt. The driver and bodyguard, both men from the CRU and with Spetsnaz training, had no chance. Men with machine pistols came from both sides of the road, and the two soldiers found themselves staring through the glass straight into the muzzles.

The senior plainclothes officer approached the rear passenger door, jerked it open, and looked inside. The man within glanced up with indifference, a touch of testiness, from the dossier he was reading.

"Marshal Koslov?" the leather-coated KGB man asked.

"Yes."

"Please dismount. Make no attempt at resistance. Order your soldiers to do the same. You are under arrest."

The burly marshal muttered an order to his driver and bodyguard and climbed out. His breath frosted in the icy air. He wondered when he would breathe the crisp air of winter again. If he was afraid he gave no sign.

"If you have no authority for this, you will answer to the Politburo, *Chekistl*." He used the contemptuous Russian word for a secret policeman.

"We act on the Politburo's orders," said the KGB man with satisfaction. He was a full colonel of the Second Chief Directorate. That was when the old marshal knew he had just run out of ammunition for the last time.

Two days later the Saudi security police quietly surrounded a modest private house in Riyadh in the deep darkness before dawn. Not quietly enough. One of them kicked over a tin can and a dog barked. A Yemeni house servant, already awake to brew the first strong dark coffee of the day, looked out and went to inform his master.

Colonel Easterhouse had been very well trained with the U.S. Airborne units. He also knew his Saudi Arabia, and that the threat of betrayal for a conspirator was never to be disregarded. His defenses were strong and always ready. By the time the great timber gate to his courtyard had come crashing down and his two Yemeni protectors had died for him, he had taken his own road to avoid the agonies he knew must await him. The security police heard the single shot as they raced up the stairs to the upper-floor living quarters.

They found him sprawled facedown in his study, an airy room furnished in exquisite Arab taste, his blood ruining a beautiful Kochan rug. The colonel in charge of the arrest group glanced around the room; his eye fell on a single Arabic word that formed the motif of a silk wallhanging behind the desk. It said, *Insh'Allah*. If it is the will of Allah.

The following day Philip Kelly himself led the FBI team that surrounded the estate in the foothills outside Austin. Cyrus Miller received Kelly courteously and listened to the reading of his rights. When told he was under arrest he began to pray loudly and earnestly, calling down the divine vengeance of his personal Friend upon the idolaters and Antichrists who so clearly failed to comprehend the will of the Almighty as expressed through the actions of His chosen vessel.

Kevin Brown was in charge of the team that took Melville Scanlon into custody almost at the same minute at his palatial home outside Houston. Different FBI teams visited Lionel Moir in Dallas, and sought to arrest Ben Salkind at Palo Alto and Peter Cobb at Pasadena. Whether by intuition or coincidence, Salkind had boarded a flight the previous day for Mexico City. Cobb was believed to be at his desk in his office at the hour scheduled for the arrest. In fact a head cold had detained him at home that morning. It was one of those chances that stultify the best-planned operations. Policemen and soldiers know them well. A loyal secretary phoned him as the FBI team sped to his private house. He rose from his bed, kissed his wife and children, and went into the garage that adjoined his house. The FBI men found him there twenty minutes later.

Four days later President John Cormack walked into the Cabinet Room and took his seat at the center of the table, the place reserved for the Chief Executive. His inner circle of Cabinet members and advisers was already in place, flanking him. They noticed that his back was straight, his head high, his eyes clear.

Across the table were ranged Lee Alexander and David Weintraub of the CIA, beside Don Edmonds, Philip Kelly, and Kevin Brown from the FBI. John Cormack nodded to them as he took his seat.

"Your reports, if you please, gentlemen."

Kevin Brown spoke first, at a glance from his Director.

"Mr. President, the log cabin in Vermont. We recovered an Armalite rifle and a Colt forty-five automatic, as described. Along with the bodies of Irving Moss and Duncan McCrea, both formerly of the CIA. They have been identified."

David Weintraub nodded in agreement. "We have tested the Colt at Quantico. The Belgian police sent us blow-up prints of the lands on the forty-five bullet they dug out of the upholstery of a Ferris wheel seat in Wavre. They check out: The Colt fired the bullet that killed the mercenary Marchais, alias Lefort. The Dutch police found a slug in the woodwork of an old barrel in the cellar beneath a bar in Den Bosch. Slightly distorted, but the lands were still visible. Same Colt forty-five. Finally, the Paris police recovered six intact bullets from the plaster of a bar in the Passage de Vautrin. We have identified these as having come from the Armalite. Both weapons were bought, under a false name, from a gun shop in Galveston, Texas. The owner has identified the buyer, from his photograph, as Irving Moss."

"So it checks."

"Yes, Mr. President, everything."

"Mr. Weintraub?"

"I regret I have to confirm that Duncan McCrea was indeed hired locally in Central America on the recommendation of Irving Moss. He was used as a gofer down there for two years, then brought to America and sent to Camp Peary for training. After Moss was fired, any of his protégés should have been checked out. They weren't. A lapse. I'm sorry."

"You were not Deputy Director of Operations in those years, Mr. Weintraub. Please go on."

"Thank you, Mr. President. We have learned from . . . sources . . . enough to confirm what the KGB *rezident* in New York told us unofficially. A certain Marshal Koslov has been detained for interrogation concerning the supplying of the belt that killed your son. Officially, he has resigned on grounds of health."

"He will confess, do you think?"

"At Lefortovo prison, sir, the KGB has its little ways," Weintraub admitted.

"Mr. Kelly?"

"Some things, Mr. President, will never be provable. There is no trace of the body of Dominique Orsini, but the Corsican police have established that two rounds of buckshot were indeed fired into a rear bedroom above a bar in Castelblanc. The Smith & Wesson pistol we issued to Special Agent Somerville must be presumed lost forever in the Prunelli River. But everything that is provable, has been proved. The whole lot. The manuscript is accurate to the last detail, sir."

"And the five men, the so-called Alamo Five?"

"We have three in custody, Mr. President. Cyrus Miller can almost certainly never stand trial. He is deemed to be clinically insane. Melville Scanlon has confessed everything, including the details of a further conspiracy to topple the monarchy of Saudi Arabia. I believe the State Department has already taken care of that side of things."

"It has," said the President. "The Saudi government has been informed and has taken appropriate measures. And the other men of the Alamo Five?"

"Salkind appears to have vanished—we believe to Latin America. Cobb was found hanged in his garage, by his own hand. Moir confirms everything admitted by Scanlon."

"No details still adrift, Mr. Kelly?"

"None that we can discern, Mr. President. In the time allowed we have checked everything in Mr. Quinn's manuscript. Names, dates, times, places, car rentals, airline tickets, apartment rentals, hotel bookings, the vehicles used, the weapons—everything. The police and immigration authorities in Ireland, Britain, Belgium, Holland, and France have sent us every record. It all checks."

President Cormack glanced briefly toward the empty chair on his side of the table.

"And my . . . my former colleague?"

The Director of the FBI nodded toward Philip Kelly.

"The last three pages of the manuscript make claims to a conversation between the two men on the night in question of which there is no confirmation, Mr. President. We still have no trace of Mr. Quinn. But we have checked the staff at the house in Georgetown. The official chauffeur was sent home on the grounds that the car would not be used again that night. Two of the staff recall being awakened around half past one by the sound of the garage doors opening. One looked out and saw the car going down the street. He thought it might have been stolen, so he went to rouse his master. He was gone—with the car.

"We have checked all the stock portfolios in his blind trusts, and there are huge holdings in a number of defense contractors whose share values would undoubtedly be affected by the terms of the Nantucket Treaty. It's true—what Quinn claims. As to what the man said, we will never know for sure. One can either believe Quinn or not."

President Cormack rose.

"Then I do, gentlemen. I do. Call off the manhunt for him, please. That is an executive order. Thank you for your efforts."

He left by the door opposite the fireplace, crossed the office of his personal secretary, asking that he not be disturbed, entered the Oval Office, and closed the door behind him.

He took his seat behind the great desk under the green-tinted windows of five-inch bulletproof glass that give onto the Rose Garden, and leaned back in the high swivel chair. It had been seventy-three days since he had last taken this seat.

On his desk was a silver-framed photograph. It showed Simon, a picture taken at Yale in the fall before he left for England. He was twenty then, his young face full of vitality and zest for life and great expectations.

The President took the picture in both hands and gazed at it a long time. Finally he opened a drawer on his left.

"Goodbye, son," he said.

He placed the photograph facedown in the drawer, closed it, and depressed a switch on his intercom.

"Send Craig Lipton in to see me, please."

When his Press Secretary arrived, the President told him he wanted one hour of prime-time television on the major channels the following evening for an address to the nation.

The landlady of the rooming house in Alexandria was sorry to lose her Canadian guest, Mr. Roger Lefevre. He was so quiet and well-behaved; no trouble at all. Not like some she could mention.

The evening he came down to settle his account and say goodbye she noticed he had shaved off his beard. She approved; it made him look much younger.

The television in her living room was on, as always. The tall man stood in the door to make his farewell. On the screen a serious-faced anchorman announced: "Ladies and gentlemen, the President of the United States."

"Are you sure you can't stay a little longer?" asked the landlady. "The President's going to speak. They say the poor man's bound to resign."

"My cab's at the door," said Quinn. "I have to go."

On the screen the face of President Cormack flashed up. He was sitting foursquare behind his desk in the Oval Office, beneath the Great Seal. He had scarcely been seen for eighty days, and viewers knew he looked older, more drawn, more lined than three months earlier. But that beaten look in the photograph that had been flashed around the world, his face as he stood beside the grave in Nantucket, was gone. He held himself erect and looked straight into the camera lens, establishing direct, if electronic, eye contact with more than 100 million Americans and many more millions around a world linked by satellite into the transmission. There was nothing weary or defeated about his posture; his voice was measured, grave but firm.

"My fellow Americans . . ." he began.

Quinn closed the front door and went down the steps to his cab.

"Dulles," he said.

Along the sidewalks the lights were bright with Christmas decorations, the store Santas ho-ho-ho-ing as best they could with a transistor radio slapped to one ear. The driver headed southwest on the Henry Shirley Memorial Highway to take a right onto River Turnpike and another to the Capital Beltway.

After several minutes Quinn noticed an increasing number of drivers pulling over to the curb to concentrate on the broadcast coming over their car radios. On the sidewalks, groups began to form, clustered around a radio. The driver of the blue-and-white cab had a pair of earphones over his head. Just onto the turnpike he yelled, "Sheeee-yit, man, I don't believe what I'm hearing."

He turned his head around, ignoring the road.

"You want me to put this on the speaker?"

"I'll catch the repeat later," said Quinn.

"I could pull over, man."

"Drive on," said Quinn.

At Dulles International, Quinn paid off the cab and strode through the doors toward British Airways check-in. Across the concourse most of the passengers and half the staff were gathered around a TV set mounted on a wall. Quinn found one clerk behind the check-in desk.

"Flight Two-ten for London," he said, and put down his ticket. The clerk dragged her eyes away from the TV set and studied the ticket, punching her desktop terminal to confirm the booking.

"You're changing at London for Málaga?" she asked.

"That's right."

The voice of John Cormack came across the unusually silent hall.

"In order to destroy the Nantucket Treaty, these men believed they must first destroy me. . . ."

The clerk issued his boarding pass, staring at the screen.

"I can go through to departure?" asked Quinn.

"Oh . . . yes, sure . . . have a nice day."

Past immigration control there was a waiting area with a duty-free bar. Another television set was behind the bar. All the passengers were grouped together, staring at it.

"Because they could not get at me, they took my son, my only and much-loved son, and they killed him."

In the mobile lounge rolling out to the waiting Boeing, in the red-white-and-blue livery of British Airways, there was a man with a transistor. No one spoke. At the entrance to the airplane Quinn offered his boarding pass to a steward, who gestured him toward first class. Quinn was allowing himself the luxury by using up the last of his Russian money. He heard the President's voice coming from the mobile lounge behind him as he ducked his head into the cabin.

"That is what happened. Now it is over. But of this I give you my word. Fellow Americans, you have a President again. . . ."

Quinn buckled himself into the window seat, declined a glass of champagne, and asked for red wine instead. He accepted a copy of the *Washington Post* and began to read. The aisle seat beside him remained empty at takeoff.

The 747 lifted off and turned her nose toward the Atlantic and Europe. All around Quinn there was an excited buzz as incredulous passengers discussed the presidential speech, which had lasted almost an hour. Quinn sat in silence and read his newspaper.

The lead article on the front page announced the broadcast the world had just heard, assuring readers that the President would use the occasion to inform the world of his departure from office.

"Is there anything else I can offer you, sir, anything at all?" drawled a honeyed voice in his ear.

He turned and grinned with relief. Sam stood in the aisle, leaning over him.

"Just you, baby."

He folded the paper on his lap. On the back page was a story neither of them noticed. It said, in the strange code of headline writers: VIET VETS XMAS WINDFALL. The subhead amplified the code: PARAPLEGIC HOSPITAL GETS NO-NAME $5M.

Sam sat down in the aisle seat.

"Got your message, Mr. Quinn. And yes, I will come to Spain with you. And yes, I will marry you."

"Good," he said. "I hate indecision."

"This place where you live . . . what's it like?"

"Small place, little white houses, little old church, little old priest . . ."

"Just so long as he recalls the words of the marriage ceremony."

She reached her arms behind his head and pulled it down to her own for a long lingering kiss. The newspaper slipped off his lap and fell to the floor, back page upward. A stewardess, smiling indulgently, retrieved it. She failed to notice, nor would she have cared if she had, the lead story on the page. It was headed:

PRIVATE FUNERAL FOR TREASURY SECRETARY HUBERT REED: CONTINUING MYSTERY OF LATE-NIGHT DRIVE INTO POTOMAC.